Born i...   ...e
War...   ...M's
...in...   ...at
histori...   ...write.

Over the course of her long and distinguished writing career,
Valerie has written many works of historical fiction, most
recently *The House of Lanyon*.

Still living in London, Valerie frequently visits Exmoor, the
setting featured in *The House of Allerbrook*.

THE *House* of ALLERBROOK

VALERIE ANAND

MIRA

MIRA is a registered trademark of Harlequin Enterprises Limited, used under licence.

MIRA Books, Eton House, 18-24 Paradise Road, Richmond, Surrey, TW9 1SR

© Valerie Anand 2008

ISBN 978 0 7783 0297 1

60-0509

Printed in Great Britain by CPI Mackays, Chatham

ACKNOWLEDGEMENTS

I would be hard put to list all the books, pamphlets and people I have consulted while preparing this novel.

Books concerning the Tudor age include Elizabeth Jenkins's excellent work *Elizabeth the Great*, as well as books by Jane Dunn, Lady Antonia Fraser, Wallace MacCaffrey, Alison Plowden, Jasper Ridley, Anne Somerset and Alison Weir. I must also give special mention to *Elizabeth's Spymaster* by Robert Hutchinson and *Big Chief Elizabeth* by Giles Milton.

Books concerning Exmoor include *Living on Exmoor* by Hope Bourne, *The Old Farm* by Robin Stanes, *Yesterday's Exmoor* by Hazel Eardley-Wilmot, *Devon Families* by Rosemary Lauder and *Somerset Families* by Dr Robert Dunning.

Dr Dunning (County editor for Somerset), David Holt of North Molton, the Reverend Peter Attwood of All Saints Church, North Molton, David Bromwich (Somerset Studies Librarian) and the members of the Exmoor Society also gave me much help in my research.

V.A.

This book is dedicated, with grateful thanks, to the Lamacraft family in Somerset, from whom, in bygone years, I many times hired horses to ride on and around Exmoor.

Without them, this book would probably never have been written.

THE House of ALLERBROOK

Part One

THE RELUCTANT MAID OF HONOUR
1535–1540

CHAPTER ONE
New Gowns For Court
1535

Allerbrook House is a charming and unusual manorhouse in the Exmoor district of Somerset. The charm lies in the pleasant proportions, in the three gables looking out from the slate roof, echoed by the smaller, matching gable over the porch, and the two wings stretching back toward the hillside that sweeps up to the moorland ridge above.

In front, the land drops away gently, but to the west there is a steep plunge into the wooded combe where the Allerbrook River flows noisily down from its moorland source toward the village of Clicket in the valley, a mile or so away.

There is no other house of its type actually on Exmoor. It has other uncommon features, too. These include the beautiful Tudor roses (these days they are painted red and white just as they were originally) carved into the panels and window seats of the great hall, and the striking portrait of Jane Allerbrook which hangs upstairs in the east wing.

The portrait is signed *"Spenlove"* and is the only known work by this artist. Jane looks as though she is in her early forties. She is sturdily built, clear skinned and firm of feature—not a great beauty, but, like the house, possessed of charm. She is dressed in the Elizabethan style, though without excess, her ruff and farthingale modest in size. Her hair, still brown, is gathered under a silver net. Her gown is of tawny damask, open in front to reveal a cream damask kirtle, and her brown eyes are gentle and smiling.

But the painter knew his business and recorded his sitter's face in detail. There is a guarded look in those smiling eyes, as though their owner has secrets to keep, and there are little lines of worry around them, too. Well, Jane in her forties already knew the meaning of trouble.

Her original name was Jane Sweetwater. The household didn't adopt the name of Allerbrook until the 1540s. She was sixteen years of age on that day in 1535, when the family was preparing to send her elder sister, Sybil, to court to serve Queen Anne Boleyn as a maid of honour, and with only a week to go before Sybil's departure and a celebration dinner planned for the very next day, there was much anxiety in the household, because the new gowns that had been made for her had not yet been delivered.

"Eleanor," said Jane Sweetwater to her sister-in-law, "Madame La Plage is coming. I've just seen her from the parlour window."

"Thank God," said Eleanor, brushing back the strand of hair that had escaped from her coif. "I know she sent word that she'd come without fail today, but I was beginning to think that Sybil would have to attend her celebration dinner in one of her old gowns."

She wiped her forehead, which was damp. The March day was chilly enough, but she had been pulling extra benches around the table in the great hall, and the whole house seemed to be full of the steam from the kitchen. Preparations were under way for the feast tomorrow, when notable guests would gather to congratulate Sybil on her appointment to court, a great honour for the daughter of a Somerset yeoman.

Now everything that could possibly be prepared in advance was being so prepared, with much rolling and whisking and chopping by energetic maidservants, and pots and cauldrons simmering over a lively fire.

"Let me help you," said Jane contritely, looking at her harassed sister-in-law. "I should have come down before. I was doing some mending. Where are we going to seat people?"

"There'll be Sir William Carew and Lady Joan just here…and Master Thomas Stone and Mary Stone had better go opposite and they'll want their daughter, Dorothy, beside them, I expect. Then there's Ralph Palmer. He'll probably have his father with him. Now, they're family, though I've never got the relationship clear…."

"Distant cousins. I've never quite worked it out myself," Jane remarked.

"Well, we'll seat them on that side," said Eleanor, pointing. "Then there's the Lanyons from Lynmouth…."

"They're distant relations, too," Jane said.

"Yes. All from Francis's side. I'm almost relieved that my own family can't come, but my father's not in good health…. If I put Owen and Katherine Lanyon *here,* they can talk to the Carews and the Stones quite easily and…"

Outside in the courtyard, dogs were barking and geese had begun a noisy cackling.

"That's surely Madame La Plage at last," said Jane. "I'd better go and tell Sybil."

"I bring my most sincere regrets for the delay," Madame La Plage said, leading her laden pack mule into the yard and descending from her pony into the midst of the cackling geese and barking dogs, just as Eleanor hastened out to greet her. "But I will do any needful adjustments *immédiatement*."

Madame La Plage affected a French name and a French accent, but she was actually a local woman who had married one Will Beach of Porlock, a few miles west of the port of Minehead. After his death she had taken over his tailoring and dressmaking business. However, since Anne Boleyn, who'd spent many years in France, had captivated King Henry VIII, French food and styles of dress were in fashion. Mistress Beach had therefore moved herself and her business to Minehead and, with an appropriate accent, made a new start as Madame La Plage.

Most of her customers knew perfectly well that she was no more French than they were, but her work was good and she had prospered, acquiring clientele not only in Minehead but in the nearby port of Dunster, at the mouth of the River Avill, and even in Dunster Castle itself. Later she had become known more widely, even as far as Dulverton, in the very centre of the moor, and other places deep in the moorland, such as Allerbrook House, the home of the Sweetwater family, and the village of Clicket, which belonged to them.

The commission to make Sybil's new gowns was a very good one, and she had worried because she had been too busy hitherto to ride the fourteen miles (as the crow flew;

ponies had to take a longer route) from Minehead. She dismounted now with a flustered air, flapping her cloak at the livestock. "I…go away, you brute…cease flapping your wings! Be quiet, you noisy barking *animals!* Mistress Sweetwater, can you not…?"

Eleanor seized the two dogs by their respective collars and said "Shoo!" loudly to the geese just as two grooms appeared from the stable to take charge of pony and mule and unload the hampers. She sighed a little as she did so. Eleanor's family in Dorset were dignified folk who lived in an elegant manorhouse, and she was often pained by the way her husband's home had never quite shaken off its humble farming history.

Only a few generations ago it had been a simple farm, rented from a local landowner. Nowadays the Sweetwaters owned it as well as other land and had a family tomb in the church of St. Anne's in Clicket, and neither Eleanor nor her husband's two sisters had ever been asked to help spread muck on the fields or make black pudding from pig's blood and innards or go out at harvest time to stock corn behind the reapers.

But the old atmosphere still lingered. The front windows of the otherwise beautiful house overlooked a farmyard surrounded by a confused array of stables, byres, poultry houses and sheds, and infested by aggressive geese, led by a gander with such a savage peck that even the huge black tomcat, Claws, who kept the mice in order, was terrified of him.

Peggy Ames, the chief cook and housekeeper, came out in her stained working apron, brandishing a rolling pin and laughing all over her plain, cheery face, to help chase the geese away, and Madame La Plage, along with her hampers, was taken into the hall. Eleanor sent Jane to call her sister, and offered refreshments which Madame said she would welcome after her long ride. The wind had been chilly, she said. She kept her mind on her business, though, and while sipping wine, began to talk of Sybil and the new gowns.

"You will like the tawny especially, I think. It will look charming over the pale yellow kirtle. It is ideal for a girl with fair hair. Ah, she is such a pretty girl, your sister-in-law Sybil. The fashion now is all for dark ladies, of course, but such blond hair is rare, above all with brown eyes."

"Sybil is pretty enough," conceded Eleanor, just a little sourly. Her own hair was mousy and her eyes an indeterminate grey. She had never been handsome. Her dowry had got her safely married and Francis had grown fond of her, but she didn't have the looks to turn anyone's head, and she knew it. Sybil, at court, would probably have every young man in sight dedicating sonnets to her. One could only hope that she would behave herself. "She's a little greedy, I fear," Eleanor said. "She eats too much cream. I have warned her that she will grow fat, but she takes no notice."

"Perhaps her brother Master Francis should tell her, and maybe she will take notice of him. He is not here just now?"

"No, he's out exercising his horse and riding round the farms. He takes good care of his estate," Eleanor said.

Madame La Plage beamed. "Ah, his horse! He is known for his love of fine horses. He has good taste in all ways, has he not? I hope he will approve my work. Well, Mistress Sweetwater, shall we call Mistress Sybil and fit the gowns? Where is she? Most young ladies come running when new clothes are delivered!"

She and Eleanor both turned as a door opened at the end of the hall, but it was only Jane, on her own.

"Where has Sybil got to? I asked you to fetch her," said Eleanor.

"She's in her bedchamber," said Jane, sounding puzzled. "She seems upset about something."

"She's been very quiet for a while now," Eleanor said. "Can she be nervous about going to court? It's not like Sybil to be nervous. She isn't ill, is she?"

"I don't think so," said Jane. "But I think she has been crying."

"Well," said Madame La Plage, "let us see what pretty new gowns can do for her, shall we?"

"May I come, too?" asked Jane.

"Yes, of course." Eleanor had dutifully tried to love and be a mother to both her husband's young sisters, but she had never quite managed to become really fond of Sybil. Sturdy brown-haired kindhearted Jane, on the other hand, who always had a smile in her eyes, was easy to love. Sybil was affectionate enough, but she was careless. If you sent her to fetch something from another room, she'd probably bring you the wrong thing or get distracted on the way and forget her errand altogether. Now she had apparently found a new way of being difficult. What on earth was she crying about? "We'll all go," said Eleanor. "Come along."

They found Sybil reading on the window seat in her chamber. She put down her book of poems when they entered, slipped from the seat and curtsied politely to the older women. Her little pointed face was very pale, however, and her eyes were certainly red. She looked at the hampers, which Jane and Madame La Plage were carrying between them, as though they were instruments of torture, or possibly execution.

"Now, why this sad face?" said Eleanor briskly. "Come. It's an adventure, to be going to court to wait on the queen of England! Jane will help you off with what you're wearing and we will see how these fit. Madame, shall we start with the tawny gown?"

"Has the young lady no tirewoman?" Madame La Plage enquired. "Surely, at court…"

"Yes, we have found a maid for her, but she lives in Taunton. We shall pass through Taunton on the way to London and the woman will join us there. We live simply here at Allerbrook, and assist each other instead of employing tiring maids," said Eleanor with regret. She had had a maid in Dorset, but Francis had seen no need for one here. He had a parsimonious streak, except when it came to buying the fine horses he so loved.

"I'll help you," said Jane, going to her sister.

"No. No, I can do it myself," said Sybil.

At Allerbrook they mostly wore clothes of simple design except on feast days. Sybil's light yellow gown was loose and comfortable and she could draw it over her head without aid. Slowly, and it seemed with reluctance, she pulled it off and removed her kirtle and undergarments, leaving only her stays.

"Stays, too," said Madame La Plage. "New stays are included in the price and I have them here. You must have strong new stays to wear under the gowns I have made for you."

Miserably Sybil removed her stays, as well.

"But…that is not the result of too much cream!" gasped Madame La Plage.

Jane said, "Oh, Sybil, *Sybil!*"

Eleanor said, "Oh, my God!" and then clapped her hands to her mouth and burst into tears.

CHAPTER TWO
Breaking the News
1535

fterward, what Jane remembered most vividly about that dreadful day was the fear: fear on behalf of Sybil, and another, more amorphous dread that this awful discovery heralded awful changes; that nothing in their lives would ever be the same again.

It was near dusk before Francis rode in on his handsome dark chestnut horse Copper. He had been pleased with the condition of his land and stock and he came into the farmyard whistling. In the kitchen, Peggy Ames looked at the other maids, Beth and Susie, and said grimly, "Just listen to 'un! He won't be that merry for long!"

Up in the parlour in the little tower above the family chapel, Jane and Eleanor, who had been watching for Francis and had also heard the whistling, looked at each other in anguish.

"I can't imagine what he'll say!" said Eleanor. She was a cool, sensible woman as a rule, but just now she looked terrified. "He'll be so angry, and he has all the Lanyon temperament! Will he think it was my fault? That I haven't watched over the two of you as I ought?"

"But you have," said Jane unhappily. "You can't be everywhere, all the time."

"No, I can't! God's teeth, Sybil is the silliest little girl in Christendom! I'll go down and meet him...oh, I don't know how to tell him!"

Pale with anxiety, she descended the spiral stairs to the hall. Madame La Plage had long since left to go back to Minehead, and Sybil had been locked in her chamber. Francis, stepping into the hall, pulling off his red velvet hat and stripping off his gloves, greeted her and asked if his sister's gowns had come. "I'll have something to say to Madame La Plage if they haven't!"

"They're here," said Eleanor, "but..."

"Good. I hope they're suitable," Francis said. "Where's Sybil now? I want to see her in her new finery." Then he saw Peggy looking at him from the kitchen door, and must have recognized the fear in her face and Eleanor's. "God's death, what's the matter?"

"Please come up to the parlour, Francis," Eleanor said. "I have terrible news. Peggy, bring wine. Your master will need it."

"For the love of heaven, what's *happened?* Is Sybil all right?"

"It's worse than that. We must be private when I explain. Not that we can keep it secret for long—well, it isn't now. All the household knows, and Madame La Plage. Jane is in the parlour, but she knows, too. She was there when..."

"Will you stop dithering, woman!" shouted Francis as Eleanor turned and led the way back up the staircase. "*Tell* me!"

In the parlour she turned to face him, and while Jane sat

shivering in her seat by the window, Eleanor said the words that had to be said. "Sybil can't go to court. She is expecting a child. Probably in August."

Francis collapsed onto the nearest settle. "What was that? Repeat it, if you please."

"Sybil can't take up her post at court. She's with child."

Francis bore the name of Sweetwater, but another family, the Cornish Lanyons, also formed part of his ancestry. His blue eyes were inherited from his mother but otherwise he was a Lanyon—tall, handsome, strongly made and dark haired. He also possessed what was known as the Lanyon temperament. This was thoroughly Celtic, as passionate and explosive as gunpowder. Eleanor and Jane, observing Francis now, could almost hear the fuse fizzing toward the barrel, almost see the travelling flame.

The explosion came. Francis shot to his feet and crashed a fist on the back of the settle. "This is beyond belief! Who's the man? Who did it? And where's Sybil now?"

"She's locked in her chamber. I have the key," said Eleanor. "The man is Andrew Shearer."

"*Andrew Shearer?* Of Shearers Farm? My tenant? He's married!"

"Yes. We all went to the christening of his little son last November, if you recall," said Eleanor, keeping her voice steady with an effort. "That's when it happened, it seems. We went to Shearers for the celebration dinner, and stayed on after dark—do you remember? There was dancing, by candlelight. Sybil and Andrew danced together. I never noticed that they disappeared for a while, but it seems that they did. He somehow enticed her into another part of the house and...she says she hasn't seen him since, but that he'd paid her compliments before, when they met during the harvesting. We sent her out with cider for the harvesters. She says she didn't mind when he...I mean, she wasn't forced. She admits that."

"He's *married*. I can't make him wed her. I can order the Shearers off my land, of course, though they'll only get a tenancy somewhere else, and thumb their noses at me, I suppose. I can think of three Exmoor farms straightaway in need of new tenants, since we had that outbreak of smallpox last year. The trouble that brought us! Killed our chaplain and two of our farmhands! But it'll no doubt make life easier for the Shearers. I'll be throwing them out on principle, that's all. But...dear God!" shouted Francis. "Sybil's farewell dinner is tomorrow! It's too late to cancel it! The Carews have probably set off from Devon already!"

The fury in his voice was so intense that Eleanor visibly trembled and Jane began to cry. Francis swept on.

"The Stones from Clicket Hall are coming, and bringing their girl Dorothy—they want to get her to court in a year or two, when she's older! Owen Lanyon and his wife from Lynmouth, they're coming..."

His voice faded somewhat. The one branch of the family that still bore the name of Lanyon wasn't actually entitled to it. Many years ago there had been another unsanctioned baby in the clan. That child's descendants, though, still called themselves Lanyons. Francis resumed, however, as the enormity of the present situation grew larger and larger in his mind.

"Luke and Ralph Palmer are coming! They're very likely on their way by now, too. Bideford's only twenty-five miles off, but Luke's at least sixty and they'll have to take it slowly." Francis was literally clutching at his hair. "They're only distant connections but, God's elbow, it was their wealthy

London cousin who pulled the strings to get Sybil her place at court! And now this! What am I to say to them? I...we'll say Sybil's ill! And I'll give her such a beating that with luck she'll miscarry and then she can go to court after all! Yes, that's the best thing to do. I'll—"

"No!" sobbed Jane. "No, you can't! Francis, you mustn't! It could kill her. She's past four months gone."

"And no one noticed anything?" Francis spluttered. "She never told anyone?"

"She said—" Eleanor gulped "—that she kept hoping it wasn't true. She's just gone on from day to day, hoping...there are so many women in this house, Sybil and Jane and me, and the maids...no one noticed that she hasn't been using her usual cloths. She didn't have much sickness, it seems. Oh, Sybil can be so *silly!*"

"She certainly can," said Francis. "A fault I propose to cure. Give me her key, Eleanor. At once!"

"Francis, no, you mustn't." Jane was frightened but determined. "If you hurt Sybil too much, yes, she might lose the child, but if that happened she really *could* die! You can't want that!"

"I don't need to be told my business by a little girl of sixteen!"

"She might *not* lose the child," Eleanor pointed out. "And if she did, and survived and went to court, how could we trust her, after this! She might create a scandal there, and what good would that do us?"

"It's a complete disaster!" Francis groaned. "It's been trouble enough, planning for portions for my sisters. We were well-off when I was a boy, but that was before Father sold our stone quarry so as to rebuild the east wing. We've lost income without it. Letting Clicket Hall doesn't make up for it. I've worried! Getting one of the girls to court would help—there'd be all sorts of opportunities. Good contacts are worth having in a dozen ways and they can smooth the path to marriage even for a girl with a modest dowry."

"We have good contacts already," said Eleanor weakly.

"I want to do better! But now…! We can't keep it secret. You said yourself, the whole household knows—Peggy, the maidservants… Susie's courting Tim Snowe and I saw them as I came in, talking in the yard. By tomorrow all the farm-hands will know and the whole lot of them have families roundabout. And Madame La Plage will have taken the news back to Minehead!"

"Yes," agreed Eleanor dismally.

There was a dreadful silence.

"Well," said Eleanor, "all we can do is face it out, and I'm sorry, Francis, but even if she is only sixteen, Jane is right. You can't beat a young girl while she's carrying."

"I'm entitled, and the whole world would say so."

"Not if you killed her, and you might. That's *true*."

"But what are we to do?" demanded Francis. He sat down on the settle again, his head in his hands. "What are we to *do*?"

"I suggest," said Eleanor, "that we hold the dinner—without Sybil, of course—and tell our guests the truth and ask their advice. Andrew Shearer can't marry her, but perhaps they know of someone who will. Let's be candid. Then the truth can't creep up behind us years in the future and do any harm. These things…well, they do happen. Owen Lanyon's father was a love child, after all. But everyone respects Owen well enough. He won't refuse to know us, and nor will any of the others. I'm sure they won't. They're all our friends and some are kinsfolk. They'll want to help."

After a very long pause, Francis said, "Very well. Very well. I'll get rid of the Shearers—that I will do. Sybil must stay in her chamber. I will neither see her nor speak to her. And we will tell the truth to our friends and family."

Eleanor said reassuringly, "We will find a way through, my dear. Somehow. You'll see."

CHAPTER THREE
A Remarkable Occasion
1535

The four families who attended that remarkable gathering at Allerbrook House on 16 March 1535 all arrived in good time, in happy expectation of a festive dinner and the pleasure of congratulating young Sybil Sweetwater on her appointment to the court.

They were startled to discover that Sybil, who should have been the centre of attention, was nowhere to be seen, while their hostess, Eleanor Sweetwater, looked harassed and her husband, Francis, their host, had a distracted expression, a bruise on his jaw and a spectacular black eye.

The first to ride in, though their home at Mohuns Ottery in Devon was the farthest away, were Sir William Carew and his wife, Lady Joan. Lady Joan was a picture of elegance, but Sir William, though he represented a leading Devonshire family, was an earthy and outspoken individual with a broad Devon accent.

Having dismounted, aimed a kick at the gander and helped his wife to alight, Sir William came up the steps to where Eleanor and Francis were waiting to welcome them, looked in candid amazement at Francis's face and said, "God save us, who've you been a'vightin', then?"

"It's a sorry story," said Francis, leading the way indoors. "I'll tell it in full when everyone's here."

"Ah, well, you'm still in your twenties—suppose you can still give an account of yourself. Wait till you get to your forties, like me." Sir William actually looked older than that, his face too flushed to be healthy and his hair and moustache already turning grey. "What's the other man look like?" he demanded.

Eleanor, who had been taught by her parents that a lady should always retain her composure, no matter what the circumstances, carried the situation off as best she could and tried to satisfy at least some of Sir William's curiosity.

"My husband had occasion this morning to order one of our tenants, Andrew Shearer, who has—well, had—a farm of ours, on the other side of the combe, to surrender his tenancy. Master Shearer took exception and there was a fight. The Shearers will be gone by tomorrow, however."

"Shearer looks worse than I do," said Francis, with a certain amount of grim humour. "But not entirely because of my fists. His wife joined in. With a frying pan. Applied to him, I mean, not to me."

"Good God! Reckon the story behind this must be interestin', sorry or not," said Carew and his wife said, "My dear Eleanor, how tiresome to have this happen just now. But where is your sweet Sybil?"

"The tale concerns her," said Francis, "and that's why I want to wait until the other guests are here before I explain in full. Meanwhile, my sister Jane will show Lady Joan to a bedchamber—ah, there you are, Jane. Look after the Lady Joan, please. But no gossiping!"

The next to arrive was Francis's distant cousin, Ralph Palmer, who rode in alone. "Your father is not with you?" Francis asked, forestalling any comments on his battered face.

Ralph, who was young and good-looking, dark haired and dark eyed, was studying his host's appearance with evident amazement, but took the social hint, restrained his curiosity and said, "No. Father is having an attack of gout and couldn't make the journey from Bideford."

"I am sorry to hear that," said Francis gravely. "Please convey our sympathy when you go home, and wish him a quick recovery."

"Certainly, Cousin," said Ralph, equally gravely. He added in a low voice, "It may be as well that he can't be here. I am sorry for him, but he is still very interested in the Lutheran teachings and it can be, well, uncomfortable when he insists on talking about them to people he doesn't know well."

Ralph himself was a merry soul with a flirtatious reputation, but his father, Luke Palmer, at sixty, was a known blight on even the happiest occasions. Luke's principal interest in life was religion and being what he called godly and most other people called tediously righteous. He disapproved of dancing and he hardly ever smiled.

His interest in the new Lutheran heresy which was beginning to be called Protestantism was also a worry to his relatives. It was an unsafe point of view, since some prominent Protestants had been put unpleasantly to death. Conversation with Luke Palmer could be embarrassing at the best of times, which this certainly was not. Francis Sweetwater would not have dreamed of saying so aloud, but he was not sorry to be spared both Luke's tendency to heretical remarks and his probable comments on Sybil.

The next party to arrive was the Stone family, consisting of Master Thomas Stone, his wife, Mary, and their daughter, Dorothy. The Stones had just taken on the lease of Clicket Hall after the previous tenant's death.

Clicket Hall, which stood on a knoll overlooking Clicket, a mile away down Allerbrook Combe, had once been called Sweetwater House and had been the home of the Sweetwaters until they decided that they liked Allerbrook House better. Francis had changed the name to Clicket Hall because first-time visitors were often confused into turning up there instead of riding on up the combe. The Stones had leased the hall because Mistress Mary Stone had cousins in the district and wished to see them sometimes. Thomas Stone, however, was actually the owner of extensive property in Kent and was better educated, better connected and a great deal better off than Francis.

Since the Stones were new to Clicket and had not hitherto met any of Francis's womenfolk, the first thing Master Stone did was to assume that Jane was Sybil, and greet her with kind congratulations.

"I'm afraid this is my younger sister, Jane," said Francis. "You will not after all meet Sybil today. A most unfortunate thing has occurred—involving Sybil and also involving me in a fight this morning, hence my half-closed eye. This is my wife, Eleanor…"

"Isn't Sybil going to court after all, then?" asked Dorothy. She was sixteen, short and pale and somewhat overplump. She was dressed in crimson, which was too bright for her complexion. Her tone, regrettably, suggested pleasure in the girl's trouble, rather than friendly concern for another's disappointment.

Her mother and father frowned her into silence and Dorothy subsided, looking sulky. Francis, however, said, "Well, to my regret, Mistress Dorothy is right. Our plans for Sybil have had to change. Do please come into the hall. Seat yourselves around the hearth."

Hard on the heels of the Stone family came the last arrivals, the dignified, bearded merchant Master Owen Lanyon, whose father had been the illegitimate Lanyon of bygone years. He had journeyed from the Exmoor port of Lynmouth, bringing his equally dignified wife, Katherine, and their fifteen-year-old son, Idwal. Both Owen and Idwal had red hair, and if Owen's was fading now, Idwal's looked vivid enough to set a house on fire. They civilly ignored Francis's face but spoke approvingly of the pleasant aroma of roast mutton which was drifting out of the kitchen.

"One of my tenants, Harry Hudd, donated a haunch and shoulder of mutton for the occasion," Francis said. "Very generous of him."

"Will he be with us today?" Mistress Stone enquired.

"No, not today," said Francis, thinking of Master Hudd's rough accent and florid, gap-toothed face. "It wouldn't be suitable."

To begin with, however, although the dinner table waited in the centre of the hall, set with white napery and silver plate, Francis assembled everyone around the hearth, where a good fire was crackling. Peggy came bustling out of the kitchen with Beth and Susie, and handed around wine, cider and small pewter dishes full of sweetmeats.

"We have a good dinner for you," Francis told the guests. "But what I have to tell you won't fit in with chitchat across the roast. I only hope you don't all walk out in horror when you've heard what I have to say, and leave the meal uneaten!"

"It sounds," said Owen in his deep, slow voice, "as if you're going to tell us of a scandal."

Ralph, whose good looks included excellent teeth, grinned and said, "Are any of us likely to walk out in a pet? We all know the world. And we're all agog with interest, aren't we? *Is* it scandal?"

"Well, let's hear what Francis has to say," said Thomas Stone in a practical voice. "Should Dorothy be here?" he added, glancing at his daughter. "She's only sixteen."

Dorothy glowered but held her tongue. Francis nodded to where Jane had seated herself apart, on a window seat. "So is my sister Jane and she knows all about it," he said.

"Very well." Thomas exchanged looks with his wife and then shrugged. "Dorothy may stay."

Dorothy's expression changed from sullen to pleased. Francis took up a position with his back to the fire, cleared his throat and embarked on the unhappy business of explaining.

Jane sat quietly listening, hands clasped on her lap. She had been presented with the tawny gown and yellow kirtle originally meant for Sybil. Though younger, Jane was the same height as her sister, and the clothes fitted her quite well. Madame La Plage had had to make only very minor adjustments before she went home.

"Please, I don't want Sybil's gown," Jane had said, while Sybil wept forlornly, out of fear for her future and grief at her lost hopes. Eleanor would not listen and so here Jane was, whether she liked it or not, at what should have been Sybil's farewell dinner, dressed in what should have been Sybil's gown, uneasy in the first farthingale she had ever worn, and miserably embarrassed. Originally these important guests,

landowners, a prosperous merchant, even a knight and his
lady, had been invited to do honour to Sybil. Now it felt as
though they had become her judges.

Francis finished his speech and then looked gravely at
Ralph Palmer. "I feel especially bad about you, Ralph,
since it was your cousin Edmund, a kinsman to me just as
you are, who so kindly used his influence at court to
obtain Sybil's appointment for her. She has failed you
both. I feel that in some way I, too, have failed you both.
I am sorry."

Ralph shook his head. "I can't see that you're responsible,
Francis. I was going to London as part of Sybil's escort. I will
see my cousin Edmund there and if you wish, I'll tell him
that the girl isn't strong enough for court life. Maybe," he
added, with a smiling glance toward Jane, "I could say that
there's a younger sister coming along, who'll be ready for
court in a year or two."

"That is kind indeed, Ralph," said Eleanor. "We all appreciate it."

Oh, no. As the eyes of the company turned to her, Jane
shrank back into her window seat. The eyes were friendly,
but they frightened her. She didn't want to be taken away
from the dark moors and the green combes of home, which
she loved. Sending a girl to court, with the necessary gowns
and jewellery, was expensive. Hitherto, the plan had concerned only Sybil. But now…inside her heavy skirts and the
unfamiliar farthingale, she shivered.

Still, for the moment, the danger wasn't immediate.
Francis smiled at her, too, but then said, "We will think about
that later. Meanwhile, I want to ask you all for your advice.
What am I to do with Sybil? Some provision must be made
for her, but I can't condone what she has done."

There was a pause. Owen and Katherine whispered together, but said nothing aloud. Mary Stone was the first to speak.

"I agree with Master Sweetwater." Mary was fat and pallid, with a voice full of phlegm. Her amethyst-coloured damask was expensive but stretched so tightly around her ample form that it formed deep creases across her stomach. She offered a depressing suggestion of what Dorothy might turn into eventually. The sweetmeats had been passing unobtrusively around throughout the whole business and Mary's plump white fingers had helped themselves liberally. She licked sugar off her fingertips and said, "If she were our girl, she'd find herself turned out and depending on the parish. Isn't that so, Thomas?"

"I might not go that far," said Stone, "but I'd not keep her at home."

"Nor me," said William Carew. "Young folk can be the devil and all. What my youngest boy put us through—I swear it's why my hair's goin' badger-grey afore its time. Pert, forward brat, Peter was. Played truant when I put 'un to school—I was sent for to deal with 'un more than once. Got him a post as a page at the French court later on, and he behaved so bad, he ended up demoted to stable boy."

"Peter's doing well now, though," said Lady Joan mildly, also licking sugar off her fingers but with more delicacy than Mary Stone. "He's in England, at the royal court. He went into the French army when he was old enough and we heard nothing of him for so long, we thought he was dead, and then he just came home one day! What a surprise!"

"If he's made good, it's because I stood no nonsense and nor did the Frenchies," said Sir William. "And you can't stand for this, Sweetwater. I don't say throw her on the parish, but you can't keep her at home. We wouldn't. We might take the child in if one of our men sires a bastard, we support it or give it a home—our blood, after all. But the woman has to shift for herself. That's how the world is."

"Marry her off, that's the best thing," said Stone.

"Yes," Francis said. "We'd thought of that. The only problem is, who can we find to marry her? Andrew Shearer obviously can't."

"What was that you said about his wife hitting 'un with a frypan?" enquired Sir William Carew with interest. "Just what happened when you went to see the Shearers, Francis?"

"I told Shearer what I thought of him, seducing a young girl—and his landlord's sister at that—at the christening of his own son," said Francis. "He started denying it and suggesting that maybe he hadn't been the only one...you know the sort of thing..."

There were nods and murmurs of *Aye, we know, we've all heard that one.*

"That I knew wasn't true," Francis continued. "Oh, Sybil's a silly girl, too easily impressed. We think now that it's as well she isn't going to court—too many temptations there! But I watch over my sisters and she's had little chance to play the fool, and in any case, she's not a liar. And the timing's right, if she's to have the babe in August, as she says. Eleanor here says that by the look of her, August is very likely right."

"Yes. That christening party fits in," Eleanor said.

"So I told Shearer I believed her and not him and aimed a punch at him. He hit back and we were fighting in the kitchen when his wife came charging in—and I do mean charging." For a moment, despite the unhappy situation, Francis grinned. "In she came, like a whole squadron of cavalry. *I've been a-listening! So you've been at it again, have you,*

you lecherous hound! That's what she said. Then she grabbed a frying pan off a hook on the wall and landed him a beauty on top of his head. He sat down on the floor looking dazed and I said to her, sorry, but the two of them had to pack up and be off the farm double-quick. I want new, decent tenants. She cried and he sat there rubbing his head and cursing but I wouldn't give in. They've kin in Barnstaple and that's where they're going. The stock's theirs. I settled to sell the animals and send them the money. I never want to see or hear of them again after that. I gathered from a few more remarks his wife threw at him that he's left other by-blows scattered around."

"Lively goings-on," remarked Ralph. "But as for finding the girl a husband..."

"Got an unmarried tenant that might do?" Sir William enquired.

"Harry Hudd's a widower," said Eleanor. "He rents Rixons, down the hill from here. He's looking for another wife. Only..."

"I know Harry," Francis said. "He's a rough type but he's respectable. As his landlord, I could order him—or pay him—but he wouldn't like the kind of talk there'd be if he married a girl in Sybil's condition. There'd be folk saying it must be his, for one thing, and for another, he's not the sort to want to rear another man's child. No, I can't offer Sybil to Hudd. It's not fair on him."

Neither of the Lanyons had so far commented, though they had gone on whispering to each other. Owen Lanyon now spoke up.

"I've a suggestion. Not about marriage—I don't know anyone suitable and I'm not offering Idwal here." Idwal, who had been looking worried, passed a hand over his fiery hair in

a gesture of relief. "But we live at Lynmouth, a good way off—
nigh on twelve miles if you're a crow and farther on a horse.
No one there'll know who Sybil is. She can come to us."

"Are you sure? That's a very generous offer," Francis said.

"She's old enough to have been married." Katherine,
straight of back and stout of midriff, though not as massively
so as Mary Stone, nodded in agreement. "We could say that
she's a distant kinswoman, which she is, and that she's a
young widow. That smallpox last year took a lot of lives."

"We'll not make a pet of her—don't think that," Owen
said. "What she's done was wrong and she has to realize it.
But we won't ill-treat her either, or her baby. They'll have
a home with us. Katherine can always use another pair of
hands about the house. What about it?"

Jane cleared her throat and they all turned. "You want to
say something, Jane?" said Francis.

"Need Sybil go away forever?" Jane asked. "If…if Master
and Mistress Lanyon could look after her until the baby's
born, and if, maybe, we can find someone who'd like to
foster the child, couldn't Sybil come back then? She's my
sister. I'll miss her so much and she'll feel so unhappy, cast
out from her home."

"You'd have missed her if she went to court, and as for
being unhappy, she's brought that on herself," said Francis.
"No, Jane. Sybil must leave this house, and for good. Your
affection for your sister is creditable, of course, but I shall not
change my mind. What our parents would have said to her
behaviour, I shudder to think."

"We have an answer now, at least," said Eleanor. "We are
grateful, Master Lanyon." Looking around, she saw Peggy
hovering restively at the door to the kitchen. "I think," she
said, "that the feast is ready."

* * *

Dinner had been served at half past two. It was not as prolonged as it would have been in more cheerful circumstances. The meal was over inside two hours. However, the March darkness still fell quite early and most of the guests were to stay overnight and leave in the morning. Only the Stones went home that evening, since they had to go only a mile down the combe to Clicket. After they had gone, Francis discovered that Jane had slipped out of the house. He found her leaning on the gate of the field where the Sweetwaters grazed their horses.

"So here you are. I was afraid you'd gone roaming up to the ridge, and it's too late in the day for that."

"I just wanted to be by myself for a while," Jane said. Against the background of tussocky grass and grazing horses and soaring moorland, her damask finery was incongruous.

The narrow path from the rear of the house led past the small mews where Francis kept his two hawks and on past the field to join the track that ran up the side of the combe to the ridge. There the Allerbrook River had its springs in a spongy bog, and there were ring ouzels and curlews, and occasionally an adder slipping away through the grass from the sound of hooves or footfalls. Sybil, who was lazy, never walked up to the ridge, but Jane sometimes did, liking the solitude.

"I wanted to tell you," said Francis, "that when the Lanyons leave tomorrow, taking Sybil with them, I will allow you to say goodbye to her if you wish."

"I *do* wish!" said Jane. She turned to him. "Of course I want to say goodbye to her. I can't bear it that you're sending her away forever!"

"If she had gone to court and then married someone from the other side of the country, you might never have seen her again. You may make your farewells, but once Sybil goes, she is out of our lives for good. Remember that! Now, come indoors. After supper I want you to play your lute for us."

"Francis…"

"Yes, what is it?"

"Today someone suggested I might go to court instead. I don't want to, one little bit."

"Listen to me, Jane. You and Sybil were born into a good family, into a comfortable life in a house where you have had fine clothes and no hard work—every indulgence. Do you think you can have all that and not give something back? Sybil has thrown away her chance to be of use to her family. I trust you don't want to throw yours away, as well!" He laughed. "You're still very young. When you're older, you'll feel differently, I promise. If Palmer's cousin finds a post for you later on, believe me, you'll be delighted with it."

Jane was silent, still leaning on the gate. The sun had come out as evening approached, and as it set, it shed a softness over everything, so that the green meadow was tinged with gold and faintly dappled with the shadows of the tussocks.

There were things she knew Francis would not understand. Their father would have done, but Johnny Sweetwater had died two years ago, struck down by a fever after getting soaked and frozen while bringing sheep in to safety from an unexpected snowstorm. Her mother had gone two years earlier, from some internal malady that no physician could explain. Since then, Jane and Sybil had been in the care of their elder brother and his wife, and no one could say that Francis or Eleanor had been anything but conscientious and kind, but they were not like Father.

He had loved Allerbrook, loved the racing waters in the

combe, and the moor with its varying moods, and the yearly cycle of the farm. And so did Jane. She did not want to go away to court, and her father would have known. He would have been less harsh with Sybil, too. Angry, yes, but perhaps—not so unforgiving. There would have been hope for Sybil in the end.

Francis had a hardness in him which their father had lacked. If he wanted her to go to court, then go she would. And if she cried for Sybil, she had better do it secretly, in bed. "I'll be glad to play my lute after supper," she said, and followed Francis obediently indoors.

At Richmond Palace, by the River Thames a little to the west of London, the atmosphere was fraught. Queen Anne Boleyn was the cause. Her high-pitched voice and shrill laughter had been heard less than usual that day, but she gave the impression of being like a wound crossbow, which might at any moment release a bolt, and who knew which one of them would be the target?

King Henry, who was planning improvements to the private rooms at Greenwich Palace, miles downstream to the east, was engaged all day with architects and did not see the queen until he joined her for supper. Most of the conversation then concerned the choice of wall hangings for the refurbished rooms and Queen Anne took part amiably enough though those who knew her well sensed that her apparent good humour had much in common with a set of gilded bars on a cage containing an irascible tigress.

When the meal was over, in her most gracious and persuasive tones Anne invited Henry to join a game of cards with her and some other friends.

As the darkness closed in, the group settled in a snug, tapestried chamber, lit by firelight, candles and lamps, scented by sweet lamp-oils, and the rosemary in the rushes on the floor.

There, in the flickering half-light, as the cards were dealt, Anne employed them to send a secret message to Henry.

It was one of their private games, this exchange of signals that only they could read. To hold the cards in one's right hand and pensively flick the leftmost card with the other hand was to say, *I love you*. For him to run a forefinger slowly and sensually across the edge of the fan of cards was to say, *I desire you. I will come tonight*. For her to do the same was an invitation. *Please come tonight. I will be awake and waiting*. For either of them to flick the face of each card in turn with the nail of a forefinger was to reply, *You will be welcome* or *I will come*.

In the course of the evening's play she fingered the edge of her cards four times, lingeringly, invitingly. But at no point did the king's small greenish-grey eyes meet her dark ones; at no point did the square bearded face above the slashed velvet doublet show any awareness of her except as a fellow player in the game. Nor did his thick forefinger ever flick the face of any card at all.

What am I to do? I have borne him one daughter and lost one male infant. He is turning away from me. He had a mistress last year, I know he did, and she wasn't the first. I will only win him back if I give him a son, and how can I give him a son if he will not make love to me? Or if he can't?

The previous night Henry had failed her. She had used every art she could think of to help him, without success. Now it seemed he was refusing even to try. Perhaps he was ashamed. But she was afraid, because she knew he would blame her both for his failure and her own. Her dreadful failure, in his eyes, to produce a prince to follow him.

He had blamed her openly last night. He had said, "If only you were a real woman. If only you could have a healthy child every year, and half of them sons, like other women! If you were a real woman, I'd be a real man!"

"I *am* a real woman!" she had shouted. "What else could I be?"

"A witch," said King Henry nastily. "Or a whore."

Oh, God, make him come to me tonight and make him able. Let us make a sturdy son. Because if we don't...

If we don't make a son, I shall be blamed and blamed and blamed. I've given him a sweet red-haired Tudor daughter, but what use is a daughter? Elizabeth can't be his heir, any more than her sister Mary can. He told his first wife, Catherine of Aragon, that for a king to have only daughters was the same as being childless altogether. But how can a woman choose whether her babies are boys or girls? Unjust, unjust! I could kill him! Or I could kill God, for denying me this one thing that I need, that he needs, so badly.

Henry was thinking, *Candlelight doesn't suit her. It suits most women, but it makes her look weird. Like a sorceress. Maybe she is a sorceress. I wanted her so much. I've turned the church upside down for her, broken away from the Pope, changed the ritual, started closing down monasteries...not that the monks don't deserve it, fat, luxurious layabouts that most of them are. But how did she make me want her to that point, just the same? Was it witchery? If she doesn't stop fingering those cards, I'll get up and walk out of this room. We need another signal. One that says No, stop it.*

I'm getting tired of her, and my other queen is still alive. Two unwanted queens and no son. Was ever a man so accursed?

CHAPTER FOUR
A Port in a Storm
1535

"There's no room here for idle hands," Katherine said to Sybil a matter of minutes after their arrival in Lynmouth.

Sybil had made the journey on a pillion behind a groom and they had travelled slowly, but she was tired. By the time they were on the steep track down into the little harbour village of Lynmouth at the base of its towering cliffs, she was longing for a quiet bedchamber with a cup of wine to restore her.

At the door of the house, just before the foot of the hill, they dismounted and servants came out to deal with panniers and horses. The main door opened straight into a big panelled parlour. Sybil had seen it before. When her parents were alive, the Allerbrooks had once or twice attended Christmas revels at the Lanyons' home. Now, however, she paused uncertainly, wondering where to go, until Katherine tapped her arm and said, "Follow me."

The house was old and creaky and tall. Katherine led the way up a steep and somewhat rickety staircase to an attic room. There were no luxuries here, no hearth or bed-hangings. There was a clothespress, a window seat that lifted to reveal a chest below, one small shelf with a candlestick on it and a plain truckle bed with no bedding.

"Your things will be fetched up presently and I'll have the bed made up," Katherine said. "For now, just take off your cloak and hat and leave them here, and then come down to the dining parlour. Do you remember where it is?"

No rest, then. Not even a wash! She went down to the dining parlour, which led out of the main parlour, and found that food was being set out. She was not, however, to eat anything yet.

"You can serve us while we eat and leave the other maids free to get on with other things," Katherine said. Sybil stared at her and that was the moment when Katherine said, "There's no room here for idle hands. Everyone's always busy," she added. "You can eat when we've finished."

She was presented to the servants as Mistress Sybil Waters, a young widow, a relative, but without means. "We've never known anyone called Waters, so as a name it won't cause confusion," Owen said.

Sybil was willing enough to acquiesce, but the groom who had accompanied the party to Allerbrook certainly knew the truth, and she had no doubt that he would soon tell the three maids and the manservant Perkins all about it. If this was a port in a storm, it also promised to be a port in a hostile country.

The days that followed were harsh. Katherine, however well-bred in society, was less fastidious in private, where she

raised her voice whenever she pleased. Only Owen was
exempt. His wife shouted at everyone else and handed out
frequent slaps, and Sybil was sure that she received more than
her fair share. At Allerbrook such things were rare. At Allerbrook, too, people often smiled. If only, in Lynmouth,
someone now and then would smile at her. But no one ever
did and on top of that, there was the work.

Rooms must be dusted, clothes mended, onions peeled,
loaves shaped, pots stirred, fish gutted, stores counted, floors
swept, dishes washed, guests waited on, and Sybil was called
upon to perform these tasks, for all the world as though she
were a maidservant instead of a kinswoman.

Owen belonged to a consortium of merchants, but he had
a ship of his own and often sailed abroad to buy dyes and
spices and bales of silk in person, rather than leave it to
agents. He and Idwal were often away from home on trading
expeditions, and the first time the two of them set off, Sybil
hoped that there might be less to do. She was wrong. Left
in command, Katherine became not so much a conscientious housewife as a slave driver.

When the men were away, she said, that was the time to
get some real work done. New shirts must be made for
husband and son, and a spell of spring sunshine inspired her
to have all the linen in the house, both bed linen and undergarments, thoroughly washed and put out to dry.

Never before had Sybil been asked to work so long or so
hard. At home she sometimes helped in the kitchen and
dairy, but she had had time to herself to enjoy books—
poetry, travel and devotional works. In the evenings they
would all take turns with the lute and there might be dancing
or cards or backgammon.

She had realized that life at court would be different, but

there she had hoped to find glamour, to wear fashionable clothes, to attend masques and tournaments. There was no glamour and precious little merriment in her life now. There wasn't even time to read. She had pushed two books into her panniers, but she had not had a moment to open either of them.

At times she was so tired that she could scarcely force her feet to walk, and she would stumble off to bed as soon as she could after supper had been eaten and she had helped to wash the platters. And oh, the aching, desperate need for somebody to *smile* at her.

She was not asked to do heavy tasks like carrying full buckets about, but it seemed to her that the Lanyons were still, stealthily, creating conditions which might bring on a miscarriage. And that Francis had probably instructed them to do so.

Her back ached constantly and the calling of the gulls as they wheeled and soared above Lynmouth, free as the wind and gliding on it with outspread wings, was like mocking laughter. Now, lying on her pallet at the end of another dreadful day in which one menial task had followed another in pitiless procession, Sybil tossed unhappily, unable to find a position which would accommodate her swelling abdomen in comfort.

"All this," she said aloud, "all this just because that Andrew Shearer got me giggly at his son's christening party, plying me with cider, and then said, come and see how the red calf's grown, that was born so late this year. I don't even like Andrew Shearer!"

Not that Shearer was ugly. He had flint-coloured eyes but they could glint with amusement, and he had a knack of fixing his gaze on someone in a way that made the someone feel as though they were the only person in his world. His narrow face was shapely enough, and on the night of the celebration his black hair, though overlong as usual, wasn't untidy as it normally was, but carefully combed.

He had been persuasive, refilling her tankard with cider and looking at her, watching her, with those bright, flinty eyes. Then, before she knew what was happening, he'd put an arm around her, steered her out of the room where the others were dancing, across the central passage and into the adjoining byre, dark except for a glimmer of starlight through a gap under the eaves and full of the warm, pungent smell of cattle and horses.

There'd been no more talk of the red calf then—not that they could have seen it in the gloom, anyway. Instead, Andrew Shearer had put his mouth over hers and gripped her tightly and somehow slid them both down onto a pile of straw in a vacant stall.

She'd been fuddled and silly. The Shearers' home-brewed cider was very strong and she knew she had drunk too much of it. She managed a feeble protest, of which he took no notice. He murmured soothingly and told her that she was adorable and petted her in a way which made her feel very strange, as though she wanted him to go on doing it, and then she'd been squashed beneath him and something rather painful but also rather exciting was happening....

And then it was all over, and he was kissing her and saying *Thank you, sweeting. Now we'd better get back to the others before you're missed,* and a moment later they were back in the main room on the other side of the passageway.

At once Harry Hudd, that awful old man from Rixons, who smelt and had gaps in his teeth and a wind-reddened face that went all shiny when he drank cider and almost purple when anything annoyed him, was asking her to dance and Andrew was laughing and pushing her at him, and there she was, dancing, though she felt very peculiar, slightly sore and oddly wet. And that was that. Except that it wasn't because the next time she should have started a course, she didn't.

Such a little thing. A few foolish moments in the dark byre with its animal smell and the rustle of shifting hoofs, and the gleam now and then of an incurious equine or bovine eye. And now she'd lost both her home and her chance of a thrilling life at court, and come to this.

She had been given a pillow, stuffed with crackly straw but at least covered in smooth linen because that was the only kind of linen ever found in the Lanyon household. She drew it to her, put her arms around it as though it were a dear friend, pressed her nose into it and cried.

At Allerbrook Jane, too, had found her daily life subject to change. Eleanor had suddenly begun to discourage her from spending too much time in the open air. "If you're going to court one day, we don't want you having a sunburnt complexion. You'll need to look like a lady. Ladies have pale skin and soft hands and keep their hair tidy. You should be practising your embroidery and music. The standard will be high at court."

However, on the July day when Francis went out early with the young groom Tim Snowe and wouldn't tell Jane where he was going (though Eleanor knew, to judge from her secretive smile), no one seemed to mind what Jane was doing. Eleanor was asking Peggy and the maids to help her move stools and tables about in one of the downstairs rooms off the hall, but she didn't seem to want her young sister-in-law at all.

Jane promptly seized the chance to be out of doors, tossing grain to the chickens and geese and searching for eggs, and stealing a walk up to the ridge.

She was outside again, giving the poultry their evening meal and wondering whether Francis would be back for supper, when he came riding up from the combe on Copper, followed by a surprising procession.

Just behind him was an elderly man she had never seen before, on a stout, mealynosed Exmoor pony. Next came Tim Snowe, on the Allerbrook pony he usually used and leading a strange pack mule. Behind the mule came two packhorses, each carrying a large package done up in hides and rope. The horses were led by a groom apiece, trudging along on foot and checking every now and then that the package in his care wasn't slipping.

"What in the world…?" said Jane, going to the gate, her grain basket on her arm.

"Oh, there you are, Francis! I was beginning to be anxious, but I see you had to take it slowly," said Eleanor, appearing from the house. "And is this Master Corby? Welcome, sir. I take it that the packhorses are carrying the new virginals?"

"Yes, madam," said the elderly man. "All in good order, we hope and trust. I will assemble the instrument myself."

"Please come in. And here is your pupil," said Eleanor. "This is my sister-in-law, Jane Sweetwater. Make your curtsy, Jane. This gentleman is a musician by profession and he has come to teach you to play the virginals. Proficiency in music is something that you'll need when you go to court."

So it was going to happen, and Francis was so determined to make it happen that he was willing to spend money on virginals and a tutor. Jane, who liked music, didn't mind learning a new instrument, and Master Corby turned out to be a patient and agreeable instructor. It was the purpose behind the lessons that frightened her.

Just once she made a further attempt to protest. After she had practised daily on the virginals for a month, Master Corby invited Francis and Eleanor to listen while she played a simple melody. "I think you will be pleased," he said to them. "A little polishing, and she'll be an ornament to the court when she gets there."

"But," said Jane, seating herself, gathering up her courage and addressing the keyboard rather than her relatives, "I have no real wish to go to court. I would be so very happy to play music here at home, when anyone wants to dance, or to play at our Christmas and harvest revels. I am not…not eager for advancement in society."

"Well," said Francis, "let us hear how well you perform. Then we will talk privately."

Afterward, when Master Corby, with a tactful smile, had left the room, Francis said, "My dear sister, it is time you accustomed yourself to the idea of going to court. Sybil has failed us and you are her natural replacement."

"We have been in touch with Ralph Palmer's cousin, Sir Edmund Flaxton," said Eleanor. "He has sent commiserations for Sybil's ill health and he is willing to obtain an appointment for you if he can."

Francis nodded. "Do well, attract the right kind of notice, make worthwhile friends and you could become the route by which influence and wealth are drawn toward us all, and you might even find yourself a titled bridegroom!"

It was no use arguing. Francis could be severe when he was angry. Her duty was being made clear to her. There would be no escape.

"Broth," said Katherine Lanyon shortly, putting her head into the kitchen where a pot was bubbling on the trivet over the fire and giving off an appetizing aroma. "Take her some mutton broth, and some hot milk, as well."

Withdrawing from the kitchen, she marched into the parlour, stripping off her stained apron as she went. Owen, who was sitting by the window, shirtsleeved in a shaft of sunlight and playing chess against himself, got to his feet. "Is it over already?"

"Didn't you hear it squalling? Yes, it's over," said Katherine, sitting down on the nearest settle. "Where's Idwal?"

"I sent him to the jetty to see that consignment of ironware loaded properly. Well, Sybil hasn't taken long."

"No, she hasn't! Oh, it's so unfair!" Katherine cried. "I almost died bringing Idwal into the world. Three days and nights of agony and I've never conceived since. Yet I was a decent, honest young wife, bearing her husband's son. While this little hussy…!"

"I wouldn't call her that," said Owen mildly. "I fancy she only made the one mistake."

"That kind of mistake is the same whether it's once or twenty times!" snapped Katherine. "She *deserved* what I went through, but does it happen to her? No, it does not. She abandons the dinner table, saying she has a stomach-ache, and before supper she's slipped a great big bawling boy into the world as easily as though it were nothing at all, and now she's sitting up and asking for something to eat, and I'm waiting on her!"

"What does she want to call him?" Owen asked.

"Stephen," she said. "There was a Stephen in the family years ago, it seems, and she likes the name."

"Well, if he thrives, he could be an asset to the business one day," said Owen.

CHAPTER FIVE
The Blemished Queen
1535

*T*he court rarely stayed in one place long. It took only a few weeks for a palace's privies and cesspits to start stinking and then, to escape the smell, King Henry and his six-hundred-strong entourage would be off.

In a flurry of dismantling, they would pack up their goods, their clothes and ornaments and toiletries and workboxes, their books, their chess and backgammon sets, and in the case of the more important folk, their favourite tapestries, bed-coverings and items of furniture, including beds complete with their hangings, and depart, generally by water, since most of the palaces were along the River Thames or not far from it. Horses were sent by land, and there were wagons and pack animals to convey goods by land when this was required.

Everyone in the royal retinue was used to its gypsying habits, but the same problems appeared every time. Anne Boleyn, who had been at court long before she became queen, was well accustomed to them. Early in her reign she remarked to a newly appointed young lady-in-waiting called Jane Seymour that never, *never* had the court managed a move without somebody's precious Florentine tapestry or sandalwood workbox or priceless ivory chess set or irreplaceable illuminated prayer book falling into the river or off a pack saddle.

"And when we go on the summer progress, it's worse," the queen had said irritably. "We move once a week and sometimes oftener. It's hell."

But the progress in the summer of 1535, through some of the southwest counties, was not hell for Jane Seymour because it included her family home, Wolf Hall. For the few days they spent there, she could be with her parents, at ease in what, to her, was a happy and informal world.

Not that Wolf Hall was so very informal. It stood amid farmland, but the fields did not press close to the house, which was surrounded instead by parkland and formal gardens. Sir John Seymour had a solid, gentlemanly background and Lady Margery was descended from King Edward III. They were well aware of their status. The brief stay made by King Henry that late summer should have been a very pleasant one. Unfortunately...

"My dear child, what in the world is the matter?" Sir John, strolling through the beautifully shaped yews of the topiary garden, was horrified to come upon his daughter, sitting alone on a bench and sobbing, her fists balled into her eyes as though she were an infant.

Jane lowered her hands unwillingly and he sat down beside her, taking them in his. "What *is* it?"

Jane gulped and said, "The king and queen are shut in their bedchamber and they're quarrelling."

"But, my dear daughter, why should *you* cry about it? I daresay it's embarrassing, but it's their business."

"They're quarrelling," said Jane wretchedly, "about *me*."

"I saw you!" said Anne Boleyn furiously, for the fourth time that morning. "I *saw* you with my own eyes!" She knew that she was doing herself no good by all these histrionics, but she couldn't help herself. The anger and—yes—the fear had been building up inside her for so long. Now it had broken loose and she couldn't stop it. "I was in the gallery and I looked out over the knot garden and there you were..."

"It's a very pretty garden!" Henry snapped. "Even this late in the summer. I was admiring it. Mistress Seymour was walking there as well and I stopped and remarked upon the flowers. Is there anything wrong in that?"

"There is when you take her hand and lead her to a seat and sit beside her, smiling at her!"

"Would you expect me to scowl at her? She is one of your ladies and she is also the daughter of our hosts! And a very sweet, modest little thing she is! I did nothing more than sit and make conversation with her!"

"And you held her hand throughout!" shrieked Anne.

"Oh, for the love of God, will you have done?"

Across the width of the spacious bedchamber the two of them glared at each other—King Henry with feet apart and hands on hips, Queen Anne twisting her hands together and trying not to burst into tears.

And to think I was once out of my mind for love of her! Henry said to himself, staring at the termagant in front of him.

So short a time ago, she had been his one desire. He had adored her, lusted for her. He had written love letters to her, created songs and poems for her; in the gardens of Hever,

her family home in Kent, he had knelt at her feet to plead
with her. What on earth had possessed him? Look at her!
Thin as a broom handle, her face drawn into lines of dis-
content, black hair escaping untidily from its expensive
jewelled cap, dark eyes hard with rage.

Listening to her was no better than looking at her. Had he
really ever raved about the beauty of her voice? She was as shrill
as a bad-tempered cat. And look at those twisting hands! There
was a tiny outgrowth at the base of one little finger, a little extra
fingertip, even to the miniature nail. She was ashamed of it and
wore long sleeves to conceal it. Once, in their courting days,
when he caught sight of it, she had cried and said she hated it,
and he had kissed it and called it sweet. Now he thought it an
ugly blemish and recoiled from it. Suddenly he lost his temper.

"I have had enough! Half the morning I have been in here
with you, listening while you screech at me! All because yesterday afternoon I spoke pleasantly to a shy young girl. She
is timid. She was nervous of being alone with her king and
I wished to make her mind easy. I will not be accused
of…well, what *are* you accusing me of, if anything?"

"I'm not accusing you!" There was a point past which
Anne dared not go. She did not know quite what she feared,
except that it was the sense of power that emanated from King
Henry. He couldn't divorce her as he had her predecessor,
Catherine of Aragon. He'd never get away with that twice.
Catherine was still alive, after all. They'd laugh at him in the
streets if he tried to take a third bride while he still had two
wives living. Anne knew the people of England had no love
for her. She'd heard the names they called her. *That witch, Nan
Bullen,* they said, giving her surname the old English pronun-
ciation rather than the French one, which she preferred.
Another name they had for her was The Concubine.

All the same, she couldn't imagine them letting Henry, their leader under God, play with the sacrament of marriage as though it were a tennis ball. If she couldn't mend this breach between them, if he wanted to be rid of her and marry again...what *would* he do?

What, indeed? *That* was the cause of the fear. It lay deep in her mind, like a dark, frightening well that she didn't want to look into. The only thing that would release him from her would be her death. And when a man had as much power as Henry had, and such a very great determination to get himself a son, one way or another...

The tears spilled over despite all her efforts to restrain them. She went to the great bed and threw herself down on it, weeping. Henry found himself moved by pity against his will. He went to her and put a hand on her shoulder. Her unblemished hand came up to cover his.

"I want to give you a son," Anne sobbed. "I want to give you a son, so very, very much."

Her despair, her defencelessness, stirred him as he had not been stirred for a long time, or not by her. He lifted her, and her thin form felt birdlike. He could have cracked those slender bones in his two hands. He forgot the aversion which had overwhelmed him only a few moments ago. His loins awoke. "Well, there's only one way to go about that," he said.

"The one thing none of us must do," said Sir John Seymour firmly to his daughter, "is offend the king." He was tired. His sixtieth birthday was behind him and he was feeling his years. "We should have got you married before this, I suppose," he said. "You are already in your mid-twenties. Only, your mother hoped you would stand a better chance of a really fine match if you were at court. We didn't expect this."

"There isn't really any *this*," said Jane Seymour unhappily. "But the queen thinks there is."

"Let us hope she is wrong, just a jealous woman seeing what isn't really there. But if it *is* there…well, my dear, neither I nor your mother would want you to be anything but modest and virtuous. But in the last resort, if the only alternative is to make the king angry—well, don't. That would be unwise. To annoy the king," said Sir John warningly, "could be dangerous."

CHAPTER SIX
Terrifying Ambition
1536

*I*t was the month of May, 1536, and out of doors the world was burgeoning. Now was the time when cows were milked three times a day and on the moor the ponies were dropping their foals. The skies were full of singing skylarks, and in Allerbrook combe the woods echoed with birdsong and the soft call of the wood pigeons. Every part of Jane's being wanted to be out there, among it all, but these days she rarely had the chance. Life now seemed to be all fine sewing, music and dancing.

She was being relentlessly groomed for court life. The day was coming nearer and nearer when she would be exiled from Allerbrook, perhaps forever. She knew very well that Francis and Eleanor hoped that once at court, she would take the eye of some suitable young man, and marry him. Then she would live wherever his family home might be, even if it was at the other end of England.

It was in her nature to be compliant, and certainly it was in her interests. Both Francis and Eleanor could make themselves unpleasant if crossed. But inside, she was afraid and rebellious and longed to find a way of escape. Except that there didn't seem to be one.

Master Corby was pleased with her progress on the virginals, except that he said she put a little too much passion into her fingers. The passion came from anger and unhappiness, but it was no use telling him that. At the close of yet another music lesson, she went as she had been bidden to do, to join Eleanor, who was sewing in the parlour above the family chapel, settled in a window seat for the sake of the daylight, her workbox open on a table in front of her.

Eleanor looked a trifle wan and was putting in her stitches in an unusually languid fashion. Jane looked at her pale face and slow movements with some concern and said, "Eleanor, are you well?"

Eleanor, however, glanced up with a smile and said, "I had a restless night, that's all. I've started on a new altar cloth. Come and help. You can embroider at the other end."

"Where's Francis today?" Jane asked. "I saw him ride off this morning. From the path he took, I thought he might be going to Dulverton."

"Yes, he was," Eleanor said. "To talk to a possible replacement for our poor chaplain. I like to have proper family prayers on weekdays—it keeps a household together in my opinion. I hope Francis brings someone back with him. Listen! The dogs are barking. Is he coming now?"

The window beside Eleanor didn't overlook the yard. Jane went to one that did, throwing it open in order to look out. "Yes, it is. He's on his own, though. And Eleanor, the horse is lathered! He never brings a horse in sweating as a rule. Something must have happened! I'll just run down…"

"No, you won't. Sit down," said Eleanor. "No doubt he'll appear in a moment and tell us all about it. A young lady shouldn't rush about, asking questions. Come and sew with me."

Reluctantly Jane seated herself and threaded her needle. Down in the yard, Francis was speaking to someone, probably Tim Snowe. A door slammed, however, as he came indoors and then they heard him call to Peggy, asking where his wife and sister were. A moment later he came racing up the stairs to the parlour. He flung the door open dramatically and stood in the doorway, breathless, so that both of them paused, needles poised, and looked at him in astonishment.

"It's the queen!" he said.

"The queen?" Eleanor asked. On the stairs behind Francis, Peggy and the maids appeared, eyes wide.

"She's been arrested," said Francis. "Dulverton's buzzing with it. There's been a King's Messenger with a proclamation. Queen Anne's in the Tower of London, charged with treason. For taking lovers. She's going to be tried. It's a capital charge. It…it's…"

"But that's incredible!" said Eleanor, shocked, her languor quite vanished. "She's…the *queen!*"

"The king's wanted to get rid of her ever since she lost that last pregnancy, the one she must have started last summer, on progress. Ralph Palmer knows all the gossip. He went to London again in February to see his cousin Flaxton and he told me the rumours when he visited us last month. I doubt if anyone will ever know the truth, but I wouldn't place any heavy bets on her being found innocent," said Francis. "Even if she is."

There was a silence. Then Eleanor said, "What about our chaplain?"

"Dr. Amyas Spenlove will join us in a few days. He was chaplain to a man who recently died and made him the executor of his will. He has business to finish before he leaves Dulverton. You'll like him, I think."

"We'll be glad to see him. But this news about the queen," said Eleanor. "It's dreadful!"

For the rest of her life Jane was ashamed of the thoughts that went through her head as she sat listening.

If there is no queen of England, then there'll be no need for ladies-in-waiting or maids of honour. I can stay here.

In the days that followed, news came in successive waves, like a swiftly rising tide.

King Henry, determined now to rid himself forever of the harpy into which his once-adored Anne had turned, wanted his subjects to understand why he was ridding himself of her and how, and wanted them to know, too, that the new marriage he had in mind was lawful. King's Messengers and town criers were kept busy. Vicars, too, took up the task, repeating the latest announcements from their pulpits. Even the Gypsies who wandered the roads and the charcoal burners who often spent weeks deep in the forests encountered the news before many days had passed.

Yes, the queen was in the Tower. She had been tried, along with her so-called lovers. One of them was her personal musician, whose name was Mark Smeaton. Another was her own brother George. She had been accused of incest as well as adultery. They had all been sentenced to death. The men had been executed but the queen was still alive.

Queen Anne, the last to die, went to the block on Tower Green on May 19. She was executed with a sword, wielded by a professional headsman brought from France for the purpose on Henry's orders. There was no professional headsman in England accustomed to use the sword, and executions by axe could be very butcherly. Sometimes it took several blows to finish the victim off. The sword, properly handled, was instantaneous.

Cynical people remarked that King Henry evidently wished to be as merciful as he could—as long as he wasn't left with a living ex-wife whose existence might call the legality of a new marriage into question.

He had enough of that with Queen Catherine, said the knowing voices in the taverns and marketplaces. *Well, Catherine of Aragon is dead now, poor soul, and so is Nan Bullen. Never cared for the Bullen witch myself, but I don't think she got justice.*

Nor me. Can't believe she ever went with her brother, or played the fool with some court minstrel. I mean, I ask you, five of them! If it were just one, well, a fellow might believe it, but five—and her the queen, and adultery for a queen is high treason! She'd have to be out of her mind.

Ah. You're right there. Whatever next, that's what we're all wondering.

Jane heard of the queen's death from Father Anthony Drew, the vicar of Clicket, on the Sunday following, and shuddered. That Sunday was a particularly lovely May day, more beautiful even than the day when Francis had brought home the news of the queen's arrest. Rain in the night had been followed at daybreak by drifting early mist and then sudden, lavish sunshine. The tree-hung ride down the combe to Clicket was dappled with it, as though by a scattering of gold coins, and vegetation was growing almost while one watched. Long grass and cow parsley and red valerian overhung the edges of the lanes and the meadowsweet had come out early. May was no month for dying.

Whatever next? Everyone was asking that, and the answer came soon enough. On May 20, the day after Queen Anne's head had rolled into the straw, King Henry had been betrothed to her former lady-in-waiting Jane Seymour.

On May 30, he married her.

Francis and Jane heard the wedding announced by the Dulverton town crier. Eleanor was not with them. She had of late seemed more and more out of sorts and now they knew why. She had been with child, but something had gone amiss and she had miscarried. She was in bed, with Peggy looking after her, while the new chaplain, Dr. Spenlove, took charge of the house. He was cheerful and competent and had very quickly established himself as someone who could deputize for Francis when required.

"It's a relief to have him," Francis said to Jane. "I feel easy about going to Dulverton, and I really must. I've half a dozen things to do there. Come with me." And with that, they set off on the seven-mile ride to the little town, among other things to order supplies of wine from a vintner there, and buy linen to make new shirts for Francis.

On arrival, they heard the loud bell and the stentorian voice of the crier and went toward the sound. They sat on their mounts in the midst of a crowd, listening. When the crier ended his announcement of King Henry's new marriage, Francis, turning to Jane, said something that terrified her.

"So the new queen's one of the old one's ladies-in-waiting. It's a thousand pities Sybil didn't behave herself better, or you weren't a bit older. If one of you had been at court, why, the next queen could have been you!"

He wasn't joking. Jane knew it at once. He meant what he said. He was harbouring hair-raising ambitions. He was seriously imagining himself as the brother-in-law of King Henry, with one of his sisters on a throne.

"It might be dangerous," she said, and knew that her voice was trembling. "Look what happened to Queen Anne!"

"Well, I don't believe it would ever happen to you, though I can't say the same of Sybil," Francis said. "Everyone says there was no truth in the charges, but who can really know? Maybe there was."

"Even with her own brother?" said Jane.

"Yes. I grant you that's hard to believe," Francis agreed. "But all the same, I feel that perhaps Queen Anne was…shall we say, not quite trustworthy. What happened to her isn't likely to happen to anyone else."

They rode slowly homeward, their various purchases stowed in saddlebags. The moorland tracks were narrow, but when Jane saw a chance to edge her pony up alongside Francis, she seized it.

"Francis, I want to ask you something."

"Of course. What is it?"

"Please can you tell me how Sybil is? I haven't seen her or heard a word about her since she went away. The Lanyons haven't visited us, but I know you've seen Master Owen, more than once. I heard you tell Eleanor you'd seen him last year at a fair somewhere…."

"Dunster," said Francis. "Where the castle is. During the

fair, Owen and Katherine dined at Dunster Castle as guests of the Luttrell family. Owen's a successful man these days."

"He must have mentioned Sybil, or you must have asked after her, surely! How is she? Did she have the baby safely? I want to know."

"Sybil is nothing to do with you, Jane. Not anymore."

"But she is! She's my sister, whatever she's done, and if there's a child, it's my niece or my nephew. And yours, too!"

Francis relented a little. "Sybil had a boy child last August. He has been named Stephen. They are still with the Lanyons. They are perfectly safe and there's no need for you to worry about them."

"I'd like to visit them. I'd like to see Sybil again."

"No, Jane. I can't allow that." Francis spoke sharply. "Your life is going to take a very different course from hers, believe me. With a new queen on the throne, there may well be a need for new maids of honour. I'd like to see you become one of them. I want to bring our family up in the world, Jane. And it's a hard world. Life was cosier, perhaps, for our forebears. The world is wider now, and colder. You want to stay at Allerbrook, I know, but sometimes, my sister, sacrifices must be made."

No, prayed Jane, silently but passionately, to God in the sky above, to fate, to Providence—if necessary, to the ancient gods who had been worshipped by the long-departed people who had left their strange marks upon the moor in the form of upright stones and the barrow mounds where they buried their chieftains. There was a barrow on top of the ridge. When she had been free to take walks, she had liked standing on top of it. The view from there was so immense. *No, and no and no. I don't want to go. Don't make me go. Stop Francis from sending me. Please!*

★ ★ ★

Her prayers were apparently answered. Word came from London that there were no vacancies for maids of honour or ladies-in-waiting. Queen Jane Seymour had all the ladies and maids that she required.

"Well, the queen's little namesake is still young," said Thomas Stone, arriving for the Christmas revel at Allerbrook and greeting Jane with a kiss. "Plenty of time. Maids of honour marry, ladies-in-waiting go home to produce children. Vacancies will arise sooner or later. I fully intend to get Dorothy a place at court one day."

He and his family had been away on their principal estate in Kent, but had come to Somerset for Christmas so that Mistress Mary Stone could visit her cousins in Porlock, though not stay with them.

"We get on their nerves if we stay long," Thomas confided, "and there are no girls there of Dorothy's age. Still, family is family and besides, here in Somerset we can stay at Clicket Hall, which we like very much, and Dorothy can have Jane for company sometimes. Isn't that so, Dorothy?"

"Yes, of course," said Dorothy dutifully. Jane tried not to sigh. She did not enjoy spending time with Dorothy Stone, who seemed to her very dull and was inclined to take offence easily. She longed for Sybil instead.

CHAPTER SEVEN
Avenue of Escape
1536–1537

Sybil, at that very moment, was longing with all her heart for Jane.

She had been missing her sister more and more. Jane had been the one person at home who hadn't condemned her, who had kissed her goodbye and wished her well. Dear, dear Jane. Vaguely, as she rode away with her new guardians, she had hoped that one day, somehow, she and her sister would be together again, but it hadn't happened. It seemed that her presence in the Lanyon house had changed the relationship between the two families. She knew from overhearing talk between Master Owen and Mistress Katherine that Owen often met Francis, out in the world, frequently at fairs where goods and animals were bought and sold. But it seemed that they had decided to keep their womenfolk apart.

In Lynmouth, Katherine and Owen had duly presented

Sybil to their neighbours as a young widow and Stephen had been correctly baptized in the church at Lynmouth. But there had been no celebration to follow. Sybil, it seemed, was to be kept out of the public eye. One of the maidservants told her, spitefully, that Katherine had put it about that she had no dowry because her husband had been poor, and was in any case devoted to his memory and did not intend to remarry.

Sometimes Sybil wished she were really a servant. They were paid and they had time off now and then. She did not.

She was permitted to look after Stephen, but she was encouraged to begin weaning him as soon as possible.

"Children should not be nursed for too long," Katherine said. "Life is too busy for that."

Sybil's constant busyness was Katherine's fault, but Sybil was afraid to say so.

By the time her second Christmas at Lynmouth arrived, he was nearly seventeen months old, toddling energetically, and making his opinions felt in loud, indignant roars every time he fell down—which was fairly often—or was denied something to which he had taken a fancy, such as a shiny knife or a gold coin carelessly left on a table.

Both Katherine and Owen repeatedly told Sybil to make him behave and she tried, anxiously, but with little success. She had originally hoped that Idwal, who though younger than Sybil was certainly nearer to her in age than his parents were, might be a friend, but he frankly disliked both her and Stephen and if he could get either of them into trouble, he would.

When that second Christmas came, she wondered wistfully if this time there would be some contact with her own family, but there was not, although the weather was good and there was no bar to travelling. The Lanyons stayed in

Lynmouth for their Yuletide revels. They let her share in them, but in a limited fashion. It was taken for granted that she would help to wait on the other guests and though Owen, rendered genial by Christmas good cheer, gave her permission to dance, Katherine watched to make sure that no unmarried man danced with her more than once.

The following spring, it was given out one Sunday in church that Queen Jane Seymour was with child, and the congregation were asked to pray for the birth of a healthy prince to be the heir to the kingdom. The Lanyons seemed pleased to hear the news and when they went home, Owen declared that they must have a special dinner to celebrate. "Kate, send someone out to buy a good haunch of something, and we'll make an occasion of it."

If Queen Jane did have a boy, Sybil thought, church bells would ring throughout the land. A boy child born to a queen was a marvel, a joy. A boy child born to Sybil Sweet-water might well be stronger, more handsome, cleverer, but he would never be regarded as anything but a mistake and was condemned as a nuisance when he bellowed. That night she cried herself to sleep.

She had done that before, of course, but this time her misery came from a new and greater depth. In the morning she brushed the best of her plain brown gowns, combed her fair hair back, put on a clean coif and went to speak to Master Owen.

Owen Lanyon was preparing for another foreign voyage, and his packed belongings were piled just inside the street door. Idwal was down at the ship, making sure that all was ready. They were to sail to Bristol and then leave for Venice in company with other ships, as a safeguard against pirates. Owen himself was in the small room he used as an office, writing, which he continued to do even after he had answered her timid knock with the call to enter.

Sybil closed the door behind her and stood hesitating, until at length he glanced around and said, "Sit down. I won't be long. I'm writing to your brother, as it happens."

"Is there any chance of...of me seeing him? I never have, not since I came here." Sybil sat down nervously on the nearest stool.

"No, Sybil. There is not." Owen sanded the letter and blew the sand off. "I'm just giving him some information, in haste, before I set off for Venice. I was in Dunster the other day and I heard some news that may interest your brother. Cleeve Abbey, near Washford, is going to be dissolved after all."

"Oh," said Sybil a little blankly.

"Come, now. You know, surely, that the English church has broken free from the Pope and that it has meant retribution at last for the monasteries which for so long have been places of scandal, as well as much too rich." His sardonic tone suggested that he didn't entirely sympathize with King Henry's reforming zeal, or believe that its roots lay in a genuine desire for piety and morality.

Sybil said, "Oh, yes. Father Anthony Drew explained it to us. It was so the king could be free to marry Queen Anne. Only, she didn't have a son and so..."

"Hush," said Owen. "His Majesty has for many years been more and more shocked by the mismanagement of the church by Rome, and the sad laxity in the monasteries of England. Any other reason would be unthinkable. Anyway, it's wiser not to comment on the king's affairs, even in private, to members of one's own family. It's said that he has informers in many houses and who knows which? Never mind that now. The point is that the monks of Cleeve...you know where Cleeve and Washford are?"

"Yes, up the coast, to the east of Minehead. The monks are Cistercians."

"Quite. They keep sheep and the abbot has a house in Dunster, where he stays when he's there doing business in the wool trade. When the king's receiver disposes of the abbey, the sheep will come up for sale along with everything else. It will be proclaimed, of course, but since your brother runs a big flock, I thought he might like to know in advance. Those monks are clever shepherds. Their sheep are some of the best in the county. Francis might want to buy some of them and I'm giving him a chance to get in first."

"Yes, I see," said Sybil bleakly, understanding but not able to summon up any great excitement about extra sheep for Allerbrook.

As though he had read her thoughts, Owen said quite gently, "You have just asked if you can visit your brother, or if he wishes to visit you. Perhaps I should explain why the answer is no. Francis has handed you into our care and—I am sorry, Sybil—but to him, you are as one who is dead. You are not badly off, living here, you know."

"That isn't all that I came to ask," said Sybil. "I...I just wondered...if there were any chance...that you and Mistress Lanyon might...might arrange a marriage for me. With someone who wouldn't mind Stephen, who would be a father to him, of course."

There. It was out.

"Marriage," said Owen thoughtfully. "A husband and home of your own. A father for Stephen and a lawful father for any other children you might produce. Yes, a very natural wish and not impossible, for although, I'm sorry to say, most of Lynmouth knows or guesses by now that you are not a widow, there are men who would be happy to take you on, since you have proved yourself able to bear children, and that's something to be valued. But…"

"But?"

"Your brother absolutely forbade it, and one thing that *I* value is my friendship with him. He and I meet quite often. His orders were that you were to remain in our care and that since you would be perfectly safe under our roof, he had after due consideration decided that you should not marry because—" his voice hardened "—once a girl turns wanton, she is likely to remain so and is not, therefore, fit to be a wife."

"But…"

"No buts. Whether I fully agree with your brother or not isn't the point. I will do nothing to jeopardize my friendship with him. Be glad that you and your child have a home here. Now, please leave me. I have much to do before I sail. Ask Perkins to come here. I need him to take this letter to Allerbrook."

"Couldn't I even…?"

"Write a letter of your own and send it with mine? No, Sybil. And that's final."

So that was that. Sybil, ignoring the fact that she had a whole string of domestic tasks awaiting her, went up to the room where Stephen was playing with some little painted bricks which had once belonged to Idwal. She stood looking at him.

She didn't love him. She had attended to his needs, obeying ancient instinct, but it wasn't love. There were times when she almost hated him. But for him, she would have gone to court. But for him, no one would ever have known that she and Andrew Shearer had coupled in the straw at that christening party. But for Stephen…

He would be all right here. Katherine would look after him. She didn't like him much, but she was a responsible woman, and she'd reared one son; she ought to know how to manage.

Sybil had had enough. Maidservants were paid and had days off, and if they got a chance to marry, they took it. She'd rather be a maidservant than live like this.

It was a busy time of year on farms, with the extra milking to do, more eggs to collect and weeds capable of choking a vegetable bed almost overnight. Next month there would be shearing and haymaking, too. It ought to be possible to find employment.

She thought about the locality. Above Lynmouth towered the cliffs; she must begin by climbing up to Lynton, the little town at the top. Beyond that, if one went on, inland and uphill, lay the open moor and there were few farms there, but there were some in the combes around the edges. If she turned east and followed the East Lyn River, surely she would come to farmsteads, to places where extra hands might be needed.

They could have Sybil's hands, and pay for them. She was leaving. First thing tomorrow morning.

"Gone?" said Eleanor after she and Jane had listened in horror to Francis as he stood in the hall and read them the contents of the second letter in two days to come from Lynmouth.

Perkins, the Lanyons' hardworking manservant, had on re- turning to Lynmouth after delivering Owen Lanyon's news about the sale of Cleeve Abbey, found himself obliged to go back to Allerbrook again the very next morning, bearing a further missive, penned by Katherine in frantic haste. Owen and Idwal had left for Bristol and would probably have sailed for Venice before the news could catch up with them but Sybil's family at least could be informed. "She can't have gone!" Eleanor protested. "Where would she go? What happened?"

"Aye, what? It's not right, a young girl like that, wanderin' on the moor all alone!" Peggy gasped. She and the maids were also present and listening with scandalized expressions. "It's dangerous, that sort of thing," Peggy added.

Perkins, standing deferentially to one side, spoke up. "The mistress thinks that the girl ran off early today. She was in the house last night, right enough. But today the little boy Stephen started calling out for his mother, and we found Mistress Sybil wasn't there. Her things were gone from her room and some food from the kitchen and a water flask."

"Someone must search for her!" Jane cried. "Somebody will have seen her. She shouldn't be hard to find, surely?"

"Yes. She *must* be found, before something happens to her!" agreed Eleanor anxiously.

"Mistress Katherine is getting a few folk together and sending them to enquire up in Lynton and round about," Perkins said.

"Quite." Francis nodded. "I certainly hope she will be found and brought back. But there's nothing we can do from here. There never is anyone to spare at this time of year. We'll pray for her, naturally. She is even more foolish than I thought. First she throws away her chances of going to court. Now she throws away the only home and shelter that she has. However did I come to be saddled with such a ridiculous sister?"

"Oh, how can you be so unkind!" wailed Jane.

Francis looked at her coldly. "There is no unkindness. On the contrary, she has always been treated more gently than she ever deserved and see how she repays it. Peggy, take Perkins to the kitchen and see that he has refreshment. His horse must have some rest, as well."

"You care more for the horse than for Sybil!" Jane shouted.

"Mind your manners, sister," said Francis. "And yes, an honest horse is to my mind worth more than a silly, light-skirt wench."

At Stonecrop Farm, just above Porlock, the days at this time of year began at cockcrow. Bess and Ambrose Reeve rose as usual shortly after the sun, splashed their faces and dressed quickly. Bess dragged a comb through her greying hair and bundled it under a cap. Downstairs, their daughter Alison and the maidservant Marian were already astir, waking up the banked fire in the kitchen, while the farmhands were pulling on their boots, about to go and feed the plough oxen and the pigs. Ambrose went to help them.

The morning was fine, the grass asparkle with dew. Bess and Alison collected pails and set off for the field where the cows were grazing, to milk them out of doors. Two of the dogs went with them, not barking loudly, because they had been trained to be quiet when near the sheep and cattle, but sometimes woofing softly, running here and there with noses to the ground.

Until, as they passed the haybarn, one of the dogs stiffened, pointed his pewter-coloured nose at the barn, and in defiance of all his careful training, started to bark very noisily indeed.

"Now, what's amiss with you? Be quiet!" Alison seized his collar.

"He never does this as a rule. Now Brindle's started! There's something wrong in that barn," said Bess. "Be a vagabond or something in there, if it b'ain't a fox. Put thy pail down, Alison, and come along."

"But Mother, if there's a wild man in there…an outlaw…"

"We've got the dogs. Go and fetch a hayfork! That'll be enough."

Sybil, curled miserably in the hay, had barely slipped beneath the surface of sleep, because her empty stomach wouldn't let her. She woke suddenly, to find two women, both in brown working gowns and white aprons, standing over her. The younger of the pair was grasping a two-pronged hayfork. The second one was middle-aged and standing with arms akimbo. A grey lurcher and a brown-and-white sheepdog stood beside them, growling. Sybil sat up, pulling herself farther away from the threatening points of the hayfork.

"It's all right, Alison. It's just a lass," said the older woman. "Quiet! Down!" she added to the dogs.

They stopped growling and lay down, but Alison continued to hold her hayfork at the ready and demanded, "What be you a-doin' yur?"

"I just…I just wanted somewhere to sleep. I was cold and it was so late. I meant to come to the house this morning." Sybil was trembling.

"What be you at, wandering about and sleepin' in barns?" Bess asked, though not roughly. The sunlight slanting in behind her through the open door had shown her how young Sybil was, and how white her face.

"I…I ran away," said Sybil. "I took food with me but I'd eaten it all by yesterday morning. I've been looking for work, but I couldn't even find a farm till last night. I saw candlelight…from one of your windows, but it went out before I got close. The barn wasn't locked. I'm sorry. Oh," said Sybil, bursting into tears, "I'm so *hungry!*"

"Well," said Bess, "young wenches dyin' of starvation in one of our barns, that's somethin' we wouldn't care for. 'Ee'd better come in for some breakfast. Then we'll hear thy story. But it had better be the truth, now. Liars b'ain't welcome at Stonecrop."

In the kitchen Bess despatched Marian with Alison to see to the milking, telling them to send Ambrose back indoors while they were about it. She then fried a piece of bread and an egg, filled a beaker with ale and handed it to Sybil. "But eat slowly, or thy guts'll complain," she warned.

Ambrose, large, gaitered and puzzled, appeared while Sybil was in the midst of eating and Bess did the basic explaining while he listened, pulling off his cap and scratching his thin white hair. At the end, by which time Sybil had finished, he, like Bess, asked for her story.

Sybil was too tired and frightened to lie, and didn't, except that she begged them not to ask where her original home had been, and clung to the name of Sybil Waters, which the Lanyons had given her. "I walked and walked," she said, coming to the end of her account. "Miles from Lynmouth, miles up the East Lyn, trying to find somewhere. All day I walked and then when it got dark, I tried to sleep in a patch of trees, but there were things rustling, and I saw eyes…."

"Fox or weasel, no doubt," said Ambrose with a snort. "Christ, girl, you were a fool to run off like that. And leavin' thy babby!"

"No one'll hurt Stephen. They'll look after him in Lynmouth," said Sybil. "But I can't go back. I won't go back! I'd rather walk into the sea and finish it all. I was used as a slave, just a slave, not a penny in wages and nothing was going to change, ever, for the rest of my life!"

"All right, be calm," said Ambrose.

"We don't need help in the house," Bess said. "Wouldn't mind help with the milkin' and the dairy. You any good at that?"

"I can milk and make butter," offered Sybil, who had occasionally done so at Allerbrook. "But can I have a proper job? With a wage, and if anyone wants to marry me, can I say yes?"

"What do you think this here place is?" Ambrose enquired. "It b'ain't no dungeon. From what 'ee's told us and the way thee speaks, our farmhands won't be thy kind of bridegroom. But work, and 'ee'll be paid, only there's to be no more gettin' thyself into trouble. We don't stand for that here. Decent folk, we are. Today 'ee'd better take some rest. Got any clothes apart from that grubby lot 'ee's wearin'?"

"I had some in a bundle...." Sybil looked confused.

"I've got it here," said Bess. "The bundle, I mean. It wur with her in the hay."

"Then 'ee'd best change, take a bit of rest and wash all them messy clothes," said Ambrose. "Tomorrow, we'll see."

"She's at a farm called Stonecrop, just above Porlock, on the west side," said Francis, coming into the dairy where Jane and Eleanor were skimming cream. He was holding yet another letter from Katherine in his hand. "She got herself taken on as a dairymaid there, it seems. She told them that Katherine treated her like a slave. She's still calling herself Sybil Waters."

"The mistress is furious," said Perkins from the doorway behind Francis. "Says she won't have Mistress Sybil back, that she never used her as a slave. She says she cared for Sybil like a daughter and she can hardly believe in such ingratitude. She'll keep the boy, Stephen. Seems Master Owen thinks he might be trained up as a sailor...."

"I wouldn't agree to have him back here in any case," said Francis.

"Well, it doesn't arise," said Perkins. "But the mistress says she'll have naught to do with Mistress Sybil and the Stone-crop people are welcome to her."

"How was she found?" Jane asked.

"I found her, mistress. I'd been riding out each day, first this direction, then that, and eventually I came across the place. It's in Culbone parish—there's a tiny little hamlet and a little church, both called Culbone, not far away, down in the woods toward the sea. The farm's up on the edge of the moors, though, away from the woods. Bleak kind of place. She looked tired," he said with some compassion, "and I reckon she works as hard there as she ever did with us, but she told me she was happy and that she was being paid. I suppose that's a point. She can go to Porlock now and again and buy herself the sort of gewgaws women like."

"Francis," pleaded Jane, "couldn't Sybil come home?"

Francis flushed an angry red and Eleanor said, "Better not. At least we know that Sybil is safe with respectable people."

"Quite. I've said I won't have her back and I keep my word," Francis said coldly. "As for you, Jane, you should put your mind to your own future. And if you don't like it, blame Sybil. If she had behaved herself, I wouldn't be sending you to court. One sister there is an investment, but two would be an extravagance. However, as things are, it's your duty to me."

Jane, also recognizing the signs of Francis's temper, said

no more, but that night she knelt by her bed and once more prayed that no court vacancy would ever arise.

For some time, it seemed that her prayers were still being heard, for no vacancy came about and in late October the news reached them that the queen had borne the king the son he wanted, and had then died. There was no queen at court now, needing ladies to attend her.

Jane, mindful of the health of her soul, did not this time let herself feel glad that another young woman had lost her life. But the sense of freedom, of safety, of knowing for certain that she could not now be sent to the court, was immense.

Until the January of 1540, when King Henry, for the fourth time, got married.

CHAPTER EIGHT
The Icy Welcome
1540

"There's Greenwich Palace," said Ralph Palmer to Jane, standing in the bows of the hired barge which was bringing the party to the court. "See— those towers and turrets—against the sky, to the right."

"So we're nearly there," said Jane bleakly.

"I wonder what this new Queen Anna is like," said Dorothy Stone, emerging from the little covered cabin amidships, pulling her furred cloak around her more tightly and thrusting herself determinedly into the conversation, as she had been doing whenever she saw Jane and Ralph in anything like private talk. Jane glanced at her with irritation.

She had known Ralph all her life, as a kinsman, albeit a distant one. She understood now that their common ancestor had been Ralph's great-grandfather and Jane's great-great-grandfather. Their cousinship was therefore remote and Ralph was certainly handsome, but the simple fact that they had known each other since childhood was enough to make Jane regard him as a brother rather than a possible suitor.

She knew, too, that his family, especially his stern father, Luke, and the wealthy London cousin, Sir Edmund Flaxton, to whom she owed her appointment to court, intended him to make a grand marriage or at least a moneyed one, and Ralph would not cross his family's wishes. The Sweetwaters were not as wealthy as they used to be and certainly were nowhere near as rich as the Stones. Ralph's father was acquainted with Thomas Stone and Francis had told her, before she left home, that there was talk of betrothing Ralph to Dorothy.

"Once Dorothy has had a little court burnish, of course," Francis said. "She's a pallid little thing and hardly ever has a word to say for herself. You and she will travel there together."

"Very well," said Jane without enthusiasm.

"I can't escort you," Francis said. "I have too much to see to here, but Dr. Spenlove and Eleanor will accompany you. Dorothy's father is going with her and Ralph is going to court, too, and will also be in the party. Now, Jane, make sure you don't—er—upset the plans for Ralph and Dorothy in any way. You know what I mean."

She knew perfectly well what he meant, but could not see that merely talking to Ralph, as she had talked to him a thousand times already, was going to upset anything. Dorothy's attitude was embarrassing and a nuisance. Well, it was cold out here on the river anyway. Quietly she withdrew to the cabin in Dorothy's stead.

It was January, a terrible month for travelling. They should have set out sooner but their departure had been delayed by storms, and the journey had been slow. Floods after heavy rain had repeatedly forced them out of their way, and then the weather had turned bitter, with winds that penetrated the sturdiest riding cloaks as though they were made of tissue paper.

When they left their horses at Kingston and hired barges instead, Jane hoped the Thames would be warmer, but it was worse, with a leaden sky reflected in the water, and sleet on the wind. She had wondered at times if this arctic journey would ever end. *Not that I wanted to start out on it in the first place,* she said to herself, sitting down disconsolately in the cabin.

She was not alone in it, since Eleanor was there, and so was Dr. Amyas Spenlove, the chaplain who for the past three years or so had led daily prayers at Allerbrook. He was by nature rubicund and jolly, but didn't seem so just now. On the contrary, he looked pinched and unhappy. Dr. Spenlove was an indoor man. In a world where printing had turned the making of illuminated manuscripts into a dying art, there were still people who loved them, and creating the colourful pages was Spenlove's hobby. Over the years he had become quite well known. At the moment he was preparing a set of the four Gospels for a Taunton gentleman.

In his room at Allerbrook he had a cupboard full of pigments and fixatives and a locked drawer containing gold and silver leaf, and a smeary table to work on. He hated being separated from his hobby and he hated cold weather. He was also, as Jane knew, sorry for her. She had admitted to him, as they rode, that she loved Allerbrook and did not want to leave it to go to court, and although he had said all the expected things, such as "You'll enjoy yourself once you're there," she had seen sympathy in his eyes. He wasn't liking this journey at all, either on her behalf or his own.

Also in the cabin were the two middle-aged tirewomen Thomas Stone and Francis had found in Taunton.

"Maid of honour is a dignified post. You must have your own woman servant," Francis had told Jane. "Thomas Stone is looking for one for Dorothy, as well. We'll choose sensible women, skilled at their work and not too young."

Eleanor and the two sensible women were talking together just now and they all smiled at Jane as she stooped her head under the cabin door, but although she smiled back, she sat down as far apart from them as the cramped conditions would allow. Eleanor glanced at her thoughtfully, but let her be, for which Jane was grateful.

At home there would be a roaring fire in the hall on a day like this, the sheep and cattle would be in the shippon, and the moors above the house would be dark and brooding and yet beautiful in their stern way. The trees in Allerbrook combe would be leafless, so that the sound of the swift Allerbrook would come up clearly, especially after the recent rain. She had not dared to protest when the news came that a place in the new queen's entourage was hers. But now, less than a fortnight after leaving home, she was so homesick that she didn't know how to endure it, and they hadn't even landed at Greenwich yet!

They were arriving now. The plash of the oars had ceased and the barge was gliding silently onward under its own momentum. Ralph appeared. "Time to go ashore," he said.

Jane obeyed, followed by the other three women and the chaplain. Dorothy was already stepping ashore on her father's arm. Through stinging sleet they all beheld the palace frontage, stretching left and right, full of windows, adorned with the towers and turrets that Ralph had pointed out. Straight ahead was a doorway, reached by a broad flight of steps. Heads bowed against the sleet, the party ran for shelter. There were guards at the top of the steps, but a large, impressive gentleman with a blond beard stepped out to greet them and led them quickly inside, into a wide vestibule.

"I've had someone looking out for new arrivals. When he said a barge was approaching, I hoped it would be you," he said.

He had a heavy mantle edged with beaver fur and a thick gold chain across the chest of his black velvet doublet, and though he was not old, he had considerable presence. Jane, concluding that he was a senior court official, promptly curtsied with cheerful informality. Ralph, however, gave a perfunctory bow and said, "Hallo, Edmund!"

"Ralph! At last!"

"This is Sir Edmund Flaxton," said Ralph, turning to the others. "My cousin—and yours as well, Jane. You're related to him in exactly the same way as you're related to me. He's younger than me, believe it or not. It's the mantle and the gold chain that give him all that gravitas."

"You're a cheeky puppy," said Sir Edmund amiably. "Behave."

"Edmund, we all want to thank you." Ralph spoke seriously and then once more addressed the new arrivals. "He's worked himself ragged to arrange your appointment here, Mistress Sweetwater, and yours, too, Mistress Stone, when your fathers and I requested it."

"We are all very grateful for your endeavours," said Thomas Stone gravely and Eleanor, who had also sunk into a deep curtsy, echoed, "Yes, most grateful" in heartfelt tones.

Ralph performed further introductions and Sir Edmund told them all to come with him. "I've an apartment in the palace and I've already bespoken some wine and hot pasties. My wife isn't here—she's at home in Kent with our little boy, Giles—but I've good servants with me. You must all be perished after travelling on water in this weather. Where did you leave your horses?"

"Kingston, to be collected on the way home," said Dr. Spenlove glumly. "We understood that stabling couldn't be provided here, and by the time we got to Kingston, the poor beasts had had enough, anyway. The journey was difficult. I fear we've arrived much later than we expected."

"Yes. You've missed the wedding, as a matter of fact. This way," said Sir Edmund.

The route to his rooms was lengthy, across courtyards through long passageways with ornate ceilings, but finally he stopped, put a key into the lock of an unobtrusive door and showed them into a well-furnished parlour with a bed-chamber visible beyond a wide archway in the farther wall. A fire sent out blessed waves of heat.

"Please sit down, everyone," Sir Edmund said. "Yes, all of you. You all look frozen." The two tirewomen had been hanging back, but accepted the invitation thankfully. "It's no wonder that you're late," their host said as they settled them-selves. "Winter travelling is so difficult. But it's a pity you took so long."

"We made what speed we could," said Thomas Stone anx-iously. "The appointments are sound, are they not? I mean…"

"Yes, yes, perfectly sound." Sir Edmund paused as two manservants came in with the wine and pasties he had men-tioned. "Here—you probably need this. You've had an icy welcome." He waited until they had been served and the servants had gone and then said, "Presently I'll call someone to show the young ladies to their quarters and introduce them to Queen Anna and the rest of her household. But I think I had better explain the situation. If you'd been here earlier, you'd have seen it develop, but as things are…"

They looked at him in surprise, waiting for him to go on. "It's very difficult," he said, "and confidential. The wedding was three days ago, on the sixth of January. Since then, alas… Oh, how hard it is to explain! I *must* warn you. It's no secret within the court, and if I don't tell you, you'll soon hear everything, but all the same, it must *not* be bruited about outside. The king is not pleased with his bargain. I must also tell you that Queen Anna herself seems unaware of this. She is, I think, a very decent and…and innocent lady."

"What are you talking about?" asked Thomas. "You're not making yourself clear."

Sir Edmund looked at him and turned red.

"You mean," said Ralph shrewdly, "that the marriage is no marriage and may not hold?"

"King Henry tried his best to get out of it before the vows were taken," said Sir Edmund. "There was some talk of a pre-contract. But Queen Anna took an oath that it was untrue and that she was free to marry, and so that way of escape was blocked. You young ladies are coming into a delicate situation. You must walk carefully and watch your tongues, and how long there will be a queen in need of maids of honour or ladies-in-waiting, I wouldn't like to guess."

"But he can't…he wouldn't…!" gasped Eleanor.

"If there has been no carnal knowledge," said Thomas, "he won't need to do anything drastic. There could be an annulment. He certainly can't behead the daughter of a noble European house, even if he manages to…er…invent…"

"Hmm," said Ralph. "I'd heard that when His Majesty first began seeking a bride to replace Jane Seymour, Christina, the daughter of the Duchess of Milan, said she'd only marry him if she had two heads and therefore a neck to spare."

"No one's hiding behind any of my tapestries," said Sir Edmund, "but there are things it isn't advisable to say out loud. Tread carefully, cousin Ralph."

He looked at Jane and Dorothy. "And be kind to Queen Anna. Protect her as long as you can. She, too, has had an icy welcome and she doesn't deserve it. As a matter of fact, she is winning hearts at court and elsewhere. She is kind to her household and charitable to the poor. The only heart she can't win, apparently, is King Henry's!"

CHAPTER NINE
Strange New World
1540

*J*ane's first impressions of life at court were blurred by bewilderment and loneliness. Of those who had come with her, Dorothy was soon the only one left and she had never been close to Dorothy. Thomas Stone, Dr. Spenlove and Eleanor left for home almost at once. Ralph stayed for two weeks, but was then taken away by Sir Edmund to a house party in Kent. After that, to all intents and purposes, Jane was alone.

She liked the new queen, though. Anna of Cleves was not beautiful, since her complexion was lustreless and her eyes heavy lidded, but she had a sweet smile and gracious manners. When Dorothy remarked to Jane that the new queen was ugly and had hardly any English, she received a sharp answer.

"She's in a foreign country, trying to find her feet, and *I* think she's got a lovely smile," snapped Jane. "If you had to go and live in Germany, I wonder how fast you'd learn the language?"

And if there had ever been the faintest hope that because they, too, were finding their feet in a strange new world, Dorothy and Jane would draw together and make friends, it died at that moment.

Mistress Lowe, the stately matron in charge of the maids of honour, was more than a little intimidating. One of the first things that she impressed on the new arrivals was how much there was to learn. There was a routine to get used to, protocol to study and crowds of people whose identities had to be memorized just like the details of the routine.

Mistress Lowe undertook the introductions, to the court officials, the other ladies and maids of honour. There were so many that they made Jane feel dizzy.

"Mistress Sweetwater, Mistress Stone, these ladies have come from Cleves, to serve Queen Anna. This is Gertrude, this is Hanna, this is Eva…"

Of the German women, only Hanna had any English to speak of, and to Jane, they all looked alike—heavily built and dowdy. But the English women at the queen's side were nearly as confusing. *How will I ever remember all these names?* Jane wondered in a panic as she and Dorothy were introduced to Mary, to Elizabeth, to another Mary, to Susanna and Elise. "And this is Madam Elizabeth, the king's daughter."

Madam Elizabeth was a small, solemn, redheaded girl, and she at least would be easy to remember, though in the event, Jane saw little of her, since she had her own apartments and rarely came into the presence of either the queen or the king. Another who was easy to remember, however, and was very much part of the queen's entourage, was "Kate Howard, our youngest maid of honour."

Kate Howard looked no more than fifteen and was as pretty as a rose, with winning manners. "You are a good girl," Mistress Lowe said to her once when she had managed to soothe the hurt feelings of Hanna, who was sensitive. "You are like oil in a stiff lock."

The maids of honour were supposed always to be near their mistress and ready to run errands. Jane found this hair-raising at first, as she was never sure where she was supposed to go or how to recognize whoever it was she was supposed to speak to. The principal officials, who carried white sticks as a sign of office and were actually called White Staves, all looked as dignified as emperors, while their supporting staff, who worked in a perfect warren of rooms, seemed as numerous as an army.

There was a huge department called Greencloth Accounting—because of the green-covered table at which daily conferences were held—which was entirely devoted to ordering food supplies, paying the suppliers, planning menus and dispensing the ingredients to the kitchens. Queen Anna sometimes wished for dishes not familiar to the English cooks, and Jane's first errand was to the Greencloth Department, armed with a recipe, written out in English by the bilingual Hanna.

She lost her way three times and when she did find the right place, though people were polite and accepted the recipe she presented to them, she felt presumptuous, like a small child trying to give instruction to adults.

Other errands took her outside the palace. Sometimes, with other ladies, Jane went by river into London to look at merchants' goods and place orders. It was not a pleasure. The court was crowded enough and at times smelly with a distasteful mingling of body odours and cloying perfumes, but London streets were worse. They were a chaos of thronging people and lofty horsemen who seemed prepared to ride down anyone who got in their way; the streets were littered with horse droppings and human ordure flung from windows, and the stench was like a hand clutching at her throat.

But there were more and worse unpleasantnesses to come, as Jane discovered, and oddly enough, her carefully acquired skill at music was responsible. Queen Anna quite soon learned from someone, probably Sir Edmund Flaxton, that young Mistress Sweetwater played the virginals well. There came an evening when, in the queen's private rooms, which contained musical instruments, the queen, with gestures and halting phrases, asked Jane to perform for her.

The queen took supper apart, with a select group of attendants and courtiers. But the day after Jane's debut as a musician she was told that she and pretty little Kate Howard had been invited to join the inner circle that evening, as guests. Dorothy was not included, which made her glower.

Jane was instructed to dress with care, and her tirewoman Lisa helped her put on a tawny damask very like the one which had once been meant for Sybil. "The colour suits you well, madam," Lisa said.

A page showed her to the dining chamber, which proved to be a small but luxurious hall, hung with glowing tapestries and lit by innumerable candles. And this evening the king was present, seated beside his wife. For the first time, Jane beheld King Henry VIII of England.

She was near enough to see and hear him clearly. He was broad chested and strong voiced, jewelled and befurred, a powerfully dominant presence even when he was doing nothing more remarkable than saying good evening to his table companions. He was also, as far as Jane was concerned, heavily jowled and overweight. He reminded her of a bear she had once seen at a fair in Minehead, a lumbering thing with the same small, angry eyes. She pitied the poor queen, if Anna had to endure that hulking body on top of her at night. If Sir Edmund were correct, of course, perhaps she was spared it. In her place, Jane would have been thankful.

"You are new to the court, are you not?" said a voice in her ear, and she turned to find that her right-hand neighbour was addressing her. It was a man, and to her surprise his voice held a trace of the familiar west country accent. She looked at him with interest. He was not unlike Ralph, except that his hair was dark brown rather than black and he had a beard, which Ralph had not, and a more aquiline nose. He seemed older, too. He was smiling pleasantly at her and she smiled back.

"Yes, sir, very new. Everything is still very strange. I know hardly anyone yet."

"My name is Peter Carew. And you are…?"

"Jane. Jane Sweetwater. Master Carew, was Sir William Carew of Mohuns Ottery in Devon a relative of yours? He was a friend of my family."

"He was indeed, and I know who you are now, though we haven't met before. My father spoke of the Sweetwaters sometimes. I am Sir William's youngest son and was one of his biggest problems, until I went off with the French army and vanished," said Peter Carew cheerfully, and chuckled.

Across the table Kate Howard called out, "What's the joke?"

"My family history," said Carew, grinning. "I was sent abroad when I was young and eventually disappeared so thoroughly that my parents thought I was dead. When I came back to England and went to see them before joining the court, I gave my mother such a shock that she fainted. *Peter,* she said, *you're dead! You've come back from the grave!* And then she sat down on the nearest seat and rolled up her eyes and passed out. *You cause trouble even by walking through a door!* my father said to me."

Jane was working it out. At that dreadful dinner that should have been for Sybil, Sir William Carew had mentioned a son, Peter, and had described him as a pert, forward brat who, when sent out in the world, had got himself demoted from page to stable boy because of misbehaviour. This must be the same Peter Carew. He seemed to be a sufficiently dignified and responsible young gentleman now. He couldn't really be much older than Ralph. Was it the beard that made him seem so? No, it was something in the man himself. He had gone adventuring; he had seen the world and acquired experience. That was the difference.

Kate Howard was still listening. "I'm sure," she said wickedly, "that you could cause all sorts of trouble if you wanted to."

"Minx," said Carew amiably, but kept his attention on Jane. "You haven't been here long enough to realize, I suppose, but the court's a strange place just now."

"I know," said Jane in a low voice.

"I like Queen Anna," Carew said. "I was with the escort that went to meet her at Calais. But then…" He shook his head and ceased talking, because servants were coming around with dishes and could have overheard. Before supper, Mistress Lowe had warned Jane that some of the deferential persons now recommending a spicy mutton stew were paid to report questionable remarks and opinions to Thomas Cromwell, the king's most trusted aide.

As the servers withdrew, Carew, as though he knew what Jane was thinking, remarked, "The man who has gone up to the king and is speaking to him now is Thomas Cromwell. He is a great power in the land."

"The heavyset man in the dark clothes?"

"Yes. Not a fellow to cross, believe me," said Carew.

"And the tall man three seats along from the king," said Kate Howard, leaning across to interrupt, "the one with the long face and the long nose, is my uncle, Thomas Howard, Duke of Norfolk. I don't like him."

"Pert, that's what you are," said Carew. Turning back to Jane, he said quietly, "Cromwell isn't as much in favour as he was. He did more than anyone to organize the marriage, and, well…"

"Perhaps it will be better when the queen has learned English," said Jane. "It must be difficult when husband and wife can't talk to each other properly." The queen's lady, Hanna, was seated near her mistress, probably so that she could act as interpreter. She seemed to be doing so now. Somewhat to Jane's discomfort, she also kept glancing toward Jane herself.

Carew, who had not noticed, recalled Jane's attention. "It's not just that. There are feelings no one can command. As I was saying, I was in the escort that brought Queen Anna from Calais. We got her as far as Rochester, in Kent, and then King Henry arrived, galloping on horseback, dressed as a gentleman but not as a king. He wanted to surprise her, to play the passionate lover. He was as eager as a boy," said Carew, still speaking low, though no one, surely, thought Jane, could think it treasonable to say that King Henry had romantic leanings.

"What happened?" she asked.

"Cromwell was with him, but the king was shown to her rooms on his own, as though he were just another noble visitor. When he came out… Well, I saw his face, and then I heard him say to Cromwell, *I like her not*. He didn't mean her lack of English, Jane. He meant something—much more earthy. I suppose he did his best. He changed into more royal-looking clothes, had himself announced again, this time as the king, and went through the motions of being delighted with her."

"I see," said Jane, remembering what Sir Edmund had told them when she and her companions first arrived.

"He had to go through with it," Carew said. "You can't fetch the daughter of a powerful foreign duke over to England, then turn up your nose and send her back as though she were goods supplied on approval, and didn't meet your standards. It could cause all kinds of diplomatic repercussions—even destroy alliances. Every king needs his allies, just in case. Besides, it would have been rude and unkind. King Henry can be chivalrous. Well, I think he tried to be," said Carew, his voice now very cautious. "But not, I fancy, successfully, and however well she learns English—well, I fear he will end up risking the diplomatic upheavals. And, of course, there are all these absurd religious problems."

He glanced at her face and laughed again. "Oh, what *is* it?" cried Kate Howard, abruptly interrupting her own right-hand neighbour, who had been trying to talk to her about an entertainment which was scheduled for the next day. "Do share the joke!"

"It's no joke," said Carew brusquely, and kept his eyes on Jane's face. "You don't know what I'm talking about, do you? The point is that though the king has broken away from Rome, so that we have prayers in English instead of Latin and no more worshipping of idols in what we all now call the popish style, nevertheless, the church in England is still much what it was in other ways. The heresies of Martin Luther are still heresies. The queen has been docile in religious matters and worships just as the king does, but she comes from a Lutheran country. There are people who fear that her influence, if she were ever to acquire any, would be pernicious."

"Oh, I see," said Jane, who didn't. Ralph's father, Luke, was said to admire the teachings of a German called Martin Luther, but she had never been clear about what they were.

"Shhh!" said the man on Peter's other side. "The king wants to say something."

They looked toward the top table, whereupon Jane discovered that she and Kate Howard were the object of the royal attention. King Henry, in fact, was raising a goblet to them both.

"We have two young ladies here this evening who have not supped in our company before! Welcome, Mistress Kate Howard, Mistress Jane Sweetwater!"

"Stand up! Stand straight!" hissed Thomas Cromwell, suddenly appearing beside the lower table and making *get up at once* gestures at Kate and Jane.

"A toast!" boomed the genial monster in the seat of honour. "A toast to youth and beauty and gracious womanly charm. To Kate Howard, to Jane Sweetwater. Health and long life!"

Glasses and goblets were raised. The toast was drunk. "Sit down," muttered Cromwell.

They sat, but His Majesty hadn't finished. "Which one of you is Jane Sweetwater?" he demanded, and a prod from Cromwell brought Jane to her feet once more.

"My queen tells me that you play the virginals well," rumbled King Henry. "This evening, dear Mistress Sweetwater, you must play once more, for both of us."

Kate Howard, in her frivolous way, laughed again. It was a pretty and natural sound, different from the carefully cultivated laughter of many of the court ladies, who used mirth, as often as not, as a way of expressing polite scorn.

But three seats away from Henry, Kate's uncle, the Duke of Norfolk, turned what his niece, accurately enough, had described as his long face and his long nose toward Jane, stared at her with cold dark eyes, and without either speaking or moving, exuded toward her the information that he at least did not wish her well.

It was an interminable evening. There was dancing immediately after supper, but the king danced only once with his wife. Jane, on the contrary, and to her alarm, was twice led onto the floor by King Henry. He smelt of rancid sweat and sandalwood soap—no doubt meant to disguise the sweat, which it hadn't—and his big beefy hands were hot. Once more she saw Norfolk looking at her with dislike, although Kate Howard, too, was invited to dance twice. After that, both of them were bidden to accompany the queen to her quarters, where Henry presently joined them, and with Kate to turn the pages of the music for her, Jane was commanded to play.

Both king and queen applauded and asked for more. It was late before she reached her bed. She found poor Lisa drooping in a seat in the dormitory.

"I'm sorry, madam," Lisa said, helping her to undress. "I'm supposed to be a tirewoman but just now a tired woman is what I feel like."

"So do I. I hope we can both rest a little tomorrow," said Jane, much concerned.

"I heard that the king was there tonight. Did you dance with him?"

"Yes," said Jane gloomily. "And played music for him and the queen afterward."

A pattern which was to be repeated time after time throughout the weeks that followed, with Henry's beefy hands growing, it seemed, hotter and more embarrassingly enquiring during every dance, and Henry's compliments, on her footwork, her music and her appearance, more lavish and disquieting. Until the second of May, when King Henry kissed her.

I've been the biggest fool in Christendom, Sybil told herself as she scrambled out of bed and into her clothes and down the stairs of Stonecrop farmhouse, in order to plunge out into the cold and dark of a February morning to feed the sow and the poultry before breakfast.

She had thought she was to be a dairymaid, but Stonecrop was short of hands and everyone seemed to do everything, as required. After breakfast she and Alison must muck out the stable and byre, and pile the steamy result on the enormous midden. Every kind of bodily waste, animal or human, went onto that midden, and before very long, Alison had said, they'd be taking the stinking stuff to the fields in baskets on their backs, and spreading it to fertilize the earth before the spring ploughing.

She seemed to be permanently wet, cold and filthy. At Lynmouth she had worked but indoors, at least. And what was happening to Stephen all this time? She'd thought she didn't care about him, but now she was constantly wondering how he was, whether he missed her, was looking for her, crying for her…

I don't wish he'd never been born, said Sybil to herself, shovelling horse dung. *I just wish that I hadn't.*

CHAPTER TEN
Fearful Majesty
1540

ourt life did of course have its good moments. Jane attended a tournament and marvelled at the immense horses and heavily armoured riders as they charged each other, separated by a brightly coloured barrier but reaching across it with lethal-looking lances. She also liked walking in the grounds with the Queen and enjoyed dancing when King Henry wasn't there. When he was, he never failed to partner her at least once.

Peter Carew sometimes danced with her, which was much more agreeable, or strolled beside her when queen and courtiers went walking. It was from Peter that she learned that she was not imagining the unfriendly looks she kept receiving from the Duke of Norfolk.

"He saw before the wedding that this marriage was going to be a catastrophe," Carew said. "And straightaway he started getting notions about his niece. The gossip is that he'd put her into Henry's bed himself if he got the chance. As a mistress or even a wife, if Henry manages to get out of this toil he's in—and he might, from all I hear."

Jane had heard the same thing, mainly from Hanna, who sometimes, worriedly, talked to the English ladies.

"The king sometimes sleeps in her chamber," Hanna had said, "but all he does is kiss her good-night, and then kiss her good-morning and leave her. On the first night he fumbled about in a way she did not like, but from what she says, it came to naught and he doesn't do even that now. She says she hopes for children, but, poor soul, she does not know how children are made. We do not tell her, for that is for the King to do. Besides, it is no use for her to know—things—if he will not do his part. We are anxious for her."

It seemed to Jane that the few happy occasions would always be overshadowed by things that were not happy at all. The miserable royal marriage was one of these. Her home-sickness was another and she was made uncomfortable by Dorothy's obvious resentment because the king never solic-ited her hand in dancing. Carew didn't either. Dorothy, in fact, was a wallflower.

Matters worsened rapidly when the court moved upstream to London and Whitehall Palace for the May Day celebrations.

It was Jane's first experience of the strange mixture of order and chaos which was King Henry's court on the move. Instructions were exact. All personal belongings must be clearly labelled. Porters would take everything to the barges that were to transport baggage to Whitehall. Only the most important people could take furniture and bedding and hangings; the rest must accept what they found awaiting them at the other end.

Jane made sure that her goods were carefully labelled, but Lisa panicked slightly at the idea of their things being borne away to be piled up in the barge with other hampers and bundles, and prayed aloud that nothing would get lost or broken. However, the journey, though chilly, was accomplished without incident. But when the maids of honour had been shown to their new dormitory and the baggage was brought in, Jane's biggest hamper wasn't there.

"Oh, madam, I knew something would go wrong with your things. I *knew* it!" wailed Lisa.

"Well, it isn't your fault," Jane said soothingly. "Or mine, either," she added, frowning. "My brother painted my name on all my hampers and boxes before I left home and I stuck two labels on each piece of luggage, as well. I begged some glue from the Greencloth room. They keep it so that the kitchen staff can mend pots and pans and so on. Look, you can see them on the other things. I can't understand it."

Appealed to, Mistress Lowe said there was a room where unlabelled baggage was put until it was claimed, but when Jane and Lisa followed her directions, with difficulty, since Whitehall was a tangled maze of courtyards and separate buildings, they found that the room was now part of an extended Greencloth office and no one seemed to know where mislaid baggage had been stowed. A little later Peter Carew, finding Lisa and Jane down on the landing stage distractedly peering around, asked what they were about.

"I wondered if a hamper of mine had been left here by mistake," Jane said. "It hasn't been brought to our dormitory."

"There's a room where unidentified luggage is put," said Carew comfortingly. "Come. I'll show you."

"We've been there," said Jane. "But it's being used for something else—there are clerks in it."

"I don't mean that one, I mean the new one. It's been changed. No one ever remembers to tell anyone anything in this court! Details are always going wrong. Come with me."

He led them to the right place, and the missing hamper was there. "The labels must have been torn off by accident, madam," Lisa said. "I saw the way the porters just toss things about. Disgraceful, it is."

"But both labels have come off—and they've been *ripped* off," said Jane, examining the hamper. "There are just scraps of them left, and look! Someone's splashed something over the place where Francis painted my name. It's been covered over by—well, it looks like ink."

"Is there someone at court who doesn't like you, Mistress Sweetwater?" Carew asked, quite seriously.

"It's a woman, if so," said Lisa. "This is what spiteful women do. And I can put a name to the hussy, as well!"

"Leave it," said Jane. "Let's just take the hamper to the dormitory and not speak of this. I've got my property back. Master Carew, I must thank you for your help."

"I'm always willing to assist a young lady in distress," Carew said. He added suddenly and cryptically, "Remember that. Especially if there is spitefulness about."

He left them before Jane could ask him what he meant. She asked Lisa instead, as they were carrying the hamper into the empty dormitory. "I don't understand," she said in puzzlement.

"I do," said Lisa. "And I can put a name to the girl who did it."

"Who?"

Lisa opened her mouth to reply, but closed it as the door opened and Dorothy came in with her tirewoman Madge. "So you found your things after all," said Dorothy rudely.

"You ought to take more care with your labels. Fancy gluing them on so feebly that they just fall off."

Madge, who was very partisan as far as her young mistress was concerned, turned away quickly, but not quickly enough to hide a sly, smug smile. Jane looked at Lisa, who nodded.

"Start the unpacking," said Jane, and turned grimly to face Dorothy.

"I took every care. Most people tie their labels on, so how did you know I used glue? I didn't announce it and you weren't in the room when I was sticking them on. They were wrenched off deliberately and where my name was painted on the wicker, someone has blanked it out with ink. Now, I wonder who did that?"

Dorothy coloured but tossed her head. "It wasn't me, if that's what you mean."

"No?"

"Oh, don't put on such righteous, haughty airs! Just because the king and Master Carew both dance with you…"

"Dorothy, what in the world is the matter with you? You surely don't care whether you dance with the king or not." It was incredible to Jane that anyone could actually wish to be physically close to the malodorous Henry. "And you have a handsome man of your own. Aren't you going to marry Ralph Palmer?"

"There's an understanding. We're not formally betrothed yet and if we ever do marry, Ralph Palmer will be marrying my dowry, not me," Dorothy retorted. "If yours were bigger, he'd take you instead and he'd probably rather. I saw him looking at you sometimes on the way here."

"Oh, *Dorothy!*" said Jane helplessly.

She worried about it all through the May Day celebrations, with their tournaments and masques. On the following day Queen Anna said to her, in her slow English, "Hanna has written…how to make a dish I like. It is like a cake made with rice and covered in…bread in tiny bits…."

"Crumbs?" said Jane.

"Yes, so. Crumbs. And fried and served with cold, sharp stewed apples. Very good. Hanna does not like talking…to English officials. Take this to the kitchen and explain. I wish it tomorrow at supper."

I don't like giving orders to officials, either, Jane thought, but orders from the queen must be obeyed. However, the White Stave she spoke to in the Greencloth room was not one of the overdignified ones and was kind enough to tell her a quicker way back to the queen's apartments.

"Whitehall is confusing, I know. But—" he pointed through a window "—you can cut through that building there. It has a small council chamber downstairs and the king is in conference there now, but there is a staircase just inside the door and no one will mind if you go up one floor and walk through the upstairs gallery. At the far end is another staircase and you can go down to a courtyard. The side door to the queen's lodging is just a few steps to your left."

Jane was glad of the guidance, since the good May Day weather had now given way to rain. She found the building the White Stave had pointed out and went up to the gallery, a wide and handsome place with a long row of windows. Settles with arm-ends shaped like lions' heads and crimson cushions with gold fringes strewn on the seats, stood here and there, and oak chests with gold-inlaid carvings were placed between the windows. Rain blew against the diamond-leaded panes and she was glad to be on the indoor side of them.

Then, as she was walking through the gallery, a figure she

decidedly did not want to meet entered through a small door near the far end. The conference, presumably, was over. At any rate, King Henry had left it.

He had seen her. There was nothing to do but stand aside and curtsy. He seemed to be on his own and he looked angry. She kept her eyes down as he approached, hoping he would just walk past, but instead he stopped, stretched one of those beefy hands down, slipped it under her elbow and raised her.

"Mistress Jane! You're a healing sight for a harassed man. My nobles! All hummings and hawings and protocol and…ah well, never mind. Come and cheer me for a little." He led her to the nearest settle and she found herself obliged to sit on it beside him. His thick, powerful arm went around her.

"There is something you must know," he said. "Something that I suspect all you ladies have guessed anyway. Queen Anna and I…are not more than friends. I am seeking a way to dissolve the union, without harming her. I wish her to be respected and provided for and treated as my sister— but we cannot go on pretending to be man and wife. Cromwell is making every possible difficulty, damn the man. Others, not you, will have the task of telling the queen, but I want you to *know.* Can you guess why?"

With that, the powerful arm tightened and turned her to face him, and the big square countenance came close and his mouth clamped itself over hers. She dared not struggle, but the feel of his fat tongue forcing its way into her own mouth made her want to retch. She controlled the urge with a gigantic effort as he nuzzled and sucked. He had been drinking wine and the taste was on his tongue. Secondhand wine, thought Jane wildly, was horrible. There were tears in her eyes. The whole ghastly business seemed to go on forever.

He let her go at last, but put a thick forefinger on one of her eyebrows and said, "Dear little Jane. Are these tears? Have I moved you so much?"

"I…I am overwhelmed," Jane found herself stammering. She blurted out something else, about fearful majesty, and he laughed and began to fumble at her clothes. "Please," said Jane. "Please…sir…Your Majesty…"

Rescue came, but not in an agreeable form. She had been longing for it, but would have preferred it not to come in the shape either of the Duke of Norfolk or Thomas Cromwell. They, however, were both in the group of men who now followed Henry into the gallery and came striding toward them. Norfolk's expression as he looked at her was that of a bird of prey eyeing a mouse.

Henry freed her and stood up. "Well, gentlemen. I left you to further deliberations. I hope you have some sensible suggestions to make to me now." He smiled at Jane. "Go back to Queen Anna, but…" His voice dropped. "No word of this happy encounter. You understand? We will talk more in due time. Yes, Sir Thomas? What have you to tell me?"

Jane was dismissed. She was obliged to pass Norfolk and his companions, which shouldn't have been difficult because the gallery was so wide. But Cromwell had instantly engaged the king in earnest conversation and Henry had turned away from her. He did not see Norfolk shoot out a hand and grip her shoulder, spinning her around to look at him.

"Slut," said Norfolk softly. Then he let her go and she was on her way again, with tears once more in her eyes.

She found the stair at the end of the gallery and ran down it, thrusting open the door at the foot and fleeing out into the rain. The side door to the queen's lodgings was only a few yards away and she hastened to it, with mingled rain and tears almost blinding her.

Just inside the door she stopped short, leaning against the wall. She felt breathless and her heart was hammering. Never had she wished more ardently that she could be back at home, sewing with Eleanor in the parlour with its view of the brown and purple moorlands, or riding down green-shadowed Allerbrook combe.

Inside her, something seemed to have snapped. *I can't stay here. I can't stay at this court,* said Jane to herself. The door through which she had just come opened again and Peter Carew came striding in.

"Jane! I saw you running in here as if you were in a panic and, well, here you are, propped against a wall and…" He came toward her, looking at her keenly. "You're crying. Jane, what's amiss?"

"King Henry," said Jane miserably. Peter looked bewildered.

"I met him in a gallery and he kissed me. And he wants to divorce Queen Anna. Did you know?"

"Most of the court knows, except for the queen herself."

"I can't bear it. I daren't stay here. I'm going home. I'll take Lisa with me. Where's the best place to hire horses from, to start us on our way?"

"Good God, you can't go off with only Lisa as an escort!"

"I must. After what happened in that gallery, I *must!* I don't suppose I'll be granted permission, so I'll just go."

"No, you won't…no, listen! You're right to want to get away, unless you're prepared to end up as another concubine, in wedlock or out of it, living in luxury and the target of spite and not only from the other girls. The Duke of Norfolk wouldn't be your friend either. I told you I'm always willing to help a young lady in distress. And I've always had a liking," he added with a grin, "for doing lawless things, especially in a good cause. As it happens, I'm leaving the court myself tomorrow—with permission—to visit my mother in Devon. She's been lonely since my father died."

"But how…what…?"

"*Listen*. Let me think. Yes, I know. I'm good at getting into trouble and getting out of it as well, but there's no need to ask for it. Here's what you must do…"

"I'd better leave word of some sort," Jane said as his instructions ended. "I'm part of the queen's household. She'll feel responsible. She might send after me! Maybe King Henry will, too!"

"King Henry," said Peter, though he kept his voice down, "is still officially a married man, and—this is treason, of course, kindly don't repeat it—what with putting Queen Catherine aside, beheading Queen Anne and now planning to annul his present consort, he's getting a reputation. If he goes chasing, either personally or by proxy, after an errant maid of honour, there'll be talk and even laughter. He won't want that! Leave a note for the queen. Don't mention the king. Say you were homesick. Say you're going home with a reliable escort. That should reduce the chance of any pursuit. Can you trust your tirewoman?"

"Lisa? Yes."

"Does she need to travel by pillion or can she ride?"

"Lisa rides very well. You won't fail me?"

"I won't fail you. I love an adventure," said Peter, laughing. "Oh, and don't worry. You will travel as my sister and I shall not treat you as anything else. I'll bring you home unharmed, I promise."

CHAPTER ELEVEN
The Wrong Response
1540

Afterward, Jane marvelled at how smoothly it went. The following evening, as Peter had suggested, she pretended to feel unwell. In the morning the other maids of honour went to the chapel with their tirewomen, but Jane, still complaining of illness, stayed behind with Lisa to look after her. Once everyone else was out of sight, she rose and prepared a note while Lisa packed a hamper with essentials. Then she put the note half under her pillow. It would be found, but with luck, not for some time.

Because the hamper was heavy, she helped Lisa carry it outside and down to the landing stage. They were stopped only once, by a White Stave who was not for some reason in the chapel, and who called to them, quite jovially, to ask where they were going. Jane had planned for this sort of thing and answered unflinchingly that they were on a charitable errand for the queen.

"What's in the hamper, then? Clothes for the poor?"

"Yes," said Jane, and opened the lid to show the respectable but dull cloak she had deliberately put on top. Queen Anna collected plain and hard-wearing items of clothing to be sent to the people responsible for distributing charity: the vicars, mayors, parish overseers in charge of housing orphans and apprenticing them to trades. The White Stave nodded, smiled and stepped back to let them pass.

"Come, Lisa," said Jane briskly. "We should hurry. We mustn't be late back." Whereupon the White Stave escorted them to the landing stage in person and hailed a boatman for them.

Jane gave the boatman his instructions while Lisa, who had grasped her conspirator's role very well, busily thanked the White Stave and prevented him from hearing the words *White Bull Inn.* They boarded and waved goodbye to him and then they were off on time, making for the inn three miles upstream. Peter Carew was there, as he had said he would be. He introduced them to the landlord as his sister and her woman servant, and since neither of them had breakfasted, ordered refreshments. After that, the two grooms who were with him saddled the horses he had hired and they set out again, by road.

Jane was still afraid of possible pursuit, but Carew was not. There was something very resolute about him, Jane thought.

"The court's like a rabbit warren," he said, "especially at Whitehall. Everyone will think you're just somewhere else. By the time your note is found, we'll be leagues away. Don't be anxious."

He added, as they rode on, "That landlord thinks you're

my sister, but the grooms know who you are and that you're escaping from the court to protect your good name. They approve. Have no fear of any of us."

It took eight days of steady riding, but there were no alarms and Peter never seemed uncertain of the road. "How is it that you know your way about so thoroughly? I thought you'd been abroad for years!" Jane asked him once.

"I was, but since I've been back, I've travelled with the court on royal progresses and besides, I always make sure I understand the world I'm living in and how to get from here to there. You never know when it may come in useful."

He grinned at her, a bold, adventurer's grin. Combined with his air of experience and maturity, it created a heady attraction. Jane, looking at his strong brown face with its aquiline nose and shapely chin, experienced a curious physical sensation, as though a warm and powerful hand had gripped her guts and jerked.

This would never do. She must not indulge such feelings. She had no business to have them. She must not fall in love with Peter Carew! He came, and she knew it, from a family even more in the habit of making wealthy marriages than Ralph's. A Sweetwater wouldn't qualify. That was the way of the world.

Peter showed no sign of falling in love in return. Both he and his grooms showed Jane and Lisa the utmost respect. Jane knew she must be grateful for this and quelled the regrettable part of her that seemed, mysteriously, to be wishing the contrary. She kept Lisa always by her side and guarded her tongue, to the point, she sometimes thought, of seeming dull and prim. On the morning of the ninth day, she came home.

When she was once more within sight of the Exmoor hills, she felt a relief so great that she could almost have fallen from the saddle to kiss the ground beneath. It was raining, but the soft drizzle of Somerset felt like a caress. The very village seemed to welcome her. She looked with delight at the tower of St. Anne's church, built of pale Caen stone, imported for the purpose long ago by one of Jane's own forebears. And there on its knoll stood Clicket Hall, which was similar to Allerbrook House but older, the battlements of its small tower more genuine looking and less ornamental than Allerbrook's.

Even the thatched houses of the village seemed to smile at her. This was home. She would *never* go back to the court. The king would probably turn his attention to poor little Kate Howard now and she pitied the girl, but Kate must look after herself. Jane Sweetwater had escaped, and forever.

They started up the combe under the dripping trees, the pinkish mud of the track squelching beneath the horses' hooves and splashing up their legs. The main track to Allerbrook House led off to the left about two-thirds of the way up to the ridge. Then the house was in sight, with smoke drifting from the chimneys. "Home!" said Jane ecstatically. Peter, who had a bigger horse, looked down at her and laughed.

"You would never survive years abroad, would you? You're no wanderer. Not like me."

The thought shot through her mind that if she had Peter Carew for company, perhaps she could bear to travel; perhaps, with him, everything would seem different. But she mustn't say that, or even let her eyes betray it. "Here we are," he was saying. "Your very own gate."

"Our very own dogs and geese, as well!" said Jane as the usual cacophony broke out to welcome them.

It brought Francis out of the house at once. He came across the yard at a run, holding a coat over his head.

"God's teeth! *Jane!* What are you doing here? And who is this?" He stared inimically at Carew.

"I'm Peter, the youngest son of your old friend Sir William Carew. I have escorted Mistress Jane all the way from Whitehall Palace. She has come home of her own free will and for a good and honourable reason. She'll tell you all about it herself. Master Sweetwater, I don't want to impose on you, but we've been on the road since early this morning. The horses need rest and fodder and both I and my grooms would welcome something to eat. I'm not inviting myself to dine, but…"

"You'd better dine," said Francis shortly. "And of course we'll take care of the horses. Get down and come inside."

His voice was brusque, and as he helped Jane to alight she looked into his face and saw no friendly welcome there. His blue eyes were cold. He turned away as soon as she was safely down and led the way indoors without looking back. The maids came out to meet her, but their welcome seemed muted and the house felt curiously empty.

Master Corby, she knew, had left his post and gone away, but neither Dr. Spenlove nor Eleanor appeared from anywhere to greet her, and why was there a goshawk in the hall? Francis had set up a perch for her; clearly keeping her there was now a regular thing. There were mutes splashed on the floor amid the rushes. Eleanor would hate that! Where *was* Eleanor? Timidly, as she pulled her drenched cloak off, she addressed Francis's back and asked.

For a moment he didn't answer. Then he turned and she saw that his jaw was clenched and that his eyes had tears in them. "She's in the family tomb in St. Anne's, my dear. She died a week ago. Dr. Spenlove is down in Clicket now, talking to the mason about extra wording to go on the side of the tomb. I meant to write to you today."

It had been a chill, nothing more. Over dinner, which Peggy had hastily enlarged for the visitors by frying a lot of sausages and onions and cutting extra bread, Francis explained. They had been buying goods in Dulverton. The weather had turned suddenly treacherous and Eleanor had been both wet and cold when she came home.

"She'd had a cold just before. She still had a cough. We set out in sunshine—it should have done her good. Instead— she relapsed. She was dead inside a week," said Francis shortly. It was as though he were angry as well as grieving.

With obvious sincerity Carew expressed condolences. Jane, both grief-stricken and shocked, shed tears and exclaimed, "Oh, *Francis!*"

Francis, however, merely nodded coldly. The hall was warm and the food welcome, but there was a stiff atmosphere around the table which didn't seem to be connected to Eleanor's death. When Jane caught Peter Carew's eye, she saw that he had noticed the awkwardness, as well. In an attempt to lighten the air, she said, "It's as well I'm here. I can take charge of the house and look after you, Francis."

"I was managing very well, thank you," said Francis, still in a voice which seemed to hold fury as much as sorrow.

Peter Carew glanced at him thoughtfully, but maintained a tactful silence. After the meal, having been assured that the horses had been groomed and given food, he took his leave and with the grooms, rode off on the last stage of his own journey home to Devon. His home in Mohuns Ottery was still a long way off.

"He was very kind," said Jane as she and Francis stood at the door to watch them go. She wished Peter could have stayed. He had felt like a bulwark against whatever it was that was so angering Francis. "He took every care of Lisa and myself and behaved…behaved in a very gentlemanly way. I haven't told you yet why I've come home."

"No," Francis agreed. "And now, my dear sister, send your woman to unpack your belongings and let us sit by the hall fire, and then you can do your explaining. And by all the saints, your excuse had better be good."

"You complete fool," said Francis when he had heard her story. "You unmitigated wantwit! I don't suppose it will be any use to send you back. Very likely the court wouldn't have you! I suppose I'll have to send to Taunton to hire a messenger to let Queen Anna know you've reached your home safely. Thank you so much, Jane, for putting me to so much trouble, and for ruining your chances and mine."

"Francis, what are you talking about?"

"You had a unique opportunity, my girl. Rumours get around. They reach us here, far from London though we are. Ralph Palmer is back in the west country now and he brought a tale or two. And there have been others. I went to a fair at Dunster just before Eleanor died. The Luttrells seem to be basing themselves at East Quantoxhead mostly now, but I came across the steward they've left at Dunster Castle. He hears from them and *they* hear plenty of news from the court. He says that the king hasn't taken to his new queen. And now you tell me he's had his eyes on you! By the sound of it, you could have become his mistress if you'd gone about it the right way."

"But…you wouldn't want me to do that! Francis, you

couldn't!" It was the last kind of welcome she had expected.
It was altogether the wrong response. "You were so angry
with Sybil when…"

"Sybil played the whore with one of my tenants! A man
of no importance! *You* could have had the favour of the king!
Think what rewards he might have given you, and your
family! In fact, if the Luttrells' steward was right, the king
means to get out of that marriage. Maybe you'd have had a
chance to be something more than a mistress, and think what
that could do for us!"

"Yes, I could end up headless!"

"Nonsense. You would have more sense. I told you that
before."

"I don't believe poor Anne Boleyn ever did the things they
said she did. She just didn't have a son, that's all. No woman
can guarantee that!"

"And many women do have sons! Why shouldn't you?
But you had to panic like a silly milkmaid and run away!"

"I can't believe this," said Jane despairingly. "Francis, you
can't have wanted me to…to…"

"It could have sent our fortunes soaring. I grieve for
Eleanor. I miss her every day and I'll mourn her decently.
But in time I'll look for another wife, and with you at the
king's side, I might have looked high. I might have been
given a valuable appointment, a title! We live in a harsh
world, full of competition—didn't I say something like that
to you before? But now, thanks to you, in King Henry's eyes
I'll be just the brother of the girl who said no. What am I
going to do with you?"

There was a silence, furious and disappointed on Francis's
side, furious and frightened on Jane's. It went on until the
sound of honking and barking outside announced that a new
visitor had come. Francis got up and went to the window.

"Ah. It's Harry Hudd. He had an errand to Exford and I asked him, while he was about it, to look at a young horse I'd heard of, a very uncommon colour, apparently. Copper's getting old. I told Harry to buy on my behalf if the animal was sound. Why, yes." Francis, for the first time since Jane's return, sounded pleased. "Come and look. There's a man in Exford who breeds unusual-looking horses. He bought a stallion from Iceland—not a large animal, but he's been crossing him with bigger mares and this is one of the results. Look at that."

Jane joined him at the window. Harry Hudd, as red faced and gap-toothed as ever, was in the farmyard, swearing at the gander while simultaneously dismounting from his Exmoor gelding and grasping the halter of a striking young horse, nearly sixteen hands tall and gleaming black, except for its mane and tail which were silvery white.

"Harry's a good reliable man," Francis said, "though I grant you he's no beauty." He paused, and then, as one to whom an interesting new idea has occurred, he said, "He's been talking for a couple of years of getting married again but the trouble is, he hasn't been able to find a young woman willing to take him. He wants a young wife. He's a bit like the king—feels the need of a son."

At which moment, Jane became sickeningly aware of two things.

One was that she wished wholeheartedly that she had journeyed on to Mohuns Ottery with Peter Carew. She had tried not to fall in love with him, but at some point on the ride to Somerset she had given him her heart and he had ridden away with it. She was *in love* with Peter Carew and more than that; she *loved* him, which was not the same thing

at all, but much bigger. It was the *for better for worse* love that
could hold for a lifetime and face, with sorrow but not
dismay, the inevitable end of life, in illness and old age.
There was nothing to be done about it. Weirdly, it could well
have been easier for her to marry the king than a Carew.

Marriage to Peter was a dream that could not be realized.
It was also a dream that would not die until she did.

The other was that Francis was very angry with her indeed
and that he had seen a way, a most appalling way, of getting
his revenge.

Part Two

THE SILENT OATH
1540–1541

CHAPTER TWELVE
Bad Dreams Can Come True
1540

*I*t had been a bad dream. Just a bad dream, nothing more. Opening her eyes on a September dawn, Jane wondered how she could possibly have dreamed that she was married to Harry Hudd and living at Rixons Farm, no longer a Sweetwater lady entitled to spend all day on fine embroidery if she chose, but working from daybreak to nightfall and spending the night in the bed of an unprepossessing middle-aged farmer. What a silly fantasy! Of all the absurd...

She woke up fully and, not for the first time, discovered that the bad dream was real. She really was in Harry Hudd's lumpy bed and beside her, Harry was just waking up. He opened first one watery blue eye and then the other and grinned his gap-toothed grin. "Ah. Me liddle darling. Just time afore the milkin', eh?" he said in a throaty tone that she recognized all too well.

He rolled on top of her, groping beneath the covers. She tried, as she had often tried before, to close her eyes and pretend that this wasn't Harry but Peter Carew, but her bed-fellow, with his animal odour and his pawing and thrusting and complete absence of anything that could be described as tenderness, could not be anyone but Harry.

She could only lie there and resign herself. Fortunately, he never seemed to expect any kind of response from her, which was just as well, for she couldn't imagine giving it.

Francis had arranged it, as she had feared he would, but all the same, Francis was not the only one to blame. Her crime was no crime in most people's eyes, and at heart he knew it. He might never have gone through with this had it not been for Dorothy. Jane was not cruel by nature, but if Dorothy were ever arrested and taken into the depths of the Tower of London and racked, and Jane had the power to rescue her, she didn't think she'd use it. Dorothy had blocked her way of escape. Dorothy, as much as—or perhaps more than—Francis, was responsible for this.

The shock of Dorothy's behaviour had been all the worse because at first Francis, angry as he was, had refrained from criticizing Jane in front of other members of the household, and she had begun to think that after all, life might settle down.

She tried to be useful. She missed Eleanor badly, but at least Lisa was allowed to stay as her maid and companion, and otherwise the household was almost as it had been before she left for court. Susie, now married to the groom Tim Snowe and expecting a child, was rearing poultry at his cottage, and had been replaced by Letty, from Clicket. Letty was thin, wiry, hardworking and unlikely to marry. She had had an understanding with a lad in Clicket but he had backed out after smallpox marked her face.

"I'm the same girl now as I was afore I got pockmarked, but he were too daft to know it. I'll never give another man the time of day as long as I live," Letty had said when she first came to Allerbrook. Pockmarked or not, she was a good cook and as handy with a hoe or a pitchfork as any man. Jane and Letty liked each other and worked well together.

Dr. Spenlove, who had always been Jane's friend, was still there. Spenlove openly congratulated her on her good sense in fleeing the king's advances. Spenlove, more than anyone, might have helped to reconcile Francis to his sister's return home.

But then Thomas and Mary Stone, who had been away in Kent, reappeared, opened Clicket Hall, announced that Dorothy was coming home from court to be formally betrothed to Ralph Palmer and issued invitations to a celebration dinner in June.

That betrothal dinner also featured from time to time in Jane's dreams, or rather nightmares. With the Stones as with his own household, Francis kept up the pretence that all was well between himself and his sister, and when they both received invitations, he accepted them. Jane set off for the party in good spirits.

They found a houseful of guests at Clicket Hall. Thomas, the host, was well dressed and genial; Mary, though fatter than ever and bulging out of her silk dress, glowed with pride at her daughter's catch. It promised to be a most happy occasion.

Except that this time Luke Palmer had been well enough to accompany his son Ralph. Ralph, dark and debonair, was very much the dutiful son, helping his elderly father out of the saddle and offering him an arm into the house. Not that Luke Palmer seemed to need help. He had taken a physician's advice, adopted a rigorous diet and overcome his gout. He had ridden all the way from Bideford. He clearly approved of Dorothy. But it was Luke Palmer who caused the atmosphere to deteriorate, when he rose to his feet halfway through the feast and made a startling speech.

In it, he expressed conventional good wishes to the couple, but then declared roundly that if Ralph were ever unfaithful to his charming bride he, Luke, would spread the news of this behaviour from one side of the country to the other and right through the royal court.

"And that won't be all, either," he had added, looking as grimly at his son as though Ralph had already assembled a harem and declared that he meant to install it under his marital roof. "I've driven the old Adam out of him before and I will again if I have to. Mistress Dorothy, if you ever need a champion, come to me."

Ralph turned beetroot and Dorothy's face almost matched the crimson damask in which she was once more most unsuitably dressed. Everyone else took refuge in a shattered silence. Such remarks, people commented afterward, were in extremely bad taste and typical of Luke Palmer.

The normal atmosphere of a betrothal feast did presently show signs of recovery, with Dorothy, now smiling again, as the centre of attention, but there was more embarrassment to come. Triumphant at being betrothed to so handsome a fellow as Ralph, and full of her recent sojourn at court, Dorothy, who had once had so little to say for herself, became talkative.

There had been plague in London, she said. Her tirewoman Madge had fallen victim to it, though fortunately while she was off duty for a few days, visiting relatives in London. "The outbreak was mainly in the town," Dorothy said. "But I was glad to come home, though in fact, King Henry has sent the queen and her women to Richmond

Palace. To be out of harm's way, he *said*," she added with a knowing smile. "But it's really to get her out of *his* way. He's courting Kate Howard nowadays."

"You were privy to what the king was thinking, then?" Ralph said, amused, and winked wickedly at Jane. "Didn't have his eye on *you,* did he?"

Luke didn't see the wink, but Dorothy did and shot a resentful glance at Jane. Jane, at that moment, felt sorry for her and could almost understand Luke Palmer's anxiety on his future daughter-in-law's behalf. To Ralph, clearly, she was no more than the accompaniment to a valuable dowry, which he would sequester for his own use.

And then Thomas Stone said, "It's natural for a king to flirt a little. It may not be serious. He tried to flirt with your sister, didn't he, Francis, which is why she's with us now. She ran away from him."·

"Oh, *Jane,*" said Dorothy, and laughed in that carefully modulated way that court ladies used for putting each other down. Jane felt herself bristling.

"What do you mean, Dorothy?" her mother asked.

"I'm sorry. I won't say any more," Dorothy replied, holding out her goblet for some more wine.

"No, come along," said Francis. "What's in your mind, Dorothy?"

Dorothy shook her head, but her eyes gleamed with malice, and Mary Stone, with maddening obtuseness, chose to be persistent. "Dorothy, you can't say just a little and then stop. You must tell us what you mean."

Dorothy looked at Jane. "Well, the king did dance with you once or twice, but he danced with most of the ladies at times. That wasn't really why you left the court, was it?"

"Yes, it was," said Jane, and heard the defensiveness in her own voice. It was she, not Dorothy, who sounded unconvincing.

"Oh, Jane! You know you kept losing things, and arriving late for this or that occasion and you often said how homesick you were. In the end, Queen Anna decided you'd never be a successful maid of honour and kindly arranged for you to go home. I understood, though," said Dorothy with spurious sympathy. "I missed my home, too. No one blames you. But it wasn't anything to do with the king."

"I'm afraid it was," said Jane, as coolly as she could. "I did indeed miss my home but I came back, of my own choice, for the reason I have given. My maid Lisa will bear me out."

"Oh, no doubt. I'm sure Lisa is loyal to you, and so she should be. No one would criticize her for that," said Dorothy sweetly.

It was clever, Jane thought bitterly. It was fiendishly clever, couched in terms that sounded kind, even though the intention behind it was as unkind as it could possibly get.

"Well, well," said Francis calmly. "I daresay, Jane, that you did miss your home, though you'd have got over that if you'd given yourself time. And maybe you were a little overwhelmed by a few compliments from King Henry or invitations to dance. It's all in the past now. Let us not talk of this anymore. Has anyone else had trouble lately with foxes trying to get at their poultry? There was a dogfox prowling after mine last week, though the dogs and the gander saw him off...."

They were home again and Jane had retired to her chamber to sit on a stool in her loose bedgown and over-robe while Lisa brushed her hair, when Francis tapped on the door and was admitted. He gave Lisa a dismissive glance and she left them together. Francis sat down on the side of the bed. "So, now we know."

"Now we know what?" Jane asked, brushing her long brown hair herself. It gave her hands something to do and stopped them from shaking. Francis looked so very forbidding.

"The real reason why you left the court. You weren't afraid of the king! You were ordered home for idleness and incompetence. You seem to have added lies to foolishness."

"You believe Dorothy, then?"

"Why should Dorothy lie? You often said you didn't want to go to court. I suspect that you simply gave way to your absurd pining for home, failed to do your duties properly and got yourself dismissed—half if not *entirely* deliberately."

"Dorothy lied because she doesn't like me," said Jane tiredly.

"That's absurd. Why ever shouldn't she?"

"I have no interest in Ralph Palmer," said Jane, deciding on candour. "But Dorothy believes he only cares for her dowry and that if mine were bigger, he'd prefer me to her. She was also jealous of the attention the king paid me! She hates me for it."

"If you have no interest in Ralph Palmer," said Francis unexpectedly, "then I'm surprised at you. He's personable enough, I would have said! Though I saw your face when Peter Carew rode away. I suppose he's the one you'd like. You can forget that, my girl. The Carews, even more than the Palmers, go in for advantageous marriages. What am I to do with you?"

"I wish you'd just try believing me, Francis! It's true I didn't really want to go to court, but I fled from it for the reasons I told you. I was *not* dismissed. Can't I be useful to you here?"

"I don't need you here, Jane. Peggy manages very well with the maids." Francis rose to his feet. "I don't know for sure whether the liar is Dorothy or you, but I'm inclined to think it's you. I don't mind keeping Lisa on, if she's willing to stay. She must be a good seamstress—tirewomen usually are. There is always work for a skilled needle in a house like this. But as for you…"

"Francis, what are you saying?"

"Harry Hudd is still looking for a young wife and you don't want to go far from home. He's a decent, honest man, Jane. He's older than you, but he's still under fifty, and he lives just down the hill. Your dowry will be more than enough for him! I shall talk to him tomorrow."

"Francis, no!" Jane could hardly believe her ears. She stared blankly at her brother. Memories flooded back—of their parents' deaths, of how Francis had hugged his sisters and they had hugged him back and they had all cried together. Now Sybil was exiled and Jane was to be thrown to—Harry Hudd and Rixons.

"Please!" Jane said to her brother's implacable eyes. "He's…he's *old* and Rixons farmhouse is awful, so cramped and dirty and…"

"The roof is sound. I've seen to that, and you can clean the house. Don't argue, Jane. I don't suppose *he* will. I wouldn't have foisted Sybil on to him, carrying another man's love child, but you're a different matter. Determinedly virtuous, according to you," said Francis with a kind of grim humour. "As far as I'm concerned, it's settled."

He left the room. That night Jane did not sleep. In the morning he went out early, riding his new horse Silvertail. He didn't return until after dinner and Peggy expressed anxiety. "Saw that new animal of his bucking as the master rode off. The master's good in the saddle, but I'd say that horse has a vicious streak."

Francis, however, reappeared at suppertime, looking pleased with himself. Over the meal, he said, "Jane, tomorrow morning you will have a caller. Wait in the courtyard at the back if the weather's fine, in the parlour if not. Don't wear brocade or damask, but look clean and tidy."

"Why? Who is the caller?"

"Wait and see," said Francis, and withdrew to his chamber before she could ask any further. Not that she needed to ask. She already knew. Ahead of her lay another sleepless night.

Next day it was sunny. Shortly after breakfast the caller duly arrived and Francis brought him to the rear courtyard, where Jane was miserably sitting on a stone bench. Harry Hudd, his cap in his hand, his wind-reddened face carefully shaved and his square body encased in the brown fustian doublet and hose which were his nearest approach to a formal suit, had come to ask Jane Sweetwater to marry him.

"I've your brother's consent. There's no need to worry about that, maid."

Worry about it? Could even Harry Hudd imagine that she would worry if Francis forbade the banns?

"I've not that much to offer, but I've got summat. Good health I've got. I'm all in workin' order and likely there'll be little ones. I reckon 'ee'd like that. Most women want childer. House b'ain't much, but I'll leave 'ee free to do whatever's best. There'll be money enough—thy dowry and a bit I've got put by, only bein' just a man, I've never known how to make a house pretty. My old wife long ago, she knew, but that's long in the past. She were sickly, that's why we had no babbies. That were her, not me. I've a good flock of sheep, all my own, and half a dozen cows in milk and I hear 'ee's handy in the dairy. Hear 'ee's good with poultry, too. We don't keep geese, but there's a duck pond...."

He went on and on, reciting the virtues of Rixons, as if she didn't know them already and as if they could possibly compensate for the shortcomings of their proprietor. At the end, she said that she must have time to think and he seemed to approve of that. Maidenly and very proper were the words he used to describe it. He'd come back the next day for her answer, he said, and bowed himself out.

"The answer will be no," said Jane to Francis when he came out to her after saying goodbye to Harry. "You can't really believe that I'll agree to this!" But she said it with fear in her voice. There were ways, and everyone knew it, of inducing unwilling daughters or sisters to marry where their families wished. Plenty of ways.

"If you don't agree," said Francis, "then you must shift for yourself. This will no longer be your home. Go to the Lanyons and ask if they'll take in another ill-behaved girl who's been ejected from Allerbrook House. Pity there aren't any nunneries left now where I could send you. But I won't have you here. Smile and do as you're bid, and I'll see it's a good wedding and I'll say it's what you want, what you've chosen. I'll add to your dowry—you'll be able to put your new home well and truly to rights. It won't be a bad bargain."

"Francis, please don't do this! What have I done that's so terrible? Refuse to become someone's mistress? Even if the man was the king, does it make any difference? Oh, what can I say to make you understand? Ask Dr. Spenlove what he thinks! He won't approve of this, you know he won't...."

"Spenlove will mind his tongue or else leave my employment."

"Francis, *please...!*"

She burst into tears, but Francis merely seized hold of her, clapped a hand over her mouth and marched her indoors. He took her to her bedchamber, pushed her in and locked the door after her. She lay on the bed for most of the day, alternately crying and trying in vain to think of a way out. She had always known that Francis had a hard streak in him. He had taken on the duty of caring for his sisters, but in Francis's mind this was balanced by their duty to obey him. He had abandoned Sybil for failing him. He would abandon Jane as easily.

She had another dreadful night, visualizing herself turned out, wandering, seeking for shelter, perhaps being taken in by the Lanyons out of charity, perhaps ending up as Sybil apparently had—a servant on a farm.

At Rixons she would at least be mistress of some kind of house, however ill-kempt; she would be a wife; and yes, there might be children. The thought of going to bed with Harry Hudd made her feel ill, but in the dark she wouldn't be able to see him. For the first time she felt real sympathy for King Henry. When confronted with Anna of Cleves, his feelings had probably been similar to Jane's now.

Harry came back the following morning for his answer. Jane, her eyes heavy and her face pale from lack of sleep, once more greeted him in the courtyard. She wore the same dress as on the previous day, a plain brown affair, opening over a green linen underskirt. It was respectable but not luxurious, nothing like the gown of a court lady.

Harry Hudd bowed, and smiled his unlovely smile and asked for his answer and Jane, trying to smile back, said yes. The wedding took place one month later, early in July, at St. Anne's in Clicket. Father Drew conducted the service. Both he and Dr. Spenlove had been astonished by her choice, as indeed had everyone else. Jane was obliged to parry astounded protests and questions from Lisa, Peggy, the maids, the grooms, neighbours and friends alike. It was pride as much as fear of Francis that made her hold up her chin and declare that this was what she wanted.

And now it was done, and here she was in the Rixons farmhouse, which had one untidy living room, a kitchen with an earth floor, and two spartan bedchambers upstairs under the thatch, and she would be Mistress Harry Hudd for as long as they both should live.

Harry, having finished what he was about, rolled out of bed and said, "Well, now. Milkin'. Can't go lazin' around here all the day long. I can hear they cows lowin' now. Up thee comes, maid," and held out a hand to her. Another day at Rixons had begun.

She tried to make the best of it. She was probably better off than little Kate Howard, who was now married to the king. There had been proclamations everywhere, announcing that Queen Anna was henceforth to be known as Lady Anna of Cleves, the king's dear sister, and would live in state but away from the court. Jane wondered if Lady Anna felt relieved, but it must have been a comedown, to be deprived of a crown. Thomas Cromwell, whom the king held responsible for the whole disaster of the Cleves marriage, had been beheaded. No, there were certainly ways in which Mistress Jane Hudd had blessings worth counting.

And there was the traditional harvest supper at Allerbrook to look forward to. Francis couldn't expect Peggy to oversee the whole thing without help, she was sure of that. The farms of Clicket parish, Sweetwater home farm, Allerbrook home farm, Hannacombes, Rixons and Greys (Shearers had been renamed after its new tenants, though Rixons still kept the name of tenants long gone) were not reaped at the same time but one after another. Everyone joined in and everyone was invited to the Allerbrook supper when all was done. She would be able, surely, for a day or two, to spend time at Allerbrook House to help Peggy out. That much of her old life was still open to her.

Lisa would be there, too, the household seamstress now. The wife of Harry Hudd did not need a maid. Jane herself could repair sheets and cushion covers and stitch Harry's shirts. But at least, at the supper, she would see Lisa, of whom she was fond.

She followed Harry downstairs to collect the milking pails and go out to the byre. They had lingered abed just long enough for the other Rixons inhabitants to rise ahead of them. There were three of these—a man and wife called Ed and Violet Hayward, and their son Tom, aged about twenty, somewhat stupid and with a disagreeable habit of sniggering at any remark that could possibly be called suggestive, but very strong, which was useful. There was a shepherd, too, Job Searle, but Job and his wife lived away from the house, in a stone hut close to the moor where the sheep ran in summer.

There was a story that when Violet was baptized, more than forty years ago, the Clicket vicar of the time had objected to the name Violet. He knew of no saint called Violet, he said, nor was it a name hallowed simply by use. Rose, yes, if they wanted a flower name, but not Violet. Violet or nothing, her parents had insisted. It meant a sweet, shy, pretty flower; what could be better for a baby girl? When the vicar persisted in arguing, her father lost his temper and shook an angry fist at him.

Since Violet's father was the village blacksmith and his fist was a massive affair at least as large as a ham, the vicar had given in. Jane was inclined, however, to think that the

reverend gentleman had had a point. *Sweet, shy* and *pretty*
were not words that could possibly be applied to Violet
Hayward, who was squat in build with straggly straw-
coloured hair and a pink piglike face. She also disliked hard
work, although this had advantages since she had at least been
friendly to Jane, welcoming another pair of hands.

She was rousing up the fire in leisurely fashion as Harry
and Jane passed through the kitchen. "B'ain't breakfast on
the go yet?" said Harry. "We'll want it straight after seein'"
to the cows." But he spoke good-humouredly. He was not
an ill-disposed man, Jane thought.

As they went out together to the byre where the cows,
wandering in from their pasture of their own accord, were
already in their stalls, she told herself to be grateful for
Harry's good temper. Indeed, he had thanked her for the
efforts she had made to clean the farmhouse and repair the
linen. "Why, 'ee's makin' a home of the place. Reckon it
was more like a pigsty afore 'ee came," he'd said once.

And Jane, glad to be praised, had not pointed out that
when she came downstairs on her first morning, sore and
miserable after a night of Harry's enthusiastic but hardly
tender lovemaking and repelled by the smell of his breath,
she had discovered a couple of piglets wandering in the
kitchen, completely ignored by the Hayward family, who
were already there.

"Oh, they come and go as they like," Violet said. "We're
used to 'un."

"Well, I'm not," said Jane, and shooed them out. Rixons
hadn't just resembled a pigsty, it had *been* one.

It was a pigsty no longer, and Harry approved. Her life
could be worse, much worse. She fetched the milking stools
from the spare stall at the end of the byre, handed one to

Harry and they set to work. Through the sound of milk going into the pails Harry suddenly said, "We wed in July, didn't we, maid? Near the start of the month, it were."

"Yes, that's right," Jane agreed.

"I remember about a week after we were wed, 'ee said to me, 'Let me be for a few days, Harry. I'm not in the right state for lovin'.'"

"Yes, I recall."

"So I let 'ee be for a week. End of that week 'ud be just after mid-July. We're in September now, just about. Six weeks or a bit more, it is, since then and 'ee's never said to me since that 'ee's not in a right state. Would it mean anythin', would you think?"

Jane straightened her back, which was aching. It was true. She was more than three weeks overdue.

She said, "I didn't want to say anything till I felt certain. But it might mean something, yes."

CHAPTER THIRTEEN
The Coming of Tobias
1540–1541

*I*n Lynmouth, five-year-old Stephen had been left unsupervised while the rest of the family were receiving guests, in the shape of the young woman Idwal was to marry, and her parents. Her father was from Bristol, where he was one of the merchants in the consortium to which Owen belonged. The adults were now graciously exchanging compliments and bowing and curtsying and Stephen had crept away.

He didn't like the girl, Frances Thornley. She'd mumbled hello to him, but in a way which meant that she didn't know what to say to this unknown child and would rather not say anything. He sensed at once that she would regard anyone's children but her own as something that merely littered the landscape.

Having got himself out of sight, Stephen made his way

down to the basement, where goods were often stored while awaiting sale or loading onto a ship. He was not supposed to go down there, but that only made the idea more attractive. He wandered inquisitively through the shadowy cellar, where the only light came from the door he had left open at the top of the basement steps, and three gratings in the ceiling. Two of these opened not onto the floor of the house above, but directly into the street. They let in light but also rainwater. There were shutters which could be slid across, and usually they were kept closed except when people were working in the basement and wanted light. Occasionally, though, someone would forget to shut them on leaving. That had happened yesterday and it had rained hard in the night. Stephen, finding a large puddle on the floor, stamped interestedly in it and enjoyed seeing the water splash up.

Tiring of this, he began to play a game with imaginary enemies, and while trying to squeeze between a row of small earthenware jars and some kegs behind them, he upset one of the jars, which rolled and broke. A scarlet powder trickled out and into the puddle, turning the water the colour of blood.

Someone shouted his name, and the light from the doorway was briefly darkened as Owen came rapidly down the steps. "I found the basement door open, Katherine!" he shouted over his shoulder as he reached the floor. "I fancy he's down here. Oh, dear heaven! Oh, you pestiferous, interfering *brat!*" He swooped on Stephen, picked him up bodily and slapped him hard. Stephen began to howl.

"Katherine!" bellowed Owen. "Come and see what he's done!"

Katherine Lanyon came down to join them, holding her skirts clear of the steps. "What's happened? Whatever…oh, how could you? You wicked boy! How many times have you been told not to come down here! Owen, is that…?"

"Yes, it is. That's most of a jar of the most expensive red dye known to man, all lost in a puddle. I think," said Owen, taking a deep breath and attempting to be fair, "that I left that grating open myself yesterday, for which I'm sorry, but it wouldn't have mattered but for this. You've got to keep a harder hand on him, Katherine."

He looked again at the reddened pool and lost his temper once more. "He's a menace! That's good money, going to waste in that puddle! He *would* go and damage merchandise that's valuable and too damned hard to get anyway! I don't know what's gone wrong with my suppliers, but I fancy someone somewhere is offering them a better deal than the English are. And then this…this infant lunatic…!"

He slapped Stephen again, even harder than before. Stephen howled anew, and far away at Stonecrop Farm, Sybil, who was sharpening scythes, was suddenly filled with the certainty that Stephen needed her.

I shouldn't have left Lynmouth, I know it! How is Stephen now? What does he look like? I should have stayed in Lynmouth, with my son.

But it was too late now for such thoughts. She must endure, and hope—and pray—and one day her chance would come.

"Thee's doin' well. Don't 'ee worry," Peggy said. "Lucky you've got me to help and not that Violet."

It was the month of May once more, just over a year since Jane had fled from Whitehall Palace. This room was far from palatial, with its rough walls of pinkish stone and curving black beams. The bed had no canopy, and she could look directly up at the thatch. There was a piece of rope hanging from the bedhead, for her to clutch and pull at when she needed. She had used it several times already and could only hope that the ordeal wouldn't go on much longer.

Peggy was there because Jane had indeed been asked—in a message brought by Tim Snowe—to help with the harvest supper at Allerbrook. At the supper, Francis had exchanged politenesses with her as though she were a mere acquaintance, and both Beth and Letty seemed awkward, not sure what manner to adopt toward this former daughter of the house who was now the wife of a mere tenant. But Peggy had been just the same as ever, and Peggy had offered to help her when her baby was born. Francis had raised no objection.

Peggy indeed had enlivened the early stages of Jane's labour by saying a few things about Francis.

"Hope this baby takes after you and not his dad. Your brother disparaged you, marryin' you off to Hudd. Aye, disparaged, that's the old word folk used to use, wasn't it, when a girl was pushed off into a marriage not good enough for her? I tell 'ee, it's done Master Francis no good."

"What do you mean?" said Jane, grabbing for the rope.

"You and Francis both said you chose to marry Hudd, but folk b'ain't stupid. It's got round, what you say about why you come home from court, and what Mistress Stone says, and most folk believe you. And they reckon that when you go claimin' you wed Harry Hudd for choice, that's like sayin' two and two make five. He's made two tries at courting a new wife, has your brother. Good families, that's what he's interested in, but they've heard how you've been treated and they don't like it."

"Peggy, you shouldn't say things like that. If Francis heard you…oh, God's teeth…!"

"You're doin' all right. He won't hear, don't worry. But

I tell 'ee, he wanted to get rid of Lisa 'cause he said she kept lookin' at him as if she didn't hold with him. She knew he'd turned against her, and when she heard that Mistress Dorothy needed a maid, she went and asked for the job and got it. Told me she was offered better pay than she ever got from your brother. I daresay she did give 'un some funny looks. She reckoned you were badly treated, too. You ought to be married to a proper young fellow like that Ralph Palmer."

"Dorothy wouldn't have liked that much!"

"Well, he's wed to Dorothy now and I just hope she can hold 'un. That horse Silvertail nearly threw your brother during the procession back from the church, by the way. Horrible animal, that horse is. Your brother keeps tryin' to train 'un into better manners but he's getting nowhere fast, if you ask me."

"The horse is an entire," said Jane. "He might be more manageable if he were gelded."

"I'd sell 'un if he were mine," said Peggy. "For dog meat!"

"Oh, *Peggy!*"

Now, as the process of giving birth neared its climax, Jane said, "I'm glad I've got you, Peggy. I don't like any of the Haywards."

"No one likes the Haywards," said Peggy. "Specially Tom. It weren't so bad when he were younger, but nowadays I don't let Beth or Letty go far, not without one of our men. We can trust ours, and Tim Snowe, he's a rock. Looks after Susie that well."

"I heard they had a little girl."

"Aye, they have, little Phoebe, and Tom Hayward, he don't go near Susie since Snowe caught him hangin' round the place ogling her and *sayin'* things—you know what I mean. Snowe knocked him flat, for all Tom's so big and hefty, and then picked 'un up and chucked 'un into a ditch. I watch over the wenches, even Letty, pocks or no pocks. Nasty creature, Tom is. Ah! We're on the move. Now, then…"

"God in heaven!" Jane shouted. "What's happening?"

"Nothing that shouldn't. Hang on to that rope. Now, a good hard push. Go on, swear if 'ee wants to. I always did. Six I had, and cursin' all the way."

"Sod it!" yelled Jane, which was a phrase neither her parents nor Francis nor Eleanor would ever have allowed her to use though Harry used it frequently and on the only occasion when he had heard it from her—when a big pan of cream had turned sour in thundery weather and seriously reduced the next day's butter production—had just laughed.

"Well done. Here we come…here…we…come! And there he is! You've got a boy, mistress, a fine, healthy boy…" A loud wail interrupted her. "Good lungs. No trouble there. Harry'll be pleased, won't he? Wanted a son, I heard. What'll you call him?"

"Harry's father was called Tobias. He said Tobias, if we had a boy."

"So, welcome little Tobias," said Peggy, busying herself with towels. "You did well, mistress. Quick and easy, believe me. Ah well, that's how it is. One comes, and one goes."

"One goes? Who's gone?" asked Jane weakly, letting go of the rope.

"Oh, of course, don't suppose the news has reached 'ee. Only reached Allerbrook this mornin' when Master Stone rode up there."

"Stone? He isn't here. Clicket Hall has been shut up for three months."

"It's open again now. Master Stone's there now—he's come to see his wife's cousins, the ones that live over at Porlock, and tell them about it. She's dead—Mary, I mean. Got too fat to move and then too fat to breathe, it seems. Came to see your brother and I heard them talkin'. Like I said, one comes and one goes. That's the way of it. My younger daughter had her first baby just two days afore her father died."

"Are Dorothy and Ralph with Master Stone?" Jane asked, dimly interested. "Is Dorothy with child yet?"

"Not that I know of, but they're not there, no. They're at Dover. Been seein' Master Peter Carew off, so Master Stone said. They've a house near Dover—it was part of Dorothy's dowry. There's real wealth in her family. Carew and Master Ralph are friends, it seems—see a lot of each other when they're both in London."

"Where was Master Carew going?" Jane asked. She had had no news of Peter Carew for so long, so very long, and yet his memory hadn't faded. She still thought of him and was parched for word of him.

"Some journey to foreign places. Venice and then Turkey, I think Master Stone said. Some secret task for the king. Now, how'd you like to hold your son?"

CHAPTER FOURTEEN
Blind Corner
1541

*H*aving Tobias was like rounding a blind corner. Jane had had no concept of the pit of love into which she fell the first time she held him. Peter Carew might be lost to her but Tobias, it seemed, had come in his stead. He was beautiful, and he brought her back into some kind of social life, because the women from Clicket and the surrounding farms began coming to call and admire him.

Many of them had been confused by her marriage. They didn't know whether to go on showing her the deference they had shown to Francis Sweetwater's sister who had been to court and mingled with royalty, or whether to treat her as simply the wife of Harry Hudd, tenant farmer. Now it was different. Most of them had children, too, and it gave them common ground with her at last. It was like joining a secret society.

Eventually, even Francis considered coming to call.

He would never admit it to Jane, but the reason lay mainly with Dr Spenlove.

Spenlove, who like most other people in Francis's circle had long since grasped most of the truth about Jane's marriage, had never attempted to reprove his employer, but he had taken, during household prayers, to including petitions to the Almighty to grant loving and forgiving hearts to all present. No one could very well object aloud to such prayers, let alone dismiss a chaplain for them, but Francis had objected in silence, because the prayers had caused twinges in his conscience. The arrival of Tobias gave him an excuse for softening his attitude to Jane, and he found this quite welcome. After all, the baby she had just produced down at Rixons was his own nephew.

He mentioned the child to Thomas Stone when the latter called on him to pay his respects and report the death of Mary Stone, and Thomas said, "When you see them, congratulate Jane and Harry for me, would you? I'd go in person, but I'm not too well myself these days. I've not felt right since Mary went."

Another good excuse to visit Rixons. Well, Jane had obeyed him in the matter of her marriage and she seemed to be doing her duty now. He was pleased to learn from Thomas that Carew had gone abroad. The man was a natural-born disturbing influence and better out of the way.

Carew was at that moment in his cabin on a ship called *Blue Water*. The ship was in the middle of the Bay of Biscay, which was living up to its bad reputation. Carew was not in the least liable to seasickness, but he was annoyed because it was hard to keep the cabin lit. There was a lantern, but it was swinging crazily from the ceiling and it was difficult to study the papers in front of him because of the way the light came and went.

He must study them, though, because they consisted of the instructions the king had given him, along with background details and names of contacts, and he would be well advised to commit as much as he could to memory. He ought to destroy the documents before reaching Venice, let alone Istanbul.

As far as anyone else on board the *Blue Water* knew, he was an alum merchant on his way to negotiate new contracts with suppliers in Venice and the Aegean. There was nothing remarkable about that. Alum was a valuable mineral, essential as a fixative for dyes. It was a convincing disguise.

Henry VIII, however, who had a businesslike side to him, had received reports that disquieted him. He was all the more inclined to concentrate on these because Kate Howard, the sweet young wife he had named his rose without a thorn, having told him delightedly that she was pregnant, had let him down by losing the baby.

"So you slip your foals, too!" he said crudely when her ladies admitted him to see her. *Just like Anne Boleyn* were the words that went through his head. *And she was a cousin of yours, come to think of it. God's teeth, does it run in the family?*

He was still in a bad temper when Peter Carew, obeying a peremptory summons to the royal apartments, was shown in. Carew did his initial bow not to Henry's face but to a broad royal back. The king was staring moodily out the window at the grounds of Hampton Court. He had heard Peter being announced, though, and turned around after a moment. "Ah. There you are. You come promptly. I like that."

His expression, however, wasn't that of a man who liked anything whatsoever and the adventurer Carew, wary enough when necessary, thought it wise simply to bow again and await instructions. Henry, who was normally affable toward people who hadn't displeased him, and aware that his ill temper was written on his face, had the grace to adjust his features, smile, sit down, invite his guest to sit down, too, and offer an explanation of sorts for his annoyance.

"I've been to a horse fair and I saw too many undersized runts. We need good horses with long legs, Peter, for messengers, for ceremonial processions, for travel in general, even for war. We still have tourneys with heavy armour but in real war, heavy armour's no use anymore. Breastplates won't protect men from cannons. The horses that weren't miserable little runts under fourteen hands," said Henry, who really had found the horse fair exasperating, "were heavy horses being sold off for draught work because they're not wanted for armoured knights anymore. They make good plough teams, as a matter of fact. They can do more in a day than oxen can...."

He seemed distracted for a moment and stopped. Peter Carew said cautiously, "Did you wish to see me about horses, sir? I maintain a small stud in Devonshire. Anything I can do..."

Henry pushed away the memory of the tears his young wife had shed at his rudeness and said, "We need horses bred for height and speed but not massiveness. Tell your horsemaster that. But I didn't call you here to discuss horses. Forgive the digression. I've just come from visiting the fair and I had it on my mind, that's all. Now, listen."

The problem on Henry's mind, it seemed, was connected with the steady rise in the power of the Ottomans who now governed Istanbul and were extending their rule. "Since my father's day," Henry said glumly, "England has opened up new trade routes. Whole new lands are being discovered. The world grows wider and wider. But not just for us! The Ottomans have insatiable enthusiasm for conquest—and it's interfering with trade. There are shortages of a number of commodities. I've had complaints from merchant companies and anxious reports from Venetian contacts."

Carew nodded. Owen Lanyon would have nodded, too. He had been infuriated and Stephen had been slapped over the loss of a scarlet dye which was an example of merchandise now becoming difficult to get.

"You're a travelled man," King Henry said now. "Go to Venice and Istanbul and find out what the Ottoman intentions are. Find out who they want to make friends with and who they're planning to gobble up next. Find out who is partnering who in the great pavane of Levantine trade. The secretariat will provide your brief. The clerks have been working on it for days."

The brief had been ready when he called in at the secretariat to ask about it, along with a passport, and his passage on the *Blue Water* had already been arranged. He had sailed within two days. He'd barely had time to pack.

The ship tilted wildly again, the lantern swung and a list of useful contacts slid off the table. Peter Carew swore. He had forgotten even the existence of Jane Hudd, née Sweetwater, left behind in far-off Somerset.

Tobias had been baptized and Jane had been churched, both occasions being attended by a number of friends, including Peggy, although not Francis. Now, a few mornings later, having fed her offspring and also the poultry, and laughed at the sight of a distracted mother hen, who had been given a clutch of duck eggs to hatch and was now panic-stricken because the duck chicks were happily taking to the pond, she was working indoors.

She was in fact attacking some cobwebby beams of the main bedchamber with a long-handled broom while Tobias, who was a quiet baby and at the moment a well-fed one, slept fatly in his crib. Violet, Jane hoped, was in the kitchen preparing dinner. The weather was bright, so all the men were out on the farm. She was free to choose her own tasks and think her own thoughts.

One thing she had learned during her marriage to Harry was that although the wedding bond gave him the right of entry to her body, what went on inside her head was still private to her and her alone. No one could control, no one could see, what happened inside anyone else's head.

If she wanted to imagine that she was cleaning a home that she shared with Peter Carew, then no one could stop her. If she were married to Peter, then no doubt he would often be away from home, but when he returned she would hear, not the clump-clump of Harry's boots crossing the farmyard but the clatter of hooves and the jingle of a bridle and…

She stopped short, broom uplifted. For from outside, she *could* hear the clatter of hooves and the jingle of a bridle. Lowering the broom, she made for the window. In the yard Francis was just dismounting from Silvertail, who was fretting at his bridle and tossing his head. Jane pushed the window open. "Francis!"

Her brother looked up. "Jane, there you are." He spoke quite casually, as though they had never been out of touch. "I decided it was time to visit you, to congratulate you and meet my new nephew. May I stable my horse and come in?"

She had been angry enough with Francis at first, heaven knew, but one couldn't go on being angry forever, and she hated being estranged from him in this way. It had hurt her that during her one visit to Allerbrook, for the harvest feast, he had behaved as though she were—not a servant exactly, but just another neighbour. Since Sybil was now out of her life, Francis was the only one of her former family that she had left.

There was Violet, going out the kitchen door to greet him. She went downstairs to join them.

It was not a long visit and it was undoubtedly awkward, since neither of them was quite sure what to say to the other. Francis did not ask her if she was happy, although he did ask if Harry was in good health. He behaved as though she had chosen this marriage herself and as though he was taking it for granted that all was well with her.

He admired Tobias and Tobias, always placid, woke up to look at his uncle and wrapped a tiny hand around the forefinger that Francis offered him. "I brought him a rattle to play with," said Francis, producing it. Tobias received the gift with contented gurgles.

"A fine child. May you have many more, just as good. Harry must be very pleased," Francis said as they went downstairs again, with Jane carrying the baby.

"Yes, he is. Will you stay to dine? He'll be in for that. I don't suppose you've seen him since he paid the rent on Lady Day."

"No, I haven't. He brought his usual tallies, about the bushels of barley and the number of yearling stock. I'd wondered if you'd introduce written records, but apparently you haven't."

"I've suggested it," said Jane somewhat stiffly. Harry could neither read nor write and didn't, he had said, want his wife showing off a skill he hadn't got himself. She had brought two books of verse with her from Allerbrook, but the moment Harry saw her reading, he had turned crimson and said, "Now, maid, there's no time for fiddle-faddles like readin' in a place like Rixons. Readin's a waste of time."

She often wondered just what Francis had said when he went to offer her to Harry as a wife. But Harry was used to thinking of women as being there to do as fathers, brothers and husbands told them. Francis had probably said he wanted a match for his sister somewhere nearby and added a few words about Jane's virtuous nature and Harry had said thank-you and when can we tie the knot? And that was that.

Now she said, "Harry prefers to go on doing things the way he's used to."

"Well, it's for him to say. I won't stop for dinner, Jane. I'll see Harry another time. I'll get my horse now. Take good care of Tobias."

Riding out of the farmyard, Francis felt relief. He had broken the deadlock. Some sort of social link could now be forged between Allerbrook and Rixons. It would be more natural to be on good terms with his own sister. When he married a new wife of his own…if he ever did…no doubt she would expect it.

The track up the hillside from Rixons to Allerbrook took a zigzag path, to minimize the gradient, and in places was sunken between banks and hedgerows of hazel and bramble with a few small trees growing through them and one or two gates, giving onto fields.

When they were young, he and Jane and Sybil had often, on sunny afternoons in early autumn, wandered along this very path with baskets, collecting nuts and blackberries. They were happy, innocent days. It was a pity they were gone.

Somewhere on his left he heard what for a moment he took to be the cry of some bird or animal. A buzzard flew up from a tree and slanted away over the opposite hedgerow. Then came another shriek and a shout, this time from unmistakably human throats, and a young woman, skirts flying, tumbled headlong over a gate to fall to the ground almost under Silvertail's hooves. Silvertail reared.

Francis, keeping his seat with difficulty, recognized the Allerbrook maidservant Beth. She was scrambling to her feet and gaping at him and as she did so, another figure burst shouting and laughing onto the scene, leaping over the gate, pouncing on Beth and flinging her to the ground. She screamed and Silvertail, further provoked by the noise, reared again and squealed. Once more Francis held on, but lost a stirrup. The new arrival then, belatedly, realized that Beth was no longer alone, let her go and stood up shamefacedly.

"Tom Hayward, what in hell's name do you think you're doing?" roared Francis.

"Oh, Master Sweetwater, thank the sweet saints in heaven you're here—he's been chasing after me. I've run all the way across Quillet Field. Oh, dear God…" Beth got breathlessly to her feet. Her pretty round face, normally a pleasant pink, was scarlet and streaked with tears. Her cap was gone and there was a bramble twig caught in her brown curls.

"I don't mean no harm. It were just a bit of fun," said Tom.

"No, it weren't!" shouted Beth, emboldened by Francis's presence. "You're allus after one or other of us and you do mean harm, you do! Master Sweetwater, he jumped out from behind a bush and got hold of me and I only just got away and what was he doing on Sweetwater land anyhow, if not prowlin' to see if he could find me or Letty?"

"How *dare* you, Tom Hayward?" There had been complaints about young Hayward before, and Francis took them seriously. His employees often grumbled at the amount of work he wanted from them, but it was known that maidservants were safe in his house. Francis, furious, raised his whip and struck. Tom flung up his arms to protect himself and yelled as the lash came down across his forearm. And Silvertail, outraged by this further loud noise so near his sensitive black ears, reared again, forelegs reaching for the sky.

This time Francis did not keep his seat.

It was Silvertail who alerted Jane to the disaster. He would rather have bolted home, but because Tom, to whom the horse had taken a dislike, was standing between him and his stable, he wheeled on his hocks, bolted the other way instead and came charging riderless into the Rixons farmyard.

Jane, who had stayed in the kitchen, ran out at the sound of the agitated hooves, saw Silvertail come to a halt in the middle of the yard, stirrups flying loose, white-ringed eyes rolling and ears flat back, shouted, "See to the horse! Look after Tobias!" at Violet and rushed off along the path that Francis had taken.

Gasping, she came at last on the scene of the accident. Francis was lying on the ground, with Tom Hayward standing there, looking stupid, and saying, "It weren't my fault. Lot of fuss all about nothing. What's wrong with 'un?" while Beth from Allerbrook knelt at Francis's side, crying and shaking his arm and begging him to speak to her. Jane threw herself down at Beth's side. "Francis!"

And knew at once that it was useless. No living human neck could be bent in that particular way.

"What happened?" she demanded.

"The horse threw 'un. He went headfirst into that tree," said Beth, pointing with a shaky finger. "Horse were upset.

We gave 'un a fright, bursting into the lane. I were runnin' away from *him*." She scowled at Tom.

"I just come on her and axed her for a kiss and she run off as if I'd got horns and a tail," said Tom sulkily. "Stupid girl."

"I'm not stupid and you wanted more than a kiss and I didn't want to give you even that but I had to kick you to get away, you…!"

"Stop that, both of you!" Jane stood up angrily. "Can't you see that Francis…that my brother…I think his neck's broken." She heard her voice tremble. "What were you doing here, off Rixons land, Tom? Looking for girls, I suppose. Well, go and find your father and Master Hudd and bring them both here. Go *on*, don't stand there like a booby!"

She watched his slow mind grasp the seriousness of the calamity. He understood at last and ran off, and she turned to Beth, who had also risen sobbing to her feet. "Beth, whatever made you come out alone? You know that Peggy's warned you not to."

"Peggy sent me! There's word from Clicket Hall—from Master Stone. Oh, everything happens at once!" Beth wailed. "The messenger said to fetch Master Francis from Rixons, that Master Stone is ill but needs to see him, something about the lease of Clicket Hall—he wants it to pass to Dorothy when he's gone or something…it sounded important. Peggy told me to run down the hill, she said I'm younger and I'd be quicker than she would, and to bring Master Francis back. I think she just forgot about Tom Hayward—after all, I'd be on Allerbrook land almost all the way. I thought to take a shortcut across Quillet…"

"All right. Never mind that now. Go back up to the house and fetch Dr. Spenlove. Is he there?"

"Yes, yes, he'm there."

"Bring him here. Hurry! I'll stay with the master."

Beth ran off, still weeping, leaving Jane alone with the rustle of wind in the hedgerow, and after a moment, as the human noises ceased, the sound of birds came from near at hand: a stonechat, a blackbird. Francis lay on the track, his face white, his neck twisted at that dreadful, unnatural angle. Only a short time ago she had been talking to him; he had been giving Tobias a finger to hold. Now he was dead and her life had just gone around another blind corner.

The sound of voices roused her. Her husband was hurrying toward her, along with Ed and Tom Hayward. She said something she had never expected to say, at least not in those heartfelt tones.

"Oh, *Harry.* I am so glad to see you."

CHAPTER FIFTEEN
Knowing One's Place
1541

*I*t was rotund little Dr. Spenlove, though, who took charge. Beth must have recovered her usual common sense by the time she reached Allerbrook House, and explained things to him properly, for he came hotfoot, and unusually solemn of face, saying that he had ordered Tim Snowe to find helpers and bring something on which to carry Francis home.

Tim and two of the other farmhands arrived shortly, carrying a hurdle. At Spenlove's behest, Harry sent Tom Hayward off again, this time to fetch his mother, Violet. "And the baby. We'll be goin' up to Allerbrook," he said. "And don't think," he added, "that 'ee've heard the last of this. Half-dead 'ee'll be when I've dealt with 'ee. Meanwhile, send your ma and my boy Toby yur as quick as 'ee can, or half-dead might be *all* dead. *Send* them. Don't want the likes of 'ee up at Allerbrook. You'll stop at Rixons and wait till I get back. Hear me?"

Tom, loose mouthed with fright, made off at speed, and Violet appeared with the baby a short time later. Spenlove had made everyone wait for them to come, then marshalled them all up the hill together, following the makeshift bier. Peggy and Letty ran distractedly out to meet them.

"Carry Master Sweetwater to his bedchamber," said Spenlove, authoritatively. "Peggy, Violet, you both understand the business of laying out. You attended to Mistress Eleanor, if I remember rightly. Kindly do the same for Master Sweetwater. Give the child to his mother, Violet. Letty, they'll want hot water to wash the master. Set some to heat. Beth, I see the hall fire is laid—light it, please, quick as you can, and then bring us some cider or ale—something to hearten us. Hot milk for Mistress Hudd. Mistress Hudd, bring the baby and sit by the hearth. The day's none too warm, for all it's sunny, and you need warmth to comfort you. You sit down, too, Master Hudd, yes and you, too, Ed Hayward. I made sure that you all came up to the house because there are things that I must tell you. They affect every one of you."

"What things?" asked Jane nervously as they sat themselves down. She was holding Tobias on her lap and joggling him gently while her mind continued to spin with shock.

It was not possible, it was just *not possible* that Francis could be dead. This was his house, his hall. Jane had not been here since the harvest supper and now, looking confusedly around her, she saw her brother's goshawk still on her perch. (There were mutes on the floor again; Eleanor would have been horrified.) In a moment Francis would join them. Little over an hour ago he had been admiring Tobias....

Beth lit the fire and fetched the drinks. The chaplain let everyone settle before saying, "I can see no point in delaying this. Disaster has struck very suddenly and we have hardly been able to take it in, but it *has* happened and already, I have no doubt, some of you will be wondering what your position is now. Wondering who will be master of Allerbrook House now that Francis Sweetwater has left us. I see no reason to waste time."

"Did he make a will?" Jane asked.

"Yes, Mistress Hudd, he did. He made a new will just after his wife died, while you were still at court. He talked its terms over with me, and I can tell you that I was sorry that your sister was cut out and tried to persuade him to change his mind, but he would not. Finally, I was a witness when he signed it in the presence of a lawyer in Dulverton. The lawyer himself was also a witness. Then when you and he...disagreed..."

"He changed it?" said Jane, cutting in. "He left Allerbrook to me to begin with, but then he took it away?" She heard the pain in her own voice.

"Here, you shouldn't go interruptin' the man like that!" said Harry.

"I'm sorry." Jane's voice shook. Though half of her mind couldn't believe that Francis was dead, the other half had indeed begun to wonder what would happen to Allerbrook. He'd hardly have bequeathed it to her, not now.

But Spenlove was smiling at her. "No. He left it to you, and he didn't change his will. Oh, he meant to—he told me as much. But he'd heard that the Dulverton lawyer, a man he knew and trusted, had just died. He'd need a new adviser, and at the time he was too busy to look for one. Finally, he said he'd leave it until he had found a new wife. He meant to marry again as soon as possible. Francis Sweetwater mourned his late wife most sincerely, but Allerbrook House needs a mistress. He said there was no point in making a new will and then having to do it all over again when he remarried. He was a young man. He didn't expect to die for many years. The old will stands and I can show you where he kept it. It's in one of the drawers of the desk he used for his accounts."

Harry stood up. "Thee'd best bring it out," he said.

They all went together, to the panelled downstairs room that Francis had used as a study. Jane was still holding Tobias in her arms. Spenlove opened a drawer beneath the table and took out a sealed cylinder of parchment. Remarking to Jane that Master Hudd was after all her husband and also that he had his hands free while hers were full of Tobias, Spenlove offered the will to Harry, who shook his head and said, "No use givin' 'un to me. I never learned to read my own name. Jane here ought to be the one. *She* can read. Give me the baby, Jane."

Jane, detecting the irritable note in his voice, also shook her head and held on to Tobias. "Dr. Spenlove, please break the seal and read the will aloud. That would be best."

So in the end, though Jane stood close enough to make out her brother's somewhat sprawling signature at the foot, it was Spenlove who unsealed the cylinder and Spenlove who announced that according to the last will and testament of Francis Richard Sweetwater, except for some modest bequests to his servants and a donation to St. Anne's church in Clicket, he had chosen—because his wife was dead and he was childless and was estranged from one of his sisters— to make his remaining sister, Jane Sweetwater, residuary legatee. "Which means," said Spenlove, "all the rest. And *that* means the Allerbrook estate."

"Master Sweetwater's gone and left all that to *us?*" Harry almost shouted it. He glanced at Jane and then around the hall, and shook his head. "But that b'ain't decent. I'm a plain man and I know my place. A man ought to stop where God put him. That's Christian humility that Father Drew gave a sermon about only a week afore last. We can't say yes to this."

"You have little choice," said Spenlove dryly. "It's what the will says and in law, it stands."

Harry crimsoned angrily and then shrugged. "We'll settle all that later. Meanwhile, I s'pose there's the funeral to see to."

Confound you, said Spenlove to himself. *I know your breed. You're going to be obstinate.*

Peggy begged them all to stay for supper, and they did. Most of the conversation concerned funeral plans and making sure that everyone who should know of the tragedy was informed. Dr. Spenlove agreed to remain in charge at Allerbrook House for the time being. When the meal was over, Jane and Harry and the Haywards went back down the hill, taking a sleepy and slightly irritable Tobias with them. They found a scared-looking Tom awaiting them. There were the usual evening tasks of milking the cows and filling mangers and locking up the poultry for the night. Tobias had to be settled, and as he was fretful, it took time. While Jane attended to this, she heard Harry order Tom to come with him, and heard the kitchen door slam behind them as her husband marched Tom out. Presently Harry came back alone. Jane did not ask questions.

As soon as possible, ignoring the whispers and curious glances from the Haywards, Harry and Jane went to their bedchamber and, having got there, locked the door behind them and sat down side by side on the bed.

Harry had taken little part in the supper conversation. But now he said, "I've attended to Tom. He'll sleep on his stomach for a few nights now. So. What happens next?" His voice was aggressive. Jane was not surprised by this, but the strength of her own resentment was so great that it startled her. What was he complaining about? What had she done wrong?

"We've been left a good inheritance," she said, and was aware that her voice had steel in it.

She folded her hands in her lap and sat staring at them, trying to appear serene, though she did not feel serene. Savage would be nearer to the truth. She had been so thankful to see Harry, down there in the lane beside Francis's body, but now…

If Harry objects to this bequest—if he says he wants to sell my home, I'll hate him forever. I'll never forgive him.

She had never known that she was capable of feeling like this, never known till now how much she cared for Aller-brook. She was horrified by her own violent thoughts. She dared not look up, dared not look into Harry's eyes in case he read her mind. She waited.

"Well," said Harry deliberately after a moment or two, "it's all been a bit of a shock, b'ain't it?"

"Yes, Harry. It's certainly been that."

"Poor old Francis."

"Yes." Jane searched within herself and to her relief found that the proper emotion of grief was actually there. "He was just riding up the hill toward home and then, all of a sudden…he can't have believed it, either. I mean, if he had time to know about it."

"Good thing he came to see 'ee. You two've not been on proper speakin' terms, have 'ee? Don't think I don't know!" His voice was rough. "You upset him, comin' home from court. He pushed you off on to me. Well, I wanted a wife and a son and if a man's got sense, he don't argue with 'un's landlord, not when the landlord's doing him a favour. Can't say 'ee've not done right by me—good maid you are, Jane. But I don't suppose I was what 'ee wanted. I don't suppose I'm what 'ee wants now. I can see that. I can't read nor write, but I b'ain't the village idiot. Only idiot hereabouts is that gurt fool Tom Hayward."

"Harry, you've always been kind to me and you mustn't think I don't…" She lost herself and started again. "I'm better off with you than I would be with some of the men I saw at court. And you've given me Tobias." She swallowed and then made herself say, "I'm perfectly happy with you."

I wonder where Peter Carew is now? Doing what? Is he in danger?

"Yes, Tobias." Harry seemed to be thinking. "This'll make a difference to him. Next, 'ee'll be sayin' the lad ought to get some schooling. I don't like the sound of that. Don't want my son thinkin' he's above me."

"If he's got to look after property one day…" Jane ventured. "I mean, he ought to learn to deal with accounts and letters and…"

"I know I'm ignorant. Just said as much, didn't I? Well, same as I said to that chaplain up at the house, that's the station in life I were born to and I b'ain't presumin' to leave it. And I don't want my son lookin' down 'un's nose at me, either!"

"He won't! I'll see to that."

"I don't doubt 'ee'll try," said Harry, sounding slightly mollified. Jane put out a hand, searching for his without looking for it, but he only took the offering momentarily before putting her hand down as though it were something he had inspected and found wanting. There was another pause and then he said, "Jane, just what is it 'ee've been left? Don't think Spenlove finished readin' it all, did he? So tell me."

Jane cleared her throat. "There's Allerbrook House and its home farm, and three other farms. Hannacombes, Greys—the place that used to be Shearers—and Rixons. That's us. There's the village—all the houses are rented from Allerbrook. There's Clicket Hall that's on lease to the Stone family, but it belongs to Allerbrook really. So does the water mill on the far side of it—that came into our family when Clicket Hall itself did. There's a home farm attached to Clicket Hall, as well. And there are two farms on the eastern side of Somerset."

"Got it all at thy tongue-tip, I see. Seems there's a good bit of land," said Harry. "Who does the accounts and sees to the taxes and whatnot?"

"Francis mostly. He liked doing things himself. He goes...no, he used to go...out with the reapers at harvest time."

"Well, I can't do any of that bar the reapin'," said Harry. "And I don't fancy livin' in that big house up there, playing lord of the manor. It wouldn't be fittin'. Gentry won't call on the likes of me, and they're right. Reckon I'd do better to sell the place, along with the home farm. Can't let it," he added ruminatively. "That'ud look daft, landlord living here at Rixons and tenants spreadin' theirselves all over the big house. But sellin'—that's different. Money'll come in handy and we can keep the rest of the land. Plenty there. Plenty for Tobias one day."

Jane coughed again. She had not been in the care of the businesslike Francis for nothing, and matters of inheritance had also been discussed at court at times. Everyone was interested in them and she knew something of the law. "Harry, you can't sell my inheritance unless I give my consent. And I won't. I don't want my old home sold."

"Don't 'ee now?" Harry spoke quite easily. "And it can't be put on the market except 'ee signs a bit of paper? I take it that's what 'ee means."

"Yes."

"You'll sign," said Harry. "Wives have to obey husbands and if 'ee says no to me, I'll beat the consent out of 'ee. No fun for either of us in that, but I'll do it. Shouldn't risk it if I were you, maid. You ought to see the state Tom Hayward's in."

Jane, still looking down at her hands, felt sick. He meant it; she knew he did and she would never be able to withstand him. Her home, which had been left to her, was going to be sold against her will. Fury again rose in her, fury that almost stopped her breath.

Careful.

"Harry, we're both tired and upset. Should we even try to decide anything yet? We'll have to hold the funeral from Allerbrook House, I suppose. That was Francis's home, after all. Shouldn't we leave deciding anything till all that's over? I think," said Jane, forcing the words out through her rage as though she were pushing a plough through heavy soil, "that we really ought to go to sleep."

They hadn't quarrelled, not exactly. But that night they slept back-to-back, and neither reached a hand toward the other.

In Allerbrook House, Dr. Amyas Spenlove was sitting up late. His bedchamber, which was in the east wing, had an austere bed without curtains and a shelf of books—theological works, some treatises on travel, history and politics and, very precious to him, a volume on the art of calligraphy and illumination.

His pigment-smeared table stood to one side, and on the wall he had a crucifix an uncle had given him when he qualified as a priest. The cross was two feet tall, and the figure was made of ivory. It was very well carved. Too well carved for comfort, Dr. Spenlove sometimes thought. The craftsman had understood the human body, understood pain.

The table held writing things, paper and parchment. Beside it was the cupboard for his pigment jars. The lockable drawer for his valuable supplies of gold and silver leaf was under the tabletop, like the drawer in Francis's study. He had completed three of the Gospels commissioned by the Taunton gentleman, and was now working on the final one, St. John.

He liked to work at night when the house was quiet. It came hard on the eyesight, but he kept a supply of good-quality candles and a pair of eyeglasses that fitted firmly on the bridge of his nose. Armed with these, he could manage very well, even by candlelight.

At the moment he was preparing to work but not, this time, with pigments, only with black ink. Before he began, he folded his hands and addressed the poor contorted ivory figure.

"I ask forgiveness, Saviour, for what I am about to do. I will break the laws of men but not the laws of justice, not the laws—I think—of God. We are told to render unto Caesar that which is Caesar's, but Harry Hudd isn't Caesar and Mistress Jane did nothing more wrong than protect her own honesty. She shouldn't be married to someone like Hudd. Perhaps I'm doing him an injustice and he will not throw Allerbrook away, but I fear that he will and I know how much Mistress Jane loves it. I've known since she told me on the way to London. I heard the tears in her voice today when she said she thought Francis must have changed his will. She will not want to lose it, but that man is capable of making her. I must act *now!* She will soon ask to see the will for herself, and whatever happens, *she* must not be a party to this. I don't think I'm wrong. I know his type. *Christian humility,* he calls it, and *knowing his place. I* call it damned obstinacy and sheer bloody-mindedness, and that sweet, decent lady shan't suffer for it."

He had brought Francis's will up from the study and it was on his table, loosely rolled. He opened it out flat, weighing down the corners with books and an inkstand. It was lucky that he hadn't actually finished reading the document aloud. When he brought the will to everyone's attention a second time, as he would now have to do, he could say with truth that the first reading had been incomplete. He really had stopped short of the final paragraph, which listed the details of the Allerbrook estate. But there was still a convenient space at the bottom, enough for two or three extra lines.

He took a sheet of paper. The first thing he had to do was practise the writing. It was Francis's own, for sure; Spenlove recognized it. It was a sprawling hand, but not elaborate. It shouldn't be hard to imitate. He would have to make sure that the colour of the ink matched precisely....

He studied the ink and the handwriting for some time and then began, thoughtfully, to trim a fresh quill before beginning to experiment.

He had no hearth in his room, but later, deep in the night, he took his candle and crept down to the kitchen. In some houses kitchenmaids slept beside their work, but at Allerbrook the girls shared a chamber in the west wing. No one was there to see him shift one of the turfs that kept the fire banked through the night, and push in some pieces of torn paper. The fire flared, consuming the new fuel, and sank once more to ember red. The evidence of his experiments was gone. Spenlove replaced the turf and stole away, well pleased with his night's work.

CHAPTER SIXTEEN
The Oath is Taken
1541

*D*r. Spenlove made the funeral arrangements and when the day came, Jane and Harry were at Allerbrook House early. The Haywards, however, were absent.

"We all know whose fault this business was," said Harry grimly to Ed on the eve of the ceremony. "If that daft son of yours knew how to keep himself to himself, there'd be no packhorse carryin' a coffin up the combe from Clicket this day. You can all stop home and get on with whatever wants doing and Tom had better do his work right or I'll skin his back for him. Again. The baby," he added, "comes with us."

At the house, Peggy and Dr. Spenlove greeted them soberly and showed them to the study. The coffin had been placed on top of the table and it was still open, so that any who wished could make their last farewells.

"We thought in here because Master Francis used to work here," Peggy said. "It's his room, like, and he were fond of it."

The hall was ready for guests, with a white cloth on the table and a good deal of cold food, covered by napkins or lids, awaiting the return of the funeral party. "And there's a couple of chickens to go on the spit," said Peggy. "Beth's stayin' back, to see to 'un. She feels kind of awkward, like, seein' how she were mixed up in how it all come about. She'll take care of little Tobias for 'ee, too, while 'ee's down at the churchyard."

"Don't know who'll come," Harry said. "Folk from Clicket, I daresay, but they won't all want to climb a mile back up the combe from the church, once he's buried. No need to overdo things, Peggy."

Peggy, however, was right and Harry quite mistaken. Ralph Palmer and Dorothy had as it happened arrived lately to visit the ailing Thomas Stone in Clicket and were the first to ride up the combe. Next, Father Anthony Drew jogged in on his mealy-nosed moor pony, black gown hoisted clear of his leggings, greying hair tidily trimmed, face serious. Tim took charge of the pony in deferential fashion, and Father Drew came into the hall, to clasp hands with Spenlove and Jane, and murmur his condolences in his deep Somerset voice.

"It'll be a good, respectful service, though one has to be careful with the wording nowadays. Seems to me the king wasn't wise, breakin' away from Rome and closing the monasteries but wantin' everything to stay the same otherwise. He still says these here Lutherans are heretics, but the fact is, cuttin' loose from Rome, it's opened the door to 'un. Folk are thinkin' and talkin' different."

"My father's been doing that for a long time," said Ralph gloomily. "I worry about him. He thinks and talks too much."

"Does he? He'd do better not to trouble his old head," Drew said. "Why should he? I have to, bein' a vicar, but I swear it's aged me ten years. I just want to take care of my flock. Well, well, I mustn't go on about my troubles. This is a sad day for you, Mistress Hudd, and for all of us. We'll all miss your brother."

Others were now crowding in: the Greys who had replaced the Shearers at the farm across the combe; Job Searle, the tall, gaunt Rixons shepherd with his wife, Jennet; Alfred the blacksmith, who was Violet Hayward's cousin, and his strident wife, Annet, who was nearly as hefty as her husband.

Among the others who made their way up the mile-long combe were John Dyer, the carpenter who had made the coffin, Hal Jones, the elderly, widowed potter, whose earthenware was in use in nearly every house for miles, Simon the Miller from the water mill, Arthur and Marjorie Wright from the White Hart inn, and Will and Betty Hannacombe from Hannacombes farm on the other side of the ridge. Hard behind them came Owen and Katherine Lanyon on horseback.

"Dr. Spenlove let us know. Idwal and Frances couldn't come—Frances is expecting and near her time. They're staying at home and keeping an eye on young Stephen. That young limb," said Owen, "gets his fingers into everything. Good day, Master Palmer. And Mistress Dorothy! Is Master Stone not with you?"

"Master Stone is very ill," Ralph said. His dark eyes were full of their old beguiling smile as he kissed Jane and then Katherine Lanyon in greeting. "His steward fetched us several days ago. We'd ridden from Dover to stay with my

father so we were at Bideford. Master Stone has trouble
with his breathing and the physician can't tell us what ails
him. He began to fail after Dorothy's mother died. Dorothy's
woman Lisa is taking care of him today."

Jane, welcoming Dorothy with the courtesy that must be
extended to guests who are attending the funeral of one's
brother, thought about fat, pallid Mary Stone and secretly
marvelled that Stone had been so stricken by her death.
Dorothy, too, was getting fat now and would probably end
up looking just like her mother. Ralph was not likely to
prove as devoted as Thomas had apparently been. Ralph's kiss
of greeting had been very enthusiastic. She suspected that
he was still a philanderer.

Turning to the Lanyons, she asked if there was any news
of Sybil.

"Not that we know of," Katherine told her. "She's still at
Stonecrop as far as we're aware. I take it that she will not be
here today?"

"No," said Jane rather blankly. In all the confusion and
with so many things to do, she had not thought of sending
word to Sybil. "No, Sybil won't be here."

"What happened to Andrew Shearer?" Owen asked. Jane
shook her head, but Arthur Wright overheard and said, "I
think he's got one of the Luttrell farms, over toward Dunster.
Someone mentioned it in the White Hart a year or two back."

Jane was not interested in the fortunes of Andrew
Shearer, who had so thoroughly shipwrecked Sybil's life.
Seeing a few more villagers arrive, she excused herself in
order to greet them. She was then surprised to see a
stranger, dressed in elegant black velvet, ride in on a good-
looking bay gelding. She was about to go out and ask who
he was when Ralph Palmer stepped past her and went out

to meet the newcomer himself. A few minutes later he returned with the stranger at his side and said, "This is Master Russell, horsemaster, from the Carew estate at Mohuns Ottery. We are acquainted. I hoped he'd come. I let him know all about it. He has something to ask you, Mistress Hudd."

"Later," said the stranger, removing his hat. He was past his first youth, though still fit looking, and he was well-spoken. "All that can come later, after the ceremony. For the moment, we're all at a funeral."

"Quite," said Jane, bewildered, and introduced Master Russell to her husband. It was almost time to set out.

It was over. The weather had held. Jane, looking— although she didn't know it—both dignified and forlorn in her square-necked black stuff gown with its plain ash-coloured kirtle, was touched to see how many of the funeral party had after all chosen to return up the combe to partake of the repast at Allerbrook House.

"You've done very well. I'm so grateful," Jane said, going into the kitchen to compliment Peggy and the other maids. "This is hardly a happy occasion, but it's a success. Thank you."

"Thing is, Mistress Hudd," Peggy said, "what happens now? That's what we're all wondering—Beth and Letty and the Snowes and me."

"I can't tell you that," said Jane, and felt the weight of depression settle in her stomach. "Not yet. We shall have to wait and see."

She went back to the hall, where Francis's wine and Peggy's cider were in circulation and Master Russell was discussing horses with Harry. She heard the word *Silvertail* and went over to them. Harry looked around as she came up to them.

"This fellow wants to buy that horse that killed your brother. If it's still an entire, that is. Is it?"

"Yes," said Jane. "It's very temperamental. If it hadn't been..."

"Who's to say? It's all over and done with now," said Harry. "Fact is, Master Russell here's made an offer."

Dr. Spenlove, tankard in hand, came to join them. "Master Russell is in charge of a small stud, it appears, and the king has sent out an edict requiring that taller horses with height and speed must be bred. Silvertail has both."

"My master Peter Carew is abroad," said Russell, "but provided funds and left me empowered to buy and sell as I thought fit, for the benefit of the stud. When my friend Ralph Palmer chanced to meet me and told me of this tragic business, he mentioned that Francis Sweetwater had owned a very striking horse that was nearly sixteen hands and was, he thought, a stallion. It sounds to me like the sort of animal I want. I also thought—very likely Mistress Hudd won't have any use for him, anyhow."

"I meant to put the brute down," said Harry, assuming ownership without reference to Jane. "But if there's a fair offer...well, if 'ee'd like to come and take a look at 'un now, sir, it's out in the meadow." He was more garrulous than usual, possibly because of Peggy's cider. "Thing is," said Harry in confiding but clearly audible tones, "I'll be needin' to sell up more than just that horse. Your master wouldn't be interested in Allerbrook House and home farm hisself, would he?"

"That I couldn't say, Master Hudd. As I explained, my employer is currently overseas and I have no means of contacting him."

Spenlove drew a deep breath and put his tankard down on the table with enough of a bang to make them look at him in surprise. "It would be of no use if you did contact him," he said. "There seems to have been a misunderstanding."

"A misunderstanding?" Jane was puzzled.

Harry frowned. "What's 'ee on about? If it's my wife's consent 'ee's worryin' about, there's no need. Jane'll do as I ask, any time, won't 'ee, maid?"

"Naturally," said Jane bleakly.

I was right. Spenlove felt himself grow hot with rage. *I knew it. I can hear the threat in his voice even if no one else can. He'll make her do as he wants. Or would. Thank God I acted in time.* Hoping that his flushed face would be put down to embarrassment, he said in flustered tones, "But I'm sure I...didn't I...?" and then appeared to brighten. "Oh yes, of course. Now I remember. I was still reading out the will the other day when you were so startled, Master Hudd, by some of the terms, when I explained them, that you burst out in astonishment. Why, I do believe I never read out the last two paragraphs at all!"

"This is private," said Russell. "Perhaps one of your grooms would show me the horse?"

Harry nodded and Spenlove said, "Tim Snowe will show you—there he is, over in the corner. And there's the Clicket vicar, Father Drew. Would you ask him to come here, please?"

Russell withdrew. Jane said, "Dr. Spenlove, what *is* all this? What's in those last paragraphs?"

"You'll see in a moment, but I want Father Drew to be with us. I feel there should be a witness. I was most remiss the other day. We were all upset, of course...ah, Father Drew. An awkward thing has occurred. I didn't mean to deal with this matter today, at the funeral, but it seems necessary. Will you and Master and Mistress Hudd come with me for a few moments, please?"

In Francis's study the table was empty now, its owner

gone forever. Beside the table, looking nervous, Dr. Spenlove took his stand.

"I can't apologize enough," he said. "I was so shaken by events…but there it is. I never actually finished reading the will, and the final paragraph in particular is important. It makes a difference, Master Hudd, to what you can and can't do. Let me see…oh, where have I put my eyeglasses?"

Father Drew, looking impatient, produced his own from a pouch sewn inside his black formal gown, and handed them over. "I daresay yours are in your room. But these here glasses magnify very well."

"I don't see how anything can make a difference," said Harry loudly. "It's for me to say what's to be done with my wife's property, b'ain't it, given she consents to any sale, and she'll do that, right enough. Didn't 'ee hear her say so?"

"It's not so simple. Not this time." Spenlove, holding Father Drew's eyeglasses in place with one hand, because Drew's nose was broader than his own, pulled out one of the drawers under the tabletop, clicked his tongue, shut it again and pulled out another. Father Drew rolled his eyes at Jane. Spenlove, looking into the second drawer, said, "Ah." He took out two scrolls, one bigger than the other.

"This small one is the pedigree for the horse Silvertail," he said to Harry. "The man Russell will want that, I daresay. This other one is the will. Now. Let me see…"

He unrolled the parchment, spread it out on the table and pointed to the text at the foot of it. "There are the two paragraphs that I never read out. Oh dear, dear, how could I have been so careless?"

"Perhaps," said Father Drew irritably, "you would give over this havering, Spenlove, and amend this here error without further delay?"

"Yes. Of course. Well, first there's a description of the estate—that doesn't matter at this moment—but then we come to this. '*To safeguard my sister Jane against later misfortune and ensure that she always has a home, I enjoin that Allerbrook House and the home farm that goes with it should not be sold in her lifetime. On her death, they are to pass to her lawful heirs, if heirs there be, in accordance with the normal laws of inheritance.*'

"It means, Master Hudd," said Spenlove gravely to Harry, "that you cannot legally sell either this house or its home farm, with or without your wife's agreement. They are to be kept and passed to your wife's children—your children, of course. Your little Tobias is the heir."

"But…that means I can't do as I like with my own!" Harry shouted.

"Well, Master Hudd, the…er…provision I've just read out is for your wife's protection and that of your children. Surely you can't object to that."

"You think I can't look after my own wife and son without this here kind of charity and…and…" Harry was at a loss for words.

Jane, gazing at the spread parchment, which Spenlove was holding open, remembered how she had looked over his shoulder as he read it out a few days before. She hadn't been close enough to read it properly, except for Francis's expansive signature, but she could remember the pattern of the text. Surely there had been a bigger space between the end of it and the loops and swirls of *Francis Sweetwater.* There was little space now; indeed, the signature seemed crowded close to the last line.

Below it were the names of the witnesses: the Dulverton lawyer, who was now dead, and Dr. Spenlove himself.

Suddenly her eyes met Spenlove's. His were greyish-blue in colour, usually bright, usually smiling. Now they were as opaque as breathed-on glass. They stared unblink-ingly into hers.

She understood. She stood motionless, silent.

"Well, there's no argument," said Father Drew easily. "You can't sell this here house, Harry, but why should you, anyhow? Don't you fancy living in a fine place like this?"

"You've been *called* to live in it," said Spenlove helpfully. "If God wanted you to stop at Rixons, He'd have made sure you did. Sometimes it's that way. Sometimes a man gets picked out and given a promotion, so to speak. Men can join an army as just plain soldiers and find themselves turned into captains. Why, you're to be congratulated! We've laid poor Master Sweetwater to rest with all respect. Now we're all looking to you to take care of us, and we know you'll do it well."

Jane, recalling pigs in the Rixons kitchen, came within a hairsbreadth of hysterical laughter. Harry looked slightly stunned. She took heart. That wording in the will was *there* and she didn't propose to ask how it had got there. As far as Harry was concerned, Francis had written it, and Jane wasn't going to quarrel with that.

"I used to help Master Sweetwater with estate business," Spenlove remarked. "I'm not usually as woolly-headed as I must have seemed over this. I can do the same for you, Master Hudd. It'll all go smoothly—you'll be amazed."

Father Drew joined in. "It's my opinion we should all go back to the hall and drink a toast to the new master. What about that?"

A few minutes later the bemused Harry was standing in the middle of the hall and having his health drunk in wine and cider. Russell, back from the paddock, pleased with what he had seen and now in possession of Silvertail's pedigree, joined in. The occasion was becoming cheerful.

Simon Miller pushed his way through the crowd to clink his goblet against Harry's. "There's something I'll want to talk to 'ee about—maybe not now, but soon. The mill wheel wants a bit of repairin'. Master Sweetwater was comin' to take a look at it this very week to see for hisself. Maybe you could find a moment."

"Replacin' or repairin'?" Harry asked. "Which?"

"Replaced 'ud be best. Repairs 'ud be just botchin'. They'd last a while and then want doin' again."

"All right. I'll ride down when I can and take a look."

"And when'll 'ee be wantin' to move up here?" That was John Dyer. "If 'ee needs a few boxes and crates and whatnot made, I'll see to it."

"Not yet. I've no tenant for Rixons. Can't just leave 'un…"

Harry showed signs once more of digging his toes in. Jane watched him warily. But now Alfred Smith was clearing his throat.

"Well, as to that, would 'ee consider my cousin Vi and her husband? Don't reckon they'll let that son of theirs give trouble, not after this. How about makin' it a condition that that gurt lump Tom goes to sea?"

"Not in my ship, he won't," said Owen Lanyon, though good-humouredly enough.

"My second boy's as handy on my patch of land as he is in the forge," remarked the blacksmith. "And he's betrothed. Elder lad'll have the forge but the younger'll have to make his way, so there'll be one young couple lookin' for work. Rixons 'ud suit them, likely as not, if extra hands are needed."

"Well, now," said Harry, his voice by this time some-what blurred due to the cider. "Maybe we could consider that...."

Secretly, in the dark folds of her mourning gown, Jane crossed the fingers of one hand. It was really going to happen. The miller, the Smiths were accepting Harry as the new master of Allerbrook and between them they were, so to speak, putting him into his seat of honour and filling up the empty space he'd have to leave at Rixons.

Standing there, looking around at the hall, so familiar and yet so strange, with Francis not there and such a crowd of solemn black-clad figures, she was swept by an extraordinary sensation. She was suddenly aware, as never before, of time and its ravages.

Only a few years ago there had been a happy family here: Francis and Eleanor, Sybil and herself. In those few years, that serene family had been ripped to pieces. Only she was still here, and the future was in the hands of Harry Hudd and, one day, of Tobias.

Others besides her must have felt like this. Time did similarly astonishing and sometimes dreadful things to everyone, however secure they had once felt, however solidly em-bedded in their own lives and families.

She looked at the friendly faces of the people around her. Here they all were; this was her community, and time would tear this to pieces, too. Oh, people would fight back; they always did, trying to defend their own, but they never won. Was the whole of human life a desperate attempt to defy time and hold back chaos?

If there was no chance of winning, it ought to mean that there was no point in fighting, but it didn't feel like that. All her instincts cried out to her to do her utmost in the gallant, useless resistance until she herself was overcome by the years. While she could, she would safeguard this household and all the people who belonged to it—indeed, all the people she cared about, who made up her world. She would keep them happy and defended.

It was like taking an oath.

"And may I ask," said Ralph Palmer as he and Dorothy rode down the combe on the way back to Clicket Hall, "why you're looking so sour?"

"I didn't know I was," said Dorothy, as usual slumping on her sidesaddle rather than sitting up straight. She was on a quiet mare. Any horse ridden by Dorothy had to be quiet; a mount with an ounce of spirit would have rid itself of her awkward, ill-balanced weight as fast as it could.

"If you looked like that at a quart of milk, it would turn on the instant," said Ralph.

He had never expected to love his wife. He had been reared to think of marriage as way of adding to the family fortunes by seeking a bride whose money and land could augment his own, and producing children to carry the family on. If one were fortunate, affection would grow. Most people hoped for that.

Dorothy had obliged with the money and land, but affection had failed to develop, though he had tried hard enough, and as for the hope of a child…

It was becoming harder and harder, in fact, to do his duty in bed. More and more, he found her pale plumpness unattractive and her passive unresponsiveness a discouragement. And yet she was jealous, always jealous of him. She was suffering it now. He knew the symptoms—that droop of the mouth, the way she wouldn't meet his eyes.

THE HOUSE OF ALLERBROOK   181

"I saw you," she said.

"Saw what?" He pushed his horse close alongside her and tried to get her to turn to him.

"Saw the way you looked at Jane Hudd. Saw how you kissed her."

"I kissed all the ladies. I kissed Katherine Lanyon."

"Not the way you kissed Jane. And I saw how long you held her hand and talked to her when we were taking our leave."

"Dorothy, please! We're cousins. We've never looked on each other as anything but close kin."

He hoped he sounded convincing. What he had just said had been true enough once, but Jane had changed. Something—marriage, was it? The birth of Tobias?—had altered her, deepened her. He was attracted now.

"You're not that close," said Dorothy. "I suppose she'll be the next in your long line of doxies."

"Dorothy!"

"About number five, I'd say, unless there have been some I didn't know about."

"You imagine things."

"No, I don't."

And no, of course she didn't. He had had affairs since their marriage. He had been as discreet as he could, but it was astounding how she always managed to ferret out his infidelities, though she didn't always succeed in identifying the women. She didn't, for instance, know that Marjorie Wright's third child, a dark-haired little girl now growing up in the White Hart amid a crowd of flaxen siblings, was Ralph's and not Arthur's. Arthur attributed the dark hair to his Welsh mother.

"Let us not quarrel," he said. "Your father is very ill. We should be thinking about him."

"Lisa thought this morning that he seemed better."
Dorothy grudgingly accepted the olive branch.

"I trust she was right."

But as they rode into the stable yard of Clicket Hall, Lisa
ran out to meet them. "Master Ralph, Mistress Dorothy,
there you are! He's taken a bad turn. He's unconscious and
his breathing...well, I've sent a groom for the physician but
he'll have to come from Dulverton and God knows how
long it'll take to get him here or what he can do when he
comes anyway...I've left a maid with Master Stone...."

Ralph was already out of his saddle and reaching to help
Dorothy from hers. "We'll go to him at once. Come, Dorothy."

They found the maid on her knees at the bedside, praying
through her tears. Thomas Stone's troubled breathing had
entirely ceased.

CHAPTER SEVENTEEN
Appointment of a Dairymaid
1541

With a feeling of great relief Ralph touched his heels to his horse and rode away from Clicket Hall. Father Drew was there and would be better than Ralph at comforting Dorothy and arranging Thomas Stone's funeral. He was thankful that for a whole day he would be astride a horse in the sun and wind of early summer and away from the sight of Dorothy's puffy, tearful face.

Ostensibly he was on his way to inform her mother's cousins in Porlock of Thomas's passing, but he had another purpose in mind, as well. He had gathered at the Allerbrook funeral the day before yesterday that Francis's sister Sybil did not yet know that he was dead. Jane, when saying goodbye to him, had remarked worriedly that she hadn't let Sybil know and must see to it but couldn't be sure when.

"I'll take word to her," he said. "You've enough on your hands. Where is she?"

"It's a place called Stonecrop Farm, near the coast, west of Porlock. I've never been to that part of the moor but I think Perkins, the Lanyons' manservant—he found her—said it was in Culbone parish. There's a little hamlet there, I think, and a small church. The farm itself is on the moors. I think that's right."

"I'll find it," Ralph said.

Some time later he found himself ruefully concluding that this might be more easily said than done. He had been to Porlock before, but not by taking the coastal route, and he had never heard of Culbone. He began by riding almost to Lynmouth, since Sybil must have started from there. Going right into Lynmouth to ask for help from the Lanyons' manservant did occur to him but Jane's instructions seemed clear enough and why waste time? Turning the other way, he took the coastal track eastward, toward Porlock. Poor girl, setting out on foot through this landscape, looking for shelter! He had never seen such a lonely district.

He rode for a long time, keeping his eyes open for farmland but without seeing any. Empty moors were on his right hand, while thick woods dropped away on his left toward the coastal cliffs. He had gone about ten miles when the sun went in and low cloud swept in from the sea, surrounding him with fog. He slowed from a trot to a walk. In this he could ride past a dozen farms without noticing them.

He rode on slowly, studying a tangled verge of ivy and brambles, looking for a likely turning. It would be to the right, if the farm was on the moorland as Jane had said. In the end it was sound and not sight that drew his attention. He heard the squeals of a piglet and then a squelching thud, and a girl's voice cried, "Come here, you horrible little beast!" and after that emitted some most unwomanly curses.

Voices were astonishingly individual and memorable, too, even if one hadn't heard them for years. Ralph pulled up and shouted, *"Sybil! Is that you?"*

"Who's that?" The voice came from closer now.

"If you're Sybil Sweetwater, I'm your cousin, Ralph Palmer! Over here!"

A shadowy figure emerged from the mist. A moment later she was beside him. He blinked and had to look twice before he was sure that his ears had not misled him, but yes, it was Sybil. Thinner than he remembered, with weather-roughened skin and a hardness in her face that had never been there before. Her dress of undyed wool was splashed with mud, and when she reached up a hand to take his in greeting, he felt calluses on it. But the hair escaping from a grubby cap was still ash-fair and still an astonishing contrast to the brown eyes.

"I was looking for you," he said. "I have news for you, though not happy news. Your sister Jane sent me. It's about your brother. I'm sorry, Sybil. There's no way to break such things gently. I'm afraid he's dead, in a riding accident. He was buried two days ago. His wife died, too, last year."

"Francis and Eleanor—both dead! No, I didn't know." Her hard expression intensified. "Well, I wouldn't have wanted to go to Francis's funeral, even if anyone had bothered to tell me in time," said Sybil. "But I'm sorry I missed Eleanor's. I suppose Francis just didn't trouble to let me know. But why didn't Jane get word to me about *him?*"

Ralph said, "Jane has had a great shock. Please forgive her. Things have been difficult for her."

"It was kind of you to come." Sybil was remembering her manners. "How is Jane? Didn't she go to court after all?"

"She went but she wasn't happy, and came home. Francis married her off to Harry Hudd at Rixons."

"He did *what?*"

"She's Mistress Hudd now, and has a little son. But she's inherited Allerbrook."

"I'm glad to hear that, at least," said Sybil waspishly. "What made Francis push her off onto Harry Hudd? Was he angry because she didn't stay at court?"

"I think so, yes."

"That sounds like my brother," Sybil said. Dismissing Francis, she added, "I long for news. I never get word of my little boy, Stephen. You know I had a little boy?"

"Yes, I know about Stephen. Francis told me a long time ago. He's still with the Lanyons. He's all right as far as I'm aware."

"Is he? He could be dead, too, for all I know! I think that's deliberate—that the Lanyons want it that way and probably so did Francis. So my dear brother is gone. Well, as I said, I am sorry about Eleanor but if you expect me to mourn for Francis, well, I shan't! I don't suppose Jane will, either!"

"I think Jane feels a natural sorrow, but in your place I don't think I'd feel very grieved, either," Ralph said thoughtfully. He swung out of the saddle and alighted beside her. "What was happening when I called to you?" he asked. "You sounded as though you were having trouble of some kind."

"Piglets," said Sybil bitterly. "I didn't shut the sty gate properly and a piglet got out. Everyone was angry with me and told me to get it back. I went after it in the fog and caught it, but it got away again, loathsome little thing, and trying to hold on to it, I slipped and fell down in some mud. I hate it when they're cross with me."

"Who are *they?*"

"The family here. The Reeve family. And Marian, their

maidservant. They're not really unkind," said Sybil, "and they do pay me, but they get annoyed if I get things wrong and sometimes I do. Not in the dairy—I can do that sort of work. But I'm not used to all the outdoor things. I get tired and make mistakes, like not shutting a sty gate as I should and then they shout at me."

"You do look tired," Ralph agreed. His dark eyes took her in, from grubby cap to the battered shoes on her feet. They were so muddy that it was impossible to tell what they were made of. "Do you get enough to eat? Does anyone hit you?"

"There's plenty of food, only sometimes I'm nearly too tired to eat it. I've been hit, yes," said Sybil grimly.

At home in Allerbrook no one had struck her since she was a small child, and those occasions had been rare and mild. Francis had sometimes made threats, but had never carried them out. As for Katherine Lanyon's slaps, Sybil now knew what minor affairs they were. The first time Ambrose had clouted her, for leaving a rake propped against the side of a stall where there was a horse, she hadn't been able to believe it. She remembered reeling against the wall of the stable, clutching her face and staring at him in horror.

"Oh, don't look at me like a rabbit at a weasel!" Ambrose had barked. "I hardly tapped 'ee. Leavin' a rake where the hoss might knock it over and step on the prongs...I ought to half kill 'ee but I'm a kind man, so just never do that again."

She never had, but she had made other mistakes just as silly, and incurred other clouts since then. They frightened her.

"You can't stay here." Ralph suddenly made up his mind. "Jane and Harry Hudd are going to move into Allerbrook House. They could take you in. Francis isn't there to say no.

Now, let's find this piglet, and then we'll go and talk to these Reeves. You can get your things together and I'll take you to your sister. My horse can carry us and your bundle, I daresay."

"What?" Sybil gaped at him. "Leave here? Go *home?*"

"Well, if the Hudds'll have you, but with Francis gone, there's a chance. Jane will want to, surely. If not, we'll think of something else."

He was already thinking of something else, as a matter of fact. If that pale hair were washed, and her skin tended for a while, and if she were dressed in something with even a trace of colour in it, she'd be nearly as lovely as she was at eighteen. Which was a great deal lovelier than Dorothy had ever been. Even as she was now, the idea of riding with Sybil held against him was very beguiling.

"Which way did the piglet go?" he said. "Is it still sucking or will it eat something solid?"

"Oh, it's well grown. It'll eat anything," said Sybil.

"Then," said Ralph, "I recommend a pail of pig swill with a really enticing smell."

Thomas Stone's cousins by marriage would just have to wait.

Bess and Ambrose Reeve turned out to be respectable if unpolished, and had a sense of responsibility toward the girl they had befriended. Bess in particular seemed suspicious of Ralph, as though she had sensed, though she couldn't possibly have seen, the kiss he had impulsively given Sybil while they hunted for the piglet.

Sybil had fetched the noisome bucket of scraps that lived by the kitchen door and was filled each day for the benefit of the sty, but stumbling about in the fog, holding the smelly thing between them and calling, "Piggy, piggy, piggy!" had made them giggle and then Sybil somehow bumped into him and they put the bucket down and kissed as though it were the most natural thing in the world.

They caught the piglet and put it back with its family and then Ralph presented himself to the Reeves. And now Bess, standing in her kitchen, hands on hips, was eyeing him as though she knew very well what had happened in the mist.

"Fact is, she b'ain't strong enough for most of what she has to do, but she's handy with milking and in the dairy and I wouldn't like to see her cast on the world or put with unreliable folk."

"She annoys us now and then," Ambrose agreed, eyeing the mud-spattered Sybil disparagingly. "But she tries."

"Yes, she does," said Bess. "She's welcome to stay. And what do we know about you, Master Palmer? You say you're kin to Sybil, but we've never heard of 'ee."

"He's my distant cousin," said Sybil. "I've known him since I was small. Father Drew of Clicket would tell you. Ralph says he'll take me to my sister Jane. It was my brother turned me out to start with, but he's dead now, Ralph says. Jane'll help me. I know she will."

"Well, we can't stop 'ee from goin'," Ambrose told her. "We don't own 'ee." He walked to the kitchen door and looked out. "Fog's clearin'—that's a mercy. If you ride off with this man, you'll be able to see where you're a'goin'. But now, see here. We won't see any wench cast on the world with no one to turn to. If things don't go well, or as 'ee expects—" here the glance he gave Ralph was decidedly hard "—in that case, come back to Stonecrop. We'll find a place for 'ee at our table and work to do."

"They'd certainly find work for me!" Sybil said with feeling as she and Ralph rode away through the last wisps of the mist, Sybil perched in front of Ralph's pommel and her

meagre bundle of belongings bouncing on his broad shoulders. "I'm grateful to you, Ralph."

"I hope I'm right to think that Jane and Harry will take
you in. But I couldn't leave you at Stonecrop!" Ralph said.

At Rixons, plans were being made for the move.

"To start with, we'll have to keep comin' down here to
see to things, till Ed gets hisself sorted out," Harry said. "It'll
be haymaking and shearing afore long. We'll be splittin' ourselves between here and Allerbrook for a while, seems to me.
Now mind, maid, you're goin' home to your fine old house,
but I want no fine lady airs. No sittin' around doin' fancy
stitchin' or readin' books of poetry. There'll be all to do."

"Yes, Harry, I know." She knew that tone of voice. His
mind was fixed and even the smallest argument would make
him flush and become angry. Whatever happened, nothing
must provoke Harry until they were firmly installed at Allerbrook and the Haywards equally firmly installed at
Rixons. Until then, she would be unwise even to ask for the
smallest boon, not even an hour on a Sunday to read or embroider. "I don't mind work," she said cheerfully.

It didn't matter anyway. She was going home. *Going home!*
"We won't need to take much from the kitchen," she said
in a practical voice. "Or bed linen, either. Violet will want
it and there's plenty at Allerbrook. I'll just need my clothes
and brush and comb and such things."

"I'm takin' my favourite tools," said Harry. "Ed's got his
own and I work better with the wood-axe and the hoe I'm
used to. Saints alive," he added, walking to the window. It was
open, as it usually was, even in winter, to let out heat and
steam and allow people to see out as well, since it had shutters
but no glass. "Who's this ridin' up our track from the village?

Ralph Palmer, by the look of 'un, but he's ridin' double. Who in heaven's name is that girl he's got in front of him?"

Jane came to his side to look at the horse as it bore its two riders up the hill and into the farmyard. Ralph pulled up, dismounted and helped his passenger down.

"I don't believe it," said Jane. "I *don't believe it*. It can't be. She looks terrible! But all the same, I think…I really think it's Sybil."

"No. Not on any account and I'm surprised at 'ee, Master Palmer, suggestin' such a thing," said Harry, and with a heavy heart, Jane once more recognized his tone. His mind was fixed about this, too.

Ralph, of course, didn't know Harry as well as she did. "Look, Master Hudd, this is your wife's sister, and she's had a bitterly hard time. She needs a bit of Christian kindness. She…"

Sybil was not present at this colloquy in the Rixons kitchen. Jane had taken one horrified look at her bedraggled sister, seized a basin, taken a jugful of water from the pan that happened just then to be heating on the fire and sent Sybil upstairs with it.

"Have a good wash—your hair, as well! Go to the room on the left at the top of the stairs—that's ours. You don't mind, do you, Harry? I must get her tidy!"

"I'd agree with 'ee there," Harry said, eyeing Sybil with disfavour. "No, I don't mind."

"Thank you." Jane bestowed a grateful smile on him. "You'll find ash and lye in pots on the washstand, Sybil. Take a fresh dress from my press. My things should fit you. Take some decent shoes and a clean cap."

"'Ee've sent her up to get clean. Well, I've no quarrel with that," Harry said now to Jane. "But stop here—or at Allerbrook—she can't. I won't have it, seein' what her past has been. She's not the sort I want about the place, and that's final. Plain and ignorant us Hudds might be, but we'm decent and we'm stayin' that way. If we give charity, it's to them as deserve it."

"But, Harry…" Jane turned to him with appeal in her voice. "I have been thinking to ask you if she couldn't come home now. There's plenty of room at Allerbrook and she's my sister, after all, and—"

"I knew it!" Harry scowled at her. "The minute you got that legacy, I knew 'ee'd start tryin' to start pushin', tryin' to take charge. I'm the one who says, maid, not thee!" He turned to Ralph. "You took her away from where she was. She's your business now. Not ours."

Jane opened her mouth again but before she could speak, he went crimson and got in first. "Mind your tongue, maid. Don't go wranglin' with me. I b'ain't never been hard with 'ee yet, but don't 'ee drive me too far. I won't give her house room and that's my last word."

Ralph looked shocked, but Harry gave him a long, hard stare. "We're man and wife and we understand each other. Jane'll see I'm right when she's had time to think."

"Don't worry," Ralph said reassuringly to Jane. "I'll look after her." His pulse was in fact throbbing with a new hope. They had both enjoyed that snatched kiss in the fog, and riding here from Stonecrop with Sybil in his arms had indeed been agreeable—in fact, exciting. Grubby and ill dressed and hard-faced as she had become, there was something about Sybil, something that explained the careless opportunism of Andrew Shearer. Her body in his embrace was not hard at all, but confiding and warm. She was like a delicious wine in a tarnished cup. He wanted to taste that wine.

"Mistress Hudd," he said, addressing Jane with formality in the presence of her husband, "would Dorothy recognize your sister?"

"She's never seen her," Jane said, swallowing down tears. "The Stones were new to Clicket when…well, you know. You were one of the guests at that dinner. Francis made Sybil stay in her room all the time and the Stones went home before she was let out. Then the Lanyons took her away with them."

"Good. Now. You'll not know it yet, perhaps," Ralph said, "but Master Thomas Stone, my father-in-law, died on the day of Francis's funeral."

"What? Oh, Ralph…Master Palmer…I'm so sorry."

"Aye. He was a well-liked man," Harry agreed. "This is a sad year for both families, it seems."

"Yes, it is," Ralph agreed. "But Dorothy and I will still be the tenants of Clicket Hall. Her father made a will, saying that he wanted her to have the lease when he was gone. In fact, he sent for Francis to get his agreement, the day that Francis was killed. Francis never reached him, but my father-in-law went ahead and signed the will. It's valid. So if I want to find a place for Sybil at Clicket Hall, I can. It's probably best," he said, thinking aloud, "if I don't present her as herself, if you follow me. But if Dorothy doesn't know her by sight, she could come, for the time being, as a…a dairy-maid, perhaps, using another name."

"She's used to dairy work," Jane agreed.

"So I gather. I won't take her back with me. She can follow me on foot. I can say I stopped at a farm for directions and heard that a girl there wanted a new situation. In fact, we do need an extra hand in the dairy at Clicket Hall. Dorothy and I have inherited all the Kent property, too, of course. You know, I might one day be able to settle Sybil in Kent. Shouldn't be difficult. I'll have plenty of money now."

"Dorothy's," Jane said, with a touch of acidity.

"The Stones' money, yes," said Ralph easily. "Money talks. A sweetener for whoever takes Sybil and a dowry for the lass, as well. Granted it's just a shadowy notion as yet, but it might work."

"I reckon she'll be recognized in Clicket. Folk there'll know her," said Harry grumpily.

"She's been gone for some time," said Ralph. "And she's changed. If she keeps her hair hidden—it's the pale hair with the brown eyes that's so striking—and doesn't go about the village too much, we might get away with it. Let us hope for the best, then. What name shall we give her? Rosie? There was a Rosie at Bideford years ago, a pretty lass."

Rosie had been not only pretty but knowledgeable. It had been Rosie who had initiated Ralph, aged sixteen, into the joys of lovemaking. He would never forget Rosie the maid-servant, with her bright come-hither eyes and their warm snugglings in the haybarn. His father would have called it wickedness, but the young Ralph had loved the whole business and they'd done it again, several times. She'd shown him how to avoid unfortunate consequences; Rosie's in-struction course in the facts of life had been comprehen-sive.

Until, disastrously, his father had caught them at it. He re-membered that with distress to this day. He was used to his father's beatings, but he had wept that time, not for his own anguish, but Rosie's and he had loathed hearing her called a whore when his father ranted about fornication. Rosie had been off the premises immediately afterward, allowed to do no more than put her few belongings in a sack. She was still sobbing and limping as she went out the farmyard gate.

She'd been all right in the end. She'd found work on a neighbouring farm and eventually married the ploughman. While Ralph, reacting finally and furiously against his father's upbringing, had found that he could attract girls with ease and proceeded to use this delightful talent, though he took great care not to let his father find out. Rosie became part of the past, but he would forever be grateful to her and he would always think that her name was the most musical sound in the world.

"Rosie," he repeated. "Rosie…Waters? She's been using the name Waters already, it seems. That's settled, then. I'll get back home in time for dinner and maybe you'd at least give Sybil a bite to eat before you send her after me. And explain what the plan is. Don't mention anything to do with making a marriage for her, in case it never happens."

With Sybil at the table it was an awkward meal. Fortunately, the Haywards had gone to visit the Searle family and were not there to complicate things. Ralph, on the other hand, would have been a help and Jane wished that he'd stayed. In his presence, Harry wouldn't have been so morose and she could have talked more freely to Sybil.

As it was, she could do little more than explain what had been arranged, and say that she hoped all would go well and that Sybil would agree to go to Clicket Hall as a servant. "It's asking rather a lot of you, but it might be for the best. Perhaps things will improve for you, gradually. I'm sure Master Palmer will see you're well treated."

"I'll make no difficulties. Don't be afraid of that," said Sybil. She made no appeal to Harry. Jane looked at her and saw, all too clearly, from her sister's worn and hardened face, how harsh life had been for her. She wanted to turn to Harry and say, *Look, hasn't she been through enough? Whatever she did that was wrong, hasn't she paid for it, with interest, over and over again?*

But Harry was in one of his implacable moods and she knew it would be useless and might even jeopardize the move back to Allerbrook.

She provided Sybil with a few extra items of clothing, and though Harry frowned, she kissed her sister goodbye very lovingly. "Don't forget. You're Rosie Waters and you were working on a farm where you just had too much to do. Too many cows to milk or something. Now, off you go."

She watched Sybil walk away, hoping that she would be all right. She would pray for her. Harry couldn't prevent that.

In Clicket Hall, Ralph was finishing his own dinner and explaining that he hadn't been able to see his father-in-law's cousins by marriage because the fog had delayed him too long. He'd have to go to Porlock again sometime. Oh, and he nearly forgot. He'd asked the way at a rough and ready farm near Porlock and heard that one of the servant girls there wanted a new place. The girl looked all right and her employers said she was a good worker in the dairy, but free to leave if she wanted.

"Anyway," he said, "I've told the girl to make her way here. If she turns up, her name's Rosie Waters—and we do need another hand in the dairy, so the steward tells me."

CHAPTER EIGHTEEN
Warm Mulled Wine
1541

On the home farm at Clicket Hall, quite close to the house itself, was a haybarn with an upper room, reached by a wooden stair with a trapdoor at the top. The room was rarely used but contained a little furniture in the shape of a bedstead, a chest and two stools. Once in a while, if there was an influx of visitors, a groom or two might sleep there; sometimes it was used to isolate servants who had fallen sick and might be contagious.

Late on a July evening it was mustily warm from the heat of the day, and dim with the approach of nightfall. A single window cast an ember-coloured patch of sunset onto the plank floor. The air was dusty, and although a pallet had been put on the bed, it was a thin, straw-filled affair that rustled.

It was a poor sort of place, but to Sybil it meant enchantment. It meant bodily satisfaction and the romance she had long missed. She had grown hard and withered with her longing and needing and now was softening again under the blessed influence of a man's desire. She had sense enough to know that desire did not mean love, but she didn't care. Desire would do. Now she sat on the thin pallet and waited, while the dull red of the sunset faded and the shadows gathered. An owl called, somewhere out in the deepening dusk. Sybil, hugging her knees, whispered to herself, "Come soon. Oh, my love. Come soon."

When at last she heard Ralph's feet on the stair, she sprang up to meet him and as he came through the trapdoor, she threw herself into his arms. In a moment they were kissing feverishly and simultaneously loosening their own and each other's clothing, disentangling themselves from it, dropping it onto the floor. Then, twined together like the strands of a single rope, they cast themselves onto the pallet.

Gloriously united with her, sweating, snuggling, laughing, nuzzling, it occurred to Ralph that, though he didn't like what he knew of the man, he owed Andrew Shearer something. Shearer had awakened this girl's appetite, this magnificent, all-powerful appetite, and then, hatefully, abandoned her to yearn and starve for what he had taught her to need. But Ralph himself was the gainer. In many years of experience, with a goodly number of women, Ralph had never encountered a response like Sybil's. Rosie was lukewarm by comparison; Dorothy always had resembled cold pottage, anyway.

With Dorothy, even at the very beginning, he had had to work to get himself to function, and could hardly manage it at all except in complete darkness. With Sybil it was all he could do, not to explode too soon, which he must not do, for he must withdraw in time to protect her from another pregnancy.

Fortunately, Sybil never kept him waiting long, and her climaxes were astounding. He sometimes had to put a hand over her mouth to muffle her cries of ecstasy.

This time there was an added intensity, because in two days, he and Dorothy were going away, and it had been hard to get to the barn this evening, with Dorothy wanting to discuss what their baggage should include. He'd finally persuaded her to go to bed early by saying she looked tired.

He had never spoken to Sybil about arranging a marriage. Now that he was her lover, he found the idea unbearable. He couldn't let her go. It was unthinkable, as long as the straw pallet rustled and Sybil's warm, joyous body surrounded him, and moonlight slanted in where the sunset had been earlier, silvering her pale hair and making her dark eyes shine and even showing the sweat on the skin that was becoming smooth again, now that she no longer had to work in the fields. He could not dream of parting from her, not now, with his whole being rising and surging toward the moment when the giant wave must break....

Her wave was breaking, too. It was the moment to get out; he was not Andrew Shearer and he meant Sybil no harm. Beneath him, Sybil was arching. Her mouth had opened for the shriek it mustn't give and he clamped his own down on hers, and her body, totally given over to its satisfaction, closed so hard on him that for a moment he couldn't escape. Then, with an effort so great that it left him gasping, he was free, and knew that he had been just a split second too late.

Silently he cursed himself. But very likely nothing would happen, anyway. The disaster with Andrew Shearer had been very bad luck. Women didn't always take, just like that. Dorothy, confound her, had never as yet shown the slightest sign of taking at all.

"Don't worry," he said soothingly as Sybil relaxed and then looked at him with eyes that were anxious and questioning in the moonlight. "Don't worry, love." He lied, to keep her happy. "I was in time. You'll be all right. I'm so sorry I have to go away soon. We're going to Bideford and then on to Kent. We won't be back till autumn maybe. But I won't forget you. I promise."

Mid-October brought gales and rainstorms and Jane, listening to the wind and rain, was glad to be by the fire in the hall at Allerbrook.

It was near the end of the afternoon. Harry was down in Clicket and Jane, for once, was embroidering. She was repairing some frayed decoration in a sleeve of her Sunday dress. Harry didn't classify keeping Sunday clothes in good order as a waste of time. Today she could practise her skill, and in familiar surroundings. It was so good to be here, so good to feel secure, part of the place again, just as she had been as a child.

The Haywards had taken charge at Rixons and installed the Smith boy and his young wife, plus a thirty-two-year-old ex-monk from a disbanded Benedictine monastery at Dunster, as helpers. Neither Harry nor Jane expected that the Haywards would ever be anything other than shiftless, but with luck, their employees would be competent. She and Harry no longer needed to lend a hand there. Best of all, Harry seemed to be taking to the life of landlord. Tobias was thriving and fortunately was a well-behaved child who didn't create disturbances. Harry was proud of him.

Harry had gone to Clicket to get new shoes for his bay Exmoor pony, Ginger. Ginger had been bred in the Allerbrook herd and carried the Allerbrook brand of two slanting lines with another crossing through them, but his wild days were far in the past. Ginger was reliability on four surefooted hooves. Master Hudd had no taste for exotic horseflesh and was thankful to be rid of Silvertail, while the aging Copper had been retired to grass. The clop of Ginger's hooves and the usual livestock noises heralded Harry's return. He came in, looking tired, but pleased to see her.

"There you be, maid. It's blowing hard out there now, fairly whistling through the combe and rippin' the leaves off the trees. Tim's seein' to Ginger. Told me to come in and get a cider, not that I didn't have one afore I started up the combe. Went into the White Hart for a drink, like I usually do. Don't want old friends thinkin' I'm fancyin' myself above them."

Jane put her work aside. "Peggy! Oh, there you are. Cider, please. The master's tired."

"Well, it 'ud be welcome." Harry relapsed onto a settle. "Somethin' interestin' happened in the inn. Thank 'ee, Peggy." He took the tankard she had brought him and took a long, grateful drink. Then he put it down and gave Jane his gappy grin. "Very interestin'! To start with, I were takin' a drink and talkin' to Job Searle, but there were a few others in there chattin', it bein' noonday, and Simon Miller was one, and suddenly Simon comes out with, *Well, I don't have land so I wouldn't know, but there's Allerbrook over there. Wonder what he thinks?* He called me Allerbrook, Jane! Not Master Hudd, but Allerbrook, like I really belonged here!"

"Well, so you do. People used to call Francis that sometimes, you know. *Ask Allerbrook,* they'd say, or *Come and meet Allerbrook.* I often heard things like that. Francis liked it, just as you did today."

"It made me feel real funny," said Harry. "And he meant it. I mean, he weren't sneerin' at me. He was callin' me Allerbrook natural-like. Anyway, Simon don't go in for sneerin'. But that ain't all. He were talkin' to the Clicket Hall head groom, about somethin' I reckon's worth thinkin' over."

"And what was that?"

"Usin' heavy horses for the plough instead of oxen. Seems that since plate armour b'ain't as useful as it was for war, what with guns and that, a lot of heavy horses are bein' sold for farm work. A horse team eats more than an ox team, but that don't matter because it can plough more land in a day, and a man can raise more feed than the horses can eat. We could make East Field twice the size it is now and put crops in!"

"It sounds like a good idea," said Jane at once. East Field, which lay, as its name declared, on the eastern side of the house, was not large and had a stretch of rough grazing just below it. "The land above it might be too steep but not the land just below. We only use that for sheep and we've plenty of grazing for them without it. Yes, why not?"

Harry finished his cider, looking pleased, and proceeded to impart some more news. "The Palmers are back at Clicket Hall. They're intendin' to stop here over Christmas. Seems Master Palmer likes the west country—feels at home here."

"Well, that's natural. He's a westcountryman, after all." Jane yearned to ask after Sybil and knew that Harry realized this perfectly well. She was also certain that even if any news of her had come his way, he probably wouldn't pass it on.

Dr. Spenlove came into the hall, pink and cheery as ever, with pigment stains on his fingers. "I think I can smell a rabbit stew being cooked. I could fancy that."

"You may be in luck. Tim shot two rabbits yesterday," said Jane. "Amyas, Harry has a very good suggestion about exchanging oxen for heavy horses. Do tell Amyas about it, Harry."

Conversation settled down to practicalities. Sometimes Jane remembered how she and Eleanor, doing their embroidery together, would talk about whatever poetry they had been reading and how when guests like Sir William Carew or Thomas Stone were present, they and Francis would talk philosophy or discuss the latest tales from the New World, to which ships from Europe were now taking colonists and explorers.

But those days were done. Harry didn't like it if she spoke of things he didn't understand. Dr. Spenlove had wider interests but he didn't mention them in Harry's hearing either, though no doubt he did when he visited Father Drew.

But at least she was here, at home. She wasn't going to grumble.

"This evening, in our usual place," Ralph said quickly, stepping into the dairy. "At about five of the clock. I'll be about the farm all day, and on the way back I'll come to the haybarn. It'll still be light. We can have a half hour, maybe a little more. Are you all right to…?"

"Yes. I'm so glad to see you back!"

Her voice was intense, a little too intense, Ralph thought, but he wanted her as much as ever. "Until this evening," he said.

An hour before supper Sybil stole out of the house. The gale snatched at her skirts, and she had to clap a hand on her cap to keep it in place as she hastened to the barn and climbed to the upper room. A fresh pallet was on the bedstead. Oh, wonderful Ralph. He had smuggled the old one away before he left for Bideford and had now replaced it with another. At night, probably, from a storeroom in the house where spare pallets were kept. He was so resourceful. *Dear* Ralph. Thank heaven for Ralph. She could trust him. He had returned to her at last, and she needed him.

He came promptly, smelling slightly of sheep, his black hair all windswept and a corn husk caught on his sleeve, but as handsome, as smiling, as beloved as ever. She went into his arms gladly, thankful to be there. She badly wanted to talk to him but he was impatient, silencing her with his mouth, eager to unite with her. She surrendered. It was a tender reunion, as though their first wild raptures had matured while they were apart, into something deeper, something warm and sweet like mulled wine.

Afterward, with their clothes in a pile on the floor beside the bed, they lay closely folded together in the stillness that always followed satisfaction. They were utterly lost in it when the footsteps sounded on the stair and the trapdoor was flung back.

They sat up, startled, as a figure rose through the opening to stand menacingly at the top. Sybil instinctively grabbed for a garment, seized the first she could find, which happened to be Ralph's shirt, and clutched it to her. It was dusk now but there was light enough to see the intruder's face. It was Dorothy.

She stood there motionless, hands linked at her waist and head high. Her eyes glittered and her whole body shook with anger.

"So I've caught you. I've suspected something ever since you first came to Clicket Hall, Rosie—if that's your name. You're slow to answer to it sometimes. I've kept watch. Chance was with me this time. I looked out of the right window at the right moment and I saw you go into the barn and then Ralph, a few minutes later. Well, well."

"I…" Ralph began, and then stopped. Sitting up, conscious of the sweat of passion still on his naked chest and Sybil there beside him, he felt a fool, and was lost for words.

"You're not the first," Dorothy said to Sybil, who stared at her, openmouthed but speechless. Dorothy turned back to her husband. "I've been loyal to you, Ralph. I have never spoken of your unfaithfulness to any other person, but now you've gone too far. I've caught you at it in our own home! Get up, please, and get dressed."

"Just a moment!" Ralph took refuge in indignation. "You can't give me orders, my lady! I am your husband!"

"You're a knave and a scoundrel and I *am* giving you orders. Young woman, give him that shirt and put on your own clothes. I do not steal the property of others and you may fetch your belongings before you leave, but leave you will, and at once. I will wait for you in the courtyard and watch your departure in person. You will leave Clicket Hall, and Clicket itself, forthwith. Never let me see your face again, even in the village. If I do, Father Drew will be told of your behaviour. You will do penance for it."

Sybil, trembling, began to whimper, a pitiful sound like a hurt puppy. Ralph wanted to take her hand, but with Dorothy's glittering gaze on him, dared not. It was almost like the moment when he and the first Rosie had been caught, he thought wildly. But no, it was not. This was his house. He had authority.

"One moment, Dorothy! Syb…Rosie can't be turned out of the house in this fashion, least of all in a gale like this, with night coming on. She has nowhere to go and she has done nothing but obey my wishes and—"

"Many people," said Dorothy, "would tell me that half the men in the kingdom play games with their maidservants while their wives look the other way. But I will not look the other way and I rather think that if I tell him of this, your father won't, either!"

"My father has no rights in this house!" shouted Ralph. "And I forbid you to tell him. Do you hear!"

"You can't stop me," said Dorothy. "I'll find a messenger when your back is turned, don't think I won't, and if you ill-use me for it, your father will be on *my* side. No rights in this house? Do you think that would weigh with him?" The scorn in her voice rang out. "I'll hold my tongue if this girl leaves Clicket today. But if she doesn't, then inform him I *will* and he'll deal with you. On our betrothal day he promised aloud, at the feast, that he would do that if ever you were unfaithful to your wife."

And so he had, and so he would. Ralph knew, all too well, what his father meant when he talked of driving out the old Adam. He had been reminding Ralph of Rosie and that other haybarn at Bideford. He would arrive, breathing fire. Ralph would not be able to withstand him; he never had been able to. Dorothy would reveal all his infidelities, not just this one, and Luke, full of moral outrage and oblivious to all matters of rights, would do to his son and to Sybil, if she were within reach, exactly what he had done, years ago, to Ralph and Rosie. Sybil must not be exposed to that, nor to the public calumny afterward. Luke had also said that he would *talk,* and he would do that, too.

And nothing would stop Dorothy from telling him. Ralph knew that he was not in any case cruel enough to use violence to intimidate her.

Beginning to scramble into his clothes, he said to Sybil, "My poor girl, for your own sake, I think you should go. I'll give you some money." He glared at Dorothy. "Don't try to stop me from doing that! She can't sleep by the wayside."

"Your money is your own," said Dorothy contemptuously. "Even when it's mine! If you want to waste it on this idle little whore, then do so."

"I'm not idle!" said Sybil tearfully.

"You're a lazy little wretch who only scours the milk pails if someone's watching you." Ralph had never found it easy to attribute any virtues at all to Dorothy, but she was in fact a good chatelaine, who watched over the work of house and dairy. "Do by all means give the little vagrant some means of support," she said. "Go and fetch it while she dresses."

"I..." Sybil looked at Ralph with desperate eyes. "I...I need to talk to you. I thought I could trust you."

"Trust him?" Dorothy laughed, and now the edge of hysteria was there. "Trust *him?* My poor child—Rosie or whatever your name is. He almost used another name just now, didn't he? If there's one man in the world you'd better not trust, it's this one here. Now, *dress!*"

Sybil obeyed, clumsily, because she was shaking so much. Ralph thrust his feet into his boots, clumsily treading on Sybil's cast-off cap in the process. She threw him a look of appeal, but he shook his head at her. "I'll get the money," he said. As he went down through the trapdoor he turned to give her one last backward glance, in which there was apology and regret but no trace of hope. Then he vanished down the stairs.

Sybil began to cry openly. Dorothy said, "Stop that. Go and fetch your own belongings. Hurry."

Shortly afterward, in the courtyard, Ralph handed money to Sybil and wished her luck, though with Dorothy standing there, he did not feel able to kiss Sybil goodbye. "There's enough there for food and lodging for a month," he said. "Find somewhere safe. God go with you."

"I fancy the devil's a likelier companion for her," said Dorothy coldly. She stood where she was to watch Sybil creep miserably out of the gate. Ralph, unable to bear it, went inside.

The air was full of the smell of supper. It made him feel sick.

CHAPTER NINETEEN
Into the Fray
1541

When the knocking on the door began, it was loud and frantic but the gale was wailing in the chimneys and blowing squalls of rain and what sounded like hailstones against the windows. It was several moments before the Allerbrook household, gathered around the supper table, realized that someone was desperately pleading to be let in.

"Bit late, b'ain't it, visitin' after supper?" Harry said, wiping custard off his chin.

"I'd better see," said Jane, getting up.

She was back in a few moments, her arm around her sister. Sybil, sickly pale, a wet cloak clutched round her and hair trailing like seaweed from under a soaked and grubby cap, seemed hardly able to walk. She carried a bundle, a few things pushed into a meal sack and tied at the neck with twine.

"Sybil!" said Harry, recognizing her, and then added, "What ails the wench? Is she drunk?"

Jane sat her sister down by the fire and said to Peggy, "Bring some cider and some stew. And a dry shawl. Take this wringing-wet cloak away. She's freezing cold."

Harry was frowning. "What's all this, then? Thought you was at Clicket Hall, milkin' cows."

"I was. But…"

Letty fetched a shawl while Peggy filled a bowl with stew and poured cider into a tankard. "Thank you," Sybil whispered. She huddled into the warm woollen fabric around her and spooned stew into her mouth, but she was avoiding Jane's eyes. Jane looked at her worriedly.

"What's happened, Syb?"

"I don't know how to tell you." Sybil scraped up the last of the stew, swallowed it and gave a scared glance toward Harry.

"Reckon 'ee'd best make a try at it," Harry said unsympathetically.

"I…I mean…oh, I can't, I don't know how to…oh, Ralph Palmer was so kind and I was grateful and…"

"Go on," said Harry ominously.

"I think," said Sybil, beginning to cry, "I think I…shall have a baby next spring. It's Ralph's. He doesn't know. I was going to tell him, but before I could get round to it… He's just come back from Kent. It must have happened just before he went away. His wife caught us. She said she'd tell his father. He's frightened of his father. He let her…he let me be just flung out."

"*Men!*" remarked Letty vindictively, rearranging the shawl more cosily around Sybil's shoulders.

"I walked up the combe," Sybil said. "It was so windy and there was a hailstorm and I've nowhere to go but here. I can't get to Stonecrop even if they'd have me—it's too far and I feel so ill...let me stay. Jane, please, let me stay!"

"I'm not sayin' throw her out into the storm," Harry said reasonably when he and Jane were alone in their chamber and Peggy was putting Sybil to bed, by Harry's orders, in the servants' wing. "She'm a maidservant nowadays and that's all. And no better than she ought to be, servant or not," Harry had said. Now he looked uncompromisingly at Jane and added, "What I'm sayin' is that she can't *stop* here. That's final."

Jane sat down on the edge of the bed. This was going to be one of the hardest things she had ever had to do. She was tired. She had put Tobias to bed as usual before the adults' supper, but the wind had disturbed him and it had been difficult to get him to sleep. Then she'd had to look after Sybil and now she must cope with Harry.

The silent oath she had taken after Francis's funeral must be kept. One look at Sybil's desperate face this evening and she knew that her sister was among those who needed her protection. No matter how angry Harry was, no matter how frightened she was herself, she must defy him.

"I am sorry, Harry. Perhaps we can make other arrangements later, but for the time being, she *must* stop here. She looks ill to me."

"No more than she deserves."

"Harry, please!"

Night had fallen now and the room was lit only by candles, but they were enough to tell her that his face had suffused.

"Let me remind 'ee once again, maid, that we stood at church door together and 'ee promised to obey me."

"I know. But I can't. It's as simple as that. I said we'll try to think of plans for her later, but not until the baby's born."

"Baby! This is the second time, b'ain't it? She's nothing but a lightskirt, that sister of yours."

"Perhaps. But she's still my sister. Harry, *please* don't be so angry. Please be kind." She was wheedling and it felt shameful, but it just might work and that was all that mattered.

"I say she goes. Tomorrow or the next day, when she's better. I grant you she looks sick after trudging up the combe, but she'll get over that and then she goes and 'ee'll accept that. I've been patient and I've some respect for a sister's feelings or I'd not be listenin' to 'ee the way I am. But I'll not…"

There were racing footsteps and a vigorous knocking at the door. "Come in!" Jane called, more relieved than anything to be interrupted.

The relief didn't last long. Peggy threw open the door and rushed in. "Better come, mistress. It's Mistress Sybil. She'm bleedin' and m'am, she'm past three months and I've seen a few like this and it's not good, it's not good at all."

"What was it? Girl or boy? Could you tell?" Sybil's voice was no more than a whisper and her face against the pillow was frighteningly white. The wind shook the shutters and found its way through, making candle flames stream and shadows dance, as though ghostly presences had gathered to watch the drama on the bed. Peggy, frantically working with wadded cloths, her hands and apron stained red, caught Jane's eye and shook her head fractionally.

"We couldn't tell. I don't think we looked."

"Poor little thing," said Sybil. "Jane…go and see Stephen, at the Lanyons', when you can. Make sure he's all right. He'll have to know."

"Know what?" said Jane with false heartiness. "He needn't know about this. You'll be able to visit him yourself soon. I'll take you. If you're afraid they won't let you see him, I promise I'll *make* them."

"Jane, sweeting. Don't be silly," said Sybil. Tears oozed from the corners of her eyes. Jane wiped them away with a napkin.

"Just a few hours ago," Sybil muttered, "I was with Ralph. I was going to tell him. I was scared but I trusted him to look after me, to think what to do. I was putting it off, but I'd have told him before we parted. Then when Dorothy came, I couldn't say it...I didn't dare...I didn't know what she might do.... I loved him, Jane. Only a few hours ago..."

She moved restlessly, turning her head from side to side, and then moved again, more violently this time. It was like a small convulsion. She whimpered. Peggy swore and snatched up a fresh cloth. The room filled with a sweet, metallic stench.

"You're all right!" Jane gripped Sybil's chilly hands in her own strong, warm ones. "I'm here. I've got hold of you. Don't be afraid."

Peggy, now muttering prayers under her breath, was striving to staunch the crimson flow. Presently, however, she stood back and looked despairingly at Jane. Against the pillow, Sybil's pale face was still, and she was silent.

"I think," said Jane wretchedly, "that I have lost my sister."

"Well, yes, the Palmers ought to be told, and her boy," Harry said grudgingly. Once again he had reddened with annoyance. "But since thee can write, I say put it all in letters and send Tim with 'un."

Jane felt not merely tired, but drained. She and Peggy had tidied that dreadful room as best they could and washed Sybil and laid her gently in clean linen and she had had a few hours' sleep, but not enough. She took a long breath and started again.

"Harry, I am sorry it displeases you, but Ralph's a cousin and I feel I must *myself* tell Ralph and Dorothy what has happened. And I must, myself, see Stephen. Sybil asked me to."

"It does displease me, maid, but I can see 'ee's obstinate."

As if you aren't, Jane thought savagely.

"All right. Take Ginger. And take Dr. Spenlove with you. That fat cob of his—what does he call it? Podge? If you push on, you'll get some weight off Podge and the two of you can get to the Lanyons and back in a day and take in Clicket Hall on the way. The wind's dropped. Weather's not bad this mornin'."

He was angry, but he was trying to be good-humoured. Harry could be generous as well as obstinate. She had to admit that.

At Clicket Hall they found Ralph and Dorothy in the throes of preparing to leave for Bideford the following day. It was a disagreeable interview.

Ralph was visibly shaken, while Dorothy exuded self-righteous satisfaction, until Jane was provoked into saying, "I think Sybil miscarried because of the shock of being cast out, into that wild gale, and getting soaked with rain and hail and having to stumble the long mile up the combe to beg us for help, not knowing if we'd give it. She was exhausted and frightened when she reached Allerbrook."

It was an accusation. Dorothy knew it and paled with anger. Spenlove said quietly, "We will see she's laid decently to rest. It might be best if neither of you were present. Good day."

"That was dreadful," Jane said as they rode away.

"I know. Well, it's over now," Spenlove said. "We must make haste. We've a long ride ahead."

The sky was still overcast but the day was dry. They made good time, and it was not yet noon when they rode down through the steep, wooded valley to Lynmouth at the foot of the cliffs.

"There's the house," Jane said, pointing. "I hope they're not all in Bristol. Idwal lives in Bristol now, but I think Owen only goes there just for business. Francis always kept in touch with Owen and that's how I know. Katherine generally stays in Lynmouth, I think."

"Stephen has well-to-do guardians," Dr. Spenlove said.

"Sybil seemed worried about him, though. She shouldn't have left him behind like that, but…" Suddenly Jane was overcome. She reined Ginger in and stopped to wipe her eyes. "I had a brother and a sister and now they're both dead. I can't believe it. I know Sybil was feckless, but she was my sister just the same."

"Well," said Spenlove, adopting a brisk tone in order to stem the tears, "here we are, to ask after your nephew, as Sybil wished. You're doing something for her."

They were welcomed with courtesy. A groom took their horses, and Perkins, who had apparently been promoted to the post of butler, showed them into the parlour and said the mistress was at home and he would fetch her. "Master Owen's in Bristol today."

The parlour was pleasant, its oak table and settles smelling of beeswax, its cushions colourful evidence of skilled and tasteful embroidery. Stylized ships, dolphins and fish were the principal motifs. Refreshments would be brought, Perkins said, and if they would be seated, he'd call Mistress Katherine.

He hurried away through an inner door, closing it after

him. Jane and Spenlove sat down. The windows looked out
on a street which just now was quiet, except for the eternal
calls of the gulls, and the atmosphere should have been
peaceful, but it was not. There was an undercurrent of
trouble in the house. After a moment Jane rose and went to
the inner door, which she knew led to the dining room. She
opened it. There was a stair at the far end and the disquiet
now resolved itself into noises from above. Somewhere
upstairs, a small child was crying, not to say bellowing, and
by the sound of it was hammering frantically on a door.

"Dr. Spenlove!" Jane said. "Listen!"

"That's Stephen," Katherine Lanyon came through the
dining chamber from another door. "Disturbances from that
quarter are common, alas. Has no one brought you any
wine or saffron cakes? What are they about in the kitchen?
Ah, Madge, there you are." A maid had just hurried in
behind her, carrying a tray. "Good," Katherine said. "Let's
all sit down and Madge, please close that door behind you.
We wish to talk and not be troubled by that child's din."

"But what's wrong with him?" Jane asked. "If that's
Stephen, it's him we've actually come to see."

She had always thought of Katherine as elegant and
gracious, a suitable wife for Owen. But now it struck her
that Katherine's grey eyes, though well-shaped and deep in
colour, were also chilly.

"We have bad news," Spenlove said. "We need to see
Stephen because although he is very young, there is something he must be told—and so must you. Let me explain."

He did so, taking on the task as he had done at Clicket
Hall. Katherine listened, pouring wine and handing saffron
cakes all the while. "I see," she said at the end. "So Sybil is
dead and in a very unhappy way. I can't say I'm surprised,

though naturally I am sorry to hear that such a tragedy has overtaken a family member, and Owen will feel the same. Stephen will just be told that his mother has fallen ill and died. You can rely on us not to burden him with the appalling truth."

"I'm sure we can," said Spenlove, "but we would like to see the child for ourselves. Mistress Hudd feels she owes it to her sister to do so."

"He is locked in his room until nightfall. He is six now, old enough to learn his letters, and we arranged for him to share a tutor with another child in Lynmouth. He goes daily to the other child's home. But today, not for the first time, he slipped away early and we found him down on the quay, listening to travellers' tales from an old sailor he's made friends with there. He is an impossible child!" said Katherine with energy and visible dislike. "Somehow or other we mean to bring him up properly, but he doesn't make it easy."

"I still want to see him. Now," said Jane firmly.

"He was told that the door would not be unfastened, and that he would have nothing to eat, though I have provided water, until supper."

"Yes, but you weren't expecting us to call, were you?" said Spenlove. "And we wish to break the sad news to him ourselves."

"I feel I must," said Jane. "And we can't wait till suppertime. I promised to be home by then."

Katherine looked at them. They waited. A silent battle of wills took place. Recognizing that they meant to be heeded, she inclined her head politely, rose to her feet and said, "Wait here."

It was some time before she reappeared. When she did so,

leading Stephen by the hand, his hair looked as though it
had been hastily combed and his face just as hastily wiped.
Not thoroughly enough, however, to remove all traces of
tears, and his knuckles were grazed, probably the result of
pounding on the door.

He had a hollowed little face, which looked somehow
older than six. He regarded the strangers with a mixture of
fear and something like anger. He almost seemed to be
trying to stare them out. He had Sybil's colouring, more or
less, since his eyes were brown, though he wasn't ash-fair as
she had been. His hair was midway between gold and brown.

Jane held out a hand to him. "Stephen, sweeting, I'm
your aunt Jane, your mother's sister. We…we have something
to tell you."

"Give him to me," said Spenlove and Katherine, releas-
ing the boy's hand, picked him up bodily and handed him
to the chaplain, who took him on his knee and settled him
firmly. "He's tall for his age," he observed. "Now, Stephen,
my dear lad, our news is sad, but it is something you must
know. It's to do with your mother."

Stephen said, "She went off and left me. She left me here.
I hate it here. I hate *them*." He scowled at Katherine. "And
I hate my mother for not taking me with her. Why didn't
she come with you? Is she dead?"

Spenlove looked staggered by this unpleasant and weirdly
mature outburst, but recovered himself. "Yes, Stephen, I am
sorry to tell you that she is. She became ill and died. She is
in God's hands now. But if she had got better, she'd have
come to visit you. She hadn't forgotten you and she did love
you. You must believe that."

"All right. I have to believe what I'm told," said Stephen.
"*They're* always saying so. I want to get down."

He began to struggle. Spenlove let him go and he went to stand in front of Jane. "You're my aunt. You've never come to see me before."

"No, Stephen. I have so much work to do at home and a little boy of my own to look after. But because of your mother's death—she came to me when she was ill—I decided I must come here and…and tell you myself."

"Oh." His small face was mutinous but behind the mutiny she saw an intense misery, and impulsively she slid to her knees and reached out to give him a hug. The feel of his body through his loose clothing gave her such a shock that she almost let go of him again. She did not, however, but held him close and said to Katherine, "He seems very thin. Why is that? Does he not eat well?"

"They don't let me eat!" Stephen yelled suddenly, tearing himself free. "I'm hungry!" He threw himself down on the floor and began to batter it with his small fists. "I'm… always…hungry!"

"What is this?" Jane demanded angrily of Katherine. "What does he mean?"

"He means," said Katherine, apparently not at all discon- certed, "that when he misbehaves, he has to miss meals. We don't beat him for his badness, though many people would. We consider him too young for that. But when he does things he should not, such as trying to avoid his lessons, or prying into things—our merchandise or our personal be- longings—or running about with a gang of other boys, playing ball as if they were crazy and even breaking windows, then he must go without food, or be given only bread and water for a while to teach him manners. He is a difficult child. If he'd been my child and Owen's," said Katherine with bitterness, "he would never have had such a wicked temperament. He must get it from Sybil and whoever his father was—one of your brother's tenants, I believe. I doubt we'll ever root it out of him."

"But he's…look at him!" Stephen's breeches came only halfway down his calves and his frenzy had made them slide upward. His legs, thus revealed, were sticklike. Spenlove picked the crying, kicking little boy up again and pushed up one of his sleeves. His arm was as thin as his legs. The hollows under his cheekbones were now explained.

"This child," said Spenlove, "is half-starved."

Jane stood up decisively. "He's clearly a trouble to you, Katherine. Don't worry—he won't trouble you again. I'm taking him back to Allerbrook."

"I'll not have it!" Harry shouted, standing in the middle of the hall, his furious face suffused as Jane had never seen it before: crimson tinged with orange. "Outside of enough, this be! From the moment I married 'ee, 'ee's tried to come the lady over me. Now 'ee've gone too far!"

Spenlove had carried Stephen into the hall and was standing behind Jane, holding the boy in his arms. Stephen was peering at Harry with an expression on his small face that was half scowl and half fright. "One moment, Master Hudd," Spenlove began. "I don't think…"

"*You* don't think! You take that brat out of my sight and get about thy godly business, chaplain! I tell 'ee—"

"Master Hudd!" said Spenlove, loudly enough to stop Harry in midsentence. "Peggy, come here!"

Peggy, as usual in times of domestic crisis, was hovering nearby. She came over to them and Spenlove handed Stephen to her. "Take him out of the hall. Look after him. This is Stephen, Mistress Sybil's son."

"Give him a warm-water wash and something to eat, whatever you're making for supper," Jane added.

"Pottage," said Peggy. "With oatmeal and pigeons and mushrooms in it. Apple fritters after." She bore Stephen away.

"Now…" Spenlove began, but Harry cut him short.

"I've had enough. Spenlove, I'll not have 'ee interferin' between man and wife. Since the day we were wed it's been one thing and then another. She wants to idle about readin' they silly books she says has poetry in, or else she'd rather do fancy sewing than proper mendin'…"

"Harry, that's not true, it's not fair…!" But Harry's glare was so ferocious that Jane could not go on. A quivering finger pointed at her.

"You get left this place and somehow or other it's all tied up so that though I'm thy husband, I can't decide what to do with 'un. So here I be, livin' up here, the which I never wanted, and since we've been here it's been worse. I've seen 'ee, readin' when 'ee thinks I'm not lookin'! Then off 'ee goes to Lynmouth. No axin' me if it's all right. Just *Harry, I'm goin'.* And now…"

"Harry, the child is half-starved. The Lanyons weren't feeding him properly. I hope," said Jane indignantly, "that I don't set eyes on Katherine or Owen again for years. No one's loved Stephen or cared about him, and for Sybil's sake I had to rescue him and…"

"I won't keep her brat here, don't think I will! I shan't—"

"Allerbrook!" Dr. Spenlove had ignored the order to remove himself, and now he used the name of Allerbrook, instead of Hudd, intentionally. Harry liked being called by the name of his house. "Please," said Spenlove persuasively. "He's a fine little boy. He could be a playmate for Tobias when Toby's a little older and—"

"That little bastard play with my son? If you think…"

"It's a little boy of six we're talking about—Allerbrook."

It was no use. "Stop tryin' to get round me with that there *Allerbrook, Allerbrook*. Yes, I've taken that name on and I'll hold to it because it's about the one good thing I've got out of all this, and what are you still doin' here, Dr. Spenlove? I thought I told 'ee to get out of this here hall, that's mine, not yours. Go and do some prayin'."

"Any praying I do this evening will be an appeal to God to soften your hard heart, Allerbrook!" Spenlove gave way to indignation. "There's room and to spare in this house…"

"That's right, rub it in, that I'm a common old farmer and not fit to rule in a place this size!"

"No one has said that, and no one is thinking it! Please be kind. That little boy…"

"Will not stay here! I say he will not!" shouted Harry.

"But there's nowhere else for him!" Jane had mustered her courage again. Once more, if she were to keep that silent oath, she must go into the fray no matter how frightened she was. Oh, dear God, why had Francis married her to Harry Hudd? If only it could have been Peter Carew. He wouldn't have treated her like this; she knew he wouldn't. Where was he? Would she ever see him again? "Harry, please, please listen. That poor child's hungry and—"

"I say he's not to have one crumb of my provender, do 'ee hear!"

"You can't mean that!"

"Yes, wife, I do mean it. You go now and tell that Peggy not one spoonful of pottage is he to have, I won't allow it, I…"

Spittle had formed at the corner of his mouth. The orange tint on his skin had deepened. "'Ee's drivin' me mad. My head's goin' as if someone's hittin' 'un with a hammer. I

never thought when I took 'ee to wife…I never thought…
never…"

His voice faded. A look of bewilderment crossed his face.
His knees buckled. Jane and Dr. Spenlove stood frozen with
horror as he fell to the rush-strewn floor of the hall and lay
there, his mouth drawn down on one side, one eye wide
open and the other closed, and the spittle still dribbling, dribbling, childishly down the side of his chin.

In a Hungarian castle called Buda, Peter Carew was attending a banquet. The host was the Turkish sultan, Suleiman
the Magnificent, who had just seized the castle from the grasp
of an unfriendly Hungarian ruler on behalf of a youthful
prince from a pro-Turkish branch of Hungarian royalty.

Peter had taken part in the siege, not exactly forgetting
his status as a merchant dealing in alum but volunteering on
the grounds that he had had military experience earlier in
life. He had enjoyed himself. To Peter Carew, nothing put
a shine on living more thoroughly than danger.

He had learned much, too. He knew now that many
luxury goods from India and other eastern lands were finding
their way westward by new routes, in an attempt to avoid
both political uncertainty and Venetian customs duties. He
was in a position to report on the more northerly European
markets where such goods might now be found. New trade
routes could be created, extending to England.

He also knew now what Suleiman's foreign policy was
like. The sultan clearly was prepared to be a good friend to
those who were friendly to him. He was worth cultivating.
Recommendations about that would also go into Peter's
report. He had done his work well, and knew it.

Though he mustn't, even now that the siege was over, let

down his guard. Tagging along with the army were a couple of Venetians who would probably prefer him not to take his information safely back to King Henry. He had had one bout of what might have been ordinary food poisoning—or might not. Now he took food only from the common dishes. He was taking care, to ensure that one day he and his report would reach England.

Dancing girls had appeared, to entertain the banqueters. He watched them appreciatively. They were lovely, brown as nuts, dark eyed as deer, graceful as ferns in a soft wind. It was a little odd that another picture kept forming in his mind, coming between him and them—a vision of a sturdy young woman with beechnut-coloured hair and brown eyes and beautiful English skin.

He had seen her dance at court, but her dancing was nothing like the sinuousness of these young girls. Yet, mysteriously, he preferred hers. He preferred a style of dancing in which he wasn't just an onlooker. He liked to take a woman's hand and match her steps to his. He would be glad to get home. Would he see Jane Sweetwater then? Perhaps not. He'd heard that she was married now, and his family would certainly expect him to marry soon, and choose someone suitably well-off and wellborn. Anyway, he would have to wait a while. It was the wrong time of year for travelling, with rain and swollen rivers and stormy seas. It was the second of November, All Souls' Day in England.

In England, King Henry VIII was reading, with horror and disbelief, a letter from the Archbishop of Canterbury telling him that his queen, his Kate Howard, his rose without a thorn, was, alas, a mass of thorns of the most vicious nature. She had had lovers before her marriage. She might even have been precontracted to one of them. And since her marriage she had become the mistress of a courtier called Tom Culpepper. It was even possible that the child she had lost had been Culpepper's.

He stood with the letter in his hands, staring at it. Just a few lines on a piece of paper, but they were as deadly as though they were a signed death warrant. They spelled the end of love, of hope, of trust.

Oh, dear God, how could You let this happen? I need a son. I need a wife who won't betray me. I'm so tired. I'll have to try again, but...

In this dreadful moment, his hurt mind opened and foreknowledge rushed in. For a few brief seconds he knew, without possibility of doubt, that he had no more than five years left to him, and that his two daughters and his one, often ailing, son were all the lawful children he would ever sire.

His mind snapped shut, rejecting this hideous certainty. It rejected Kate Howard, too. However near his death might be, she would meet hers first.

Part Three

KEEPING THE FAITH
1550–1562

CHAPTER TWENTY
The Persistent Visitor
1550

"There you are," Jane said, giving Harry's chair a twist so that he could see out of the window, and propping his stick ready to hand if he wanted it. "I'm going up to the ridge for some bilberries now. We can have bilberry pie at supper."

"Don't...don't be away long."

"I won't," said Jane. She gave him a smile and then went off to collect a basket.

In clear weather the view from the high, smooth ridge of moor behind Allerbrook House was remarkable. The gleaming line on the northern horizon was the Bristol Channel. Nearer at hand, to the northeast, was Winsford Hill with its barrow mounds, where lay the chieftains of a long-departed pagan people. There were many barrows on the moor, including one on Allerbrook Ridge itself, though those on Winsford Hill were the most famous. Everyone who lived on the moor knew them.

Beyond Winsford Hill was Dunkery, the highest point on Exmoor, with its beacon on top, ready to be lit in warning if an enemy should invade. To the west, the moorland rolled on and on, like the swell of an immense and petrified sea. Turn to the south and in clear weather the more jagged heights of Dartmoor, Devon's equivalent moorland, might be glimpsed.

To walk up to the ridge alone was something she had always loved to do and now actually needed, as a means, once in a while, of escape from a life both humdrum and difficult.

Harry had recovered from his fit very well at first, and for some years had remained sharp of mind and able to get about, though he limped and had lost the sight of his left eye. That was before the hot summer two years ago, with the peat fire that threatened their fields. Despite his disabilities and the fact that he was by then fifty-five years old, he had insisted on going out with a firebroom to join the fight against the flames. Nearly everyone from Allerbrook, Rixons and Greys had been there, and they won their battle, but afterward, Harry had had a second fit and this was the result.

Now his voice was slurred and he could walk only by leaning heavily on a stick. He was still capable of giving orders, but Jane and Tim Snowe took most of the decisions these days. Meanwhile, Harry had become a curious mixture of frustration and irritation combined with a dependence on Jane which sometimes verged on the pathetic. He could bully her no longer and sometimes she found herself secretly weeping for him. Also, she was racked with guilt for having caused the illness originally by inflicting Stephen on him, though what else she could have done she didn't know. The memory of her visit to Lynmouth and the boy's thin body in her arms remained so vivid.

Dr. Spenlove, always her friend, said roundly that if a man were going to have an apoplectic fit at all, sooner or later he would have one anyway. But the guilt remained and always would, though Harry himself had never, in fact, blamed her.

He had emerged from the critical stage of the first fit to find that his wife's small nephew was now solidly part of the household, and since he was both too unwell to argue and not, in any case, a basically cruel man, he had mumbled that no, he wouldn't after all turn the lad out of doors.

He didn't like Stephen, though, and Jane was hardly surprised. Her nephew was boisterous and disobedient and she had soon understood why he had annoyed the Lanyons.

He and Tobias had never made friends, either. Tobias, who was now nine years old, was a quiet little boy, very unlike Stephen. To begin with, because Stephen had been six when he came to Allerbrook and Tobias had been a mere infant, the two had taken little notice of each other. As Tobias grew bigger, however, this changed, first to mutual dislike and then real antipathy when Stephen, aged thirteen, dared Tobias, aged seven, to climb a small tree by the stable and walk along the ridge of the sloping stable roof.

Tobias, predictably, fell off. He landed in a midden and emerged filthy and stinking rather than injured but from then on he detested his cousin Stephen, who in turn regarded Tobias as a sissy.

Dr. Spenlove, who had taken on the task of tutoring the boys, had beaten Stephen soundly but without apparent effect. Stephen was tough as well as boisterous and not at all given to remorse.

Up here on the ridge she could leave it all behind. She

could gather her berries, enjoy the late-summer sunshine, follow the fortunes of a hovering kestrel, watch ponies grazing on the moor across the valley.

From time to time she glanced down at Allerbrook below her, with the roofs and fields of Rixons farther down still, tiny with distance. Rixons was flourishing quite well in the hands of the Haywards—mainly, Jane suspected, because the hands they had hired were competent. Nothing would ever make a hard worker out of Violet. Tom had long since been sent off to sea and Harry had remarked caustically that he didn't know who he was most sorry for—Tom or the captain and crew who would have to put up with his dim-wittedness. Just now, however, Jane was not thinking about Rixons, but about Allerbrook and the changes that Harry had wrought when he was still able to manage major decisions, before his second fit.

She had to admit that under Harry's guidance, Allerbrook had prospered. No money now was spent on goshawks or showy horses, and he had taken very good care of the sheep.

The flock had first been improved by Francis, when he bought a dozen ewes and a ram from the dissolved monastery at Cleeve, thus introducing a new and better strain into the Allerbrook sheep. Harry had made good use of it, by selective breeding. Allerbrook fleeces and surplus lambs fetched good prices nowadays.

Harry had also gone ahead with buying a team of heavy horses for draught work and had duly extended East Field, though at Jane's suggestion a slice of land close to the house had been walled around and turned into a garden. With the ground dug over with manure (the two heavy horses, Giant and Thunder, could provide plenty of that) a satisfactory garden could be made.

"Though it's got to be some use, mind," Harry had said. "So put some sensible things in it, maid, not all gillyflowers and heartsease and whatnot. Put in cabbages and onion, and don't 'ee need more space for herbs? They've got flowers and smell pretty and they're useful."

And so they were. The farm sent cabbages and onions and herbs regularly to market, and if they hardly brought in a fortune, every little bit was a help. She was standing, basket on arm, looking down at her garden when she saw a rider emerge from the trees of the combe and turn toward the house. She sighed. She knew who it was. Harry might not have continued Francis's tradition of acquiring individual-looking horses, but Ralph Palmer had something of the same inclination and he owned the only piebald for miles. The rider down there was on a piebald.

"Confound you, Ralph!" said Jane. And if she did not put the thought that followed into words, even inside her own head, it was there all the same. *I wish you were Peter. Oh, Peter, why didn't you come to see me?*

She hadn't seen him since that spring in 1540 when he'd brought her home from the court, and that was now ten years ago. All she had had was occasional news of him, mainly through Ralph Palmer.

She would never forgive Ralph for his treatment of Sybil, but like it or not, he was still the lessee of Clicket Hall and when he and Dorothy were there, normal social interactions were bound to bring them together. Nor did she really want to avoid him, for a reason that she would not, *would* not admit even to herself. He went to court at times and heard the news, which meant that he sometimes heard of Peter Carew. Since her family knew the Carews, it was reasonable for her to ask after Peter occasionally and maintaining Ralph's acquaintance gave her the chance. Only, she had encouraged him more than was perhaps wise.

It had certainly annoyed Dorothy, all the more so because Ralph insisted that he and his wife should spend half of each year at Clicket Hall. Her dislike of Jane was plain. As far back as 1543, when the one child that Dorothy did finally produce, her daughter, Blanche, was christened, Jane had attended the christening party and been so pointedly ignored by Dorothy that one or two people had commented on it.

But the need to obtain news of Peter Carew still remained. She harvested what she could.

He had gone abroad and returned, having successfully performed some unknown service for the king. Then he had distinguished himself at sea and been knighted. He was Sir Peter Carew now.

He had married, taking a wealthy bride, Margaret Tallboys, widow of a baron. Ralph had attended the wedding.

And last year Carew had come to the west country for the first time in nearly a decade. When King Henry VIII finally died, leaving his crown to young King Edward, the boy's maternal uncle Lord Somerset had been made the Protector of the Realm until the young king was of an age to rule. Lord Somerset had declared that England must turn Protestant. In the west, there had been protests and riots and Peter Carew was sent as a mediator.

According to Father Drew, who, though he had not counselled violence, had been among the protestors, the Carew notions of mediation were somewhat abrasive. Jane remembered him as capable. On the ride from London he had reassured her with his air of always knowing what to do, always getting it right. On this occasion, she gathered, he had got it spectacularly wrong. His attempt to talk a group of armed rioters into peaceable dispersal had been far too combative, and anything but calming.

As Father Drew told Jane later, "The silly fellow just inflamed them more and it's a wonder he didn't get himself shot. He almost did!"

Fortunately, Jane learned, the blacksmith responsible (who was not Alfred Smith of Clicket) was no marksman with a musket, however accurate he might be with his hammer. He missed by a safe margin. Peter had however decided on a strategic retreat and returned to court to be lambasted for his tactlessness, which had come very near to turning a minor disturbance into a full-scale rebellion.

The violence fizzled out, and now was all but forgotten. But when he first came to the west, before that confrontation, said a persistent little voice in her head, he could have called on her. If he remembered she existed at all. He probably didn't. It was absurd that she should feel like this toward a man who obviously had no feeling at all for her, had probably quite forgotten her, but there it was.

During that ride from London to Somerset, years ago, he had stamped himself on her brain and on her heart and even after so long, the image had never faded. Certainly Harry Hudd—or Harry Allerbrook as he was now known—had never had the power to print himself on top.

Well, her basket was almost full and she had better go down the hill and find out why Ralph had come to call. He was doing it too often, and it worried her.

She had known Ralph all her life and understood him very well. She also held him responsible for Sybil's death. But whether she wished to be aware of it or not, his dark good looks reminded her of Peter Carew. He lacked Carew's maturity and depth, but he had a touch of the same adventurousness. He was like—an echo.

And she was now a wife only in name. From the day of his first fit, Harry had ceased to be capable in bed. There would be no more lovemaking, no more children.

With Stephen as well as Tobias to look after, she had more than enough on her hands and knew it, but desire did not listen to reason. Busy as she was and unattractive as Harry was, there were times when she felt deprived.

There were times indeed when the deprivation was almost unbearable, especially on sleepy summer afternoons, full of cuckoos and wood pigeons, when grasshoppers creaked and bumblebees murmured in the meadows, or on warm nights when a full moon looked down on the moors and owls called hauntingly to each other and the whole world was full of mystery and dreams. Then even Harry would have been better than nothing and Carew...would have been heaven. She thought of him often, and sometimes, looking at Ralph...

She was angry with herself about that. It was shameful, appalling that Ralph, after what he had done to Sybil, could still create that physical feeling, that jerk in the guts.

And at the moment he was in Allerbrook House, probably talking to Harry, who wouldn't particularly welcome him, because he had noticed how often Ralph Palmer called and had commented on it. She had better go down and deal with things as best she could.

On entering the house, she stopped short in alarm, because it sounded as though a riot were in progress. Then the racket resolved itself into boyish yells and through the door to the east wing ran Stephen, holding a book in his hands and pursued by a furious Tobias, shouting, "Give it back or I'll kill you!"

Stephen was much the larger of the two, being fifteen now and sturdily built, while Tobias was only nine and not tall for his age. He was, however, wiry and fleet of foot, and though not normally aggressive, could lose his temper forcefully when provoked. Presumably he had been provoked now, because he was hard on Stephen's heels, and as the two of them crashed into the hall he caught up with him, flung his arms around his cousin's waist, kicked violently at Stephen's Achilles tendons and sank his teeth into his cousin's shoulder.

"Boys!" Jane shrieked. "Boys, stop it!"

They took no notice. Peggy, appearing from the direction of the kitchen, said sourly, "Try a bucket of cold water, ma'am. Just shoutin' at them won't help."

Then Ralph, who had been talking to Harry at the far end of the hall, was there. Harry was on his feet, gripping his stick, but could move only slowly. Ralph had reached the scene in a few swift strides. He grabbed Stephen by one arm and Tobias by the collar of his jacket. One good wrench, and they were separated, breathless and scarlet in the face.

"What do you think you're doing?" bellowed Ralph, shaking them. "Stop behaving like barbarians!"

"He's snatched my book on travel! I was reading and he just took it off me!"

"I'm interested in travel. I'm going to travel one day!" Stephen retorted. "Did you know that not as much as fifteen years ago, a man called Richard Hore set off from Gravesend on the Thames with two ships and went all the way to the new lands in the northwest? And he lost his ships and half his men, but got a passage home with one of the French ships that go all that way to fish…."

"Stephen!" Jane shouted. "Give Tobias his book and apologize to him!"

"Hore and his men were nearly skeletons from starvation!" Stephen said excitedly. "But they seized control of the French vessel just the same. They sailed it to Cornwall and marched through Somerset, wanting to go to London overland because they were so sick of the sea. They spent a night at Dunster Castle on the journey! They were that close to us! I wish I'd seen them. I wish I'd been old enough! *You'll* never travel, Toby. You're just interested in Allerbrook. You say yourself you don't want to travel. So why won't you lend me your book?"

"Because Dr. Spenlove said I was to read it!" Tobias tore himself free from Ralph and pushed a tangle of light brown hair out of his eyes. "It was the task he gave me while he was away and you just took the book off me!"

"Oh, you always do what the tutor tells you, don't you, you sweet little teacher's pet. You read books about religion, too, dear pious Tobias. Well, well, that rhymes! Pious Tobias! Pious Tobias! Pious—"

"I *will* kill you one day!" yelled Tobias, and would have kicked his older cousin on the shins except that Stephen dodged.

"Be quiet, both of you!" Jane marched forward and seized the book from Stephen. "How dare you behave like this? Tobias, I won't have you kicking people. As for you, Stephen, snatching your cousin's book and then making fun of him— you started this. Apologize! At once!"

Stephen visibly considered saying, "Won't!" but Ralph shook him again and he thought better of it. "All right. Sorry, Toby." It was grudging, but at least audible.

"Thank you, Ralph," said Jane and smiled at Harry, who by this time had reached them. "Toby," Jane said, "take the book and read it in the parlour. Stephen, go back to the schoolroom and get on with whatever task Dr. Spenlove set for you. No doubt he set you something to do while he is away. What was it?"

"Stupid Latin. Tenses," said Stephen. "I'd rather study French or Italian. There are people who really speak *those* languages."

"If he set you Latin then you'll do Latin," snapped Ralph. "Go and get on with it. Now!"

He and Jane watched in silence as the two boys went off in different directions. "That lad Stephen should have been sent away to school long ago," he remarked. "Why wasn't he?"

"I said no," said Harry. "Younglings should...stop at home." Peggy, who had helped him up the hall, steered him to a seat and he took it thankfully. With an impatient gesture he signed to Jane to finish the explanation.

"Harry agrees that the boys must study," Jane said. "Toby must learn to run Allerbrook and Stephen has his way to make, but Harry doesn't want to send them to school, to mix with the gentry, in case they get ideas above themselves. Spenlove teaches them."

"Spenlove seems to do it all!" said Ralph. "He's the chaplain, the land agent, the tutor and he does calligraphy and illumination, too. Where is he now? It's really him I've come to see."

"He's gone to look at our land on the other side of Somerset," said Jane. "You know we own two farms there? Harry and I have decided to sell them. Collecting rent and keeping an eye on them generally has never been convenient. We are thinking of buying something closer at hand instead. Spenlove's gone to see about selling them and I don't know when he'll be back. Why?"

"Father Drew wants to see him. I'm Father Drew's

emissary, in a way. He's worried about a rumour he's heard and he wanted Spenlove to go to Minehead to find out what was happening."

"Rumour?"

"Yes. Ever since that edict went out, turning us all into Protestants, there's been trouble rumbling and burning underground. It's like peat fire, creeping under the surface and appearing here and there, without warning, as if from nowhere."

"I know," said Jane with feeling, recalling the fire that had caused Harry's second fit.

"It's because there are people like Father Drew," said Ralph, "who cling to tradition and get involved in arguments with the likes of Peter Carew, and others who want to prise us all loose from the old ways and are prepared to go to any lengths to do it. I've noticed that all the images of Our Lady have gone from your private chapel. Very wise!"

"Dr. Spenlove has even put away the crucifix he used to keep in his room," Jane said. "And I've taken off the altar cloth that Eleanor and I embroidered and stored it in a chest. Everything's very plain now."

"Quite," said Ralph grimly. "You should be safe. Because there is apparently a faction in Minehead that's determined to make everyone conform to Protestant plainness. *That's* what the rumour is about. They've been holding public meetings, so the pedlar said who brought word of it to Clicket. Everyone was talking about it last night in the White Hart. Father Drew was there and so was I, and he asked me to come up here and see if Dr. Spenlove would go to Minehead on his behalf. He can't ride so far nowadays. I can't go to Minehead myself—I'm leaving for another tour of duty at court tomorrow and it doesn't do to be unpunctual. But I said I could call here today. Drew couldn't. He had a marriage to perform this morning and a baptism this afternoon."

As if casually, Jane moved them both farther away from Harry. "I need to go to Minehead myself soon," she said quietly. "I could go tomorrow—it's as good a day as any. I want to order some new clothes for me and the boys." She smiled. "Our usual dressmaker, Madame La Plage, will make the things. She's still in business. Like Father Drew, she doesn't ride far anymore, but her son Philip does that part of it. He'll bring the clothes out to me for fittings. While I'm about it, I expect I can find out anything that Father Drew wants to know. I'll see him first and then go on to Minehead. I won't tell Harry it's because of the rumours, in case he worries."

"Does he worry?"

"Yes, I think he does. There isn't any real danger, is there?" she asked.

"Not for a lady riding in on a simple domestic errand— at least, I shouldn't think so. But be careful. Take note of what you hear or see, but don't go making yourself conspicuous or asking questions. Who will you take as escort?"

"Tim Snowe. He's a good solid fellow," Jane said. "I'd better ask you to stay for supper. I've brought some bilberries home."

After a somewhat silent supper, at which the boys were quiet and chastened, Jane saw Ralph out. Standing beside his horse as he prepared to mount, she said, "Surely you or Father Drew could have found someone in Clicket who could go to Minehead. Why didn't you?"

Ralph, with one foot in the stirrup, said, "Don't you know?"

"No."

"I was the one who suggested Spenlove. I said because he and Drew are old friends. But really, it made an excuse to come and see you."

"I see," said Jane. "Ralph, you find too many excuses to call at Allerbrook. You mustn't. Please."

"Why not? Jane, you're still beautiful. I hate to see you like this, tied to that old man in his chair. What use is he to you? You should have a fine husband, someone who appreciates you and gives you silk dresses and will take you about and be a good-looking escort to you. This is all wrong!"

"It can't be helped." She tried to be brisk. "How is Blanche? I should have asked before. I've seen very little of her, but I glimpsed her the other day in Clicket and thought she was becoming pretty. She must be about seven years old by now."

"Blanche is very pretty, and lively as I always was, and you're prattling. Jane, I don't want to exchange social politenesses with you. I would rather comfort you, hold you, make your life warmer...."

"Ralph, please stop it! Please go."

Ralph took his foot out of the stirrup. "Can I kiss you goodbye?"

"No."

"Really?" said Ralph, and with that he took hold of her, catching her upper arms in hard brown hands and pulling her against him. "Just a kiss won't hurt anyone," he said, and with that, his mouth had covered hers.

I mustn't feel like this, I mustn't, I MUSTN'T! Jane, appalled, shouted the warning silently to herself, knowing that even if he were Peter Carew, she would have no right to let him hold her like this, and knowing also that Ralph was *not* Carew;

He pointed to the statue of the Virgin and Child which was the chapel's main feature, and to the small altar with its candles and the very pretty altar cloth which had been embroidered by loving female hands in Clicket. Jane was reminded of the one she and Eleanor had made, which was now folded away in a press.

"Women especially come here to pray, for children, if they're barren, or for their husbands if they're worried about their menfolk for any reason. They feel that Our Lady might intercede for them more willingly even than Christ, being a woman herself. What's so wrong about that? They find comfort. But now the orders are that such things are popish and I must get rid of the image and the candles. But my flock don't want me to."

"I'm sorry," said Jane with genuine sympathy.

"Poor Marjorie Wright at the White Hart, she died two days ago," Father Drew said. "Some trouble inside her that no medicines could cure. The funeral's this afternoon. She used to come and pray to Our Lady for help. She still died, but I think she found comfort here. Why shouldn't people be allowed comfort if they want it?"

"Marjorie's dead?" Jane was startled. "I knew she was ailing, but I didn't realize things were so bad."

"It happened very quickly at the end." Drew sighed. "I've a young relative who's just been appointed as vicar of All Saints, over at North Molton, on the other side of the moor. He's a Protestant, right enough, but he doesn't mind a few images of Our Lady about his place. Again, his parishioners like them and he says he'd sooner lead his flock than drive it. He wouldn't have grudged Marjorie her comfort. He's only in his twenties, but he's got sense."

He sounded so unhappy that Jane hardly knew what to say to him. "I'm so sorry for it all," she said at last.

"So am I!" Drew was shakily angry. "And now there's this trouble brewing in Minehead. It seems that someone there's gathering followers and they want to take it upon themselves to rid the west country of popish symbols. I want to know what's really happening, that's all. Mistress Allerbrook, I can't sleep at night for worrying. But I can't ride to Minehead myself. I can just about get round my parish. I've no curate. The last one walked out just *because* I wouldn't dismantle this Lady Chapel."

"I thought I hadn't seen him lately," Jane said. "Well, I'm on my way to Minehead now. I'll see what I can discover for you."

Minehead wasn't large. Surrounded by farms and parkland, it was a little cluster of houses and a few shops and businesses at the foot of the rounded headland that was known as North Hill. A few buildings extended up the hillside and the parish church in particular stood high, overlooking most of the dwellings. Inland, a hill called Grabbist stretched from its butt end at Dunster, two miles to the east, and reached out toward Minehead, where one side of it fell away into the valley between it and North Hill and the other overlooked a wider valley, with the smooth, heathery heights of Dunkery on the far side.

Just below North Hill was a small harbour, big enough for fishing boats and small merchant vessels, and close by stood a huddle of fishermen's cottages, a miniature village in its own right.

The town as a whole was a sleepy place as a rule (seamen regularly complained that it was far too sleepy and the harbour needed better maintenance) but today it was different. As Jane and Tim rode in, they saw knots of people, talking earnestly and gesticulating. When Jane called at the fabric warehouse there was hardly anyone to serve her, and the young man who eventually did seemed distracted.

Her purchases made, she told him to deliver the cloth to Madame La Plage, and then rejoined Tim so as to go on to the La Plage house herself. They took the easiest if not quite the shortest route around by the shore, where they found a crowd clustered around an orator on a makeshift platform made out of crates. He seemed to be lecturing them on the sinful nature of popishness.

It struck her that the speaker looked vaguely familiar, but she couldn't put a name to him until, as she and Tim turned their mounts away and rode toward the harbour, Tim said, "That was Andrew Shearer, shouting fit to bust his lungs on that pile of crates."

"Shearer!"

"Aye. Him as led your sister into trouble, mistress. Nasty lot, they Shearers. Never did like that family. They've got a farm not that far from here. Pity that man Andrew don't stay on it instead of making a nuisance of hisself, upsettin' crowds and disturbin' the peace."

Before they reached the harbour they turned left and clattered up a winding cobbled lane toward the parish church, St. Michael's. Madame La Plage and her serious, business-like widower son Philip lived and worked almost opposite the church. At the house she found that Philip was out, but that his mother was there, busy but also harassed, urging a restless and uneasy workforce of sempstresses to concentrate on their tasks and stop whispering.

"Not that I don't understand why they're like this," Madame La Plage said. She was close on sixty and though, as yet, she could sew well enough with the aid of eyeglasses, her back was growing humped and her throat, exposed by her fashionably square neckline, was wrinkled, like the wattle of a chicken.

"There's been talk of attacking the church," she said. "One of the girls says her own father's all for it. He says it's the orders of this young King Edward that popish images be taken out of churches and anyone who's kept them is breaking the law. There are saints' statues in niches in the wall on either side of the west door and she says her father won't look at them when he goes to church of a Sunday. She's upset. She likes the statues. Now, what can I do for you?"

Jane had made sketches of the new gown she required, and the doublets and hose she wanted for the boys, and had brought the necessary measurements. She and Madame La Plage were discussing details when they heard feet running up the cobbles, and Philip La Plage burst in, out of breath. Though only in his thirties, he was too plump for running uphill. Astonished, everyone turned to look at him, semp-stresses with needles upraised, Madame La Plage holding the piece of charcoal with which she had been improving on Jane's sketches.

"They're on the march!" Philip gasped. "They're going to march on St. Michael's!" He caught sight of Jane. "Did you come on horseback?"

"Yes. On ponies. Tim's round the back, tethering them."

"Get him in through the back door. There's real trouble coming. *Listen!*"

They were all still, ears alert. In the distance they heard it, the menacing mutter of an approaching mob. A few moments later the crowd appeared around the curve of the lane. Many were armed, mostly with staves but some with blades. Opposite, the vicar of St. Michael's had appeared at the gate of the churchyard, looking frightened, as well he might, for every single face in that crowd seemed to be distorted with hate.

There was nothing that any of them could do. They called Tim inside, glad that the ponies were safely out of sight. It was a time for lying low.

"We'd best lock ourselves in," Philip said. "And then go upstairs."

"Quite right," Tim agreed. "Especially with all these young wenches here. It'll feel safer, like."

From the window of the big front bedchamber upstairs they watched the mob arrive at the church. The vicar tried to bar their way, arms spread pleadingly wide, and was swiped out of the way by a ladder that one man was carrying instead of a weapon. The vicar fell back against the side of the gate and a hulking man with a billhook stepped in front of him and kept him there.

The crowd poured into the churchyard. It sloped steeply and they swarmed all over it, apparently seeking vantage points from which to survey their target. Then, amid shouting, the ladder was brought to the west door and put up to one of the niches and hammers were handed up. Stone chips flew. Some of the sempstresses, crowding close and peering over the shoulders of the La Plages, Jane and Tim, began to sob, with sorrow and alarm.

The noise sent frightened birds up from the trees at the top of the churchyard; a terrified cat appeared from somewhere, fleeing with ears flat back, leaped over the churchyard wall and vanished up the lane. Cheers broke out as the first image fell, and then its destroyer came down the ladder and shifted it to deal with the other. At the same time some of the crowd began to thrust their way into the church itself.

"Oh, *now* what are they doing?" said Philip La Plage, un-latching the casement window and leaning out to get a better view. Beside him, Jane, also urged on by a wish to know more, opened a second window. A new succession of crashes sounded from the church and people began to push their way out again, cheering and brandishing trophies: candlesticks, statuettes, a silver chalice and a big silver crucifix. The man with the crucifix bore his prize triumphantly down to the gate, and then, as he stepped into the lane, he looked up.

For a dreadful moment Jane found herself gazing straight down into the narrow face and flinty eyes of Andrew Shearer.

"Well, I'll be damned!" said Andrew Shearer.

Unable to stop herself, Jane said, "That's all too possible."

"Mistress Hudd—Allerbrook you call yourself now, don't you? Whose brother threw me and mine off our land!"

"You know why," said Jane.

"Mistress, don't! Be careful!" said Tim urgently from behind her.

"If a woman's an easy lay, that's her fault," Shearer retorted. "Well, well. I hear your chaplain's been good as gold and made your chapel plain, but the tale's going round that dear old Anthony Drew in Clicket village b'ain't obeyin' orders. We'll be seein' him soon. See if he's got any silver that might melt down for better uses!"

Someone behind him called out, "So he has! I told 'ee that! Seen every church on the moor, I have. But what about Dunster? That's nearer!"

Jane, peering past Shearer, recognized the speaker and knew, grimly, that he was telling the truth. He was Danny Clay, who dug clay from the Minehead shore at low tide, when the sticky grey deposits were exposed, and travelled on a regular round through the district to supply local potters. He was a scruffy little man, with an equally scruffy wife called Eva, who helped him dig. She never wore a cap and had blobs of clay forever in her straggly hair. They had a horde of children who trailed along the shore with them, wielding small spades and shovels. Jane had seen Danny in the potter's shop in Clicket, and on previous visits to Minehead she had also noted the family working on the shore at ebbtide. Everyone for miles could recognize the Clays, and Danny did indeed know every village on the moor and every church, too.

Shearer glared around at his followers, especially Danny. "There's a garrison in Dunster Castle. Reckon we'll leave Dunster alone. Clicket's different. I've a score to settle there. Anthony Drew needn't think just lockin' his pretty things in cupboards'll get him out of trouble! If we find a single candlestick, a single statue of Mary, even hung down his well in a bucket, he'll be sorry! And after that," Master Shearer added with ominous silkiness, "I've somewhere else in mind, as well. With a slender link to Clicket and a real hypocrite for a vicar. Claims to be Lutheran but don't act like it. Clicket's on the way to him."

His tone changed, to become reassuring. Master Shearer had a flexible voice and knew how to use it. "Don't 'ee fret now. I'll lead 'ee right, never fear. We'll clean the whole moor in the end." He glanced around at Jane, who was still at the window, transfixed. "And don't 'ee think of tryin' to warn anyone, woman. Won't stand for that, we won't."

"I wish I'd never looked out of that window," said Jane desperately. "It's given him ideas."

"I rather think he had them already, mistress," said Philip calmly. "But they won't reach Clicket in five minutes. It's fourteen miles off in a straight line, so my schoolmaster told us when he was showing us how to read a map, but the way the tracks wind, it adds up to twenty miles or more, and they're on foot. You can get there ahead of them easily, and warn Father Drew. There's time for you to snatch a bite of food and let the ponies have a manger before you go."

"We've got cold pies for ourselves and nosebags for the ponies," said Jane distractedly. "But you heard what Shearer said. If we let them go ahead of us, we'll have to overtake them and they'll stop us for sure!"

"No, mistress. They'll take the main track," said Tim. "Bound to. Back through Dunster and up the Avill valley. We'll go over Grabbist. Master La Plage is right. We'll do better and so will the ponies if we put somethin' in our bellies first. There's a way round the back of the town—leads up to the hill. We'll take that."

"Share our dinner," said Philip. "And save your cold pies. And we've fodder enough for the ponies."

It was like the escape from court. It could have gone horribly wrong but it did not. Tim Snowe, whom she had known for most of her life and had simply regarded as a quiet, reliable groom, now turned out to be a strategist.

Having eaten and drunk, they saddled up again and set off through the warm afternoon. The winding track up Grabbist was steep, which at first kept them to a walk, and it led through fly-ridden bracken. Jane, swatting the pests aside with a bracken frond, cursed them aloud as well as cursing the slow climb. "We'll never get there at this pace, Tim!"

"Yes, we will," said Tim imperturbably. "Wait till we'm

on top." At the summit, the path emerged onto short, sheep-nibbled grass and there was a breeze to disperse the flies. The ponies snorted and tossed their heads and cantering became possible. Presently they found themselves looking down into the valley of the Avill river. Jane drew rein. "Tim! Do you see what I see?"

"I see a crowd of ants on the track," said Tim. "Scarcely out of Dunster and they've miles ahead of them. We'll beat them easy! We'll dodge Exford and Withypool—best not be seen by too many folk. We don't want reprisals. These are bad times, mistress. Though I didn't expect this sort of thing, or I'd have counselled 'ee against goin' to Minehead at all."

"I'm glad we did go. I want to help Father Drew."

"Well, on our way, then."

They shook the ponies up again and cantered on until they reached another steep track, perilous with loose pebbles, that led down into the valley between Grabbist and Dunkery. They descended at a speed they would not normally have attempted, though the ponies, strong and sure-footed, made light of the work. In half an hour they had climbed Dunkery's heathery shoulder and were riding down the far side. Soon after that, they had bypassed the little village of Exford and taken a path toward the town of Dulverton. Clicket lay five miles to their right, on the other side of a river.

"We'll have to go through Withypool to cross the Barle," Jane said. "We can't avoid it."

"Yes, we can. We'll cross the Barle at Tarr Steps. Water b'ain't high," Tim said.

"It's a nasty ford."

"Ponies'll manage."

Tarr Steps was a bridge of uneven granite slabs and was therefore unsuitable for horses. No one knew who had made it and local legend talked of bygone giants. The river on the upstream side, however, was not very deep and though its bed was a mass of pebbles, a sensible horse with a rider who was prepared to sit still could pick its way safely across. Jane, who was riding the stolid Ginger, had crossed it on his back before and Ginger had certainly managed, but had also made it clear that he hated the slithery shingle under his hooves. This time, turning awkward for once, he tried to balk, but was finally persuaded into the water when Tim went ahead on his pony Dusty.

"No need to fret," Tim said when both ponies had reached the other side. "We've only lost a few minutes and I'd reckon we're two hours ahead of Shearer's mob."

There was a funeral in progress when they reached the church. "That'll be Marjorie Wright," Jane said. The mourners were about to leave the churchyard and as they did so, Jane and Tim rode forward to intercept Father Drew, who stopped, looking up at them. "You are back so soon! Is there any news?"

"Yes," said Jane tersely. "And it's bad. There's danger." Briefly she told him what had happened at St. Michael's, and described the threat that was now making for Clicket, led by a man with a spite against the Allerbrooks and everyone on their land.

"They're on their way now?" Drew was horrified.

"Yes. Father…" Jane dismounted so quickly that Tim Snowe was not in time to help her as he usually did. "Father, everything that they might want to destroy must be put out of sight and quickly, and not down your well, either. They've thought of that. What is there that ought to be hidden?"

"Come into the church." The priest glanced around and saw

Arthur Wright hovering. "Arthur, some important news has reached me. I can't come to the funeral gathering. I am sorry."

In words even briefer than Jane's, he explained the situation. The landlord of the White Hart, a sturdy, flaxen-haired man whose nature was normally equable, flushed with outrage. "The Lady Chapel was all that gave my poor Marge any peace. No one's goin' to harm it!"

"I think they'll try," said Drew. "But I must deal with it. Go and be host to those who have come to help you grieve."

Muttering angrily, Arthur turned away. "Do you think," Tim murmured, "that he's ever guessed about Ralph Palmer and Marjorie and that dark-haired little child of hers?"

"So you know about that? Well, forget it, Tim," said Drew sharply. "He's never guessed and never will if I have anything to do with it. He's lost her one way. Don't make him lose her twice over. Take the ponies to my stable, and then join us in the church. We've things to do."

"It feels like sacrilege," Jane said unhappily as she and Drew set about emptying the Lady Chapel of images, candles and altar cloth.

"I know. But it's only to protect things," Drew told her.

Tim joined them quickly and between the three of them, the Lady Chapel was rapidly cleared. They turned to the rest of the church, bearing silver candlesticks, altar cloths, statuettes and a heavy oak crucifix with a silver figure out to the porch.

"But that big statue of St. Anne on the left of the west door—we can't move that. It's too heavy," Father Drew moaned. "And it's fixed somehow to the wall behind. And I must save the silver communion cup. Oh, you've brought it out, Tim. What do they do with such things?"

"Melt 'un down," said Tim grimly.

"Oh, dear God. And what are *we* to do with all this?" Drew looked despairingly at the heap of beautiful objects on the floor of the porch. "Where can we hide them? Buckets down the well should have done very well, but you say they'll look there! Where else can they go?"

Jane said, "Marjorie's grave isn't filled in yet. Wrap everything well. Put the altar cloths inside a small chest or something. Put it all in the grave and shovel the earth on top. I don't think even Shearer would go grave robbing!"

An hour later, with the earth heaped concealingly over Marjorie Wright and her unexpected mass of valuable grave goods, Tim, Jane and Father Drew, sweaty and earth-stained, retreated to the vicarage beside the church, where Biddy Mayes, the elderly widow who was the vicarage house-keeper, gave them elderflower wine and wondered what the world was coming to.

Only a short time later, the invasion from Minehead marched into the street, shouting *Down with the Pope,* waving banners and grasping their assorted weaponry in a menacing fashion. Whereupon, to the horror of Father Drew as he peered from his front windows, the mourners in the White Hart, evidently alerted by Arthur Wright, poured into the street to stand between them and the door of the church and meet them face-to-face.

"Please don't, Father!" said Jane strongly as the uproar in the street outside reached a crescendo. "Stay here! You'll only get hurt. Best keep out of sight and let the storm pass. We've saved the things that matter."

"Quite right." Biddy Mayes, who tended to cluck over Father Drew as though she were a hen and her employer a wayward chick, actually barred his way as he tried to reach the door. "No, Father, you go back into your parlour and if anyone calls I'll say you're not here. You just keep away from all they barbarians out there—dear Lord preserve us, what's going on *now!*"

"Whatever it is, I've got to join in!" burst out Tim, who had been growing more and more restless. "No, don't 'ee try stoppin' me. I'm fit enough to fight if it comes to it."

"No!" Jane cried. "No, Tim, please! Think of Susie…"

"I must! I can't see this and not go to help. Thought I could, but I can't. Sorry, mistress, but there it be." He pushed past Biddy and was gone. "Let 'un go," Biddy said. "But not you, Father. No, *not* you!"

"No, I'm past it. But before God, I wish I were not," said Drew miserably. "I suppose we can go upstairs and watch from the top floor without being seen. Come on."

The vicarage was the biggest house in the village, after Clicket Hall, with an attic complete with dormer windows in the thatch. From there they could watch the ugly spectacle in the street. The two sides had joined battle and Marjorie's mourners seemed to be as well armed as their attackers. Jane, cautiously opening a dormer window, saw that although only a few pikes and blades were being used, there was much savage fighting with fists and staves and much throwing of a weird variety of missiles. There were casualties lying on the cobbles, though most of them seemed to be alive and trying to crawl to safety. It looked as if the combatants were not for the most part trying to kill, but nevertheless, there were places where blood ran in scarlet veins between the cobblestones and the yells of fury were horrifying. Danny Clay was in the forefront of the attackers, flourishing a makeshift weapon in the form of a spade, and bawling *No popery!* as though it were a war cry.

"Oh, this is vile, foul!" Father Drew was almost in tears. "I knew Arthur Wright was collecting weapons! He told me he was, when the first rumours began. He's turned the funeral party into an army! There are even women down there in the fighting. There's Annet Smith—she's got a sack of old horseshoes and she's hurling them... *hard*...that woman's built like an ox.... Oh, heaven help us, what are we to do?"

"I can see Tim!" Jane was still looking out the window. "He's fighting...oh no, oh no! He's down. Someone got him with a pike and he's down on the cobbles...!"

Flinging herself away, she tore down the stairs and out the door. If someone recognized her and there were reprisals later, as Tim had feared, it couldn't be helped. Tim must be rescued, no matter what the risk. She found as she rushed into the street that even during the brief time she had taken to get there, the situation had changed. Wright's army had been trying to keep the aggressors from getting into St. Anne's, but although reinforced by other folk from Clicket, who had run from their homes to join in, they were still out-numbered and the enemy had broken through.

They had hurled themselves into the church and no one hindered or threatened Jane as she threw herself on her knees beside Tim. He raised himself on an elbow and said, "Not dead, mistress. Don't 'ee take on. Some bugger, beggin' your pardon, slashed my calf with a pike. I'll be all right."

He tried to get to his feet, but failed. Biddy, however, had come after Jane and between them they got him up, draping his arms across their shoulders. From within the church they could hear the sounds of stone being smashed, which was probably the end of St. Anne's statue. A few of the mob were now filtering out again, but they had found little booty.

Danny Clay was waving two small gilt candlesticks which had somehow been overlooked, and that was all.

"Looks like old Drew came to 'un's senses in time," another of the intruders was saying as they went unheedingly past Tim and his helpers. Jane turned her head away, afraid of being recognized, but they never even glanced toward her. "Here, that's my brother, flat on his back there. Hey, Jeffrey, what's amiss with 'ee? Someone give me a hand…!"

"I b'ain't hurt. Just fell over, dodging a great iron horse-shoe some mad harridan threw at me. They'm all crazy papists in this place," said the fallen Jeffrey, sitting up. "Is that all 'ee found in there, Danny—them tiddly little candlesticks? Where are we off to next?"

"North Molton," said Danny as Jeffrey got to his feet. "Finish here, get some food at the inn and march straight on, he said. Fellow at Molton's a cousin of Drew or something and he's supposed to be one of us, but there's an image on the church tower that he's had no business to leave there, and more papist things inside the church. I've seen 'em! I get about, I do. We're for North Molton next. Get there afore night."

"I'll go and warn them," said Tim valiantly. "Just patch me up and…"

"You're goin' nowhere, with this great slash in your leg…hold still while I stitch it…." Biddy had reared four sons and knew a good deal about emergency doctoring. "I've washed out the dirt. It'll heal but not if you go chasin' off on a pony. Vicar of North Molton'll have to cope on his own. Supposed to be a Lutheran, b'ain't he?"

"He'll still want to protect the things his flock love," said Drew. Biddy had somehow prevented him from rushing out to Tim's aid along with her, but he had been ready with warm water when they brought him in and was now steadying Tim's injured leg while Biddy stitched the slash. "John Grede's a good decent man. But he needs to be warned, same as I was! What's going on out there now?"

Jane went to the window again. A species of truce seemed to be developing. The fighting had apparently ceased and the fallen were being ministered to. There were a couple of sad little processions going toward the inn; it looked as though at least two men were dead, but it seemed to her a miracle that the number was so low.

Arthur Wright went past in a group of people that seemed to include both Clicket and Minehead folk. The Clicket contingent were saying that the funeral feast wasn't finished and the uninvited guests from Minehead were saying they needed food and drink and would pay for it. Someone was even apologizing for the invasion.

"Looks like there was nothin' there to complain about, bar a statue that your poor old vicar probably couldn't see how to get rid of, anyhow."

"Quite. Reckon Shearer got it wrong this time...."

"He b'ain't wrong about North Molton, though. I've been to a cattle sale there and seen those popish things my own self...."

Quietly Jane closed the window. "They're going to the White Hart." She stood for a moment, coming to a decision, and then said, "Biddy, I need something to eat and drink myself, but it has to be something quick. I mustn't waste time over it. Father Drew, can I borrow your mare? Ginger's been to Minehead and back already today. If I take a fresh pony from Allerbrook, Harry will say no. He'll say send one of the grooms instead, and I can't afford all that. There's no time to lose."

"Take Bella and welcome," said Drew and Biddy, without a word, hurried into the kitchen. "I ought to go myself," the priest said miserably. "This joint evil keeps me from my proper work. I can hardly get up the combe to see Spenlove these days. You can collect Ginger when you come back. Hope Bella behaves. She can be awkward, but she's fresh, at least. I'll see word gets to Allerbrook, to say where you've gone."

"Don't fret, Father Drew," Jane said. "I'll make sure that Master Grede is warned."

"You can't go alone!" Tim expostulated, jerking himself upright on the settle on which he was lying. "Get one of the villagers to go! Drag someone out of the White Hart! It can't be you, mistress."

Biddy came back with cold meat, bread and a beaker of small ale and Jane, seizing them from her, began to consume them standing up. "We can't waste time and the White Hart's full of Shearer and his madmen, and if any of us goes in there, someone will recognize us and know what we're about and stop us. I will not be stopped. Not by anyone! Not by them or Harry or you, Tim. Don't try!"

CHAPTER TWENTY-TWO
Resourcefulness is a Virtue
1550

Jane, pushing Bella, Father Drew's flea-bitten grey mare, on up Allerbrook Combe, was tired, frightened and also, as she now realized, annoyed. The task of dealing with crises seemed to be devolving on her too often.

Sybil couldn't go to court to further Francis's ambitions, so Jane had had to go instead. Sybil and Stephen alike had needed her help and Jane had done her best for them in the face of Harry's fury. And must carry the guilt for Harry's apoplexy for the rest of her life.

Now it was Father Drew, wanting to know about the danger that threatened from Minehead, wanting to warn his kinsman in North Molton, and somehow or other it had fallen to Jane to do it. She had promised herself that she would look after everyone, but, "It's turning out to be a complicated business," she said aloud to Bella's speckled ears.

They had just reached the place where the track branched off toward Allerbrook House. As he saw her off, Father Drew had warned her that Bella's awkwardness often took the form of balking at unfamiliar routes. "I've not had her long. She's got used to visiting Dr. Spenlove at Allerbrook, but I've not yet had to take her over the ridge to Hanna-combes. I hope she won't give you trouble," he said.

Now as they reached the Allerbrook track she tried to turn that way, and when Jane pointed her up the combe instead, she stopped dead and dug in her forefeet. *"Bella!"* Jane pro-tested. "We're going straight on. We must."

Bella, front hooves firmly planted, said, *"Shan't!"* as clearly as a horse possibly could.

Jane was a gentle rider who disliked hitting horses, but this time she used her whip with vigour. The mare, outraged, put her ears back and went up the combe obediently, but flat out, long legs reaching for the ground, mane flying and muzzle extended in indignation. Fortunately, the final slope slowed Bella down and the pace steadied as they reached the top of the ridge, emerging from the trees into the sunlight. Jane pulled up and surveyed the terrain ahead.

She knew the way. North Molton lay five or six miles off, on the other side of a broad expanse of moorland. She had visited it occasionally. However, the track did not take a straight line and it wound up and down a good deal. Oh, well. The marchers would have to cope with the same delays, and she was well ahead of them. She patted Bella to show that there were no hard feelings, and pressed on, going downhill now, into the valley immediately before her, skirting the edge of Hannacombes Farm.

She hoped she wouldn't meet the Hannacombes or any farmhand who knew her, for she did not want to stop and explain herself. However, no one seemed to be about. Very likely they had all gone to Clicket to attend the funeral, since most of them had known Marjorie. Indeed, Jane thought she could remember seeing Will Hannacombe in the fighting.

She passed the farmland as briskly as she could, however. At one point Bella shied for no apparent reason, but it was probably because she had smelt an adder in the long grass by the path. Jane, gripping hard with her knees, muttered an inelegant curse.

Adders usually heard horses coming and kept themselves out of the way, but horses loathed them. Even the imperturbable Ginger had been known to shy if he sensed one. Riders had on occasion been thrown, to land on top of the snake. The moment passed, however, and presently, leaving the fields behind, she put Bella into a canter as the track climbed a gentle slope up the moorland on the other side of the valley.

All the time, she was wondering how to shorten the journey. There were places where one could cut across the moor and avoid some of the track's windings and she knew of at least two such shortcuts that wouldn't lead to bogs or sudden precipitous dips.

She was halfway along the second shortcut when a coldness at her back and a dimming of the sunlight warned her to glance over her shoulder.

A white wall of mist had wiped out all the moorland behind her, and the sun had faded to a pallid circle behind a veil of vapour. The mist was gaining on her. Even as she looked, the sun vanished altogether and the first pale wisps blew around her. Another thirty seconds, and the world about her had dwindled to a vista only a few yards across. "Oh, *damn!*" said Jane.

And she was off the track. The marchers would no doubt keep to it. They were probably on their way by now, and even if they were already high enough on the moor to be inside the cloud as she was, they would not get lost if they kept to the path. The track was well-defined, the few side paths being only narrow sheep trails.

She could only go on. Bella was showing a desire to turn around, which meant that she wanted to go home. She would know the way; horses usually did. Jane had only to slacken the reins and Bella would take her back to Clicket without hesitation. But that would never do. "On, Bella," she said. *"On!"*

They moved forward. The mist showed no sign of dissipating but it was on the move, flowing on a west wind. The visibility kept changing. When the mare suddenly stopped short, Jane sat still, peering forward, waiting for the view to improve for a moment. When it did, by a matter of a few yards, she saw that Bella had sensibly stopped almost at the edge of a place where the hill plunged downward at a hair-raisingly steep angle. Quickly Jane turned them away from it.

She halted again, trying to think. She had meant to cross a shoulder of moorland, instead of following the track, which curved around it. She had veered too far to the right, probably. Yes, she recalled that the hillsides did become much steeper in that direction. She had turned left to avoid the steep plunge. If she now rode on, slowly and carefully, she ought to find herself going gently downhill toward the track.

She did so, for what seemed a long time. Then she drew rein again, knowing that she was horribly astray. She had come face-to-face with a barrow. She should have been close to the track by now and there was no barrow near it.

All the barrows were supposed to be haunted and for a

moment, when through the blowing vapours she saw the long grass on top of it move against the wind, a stab of pure supernatural terror went through her. Then a stag sprang out of the grass and fled away into the greyness. He was a fine animal with twelve points on his antlers and he was decidedly part of the material world. Jane's accelerating heartbeat slowed down. But she still had ample cause for anxiety. "Where on earth *are* we?" she said aloud.

Summoning up all the resourcefulness she possessed, she remembered that the mist had come from the west. She wanted to go south. Judging the direction as best she could by the movement of the vapours, she urged Bella cautiously that way, only to halt in despair after a short distance. They were apparently descending into a narrow combe. Small trees had appeared, pale and ghostlike. She had no knowledge of this place. She was losing time with every moment that passed, but there was only one thing to do.

She slackened the reins and said, "Bella, go home."

Bella unhesitatingly turned around, went back up the combe, over a stretch of heather and then downhill again. Mists clearly meant nothing to her. Ten minutes later they emerged into clear air, and there was the North Molton track just ahead. Bella made for it, and pointed her nose toward home.

The cloud now was overhead, shrouding only the higher ground. Jane, facing back toward Allerbrook, could see the track winding away up a long moorland slope to vanish into the mist. Something was emerging from that mist, coming down from the hidden hillcrest. It was a crowd of tiny figures. The marchers were on their way.

She spun Bella around. "This time we keep to the track but we go fast! We must gain ground and get out of sight! *Come on, Bella!*"

Jane's urgency and fear must have communicated itself to Bella, for this time the mare didn't fight the order. She stretched out her neck, snorted and took off, galloping strongly. The shoulder of hills over which Jane had tried to ride with such disastrous results loomed on her right. The path bent around it and a moment later they were safely out of sight of the marchers and pounding onward. Even now she could hope to get there with a little while to spare. Even now she could be in time.

A quarter of an hour later they were clattering past the thatched dwellings of North Molton and then across the cobbled space before the churchyard. It sloped upward to the church, and from a niche high on the tower a stone Virgin and Child looked benignly out over the village. No one seemed to be about, but the vicarage was there to the right of the churchyard. Jane jumped from the saddle, led her mount to the door and hammered on it.

It was opened quickly and somewhat indignantly by a large lady with a cap slightly awry, a stained apron over a dark gown and a floury rolling pin in a powerful right hand. "Just what's this? A-knockin' and a-bangin' on the door as if you were Gabriel tryin' to announce Judgement Day without 'un's horn! Who be you, mistress?"

"Is Master Grede here?"

"I'm his housekeeper. Who be you and what's thy business? The master's not at home to everyone as comes a-crashin' and a-poundin'…"

"*Master Grede!*" Jane shouted at the top of her voice, causing Bella to fling up her head so that Jane had to hold tightly to the bridle. The shout produced results, however, in the shape of a dark-gowned young man who appeared behind the housekeeper, his finger still keeping a place in a book he had evidently been studying.

"What's this uproar?" He had pale, bright eyes and a pale chiselled face, in which cheekbone, jaw and nose all seemed to have a sharp edge. His voice was as sharp as his bone structure. He frowned at Jane, light brown eyebrows drawing together.

"Are you John Grede?"

"Yes."

"My name is Jane Allerbrook. I come from Father Anthony Drew of Clicket. A mob has attacked his church, wanting to destroy what they call popish symbols. He was warned just in time to hide most of them. The same rabble is on its way here, now. If there is anything in your church that they think is popish, they'll snatch it, or smash it. They're close behind me. I was delayed. I lost my way in a mist."

With relief she saw that his mind was keen-edged, too. He nodded and the frowning brows relaxed. "Ah. There have been tales of trouble. All right, Mattie." He patted the housekeeper's arm reassuringly. "How far away are they, mistress? Can you tell me?"

"They were still...let me think, about four miles from here when I saw them and that was—oh, perhaps a quarter of an hour ago."

"Then we should have a good half hour. Ah. Here come reinforcements."

Alerted by Bella's noisy hoofbeats, people were coming inquisitively across from the cottages. A wiry old man in a workman's sleeveless jerkin hurried from the churchyard, grasping a scythe with which he had presumably been trimming the grass, and a young groom with a dandy brush in his hand came around the corner from the back of the vicarage. Grede beckoned to the villagers, told the groom to take Bella and then strode to meet his parishioners, who gathered around him as he began to explain. Then he led the way into the church, with the crowd and Jane at his heels.

It was a bigger church than St. Anne's, and more shadowy, though beautiful. "They'll have hard work to do much damage to those," Grede said, pointing to the carved leaves and flowers of the roof high above them and to the handsome and beautifully carved font. "But the candlesticks on the altar will have to be hidden—yes, and that gold crucifix—"

"And what about the saints round the pulpit?" someone asked. The pulpit was seven-sided, with a niche in each side, each niche containing a gilded wooden statue of a saint.

"Yes, those, too. Let's get to it. Quickly, now!"

"But where do we hide 'un?" That was the gardener with the scythe.

"Do you have a recent grave they could be buried in?" Jane asked. "That's what Father Drew did in Clicket."

"No. We're a healthy lot hereabouts. We haven't had any funerals lately," Grede told her. He stood for a moment, frowning again. Then his face cleared and he turned to one of his flock.

"Will Fuller, haven't you just dug over half your vegetable plot? Getting too weedy, you said, didn't you? You could put sackloads of things in there, where there's turned earth already. There are spades and sacks in the lean-to alongside my stable. Will can show you where to bury the things. Then go well away, all of you, back home or about your business. You can come back here and carry on scything, Tammy. Hurry! There's hardly any time. "

Mattie the housekeeper had come to the church with the rest. It was she who said, "But what about our Virgin and her baby up on the tower? They'll be after that, too. I've heard it's happened in other places. On the orders of the king, too, shame on him, and him only a boy, tellin' us older folk what we can and can't love! There she be, with her child in her arms, lookin' out over our roofs and protectin' us from harm, but they'll take her away! We'll never see her again! They'll smash her!"

"Yes, they will!" Jane remembered what Danny Clay had said in the street at Clicket.

"If they can reach her," said Will Fuller.

"Well, my ladder's long enough." Tammy's voice was glum. "Couldn't prune they trees round the churchyard without my long ladder."

"Then get the damned thing out of sight," said John Grede roundly. "Put it in a ditch or a hayloft, anywhere! And any other ladders that might be long enough. You, Pete Thatcher!" He pointed at another of his flock. "You've got two long ladders—I know you have! Hide them! Are these folk bringing ladders with them, Mistress Allerbrook?"

"I don't think so. They had one in Minehead but I don't think they brought any to Clicket. But they've got cudgels and staves and some blades, as well."

"Oh," said Grede, and now his face was lightened by a smile, "we're not going to *fight* them. Hear that, all of you! No resistance. Let them do as they will. Take heed." He had begun to lead the way around to the stable and its lean-to, but he was talking as he went. "This is what we must do…"

Later, steering Jane into the shelter of the vicarage, he said, "I sometimes think that resourcefulness ought to be accounted among the virtues. With just a little good luck, the things my parishioners treasure will be kept from harm. Here's my parlour. My housekeeper will bring us something soon. She's gone back to her kitchen—trying to look ordinary.

"You know," he added as Jane, who had taken a spade and helped with the frenzied, top-speed digging, sat wearily down in a settle, "this is not too great a disaster. I am not fond of popish images either. Only I didn't want to go too fast. A good shepherd doesn't harry his sheep, and vicars are supposed to be like shepherds. Now the images have been removed to protect them, not to harm them, and the villagers are happy with that. They'll take to a different kind of worship more easily for it. Perhaps the treasures will stay hidden for good now." He paused, head on one side. "We were only just in time. I think your passionate Protestants are here."

"Some of them know me!" Jane, also hearing that distant but menacing mutter, was suddenly afraid. "I shouldn't be seen."

"Indeed? Then go upstairs and lock yourself into a bed-chamber. I doubt they'll intrude on my private home, but if necessary, I shall say I have a sick maidservant above stairs and that I *hope* it isn't the smallpox. I've had it and so has my housekeeper but..."

"Another example of resourcefulness!" said Jane, and then, taking his advice, retreated to yet another upper floor.

Afterward, Jane often thought with laughter of that scene in front of the church. Andrew Shearer's crowd, having discovered that there was little in the church of which they could disapprove, forgathered in front of the vicarage and, as the housekeeper had foreseen, turned their attention to the stone statue in the niche on the tower.

The villagers, who had returned to their various homes and duties, only to leave them again in order to stare at the incomers, were clustering around. John Grede had however ordered them not to resist and they were obeying him, not only with alacrity, but inventiveness. Jane, once again peering with caution from an upstairs window, noticed with delight that almost every North Molton face wore a similar expression. It was one of bovine doltishness, as though the entire population had been suddenly stricken with some form of mental blight.

They had been bright enough earlier, when they were hiding their treasures, but now anyone looking at them might well wonder how any of them ever summoned up enough intelligence to turn a furrow or memorize the paternoster. Will Fuller and Tammy were actually chewing straws.

The intruders, with Andrew Shearer and Danny Clay the most vociferous, were demanding long ladders and the villagers, their faces full of histrionic bewilderment, were turning to each other and muttering and shaking their heads helplessly. A few phrases drifted upward.

"…can't say as I knows of a ladder that'ud reach that far up…"

"…don't t'ee recall, that time that storm blew a lot of twigs or summat that stuck on the statue and we wanted to clean it and we couldn't get up there to do it? Had to wait till the next rainstorm did it for we."

"…no call for ladders that long, not hereabouts…"

"…didn't Farmer Weston have one?"

"…you'm a gurt vule. Course he did, and he went to live over the other side of Somerset and took ladders and all with 'un!"

Like Clicket, North Molton had an inn. The innkeeper was in the gathering and was now urging everyone to come back to his hostelry and enjoy some hospitality. They must all be footsore after their long march; he had cider, ale, viands of the best...

His expression was slightly less bovine than most; there was no harm, he seemed to be saying, in looking like a man who knew how to turn an honest penny. Gradually, like an ebbing tide, the crowd receded.

Jane spent the night at the vicarage and rode home the next day, quietly, having let the invaders depart ahead of her. Most of them had found lodgings in the village for the night ("And will be charged high for their beds and breakfasts," Grede observed). She went to Clicket first, with caution, but saw nothing of them. Perhaps they had gone straight back to Minehead. She told a grateful Father Drew what had happened, stabled Bella, collected Ginger and went home.

Harry gave her a relieved but resentful welcome. Father Drew had sent Biddy up the combe on foot the previous evening to tell Harry where she was, but he had clearly been anxious and certainly not approving.

Andrew Shearer together with half a dozen of his most devoted entourage, including Danny Clay and, oddly, Dorothy Palmer, presented themselves at Allerbrook one hour after Jane herself reached home.

CHAPTER TWENTY-THREE
Payment in Full
1550

*P*eggy opened the door to the deputation and was thrust aside as they surged past her. "I couldn't stop them, Mistress Allerbrook," she spluttered indignantly, scurrying into the hall after them. "They pushed me!"

They came in exuding menace. Danny Clay slammed the door behind him and barred it from inside. The Allerbrooks were at dinner and Jane was cutting up Harry's meat. He gaped in alarm and she rose, putting down her knife and placing herself protectively beside him. She signalled to Tobias and Stephen to sit still.

She maintained a calm front, while her brain whirled in panic and her heart galloped like Bella's hooves when they'd raced into North Molton. She wished Dr. Spenlove were there, but he was still on the other side of the county. Distractedly she thought that Dorothy had indeed grown like her mother, only worse. Mary Stone had been fat, pallid, greedy and inclined to self-righteousness. But she had never been spiteful nor as physically repulsive as her daughter was now. That Dorothy was wearing pink only made the impression more horrible. *She looks,* thought Jane with distaste, *like a pink slug.*

Dorothy, however, was looking at Jane with equal loathing and her voice was triumphant as she turned to Andrew Shearer and said, "There she stands. She went to North Molton ahead of you and made sure you'd find nothing. I *know* she went! Father Drew sent her. His housekeeper Biddy told me afterward. She came to Clicket Hall last evening to see her niece who works there and I exchanged a word or two with her and that's when she spoke of it."

"*Biddy* told you?" said Jane.

Dorothy's smile was horrid. "She meant no harm. She doesn't realize I don't hold with popishness any more than Master Shearer here does. But I made sure to tell him, when Master Shearer came back this morning. I was out in Clicket and I saw him coming through the street with his folk, so I went and called to him."

"And so I stayed in Clicket, 'stead of goin' on home, and kept a few friends with me," Shearer said. "We had a talk, sayin' shall us do this or shall us do that and in the end we settled to pay you a visit."

"I said burn your barley!" Danny Clay put in. Jane gasped and saw that even Tobias and Stephen were looking at each other in mutual horror. "But he's a man of chivalry, is Master Shearer," said Danny with a sneer. "Says we first got to ask what you've got to say for yourself, madam."

"We reckon we saw 'ee," said Shearer nastily. "When we came out of the mist, on the way to North Molton, we saw a rider gallopin' off ahead of us, too far off to recognize, but we take it that was you."

"What…what you…a-talkin' about?" Harry heaved himself up from his chair, groping for his stick. Pushing Jane aside, he lurched around the table. "M-my wife…she's not been away from here! Was here…all…all…" His slurred speech almost defeated him, but he forced out a few more indistinct words. "All day…all yesterday…silly lies…"

"Not lies," said Dorothy coolly. She turned to Andrew. "You know this family! You can't trust any of them."

"You can't trust any papist," said another of Shearer's companions. It was the beefy man who had brandished a billhook at the vicar of St. Michael's in Minehead.

"Quite," said Dorothy viciously. "The elder sister, Sybil, was nothing but a whore and this one's as bad. My husband's been after her, and if you ask me, he's had her. A wife can always tell."

Jane, with the memory of Ralph's kiss suddenly burning on her mouth, and the memory of the strange yearning he had awakened churning in her guts, felt herself turn scarlet, but supporters were coming to her aid. Peggy, arms akimbo, shouted, "How dare 'ee? 'Ee's a foul-minded besom!" at the top of her voice, and was echoed by Stephen as he, too, came to his feet and indignantly joined in.

"That's *right!* Filthy lies!" Stephen shouted, his voice cracking abruptly from treble to baritone. "Mistress Sybil was my mother and no one calls my mother a whore…."

"No?" said Dorothy unpleasantly. "Do you know how she died?"

"Yes," Peggy broke in. "He does. I once let it out by mistake."

"Peggy!" Jane cried.

"Sorry, ma'am, but I also told him it come about because

his ma was just too kind to say no. I told him not to hold it against her."

"I don't even remember her," said Stephen. "She ran away when I was a baby. Maybe she had her reasons. But Katherine Lanyon told me who sired me. Interesting to meet you at last, *Father.*" He scowled at Shearer. "Later, it seems, she had another lover. I don't know who that one was and I don't care. None of it matters. She was still *my mother* and I won't have her insulted."

"And no one says things about *my* mother either!" cried Tobias, who had also sprung up, and was clenching his nine-year-old fists. The effect was almost comical, except that his fury was real and the cause of it very adult, and only his lack of years and inches made him look more endearing than dangerous.

Dorothy said, "Mistress Hudd's face condemns her. Look at her. Scarlet as a poppy!"

"It's embarrassment!" Jane gasped. "To hear such things said of me…! I have *never, never* been unfaithful to my husband. I'll swear it on the Bible, on the cross, on anything…."

"Only papists swear on the cross," said Shearer.

"And what's wrong with being a papist?" shouted Tobias. "It's better than being a foul-mouthed bully!"

"And who invited 'ee here this day?" demanded Peggy. "Pushin' past me and burstin' in as if 'ee owned the place! Clear out, all of 'ee, and leave a decent household in peace!"

The beefy individual stepped forward and hit her across the face. She would have fallen, except that Stephen darted from his place and caught hold of her. She clung there, a hand to her bruised mouth. "You bloody savage!" bellowed Stephen. "Get out of our house!"

"It's not your house," said Dorothy disparagingly. "Just an orphan that's been given a roof, that's all you are." Danny Clay sniggered.

"It's his *home!*" said Peggy indistinctly. "The only one he's got, since his *father* didn't offer him one!" Glaring at Andrew Shearer, she withdrew her hand from her mouth and looked at it. It was stained with the blood from her lip where her assailant's fist had driven it against her teeth.

Shearer, who had been staring at Stephen appraisingly, laughed. "Yes, I'm findin' it interestin', too, to meet Sybil's brat. I b'ain't never been too sure he were mine."

There was a startled silence, while his audience considered this further new facet to the drama in progress. In the kitchen doorway Letty and the other maids were clustered, frightened, and out in the yard Tim Snowe and three of the other men had gathered, though they could not get in. Danny had taken up a position in front of the barred door. Peggy wiped her mouth again and glowered afresh.

"Shame on every one of 'ee! You'm a boor and she'm a harridan!" She pointed at Andrew and Dorothy in turn.

"Don't call me names!" Dorothy snapped.

"Peggy can call you all the names she likes, with my right goodwill," said Jane furiously. "If I *had* gone to warn North Molton, well, why shouldn't I? Why should anyone have to put up with all of you, behaving like barbarians, like…?"

"Like decent Protestants, keeping the laws laid down by the king!" shouted Clay.

Thump! *Thump, thump, THUMP!* Harry, pounding on the floor with his stick, brought the ugly exchange to an end. Tobias went to help him stand steady and Harry, forcing words out the side of his mouth that still functioned normally, said, "You're wrong! All wrong! Don't care what anyone told 'ee…! My wife…was *here*, I tell…tell 'ee! She wouldn't leave me…go off to Molton…lies…all lies. And she's never had aught to do with any man but me, either!"

The last sentence came out with astonishing clarity, as though his own strong feelings had burst through the physical hindrance. "I *know!* You think I'm some gurt vule as wouldn't know? I'd…have…smelt him on her. She'm honest…good woman. Good wife. No one…slanders my wife and gets away with it…bitch…tellin' lies, *lies…!*"

Abandoning Tobias's support, he staggered forward and swiped at Dorothy with his stick. Dorothy stumbled back with a shriek of fright. Shearer stepped between them and Harry, with a sudden and explicit curse, aimed a blow at him, as well. But the blow lost impetus halfway. The stick did not reach Shearer and it was Jane who cried out, horrified, as for the third time, Harry's illness struck.

Once again his cheekbones flushed reddish-orange. Once again spittle formed at the side of his mouth, and he fell, a look of wild bewilderment in his one good eye. On the floor, he jerked, drawing noisy, greedy breaths as though struggling for air. Tears ran from his eyes.

Then the breathing ceased.

Jane found herself kneeling beside him. Tobias was on the other side. Stephen and Peggy rushed to crouch by Harry, too. Blood still ran from Peggy's cut lip, but she was taking no notice. She was crying, and simultaneously feeling for the pulse in Harry's neck.

But his face had already lost its flush, was fading to a greyish tinge and Peggy, looking at Jane, slowly shook her head.

Jane stood up. "Well, Master Shearer and Mistress Palmer, are you satisfied? Do you feel you've done enough, had sufficient revenge for this crime you imagine I have committed, despite my husband's testimony to the contrary? My husband is dead. Come and see for yourselves." She stood aside for them.

There was a new kind of silence, except for an uneasy shuffling of feet and some clearing of throats. Even Danny Clay looked awkward, while Andrew Shearer had become suddenly hangdog. "We never meant *that,*" he said.

"I daresay, though I do wonder what you did mean," said Jane icily.

"To give 'ee a fright, make it clear that we can't be fooled," said the beefy individual, but not very forcibly.

"Aye. That's the truth of it," echoed Danny, apparently forgetting that he had recommended burning the barley.

They hadn't, thought Jane, really decided on their intentions at all; they had just come here on a wave of rage and excitement, urged on by Dorothy. She looked down at Harry. Grief would begin soon. She hadn't loved him, but there had been something between them, something that had sprung from sheer physical intimacy, from working side by side, from having a child together. In the end, knowing perfectly well that she really had been to North Molton, he had lied in her defence.

"I think," she said, turning to the intruders, "that you should all go."

"So do I," said Stephen belligerently. "Including my father. I don't want to acknowledge him any more than he wants to acknowledge me."

Father and son stared at each other inimically. And Jane, watching, saw their resemblance to each other suddenly flame out. Stephen was mature for a lad of fifteen. Their colouring was different, but the long yet shapely bones of their two faces and the set of their shoulders were identical.

Furthermore, they had seen it themselves. It was pulling at them, the tie of blood relationship that was stronger than any ideological loyalties.

Andrew voiced it, after a fashion. "Maybe you are my son. Looks like you are. I wish you well. Seems you're provided for, even though it's no thanks to me. Well, all right, I'm glad."

Stiffly Stephen said, "Thank you."

If they could, they would have walked away together and sat down in private to further their acquaintance over a drink, but in these circumstances it wasn't possible.

Dorothy broke in. "If you ask me—"

"We didn't," said Stephen.

"If you ask me," repeated Dorothy loudly, "I think *she's* done as much to kill Master Allerbrook as any." She pointed at Jane. "He stood up for her because he was a loyal, decent man, but I think hearing that she'd been whoring with my husband gave him a shock. I don't suppose he knew about it. But it's true!"

"It is *not* true!" Jane shouted. "You're a spiteful, wicked woman. *You're* the one who caused this—Mistress Fat Slug Palmer!"

"That's enough." Shearer took Dorothy's elbow. Jane, shuddering with rage and anguish, wondered how he could bear to feel that squashy flesh below the pale pink sleeve.

"The man is dead," Shearer said. He looked down at Harry and for once, his narrow features displayed something that resembled compassion. "Death pays all debts—and I'll not call a dead man a liar. Maybe Biddy was muddled or maybe not, but we'll not ask any further. Shall us?" He looked around at his followers and there were shamefaced murmurs of agreement, even from Danny Clay.

He turned to Stephen. "I'll not trouble 'ee in time to come, son, but I wish 'ee good luck."

"And the same to you," said Stephen. His voice was expressionless.

"And now, please," said Jane, "will you all leave this house?"

CHAPTER TWENTY-FOUR
The Signs of Danger
1551–1553

"No," said Jane resolutely to Sir Edmund Flaxton, Ralph Palmer's wealthy first cousin and her own distant relative, when, less than a year after Harry's death, he travelled all the way to Somerset to urge a second marriage on her. The Allerbrook lands amounted to a good dowry, he said, and he had found a suitable man, a good stepfather for Tobias.

"In fact, you're lucky, mistress, that your lands aren't bigger and neither Francis nor Master Hudd had any titles or high positions, or the Crown might have made young Toby its ward and sold the wardship to the best bidder. As it is, you can keep him, but he needs a man to guide him all the same. Now, this gentleman comes from Shropshire and you'd need to move there...."

"I don't want to remarry," said Jane. "Or to leave Allerbrook. My nephew Stephen is almost a man already. You mean well, but I have no need of a husband."

"Every woman needs a husband!"

"Some women have husbands they scarcely see anyway!" According to the gossip exchange in the White Hart inn in Clicket, Ralph Palmer had been furious with Dorothy for leading Shearer and his followers to Allerbrook, and since then had hardly spent a night under the same roof with his wife. "I am sorry, Sir Edmund," Jane said determinedly, " but *no.*"

Another year passed, during which, with the aid of the heavy horses, she brought more land under the plough, which meant extra corn to send to market. She did not think twice about penning a letter saying no thank you to another offer, from a distant relative in Yorkshire, who wrote offering an alliance with a neighbour.

You are so much alone, the letter said. *Your father and brother are both gone and now your husband is gone, as well. I hereby offer a proposal from our neighbour Master Humphrey Robbins, a well-respected gentleman with a house and lands near the city of York. He adheres to the old religion, but we are disturbed very little in the north. He is past his fiftieth birthday but has no infirmity beyond a stiff knee.*

He was recently widowed, as you were. He can offer good hopes of children, having already four, aged from six to thirteen. He needs someone who will guard and guide them as did his late wife....

"Past fifty and lame!" said Stephen, aghast, when shown this missive. "I'd wager that the stiff knee is ten times as bad as they pretend—and I'd wager that those four children who need a mother so badly are *troublesome* children, worse than I ever was! Dear Aunt Jane, have nothing to do with this!"

"I agree," chimed in Tobias, who since his father's death, had matured a good deal. "Please don't say yes, Mother. Please!"

"Of course I shan't," said Jane. "And that's final."

She meant it. There were still times, undoubtedly, when desire troubled her. But if the man were not Peter Carew, then she would do without. She was relieved that Ralph never visited Allerbrook these days and seemed to spend most of his time in Kent. She would remain where she was and look after her household, which needed her.

Tobias and Stephen did, now, try to put up with each other because they loved her. They even had occasional moments of accord, as they had during Shearer's intrusion and just now, when discussing this latest proposal. But they would never be real friends. Meanwhile, the times were full of trouble and unease. She must fortify Allerbrook against these things if she could.

The disquiet worsened as the months passed. The sense of impending disaster was more powerful than ever when rumour began to say that young King Edward was dying.

In Greenwich, in the May of 1553, the royal council was panicking.

It was cold for springtime. There was a hearth in the council chamber, but the meeting had been called at short notice and so disturbed was the atmosphere in the palace that no one had thought of laying a fire. Most of the gentlemen now in agitated conference around the long table were in their warmest fur-trimmed robes. Beaver jostled red fox; silver fox and ermine rubbed against the pelts of bear and lynx. Among their wearers were points of view as diverse as the original owners of the furs, but at the moment they were drawn together by mutual alarm.

"The king's physicians are in despair," said John Dudley, Duke of Northumberland, grimly, standing at the head of the table. Tall and balding and ermine-trimmed, with sharp dark eyes under high-arched brows, he was pulsating both with his authority as head of the council, and the dread of losing it.

"His Majesty is coughing up black phlegm with blood in it," he said. "He hasn't been himself since catching smallpox and measles both at once last year. There's a wise woman I've found, who thinks she can help—I've promised no reprisals if she fails. No good terrifying the woman! She's giving him a medicine that has eased things a little, but…"

"What's in it?" enquired Henry Grey of Suffolk.

"I asked her that. She gave me a whole list of things. There's arsenic among them," said Dudley. "Not much! Don't be afraid. It will help to clear his breathing, so she says. I've heard of it being used that way before. It may upset his stomach," he added callously, "but he'll have to put up with that. If he dies…"

"If he dies," said Sir William Petre, who was one of the Secretaries of State, "we shall have his sister Mary. We'll have a woman on the throne." Several red foxes had died to adorn his cloak and he himself had a pointed, foxlike face that was almost feminine. He wore a beard and kept stroking it as if to remind himself that he was male.

The other Secretary of State, young Sir William Cecil, nodded gravely. "She is next in the line of succession under King Henry's will."

"And," said Antoine de Noailles, the French ambassador, who was present by invitation, "she is half-Spanish." His voice was cool and sardonic. He had a feline air and he affected lynx fur on his cloak. He was reminding them that the French and the Spaniards were hereditary rivals, to a point that outweighed by several tons the fact that both were Catholic.

"I can tolerate a woman on the throne," said Northumberland. "But the Lady Mary…"

"She will overturn the reformed religion and she'll have support for that," said the aging Thomas Cranmer, Archbishop of Canterbury. "We've had uprisings against the Reformation. There was that absurd upheaval in the southwest, the one that Sir Peter Carew nearly managed to turn into a major catastrophe, and there have been others since, here and there. She'll call those people to her side. And then what will happen to all of us? I'm the king's godfather! I've reared him in the reformed church. She'll very likely have me in the Tower, or worse!" His voice held a quiver of fear.

In his bedchamber, Edward VI of England lay, listening to the birdsong beyond his window. His swollen, pustule-ridden body hurt in every part. Above all, his throat and chest were sore because of the cough that would not stop, that kept sleep from him at night, and brought up sputum so ugly that the sight of it made him want to vomit.

He was trying to read a prayer book, but his head throbbed and he knew that he was feverish again. The piping of the blackbird outside was a torment, in its purity and its love of life. His body was as foul, as corrupt as a body well could be and still live, but who could call this living? Nor, he knew, would he ever regain health and cleanliness and rejoin the world in which that innocent bird rejoiced. He tossed in the bed, and hurt himself in so doing, and wished he could strangle the bird, or that a cat would kill it.

In the council chamber someone had said, "What other candidates are there, besides Mary?"

Someone else mentioned her younger sister Elizabeth, who was also mentioned in King Henry's will as being in line for the throne. "There's doubt about her legitimacy," said the archbishop gloomily.

Northumberland observed that what was needed was a good Protestant princess, born in wedlock, with forebears who were also, one and all, born in wedlock, and who was a direct descendant of the royal Tudor house. As he spoke, he looked thoughtfully at Suffolk. Suffolk's wife was King Henry's niece. Henry VII had been her grandfather. "You have two unmarried daughters, haven't you?" he said. "Good girls, reared in the reformed faith?"

"They're just young wenches!" Suffolk protested. "Even the eldest, Jane, isn't quite sixteen."

"That's old enough for marriage. A queen must have a husband," Northumberland said. "I still have one unmarried son I can use." He said it casually, as though his offspring were surplus items of furniture, settles or stools perhaps, gathering dust in a lumber room and available to anyone who happened to find a purpose for them. Behind those sharp dark eyes, though, John Dudley's mind was working at top speed.

It had been said of Northumberland that he never did anything without at least three motives, and at this moment he was thinking that here was a scheme that would surely achieve three things. It would keep England Protestant, would ensure that his head and a good many others would stay safely on their owners' shoulders and would make him, in effect, the father of a king, the power behind the throne— and not that far behind it, either. His boy Guilford would do as he was told and any girl the lad married would have to obey Guilford. It would be a most triumphant coup.

CHAPTER TWENTY-FIVE
A Change in the Wind
1553

Jane looked around at her hall, at the shining glass and silver tableware and the applewood fire in the hearth, and was aware of her own healthy body in its best green velvet gown. If only, now and then, time would pause so that good moments could be properly savoured.

Christmas was coming; Dr. Spenlove was back from a journey to London on business connected with the sale of the Allerbrook wool clip, on which payment had been still owing from a London wool buyer. He was older, thinner and less jolly than in the past, but his health was still good and he had returned safely—and with the outstanding payment—despite bad weather and worse roads.

She had planned this as a welcome-home dinner and had invited Father Drew to join them, since he and Spenlove were friends. So, despite the disturbances in the world outside, here they all were, enjoying themselves and eating good food. Accidents and illnesses like those which had killed Francis and carried Eleanor and Harry away could seize on any of them, but they hadn't done so yet. The long, prying arm of the religious law could reach out and find fault with one of them, but that had not yet happened, either.

Even the creatures of Allerbrook were safe. It was cold and sleeting, but the hens were in their henhouse and the geese in the barn where they always sheltered in such weather. The horses and cattle were in their stalls; the two big dogs, Hunter and Rusty, were asleep in front of the hearth, amicably curled up with the two cats, both descendants of Claws. Inky looked like a reincarnation of his departed ancestor, but his sister had a white chest and white whiskers, and was accordingly known as Whiskers.

All safe, and in her care. Peggy was bent-backed these days, but she still worked as she always had, and still had Beth and Letty to help her. They had done much to make this feast a success. Peggy really did have a miraculous hand with cider and wheaten bread....

At this point, somewhat to Jane's irritation, Father Drew, who had been talking quietly to Spenlove, chose to introduce a discordant note. Having taken a long drink of cider, he suddenly put his tankard down with a thump and declared in despairing tones that at times he felt like giving up his vocation, running away and ceasing to be a vicar.

The gathering looked at him in bemusement. "I mean it!" he said.

"But...oh, please!" said Jane. "Why should you? Everyone in Clicket would miss you. Your health hasn't worsened further, has it?"

"My joints are more painful than they were but otherwise I am no worse. But I am tired—*tired*. It's as if churchmen are all just balls in a game of spiritual tennis. Under King Henry, it was *everyone abandon the Pope. Buy English Bibles and read them*. Then the king lost his nerve and took to saying that only priests and men of rank could read the Bible in English, and the ordinary folk who'd been told to buy them found it was against the law to have one in the house! Then we had the boy King Edward and it was *down with all popish images* and *say the mass in English*—and now it's Queen Mary and it's *bring back the old ways*. And if this Spanish marriage goes ahead, this Philip of Spain will most likely bring something more than the old rituals with him. According to Dr. Spenlove here, anyway!"

"I shouldn't have spoken of such things on this happy occasion," said Spenlove with regret. "But I was saying to Father Drew that London is full of rumours. There is much murmuring against the idea of Queen Mary marrying Philip of Spain for fear that he introduces the Inquisition here, and it is being said, in every tavern, by the boatmen on the Thames—by *everyone*—that the queen is angry because Prince Philip hesitates to come while there are so many Lutherans in the land. He thinks they are dangerous to him. The queen is saying she will deal with the heretics, and that, in her mind, includes anyone who opposes her marriage."

"But heresy can't be just that," said Jane. "And how can one be sure what heresy is, when the rules keep changing? Dr. Spenlove, I haven't asked you yet—is there any news of what is to happen to that young girl who has the same name as me, Lady Jane Grey? Is she still in the Tower?"

"Yes. She will be pardoned, I think. It was hardly her fault that her parents and Northumberland tried to put her on the throne. She's only just sixteen! The pardon won't be issued until after the Spanish marriage, though."

"The whole world's in confusion. I went to see Mistress Palmer today," said Drew. "She is very ill—she's dying. She wanted me to give her the sacrament but in English, and that's against the law now! But it's not fair to refuse the dying such a simple wish."

"She's no better, then?" Stephen enquired. At eighteen, he was tall and becoming handsome. His neatly clipped hair had golden glints in its light brown, and his long-chinned face, markedly like that of Andrew Shearer, had a look of strength. He was a contrast to Tobias, who was mousy-haired, wide of brow and chin, with a fair complexion and at twelve, did not look as though he would ever be tall.

Tobias was still a quiet boy, too. Stephen, however, never hesitated to speak when he felt like it, and had lately developed a curiously subtle way of expressing himself. He had long since told Jane that he had, eventually, bullied Peggy into naming Ralph as Sybil's final lover, but that he blamed Dorothy more than Ralph for his mother's death. His feelings for Sybil were few and equivocal, but he had told Jane that he hated Dorothy. His simple enquiry about her health was laden with hidden meanings, such as *I hope she won't recover* and *how soon can we expect the burial?*

Drew sighed. "Mistress Palmer is only thirty-five or so, but she's hugely fat, worse than ever her mother was, and nearly blind and her feet—it's as if they're rotting. I don't know where her husband is—Kent, I suppose. Never seems to be where his wife is, anyhow. That excellent woman Lisa does most of the nursing and looks after the little girl, Blanche, as well. In fact, I did use English when I gave Mistress Palmer the sacrament. She pleaded with me so. What does it matter? Why can't the authorities leave us alone?"

"They want to save our souls, I suppose," said Tobias seriously.

Jane wondered, not for the first time, whether she had been wrong when she decided to hold by Harry's decision not to send the boys to school. But then, few schools would have satisfied Stephen's desire to study navigation and read about the discoveries made by explorers, and she would not have wanted either of them bullied into hating the sight of Latin. She had heard bad reports of some schoolmasters. One day, perhaps, she would arrange for them to stay in London households, with a chance of attending court.

Meanwhile, why, oh why did Stephen have to make people uncomfortable by asking innocent-sounding questions which were really as full of spikes as a hedgehog, and why must Tobias, at only twelve, talk gravely about saving people's souls, for all the world as though he were a doctor of divinity aged seventy? She would prefer him to take more interest in the Allerbrook accounts. He seemed to have no head for figures.

"The trouble," she said mildly, "is that those who rule us don't seem able to agree on exactly how souls can be saved. I suppose all we can do is try to keep the laws, whatever they are. Father Drew, has John Grede in North Molton dug up the church treasures he had buried back in 1550?"

"He tells me he tried, but the spot wasn't marked and no one's been able to find them," said Drew. "Or so he says," he added, and to Jane's relief the company once more broke into laughter, and then sat up with expectant expressions, because while all this serious talk had been going on, Letty and Peggy had slipped out to the kitchen to fetch the next course, and it was venison.

Allerbrook had hunting rights. Some days ago Stephen

had brought down a fine young stag, and the platter now being carried in contained venison steaks. Beside the fire, the cats and dogs stirred and woke, roused by the smell of game. Hunter sat up, gazing at the table with wistful eyes. Whiskers sat up, too, twitching her nose and licking at her whiskers with a pink and yearning tongue.

"We'll share with 'ee. Don't be so greedy," Peggy said to them. "But two-legs eat afore four-legs. Just let me…why, whatever…?"

Hunter was on his feet, barking. So was Rusty. Out in the barn the geese were cackling noisily enough to be heard through the walls of both barn and house. Stephen got up. "I'll go. Whoever's come visiting without an invitation on a cold day like this?"

He strode off to open the door. Presently they heard him returning, talking to somebody as he did so. Jane sat still, not sure she quite believed what she thought she had heard. It was so unlikely. But…

Stephen and his companion came in. Jane rose to her feet. Slowly. It was difficult to breathe, as though Peggy, who helped her dress when she put on formal gowns, had drawn her stays too tight.

"I see you're dining. I'm sorry to intrude, though if you can spare a bite for me and the three men I've got with me— they're looking after the horses just now—I'd be grateful. Mistress Jane, it's good to see you again. You look well. It's been a long time," said Peter Carew, sweeping off his sleet-dampened hat and giving her a magnificent bow.

"A very long time," Jane agreed faintly. "Over thirteen years, I fancy."

He hadn't changed. There he stood, holding his hat, swinging an oiled leather cloak off his shoulders and grinning at her. He was as handsome, as much the bold adventurer as he had ever been. He exuded confidence and joy in living. He wasn't a man who had never made a mistake—she knew that well enough. But he was a man who could learn from his errors, who could grow in stature, and he had.

And she hadn't changed either. Outwardly calm and gracious, she stood there exchanging banalities with him, and loved him as much as when he had ridden away, back in 1540. He tossed the hat onto a window seat, came to her, kissed her hand and then kissed her mouth. It was a normal greeting between guest and hostess, but the feel of his hands on her shoulders, the smell of him, of horse and sweat and oiled leather, turned her knees to water and made her head reel.

"I'm here on a mission," he announced. "I'm on my way to Devon, to my home in Mohuns Ottery, and I've things to do in Exeter, but I'm seizing the chance to gather extra men on the way. It's on account of Queen Mary and this Spanish marriage. We can't have it." He said it as though he represented an authority with a perfect right of veto. "We can't have Mary trying to turn back the clock and bringing us a king from Spain, of all places. Something must be done. We've got to resist, in arms if need be. I'm collecting volunteers…."

One could not stand there in a daze. Someone might notice, for one thing. Jane, becoming a dignified hostess once more, interrupted him.

"Sir Peter, Dr. Spenlove has just returned from a long winter journey and this is his welcome-home dinner. Please be seated. We'll hear about your mission, whatever it is, presently, but let us finish dining first. Naturally, you and your companions are welcome to join us. Peggy, Beth, please set a second table for Sir Peter's men, and bring a seat for Sir Peter. Here, beside me. We have ample food and drink, I think."

Peter's men came in, more places were set and extra food was served. Carew, however, when alight with enthusiasm, could not be stopped from talking, not even by strong cider, fresh bread and venison steaks, and Stephen, intrigued by what Carew had said already, could not be stopped from encouraging him with questions.

"If you're collecting volunteers, sir, what are they going to do? Is this to be another rising on behalf of Lady Jane Grey, Suffolk's daughter? But she's a prisoner in the Tower!"

"Stephen, please! Let Sir Peter eat his dinner in peace."

"Don't worry about that. My digestion will work whether I talk at the same time or not. God's teeth, not Jane Grey!" said Carew. Elbows on table, he talked with his mouth full. "I've been to dinner with the Suffolks and met her and she's the most priggish brat I ever came across. Ruined the taste of a beautiful game pie by lecturing everyone on the wickedness of believing in transubstantiation. Well, I don't believe in it either. Bread's bread and wine's wine and that's that. I live in the real world and it doesn't work like that. But if some people like to believe it does, well, I'd leave them to it. It won't hurt me and I wouldn't ruin a good grouse-and-partridge pie for it. Or a good dish of venison. These collops are superb, Mistress Allerbrook. But that wretched girl…bah! She'd be a nightmare as a queen."

He had changed after all, Jane thought. He had become accentuated, *more* outspoken, *more* entertaining than before; there was something about him that caught one up as if on the rolling crest of an incoming breaker. He made people want to laugh, to follow him.

"Who do you want on the throne, then?" she asked.

"Oh, the younger princess, Elizabeth," said Carew, refilling his tankard with a generous hand. "I've met her, too. Protestant, but she doesn't lecture people on religion over dinner. She's King Henry's daughter, a royal lion cub. She has her father's magic. He had magic, you know. Not the transubstantiation sort, but the sort that *does* exist. The sort that draws people, makes a leader. No one could ignore King Henry."

No one can ignore you, either, Jane thought.

"She's got pale red hair, the same as his when he was young," said Carew. "And she still is young. Her hair's like golden-orange satin when it catches the light."

He sounded so lyrical that Jane found herself wishing she, too, had hair like golden-orange satin and a touch of magic.

"Ralph Palmer, your kinsman, he's joining in," he said. "He's with the forces we're collecting in the southeast. Their leader's a Kentish gentleman and Palmer has property in Kent. But he's often in London and we meet there. He says we can't just sit by and let the Spanish marriage go ahead. *We'll do no good by skulking at home and letting it happen,* he said to me. I have a feeling," Carew added, "that he doesn't like being with his wife—she's here at Clicket Hall, isn't she?—and welcomes any excuse to stay away, but I fancy his feeling against this prince of Spain is genuine enough."

Peggy clicked a disapproving tongue. The disapproval was for Ralph, as Jane well knew. Jane herself said nothing, but wondered how she could ever, even for five minutes, have been attracted by Master Palmer. He had quarrelled with Dorothy for her sake, but she hadn't wanted that and had felt uncomfortable when she learned of it. Now that his wife was mortally ill, he should have been with her.

"I'm collecting supporters in the west country," Carew

was saying. "I thought of Allerbrook. Ralph told me what you did at North Molton, Mistress Jane. I believe I can trust you not to betray me, and if this household can produce a sword–arm or two, I'd be grateful. Any offers?"

Jane asked for more details and gathered that there were several leaders of the intended rising. They had been scheming since November, in London. Carew, cautious to some extent, would not name the principal leader, but Spenlove, interrupting him in weary fashion, said, "Sir Thomas Wyatt the Younger. That's the man, isn't it?"

Carew's brows rose. "How did you know?"

"I've just been to London and you've been careless," said the chaplain shortly. "There are rumours, man, *rumours.* But folk are saying that Wyatt isn't out to put Elizabeth on the throne, just to keep Philip of Spain off it."

"Some say that, but others think differently."

"It sounds quite crazy to me," said Tobias, speaking up. "You'll all get yourselves killed. What's so wrong with the old religion, anyway? I like candles and the Latin mass myself."

"Oh, you were born old! I think you came into the world with long white whiskers, just like that cat down there!" said Stephen impatiently. "It sounds like a grand adventure to me!" His eyes danced. "Is the Princess Elizabeth in favour? Does she know of the scheme?"

"We wrote to her. She didn't answer, but perhaps that was wise," Carew said.

"I'd like to join you!" Stephen said.

I knew it, Jane thought. *I've been afraid of this from the moment I realized what Peter had come for.* "You're needed here," she said anxiously. "You help on the land. Sir Peter, we will keep your counsel, as you ask. No one shall ever know you came here tonight. But I can't spare my menfolk, least of all for such a risky enterprise as this."

"Ah, well," said Carew, draining a tankard of cider, "it was just an idea. Forget it. We'll ride on when the horses are rested. Mistress Allerbrook—that's your correct name now, is it not?—I heard that you were widowed. I am sorry. Palmer told me it came about because of what you did for John Grede. Grede and I are Protestants, but he didn't wish to rob his parishioners of the images and decorations that they were used to, and nor would I want to. Why take people's little comforts from them? You did right to help him. You have done enough, perhaps."

Carew and his men left after dinner, riding into the darkness and the sleet.

In the morning Stephen, too, had gone. He had apparently risen early and departed unseen, riding the pony Ginger, who though very elderly now, was still tough. Stephen had left a note on his bed. He was going to join Carew. He was on his way to Mohuns Ottery.

CHAPTER TWENTY-SIX
The Infection of Madness
1554

*I*n Clicket Hall, on a bitter January afternoon, Dorothy lay in her bed, as massive and helpless as a beached whale, full of pain, nearly blind, bitterly aware that she was slipping out of life, and savagely furious with Ralph Palmer, who, however, was not there to be told how much she hated him.

Father Drew was there, however, since Lisa had sent for him. On him Dorothy, though hoarse and short of breath, was loosing a comprehensive spleen.

"He ought to be here…what sort of a husband is he, that he's not here now, when I'm like this? He turned against me for telling Master Shearer how that Hudd woman at Allerbrook had cheated him, but it was Ralph who betrayed me first, going with other women and very likely one of them was Jane Hudd…."

"She's known as Jane Allerbrook now," said Father Drew.

"Bah. She's Jane Hudd as far as I'm concerned. He's always had his eye on her, and he had the gall to turn on me for telling the truth about her…. Oh God, why is this happening to me? God help me, Mary Mother of Jesus, plead for me…the pain…someone, do something…!"

Lisa was there, a beaker in her hand. "Take this. It will ease you."

"What's in it?" Father Drew asked.

"Something the physician got us from an apothecary in Taunton. It's made from a foreign poppy. I'm keeping Blanche out of the room," she added in an undertone. "This is no place for a child."

"I can hear you," said Dorothy. "If I die, Ralph will go to that Hudd woman, I know he will. She'll have him and she'll have Blanche. She shan't, she shan't! I won't die. I won't! I'll live, just to spite her. I…*oh no, oh God…!*"

The hoarse voice had been fading, but now it rose again, almost to a shriek. Pain and coma fought for supremacy in Dorothy's body and for a brief time there was an ugly struggle until the poppy medicine won. Then silence fell, and the gross, pallid body lay quiet. After a time, it became the stillness of death.

Only a few minutes after that, the messenger arrived at the gate.

A deathly silence had fallen after Stephen's departure. Even rumour seemed to have lost its tongue. Christmas came and went, a muted Yuletide. There was no feasting, of course, at Clicket Hall, where Dorothy Palmer, at that time, was nearing her end, but there were gatherings elsewhere: at Allerbrook on Christmas Day, to which all the tenants were invited, and on subsequent days at Rixons and Greys and Hannacombes.

Efforts were made at jollity, but Stephen's absence was noticeable. Despite his penchant for subtly spiky remarks, he was good company and he was a gifted dancer. Nothing was the same without him.

After disposing of the land on the far side of the county, Jane had duly bought a farm near Dunster. The Luttrells, who still owned Dunster Castle, though they rarely visited it, had put the place up for sale. In January she rode over with Tobias to see its tenants and take belated Christmas gifts to them. Then, for the first time, there was news. The tenants were acquainted with the steward of Dunster Castle, who in turn had regular news from the Luttrells, who knew virtually everything that happened in the southwest. Jane now learned that Sir Peter Carew was stirring up the people of Exeter.

He was said to have about seventy armed men in his Devon home at Mohuns Ottery. Stephen, presumably, was with them. The authorities had apparently got wind of the plot, since Carew had been ordered to London for questioning, but he had stayed resolutely put.

The Duke of Suffolk, the father of Lady Jane Grey, having been recently pardoned and released from the Tower, was in the midlands, trying to raise support for Wyatt. Fighting somewhere, sometime was expected.

Jane and Tobias, having stayed the night with their tenants, set off for home next day in a sombre mood. It was raining and the muddy tracks slowed them down. The Allerbrook household was looking out for them, for when they rode in, Tim Snowe and his young son Paul appeared immediately, looking so serious that Jane opened her mouth to ask if anything were amiss. But before she could speak, Peggy and Spenlove had opened the door and were standing anxiously in the porch. Resigning their horses to the grooms, Jane and Tobias hurried inside. "Mistress Allerbrook!" Peggy said in tones of relief. "We're that glad to see you back!"

"There's someone here to see you," Spenlove said. "Just arrived, in fact. In the hall."

"Who?" Jane demanded. She led the way inside, then stopped short at the sight of the two wan figures crouching on stools by the hearth and holding out their hands to its warmth. Their skirts were splashed with mud and their shoes and cloaks, arranged on a fireside bench, were steaming gently. Someone, probably Peggy, had sensibly given them slippers. But their white faces and their shivers spoke of something worse than being caught in the rain.

"Lisa! And—surely, little Blanche!" said Jane, astonished. "What has happened?"

"I've brought her to you, Mistress Allerbrook," said Lisa, getting to her feet and pulling Blanche up, as well. "There you are, child. Make your curtsy." Lisa had not been young when she first became Jane's tirewoman and the years were taking their visible toll. Her own curtsy was clearly inhibited by stiff knees.

"But what...?" said Jane, bemused.

"The mistress—Mistress Palmer—died two hours ago," Lisa said. "And hardly was she gone before there was a messenger from Master Palmer at the door, saying that he was going to ride with Sir Thomas Wyatt soon and hoped that God would defend the right, but he'd take leave of his family in case things went amiss, as well they might, for..."

"Gently, gently," said Dr. Spenlove. "Catch your breath."

"I have to tell it!" insisted Lisa. "The messenger took a mouthful of food, but then he took a fresh horse and rode on to Devon, to warn Sir Peter Carew that there's a warrant out for his arrest. Queen Mary's men are on their way to seize him. And there was a letter for me. It said that Master Ralph knew his wife might be dying and if she did, to bring Blanche here. He wrote that if he didn't come back, then it's in his will that you're to be her guardian, mistress, and he'd left money as well in case you have to buy her wardship. I don't think Mistress Dorothy knew about that and, just as well…oh, it was so horrible at the end…!"

Exhausted, cold and past the age for coping simultaneously with a deathbed and a downpour, Lisa burst into tears. Blanche, much the calmer of the two, put a kind arm around her and said, "Dear Lisa, don't take on."

"You poor things," said Jane. "Now, tell me, did you bring any baggage?"

"Yes," said Lisa. "We came on ponies and had our hampers on a pack mule."

"Good. You must change out of those splashed things at once. Peggy, have a bedchamber made ready. Does anyone know how far Mohuns Ottery is? I've never been there."

"Something like thirty miles," said Spenlove. "But, ma'am, why do you want to know?"

"I've got to get there," said Jane. "I've got to do all I possibly can to get Stephen out of this trouble. I want to bring him home."

It was ridiculous. Spenlove said so, Tobias said so and so did Tim Snowe. The weather was too bad, and Stephen would certainly refuse to be dragged home by his aunt. No young man of spirit would stand for such a thing. There was no point at all in Jane attempting to rescue him.

"I shan't go about it that way. I'm not so foolish," said Jane sharply. "I'll say I've come to warn Sir Peter. Who's to say the messenger who called at Clicket Hall ever got to Mohuns Ottery? His horse could have foundered or the queen's soldiers could have caught him. I'll see Sir Peter and warn him to get away and I'll ask him to disperse his men. Oh, why can't you understand? If the queen's men are after him, then all his followers are in danger, including Stephen. I have to *try!*"

"Mother," said Tobias, exasperated, "sometimes you behave like a sheepdog! Always you want to protect people, to safeguard them. But sometimes it isn't possible. You can't ride off now! It's getting dark and it's pouring!"

Rain blew against the windows again, tossed on a strong wind. "Then I leave at daybreak," said Jane.

"I'll come with you."

"No, Tobias, you're too young. But you're near in age to Blanche. Give her your company. She may be glad to have you to talk to. She's lost her mother and been taken from her home. Tim Snowe will escort me. I'll take Hazelnut—she's steady—and he can ride Dusty as usual."

"But, Mother…"

"Tobias, don't argue."

"If she insists on going, I'll accompany your mother, as well," said Spenlove wearily. "Don't worry about her."

"No, Dr. Spenlove." Jane's conscience troubled her. "I know you're working on another set of illuminated Gospels and I remember that after your journey to London before Christmas, you were very tired. This will be a long ride in the cold. You must stay here."

"The better your escort, the more weight your argument

will carry," said Spenlove gallantly. "I'm coming. The manuscript can wait awhile. I shall manage and so will Frosty."

Spenlove, though he was a short man, declined to ride Exmoor ponies because he said they made him feel as though his feet were about to scrape the ground. When his old cob Podge died, he had bought another, a white gelding which he had named Frosty, over fifteen hands. Frosty had been an inexpensive purchase because like his master, he wasn't young. But he was sound and willing enough. "I think we can face thirty miles in a good cause," said Spenlove.

The rain was gone by morning, but it had left misty weather behind it. As Jane and her companions made their way over the moorland into Devon, they kept to the lower tracks where visibility was better. It was a longer route, but safer, Jane said, remembering how she had lost her way on the ride to North Molton.

The county of Devon, bedded down for the winter, looked as though it had never heard of warfare. The red ploughland, which had the consistency of thick cream cheese, lay peacefully under the mist. Cattle and sheep grazed quietly in the meadows, which retained some greenness though not yet the emerald shoots that would signal the approach of spring. Here and there, however, were snowdrops.

"Signs of hope," Jane said, pointing to a cluster of them.

They paused for rest and food in Tiverton, to the south of the moor, and as they started out, the mists lifted. Fitful gleams of sunlight appeared. They were still several miles short of the Carew house in the district of Mohuns Ottery, however, when they saw four riders coming toward them. "They could be the queen's men," said Spenlove uneasily, reining in.

"Then we'd best ride on steady, looking innocent, like," said Tim Snowe. He added, "They'm comin' on fast."

The horsemen, helmeted, breastplated and armed, were moving at a steady canter. Jane and her companions edged their mounts to the side of the track, which at this point passed through a belt of woodland. Jane glanced at it, wondering if they could get out of sight among the trees, but the riders had already seen them and were slowing down. It was too late.

The leader was on a black horse with a narrow white blaze, and Tim let out an exclamation. "I know that horse! Rubbed it down once, and it kicked me, the brute."

The rider drew to a halt beside Jane, who looked at him and then laughed. His eyes widened in astonishment. "God's teeth—Jane Allerbrook! *Jane!* What in the world brings you here?"

"Sir Peter! I came to warn you!" She tumbled the words out without preamble. "There's a warrant out for your arrest. The queen's soldiers are hunting for you now!"

"I know. We've dodged two sets of them already. A messenger reached me this morning. The government's got hold of some of the letters that Wyatt and I wrote to various gentlemen, to raise arms and swordsmen. I've disbanded my men, except for these fellows, who've chosen to come with me, and a few others who've made for Kent to join Sir Thomas Wyatt. I hope they've got through. I had a summons to London but I didn't go. I knew then that the finger of the law was pointing at me. I'm going to get out of the country if I can. While Spanish delegations, and in due time, no doubt, Prince Philip of Spain, can just come in at will!" His voice was suddenly savage. "If I see any Spaniards coming ashore when I embark for France, I swear I'll throw every last man of them into the sea. You shouldn't be here, Jane.

It was brave of you to come, but you should go home at once, and quickly."

"If you're hoping to get away by sea, why are you coming this way?" Spenlove asked. "Exeter's your nearest port."

"Exeter's been fortified against me and I hear there are royal soldiers in every coastal town for miles along the south coast. I've been wary. I've had scouts out and they've brought me reports. But from what they say, Weymouth may still be safe—it's a good long way to the east. I've friends there. I'm making for Weymouth, by an inland route, going around the enemy, so to speak."

"Sir Peter," said Jane, "where's Stephen Sweetwater?"

"Your Stephen? On his way to Kent. Oh, my dear Jane, did you come to rescue him? He'd never have let you. He's a grand lad," said Carew with enthusiasm. "Lionhearted and merry as a jester. You should have given him some training in arms, though. I've tried to drill him with a sword, but you can't do in a month what normally takes years. I sent him off with a good, sharp-headed pike. He'll do better with that."

"Oh, Sir *Peter!*" said Jane, exasperated. "He should never have gone after you. I'd have stopped him if I could."

"Except that I fancy you couldn't. Not that lad," said Carew heartily.

Spenlove said, "Your chances of getting through to Weymouth aren't good. They'll have thought of the inland roads, too."

"They don't know the area as well as I do. I've lived abroad and in Lincolnshire for a good few years, but as a boy I knew this corner of England as well as I know the lines on my own palm."

Tim Snowe broke in. "You'd best get off that horse, Sir Peter. If I recognized it, so will others."

"Good God, a strategist in homespun!" said Carew. "And right, maybe. You're no fool, are you, fellow?"

He paused, frowning, glancing left and right as though mentally scanning alternative routes. And inside Jane, a terrifying idea had formed. It was turning itself into words and thrusting upward toward her mouth. She was going to say the words.

She daren't.

She said them anyway. "Sir Peter, if you were on a less striking horse, and got rid of your helmet so that you resembled a groom, and if you separated from these friends and came along with me and Tim Snowe here and Dr. Spenlove, you'd look as if you were part of an escort for a respectable lady on her way to visit a sick relative somewhere…somewhere toward Weymouth."

"Mistress Allerbrook, you can't do that!" Spenlove gasped.

"He once helped me to escape from the court," said Jane. "Now I'll help him if he likes. I want to."

It was as good an excuse as any. She could scarcely say out loud, *I'll do it because I love him.*

"It's treason!" said Spenlove, horrified. "If you're caught…you could burn!"

"No," said Carew. "I'd say I'd deceived her, that she didn't know who I was, that she hired me really believing I was a groom. I'd invent a convincing story, never fear."

"I believe you would!" Jane said.

Privately, she was marvelling at herself. *So this is what love means. He's married (I wonder what she's like?). I can never marry him, never be with him as I want to be, never have his children. By helping him now, I put my life in danger. In such danger, at risk of such a hideous death…will he accept? Do I want him to accept?*

Carew, however, was shaking his head. "It's a splendid offer, and just for a moment—but no, I can't agree to it, Mistress Allerbrook. Turn around and go home and pretend you never saw me."

"Yes, indeed!" agreed Spenlove. "A woman can't be caught up in this."

"Several women already are, to the peril of their lives," said Jane. The words still seemed to be coming out of her mouth by themselves. "Queen Mary, the girl Lady Jane Grey in the Tower. The Princess Elizabeth—she's been entangled. You wrote to her, you said, Sir Peter."

"Wyatt wrote the letter. Yes. But…"

"But?"

"I have seen her," Carew said, "occasionally, at court, before Queen Mary sent her away. I admire her greatly but I don't *know* her, not personally. You, lady, are someone I *know.*"

One of Carew's men said, "Excuse me, sir, but there are soldiers in the distance, coming toward us. The sun's out over there. I saw it flash on helmets and pike heads."

"What?" Carew transferred his gaze to the distance and then swore. "You're right. Her soldiers—bound to be. If they find us, we're all dead."

Jane wheeled her pony to look back along the track over which she had ridden so recently. It led out of the woodland, vanished into a dip and reappeared beyond, a narrow red line slanting up a grassy hillside. A sizable troop of horsemen was riding down it.

Decisively Carew said, "I doubt they've seen us yet. We're in shadow. But they'll be face-to-face with us soon. We'll be completely hidden from each other for a few moments while they're in the dip, though. That's our chance to get into the wood. Keep still till I give the word."

They waited, motionless, until the approaching enemy had vanished from sight. "Now!" said Carew, and spurred in among the trees.

The rest of them did the same. There were ditches to either side and Jane's mare Hazelnut almost stumbled as she crossed it, but recovered herself in time and scrambled safely, snorting, into shelter. Once inside the wood, they followed Carew's low call, guiding their mounts toward him. He led them away from the path. The trees were mostly bare of leaves but still provided cover, since there were many oaks with wide girths as well as tangled bushes overgrown with ivy. Fifty yards in, the ground sloped down toward a stream. Carew brought them to the water and then stopped.

"We're well out of sight," he said quietly. "Now, absolute silence. Don't let any of the horses neigh."

"I can hear hooves," whispered Jane.

One of Carew's men, slipping noiselessly out of his saddle, handed his reins to a colleague and crept up the slope to crouch behind a massive oak at the top. The hoofbeats came nearer, rapidly. As they drew level with the place where Carew had led his companions into the wood, Hazelnut stiffened, ears pricked, and Carew, leaning down, gripped her nostrils, stifling an imminent whinny.

The riders were past. The hoofbeats receded. Carew's man slithered down and took back his horse's bridle. "Yes. Queen's soldiers," he said briefly. "The land's alive with them, I reckon. They're like bedbugs in a cheap inn."

"Sir Peter," said Jane, and was surprised at the strength in her own voice. "What do you think of my offer now? Will you ever get through, looking as you do? Send your men off—to somewhere safe if you can—and tell them to shed their helmets and pikes. Then change onto a less outstanding horse yourself and make for Weymouth in my company, as my groom. Maybe then you'll all live to escape."

He considered her gravely and then nodded "This has changed things. I agree. But I will never see you charged with treason. If necessary, I'll say I forced you to help me."

Spenlove and Tim both began to protest, but Jane turned on them angrily. "If you are afraid, then go home. I will ride with one groom—Sir Peter. Dr. Spenlove, you mean well but you have no authority to give me orders. I am going to Weymouth."

"And how far will that be?" asked Spenlove wearily.

"By the route we'll have to take, fifty miles or so if you're a bird and a good bit more on horseback," Carew told him.

Looking back, long afterward, Jane thought that in those days of constant upheavals, of first one and then another monarch on the throne, of risings and plots and smashed statues and riots in the street, a kind of madness was in the air. It travelled on the wind, an infection of craziness, blown from one place to another, taking hold of people's minds. The offer she had made was mad; Sir Peter Carew was just as insane to adopt it. Spenlove and Snowe, who might in calmer times have carried the day, might even have borne her off to safety by kindly but determined force, found themselves giving in.

Helmets, breastplates and pikes were abandoned in the wood. Fortunately Carew and his men were all wearing serviceable buff garments, and once he had shed his armour and weapons, Sir Peter made quite a convincing groom. He looked even more authentic when he had exchanged horses with one of his men, and mounted a ewe-necked brown mare. From his new saddle, he gave his friends their instructions. He had once said to Jane, *I always make sure I understand the world I'm living in and how to get from here to there. You never know when it may come in useful.* It was very clear that he knew Devon and Dorset as though they were his own home farm. He gave orders to his three men in brisk, staccato fashion.

"Join me in Weymouth if you can. I'll take at least two days to get there myself...my friend there is Robert Harte and he has a ship called the *Pretty Doe.* Go well inland...you know a place called Crewkerne? Pass to the north of it...don't go through *any* village or town...that means avoiding bridges...you'll have to ford the Umborne Brook and the River Yarty...the best ford over Umborne..."

His instructions finished, he wished his friends well and sent them on their way. After that, riding politely behind Jane and Dr. Spenlove, and alongside Tim Snowe on his brown pony, he began his own escape to Weymouth.

"We can't avoid villages," he said. "Not if we're escorting a respectable lady like Mistress Allerbrook. We must use inns and take a more southerly route than my men. That'll look more natural. We'll pick villages without gates and guards. We'll be two nights on the road at least. It gets dark so early."

Jane had no idea what the village was called where they made their first stop. They presented themselves as Mistress Hudd from Somerset, making a hurried journey to an ailing cousin, escorted by her cousin's chaplain, who had come from Weymouth to fetch her, and two grooms.

As Mistress Hudd, Jane adopted a marked accent and said it was lucky that she did not use the fashionable modern side-saddle, but rode astride with leggings to protect her calves from the stirrup leathers. "I'm a countrywoman," she told her companions. "Prosperous but rustic."

She and Spenlove supped together in a small private chamber while Tim and Carew, having looked after the horses, ate in the kitchen. Just as Jane and Spenlove had finished and the innkeeper's wife, candle in hand, was showing them where they would sleep, half a dozen soldiers arrived, wanting food and lodgings for the night. From the turn of the stairs, Spenlove glanced down at them.

"As well for you to keep out of the way, mistress," he said. "I hope that Tim and Sir Peter do the same."

Jane hoped so, too, and slept badly. Tim and Peter were sleeping in the loft over the stable, though. Only Spenlove was sharing accommodation with the soldiers. The chance of disaster should be small, but nevertheless, she was nervous. However, no raised voices, no clashing weapons or running feet disturbed her rest, and she woke in the morning to find the inn perfectly peaceful.

She breakfasted in her chamber, taking her time so that the soldiers would set off first, and was relieved when she heard them leaving. She put her belongings together, paid the landlord and found her companions in the stableyard. As they took the road again, Carew said, "The plan is changed. We'll go north of Crewkerne after all. Snowe and I found a few things out last night, Mistress Hudd, when we were talking to the soldiers."

"You…when you were doing *what?*" Jane, appalled, jerked in her saddle and almost jagged Hazelnut's mouth

"We offered to give them a hand, rubbing down their horses," Tim said cheerfully. "Sir Peter here can talk more rustic even than me. You should have heard him, sayin' he was called Jem and whistlin' while he picked out the hooves of the sergeant's gelding."

"Were you out of your minds? Sir Peter, they're *looking* for you!"

"Well, they didn't find me," said Carew, grinning. "And we got them talking. From what they said, there are more patrols out than I thought and the danger extends farther inland than I ever imagined. So we'll take a detour to the north after all. The farther we keep from the coast, the better, until we're well to the east."

"You *talked* to them!" Jane gasped. "You…you…"

"May have saved our skins," said Carew cheerfully.

"I pray it may be so," said Spenlove fervently. "I helped the soldiers say prayers this morning," he added. "We all prayed for your speedy capture, Sir Peter. But God hears the heart, not the voice. I hope!"

"If I'd known what was going on, I wouldn't have slept for one single minute last night!" Jane declared. "And I didn't sleep for many as it was!"

CHAPTER TWENTY-SEVEN
Once, and Once Only
1554

The journey seemed long, but the weather stayed dry and they met no more soldiers until they reached Weymouth, where gate guards challenged them. However, Jane's story of a visit to a gravely ill relative, told in a broad west country accent, was accepted. Her voice shook, but simple countrywomen were apt to be nervous when questioned by guards, who saw nothing odd about it.

Once they were past the guards, Carew took them straight to the harbour, said thankfully, "The *Pretty Doe*'s here, all right," and hailed her, whereupon a big fair man with an immense beard appeared on her deck and came ashore to meet them.

At close quarters he was older than he seemed at first, for there was silver in the beard and in the untidy hair blowing around his ears, but his stride was vigorous. Carew, leaping out of his saddle, ran to hug him. "Robert Harte! Of all men, you're the one I most wanted to find."

"You're in trouble, I hear." Harte grinned at Jane. "He always was. We were at sea together when King Henry was at war with France. Carew had command of a ship called the *Great Venetian*. Seven hundred tons she was, and she'd have gone down like a stone if ever she sank and it's a marvel she didn't, the chances this man took. The French ships were trying to harry ours. He used to pick out a victim and sail straight at her. I was his first mate and he frightened the life out of me."

"I never rammed one," said Carew. "They always got out of the way in time and I let them—I'd come at them from an angle that would force them right off course. Harte, I need to know…"

"It's all right. I rarely go to sea at this time of year, but the *Pretty Doe* can sail the moment the tide is right, and three friends of yours are aboard. You sent them on ahead, I think, after meeting this good lady on the road."

"They're here? They've found you?"

"They turned the horses loose last night, somewhere just east of here—got to the sea on foot, in the dark, stole a dinghy and sneaked into the harbour here before dawn. At first light they saw the name *Pretty Doe* on this ship's hull and then they saw me on deck and hailed me. I've been freshening up her paintwork and sleeping aboard. They're an enterprising trio! You must have braved the town guards."

"We did," said Jane. "But we told them I was visiting a sick cousin and these men are my escort."

"You'd better have a sick cousin to visit," said Carew. "I'll give you a note to take to another friend of mine in Weymouth. He'll let you stay in his house for a few days and he'll retire convincingly to bed if necessary. Show us aboard, if you will, Harte. How long before we can sail?"

"An hour and a half yet till the tide's high enough. The wind's right. I've wine and good food on the ship, if you want it."

"I'll have to part from you here." Peter turned to look at Jane, his dark eyes serious. "But will you take wine with me first? While I write the note for you, to your pretend cousin?"

He did not say aloud that he wished to be left alone with her, but Harte, glancing shrewdly from one to the other, saw to it that when they were all on the ship and had greeted Carew's three friends, Sir Peter and his female companion were shown to a well-furnished cabin, with a bed and seats and a table on which were writing materials, a jug of wine, two pewter goblets and a platter of cold meat and fresh bread.

Jane poured the wine and they sat at the table to eat and drink. Carew managed with one hand while the other wrote the letter to his friend in Weymouth. Then he folded and sealed it, handed it to Jane and said, "We have an hour. We may never meet again. This could be the last time we are ever in each other's company. You've been a good friend to me, Mistress Allerbrook, a shield against enemy swords. Why? Just because I once snatched you out of King Henry's grasp?"

It was an impossible question to answer truthfully. Just to be alone with him made her pulse uneven and she knew that her eyes were fixed on him much too intently. She was trying to memorize him, inch by inch, so that she would have that memory to look at when Sir Peter Carew himself was far away.

"I ought to be angry with you," she said. "For taking Stephen."

"He's old enough to make up his own mind. That nephew of yours is a man, my dear, not a boy."

"I've plans for him, if he survives," Jane said. "I hope to get both him and my own son into good households for a year or two, maybe with chances to attend the court. I thought Sir Edmund Flaxton might help. And then—Sir Peter, did you know that Dorothy Palmer was dead?"

"No, though I know it was expected."

"Well, she's gone and I'm looking after her little girl, Blanche, until Ralph comes home, if he ever does! Blanche will be beautiful one day and she's an heiress. When she's old enough, she and Stephen might make a match of it. It would provide for him. He'll have nothing otherwise."

Carew paused before he answered and when he did, the words fell into a curious pool of quietness between them. "I hope there'll be affection between them, as well," he said.

The ship rocked a little. "The tide's rising," he said. "Our time's growing short. Don't underestimate affection in marriage, Jane."

Carefully she said, "I hope that your own marriage is happy."

"It's successful, though we've often been apart. Margaret is nobly born and wealthy. She's the daughter of a knight and the widow of a baron. She's very dignified, very honourable, very loyal. We have never quarrelled in any way. I haven't a word of complaint about Margaret."

"Are there any children?"

"No. It seems that God has not blessed her with fertility."

"I am sorry. Is she beautiful?" Jane asked.

"She's handsome enough. You're the one who's beautiful, Jane. You're lovely, and so wholesome. There's not a flaw in your skin. Your hair has the gloss of a beechnut washed by the dew. Your eyes are soft, and they shine. Are they shining for me?"

Jane, her pulse now thumping wildly, could not answer.

"Time's going," Carew said. "And we're wasting it, talking about Stephen and Blanche and Margaret. Why *did* you help me? Just gratitude? Or devotion to the Protestant cause? Or because you love me?"

One had one's dignity. "How can I love you? I hardly know you. I never saw you after you brought me back from court, until you rode in out of nowhere just before Christmas, raising men for a rebellion!"

"I think," said Carew, "that you fell in love with me on the ride home from court. I saw it in your face. I saw it again when I came to Allerbrook before Christmas. But…"

"I would never have made a suitable bride." She tried to quell that clamouring pulse and speak dispassionately, but her voice shook all the same. She raised her chin and held on determinedly to that unsteady dignity. "No title and no dowry."

"And you resent being thought unworthy for such reasons? I'm not surprised. And yet you helped me, at great risk to yourself. My dear Jane."

He rose, came to her, raised her to her feet, put his arms around her and then, as he had done in the hall at Allerbrook, he put his mouth on hers and any attempt to remain aloof and dignified was wiped out. Her body paid not the slightest attention. Without her permission it moulded itself to him; without her consent, her mouth opened under his.

When at last the kiss ended, he did not let her go. Instead, he said, "Is this what you want, Jane? Is this how I can repay you? I would be happy if so, for I have never desired a woman in my life as much as I desire you now. And it may be our only chance. It may be once, and once only. Will you seize the day? It's for you to say, not for me."

The bed was inviting, with a moleskin coverlet and smooth linen, a feather mattress and damask hangings of grey-green and soft rose. Jane did not afterward remember whether she had said *yes* to him in words, nor exactly how they came to be lying on the coverlet, nor how they shed their clothes. She heard herself, for the first time ever, use his name without any title. Over and over again she whispered, "Peter!" in gratitude and delight, knowing that a hunger many years old was at last to be satisfied, and a long emptiness filled.

It was so different from anything she had known with Harry. With Harry she had endured, obeyed and gone through the motions of affection, but after the first time, which had been uncomfortable though not as bad as she had feared, the business had been simply null, painless, but without any pleasure and usually performed when she was exhausted and longing for sleep. The strange yearning which sometimes afflicted her on languorous summer nights, after Harry's illness had ended lovemaking, had told her that something more was possible, something beyond her experience, but only now did she discover what it was.

This…it was as though her body were a shore, over which a slow tide of joy was rising, gathering strength as it advanced. At the end, it was as though some huge and astoundingly warm breaker had crashed over her and she was left throbbing with the reverberation of it, drenched in happiness. Soaked in sweat and aglow, from her damp, disordered hair to her very toes.

Presently he said, "I wish we could lie in each other's arms forever, but we can't. You must dress, and make yourself tidy enough to deceive your groom and your chaplain into thinking that all we've done is talk, and then go ashore with the letter I gave you. Once and once only, but oh, Jane, I will never forget it."

"Nor I. Nor I."

He sat up sharply. "Jane, if anything happens...as a result of this..."

"I will have to find myself another Harry Hudd," said Jane.

"Ralph Palmer told me about him. Neither of us approved. I'll write you another note, for my cousin, Thomas Carew of Haccombe, in Devon. Carews look after their kin. If you conceive, he'll see someone in my family gives the baby a home. Have the child somewhere where you're not known. Or you might marry Ralph Palmer." He was dressing and reaching for the inkstand simultaneously. "I know he likes you and he's my friend and no prude. He'd probably oblige. I'd be jealous, but it might be an answer."

"I would never marry Ralph," said Jane. "I knew that even before today. Now that I truly know the difference between you, I know it twice over. I'll take the note, just in case. Thank you. God go with you, Peter."

"And with you."

She did not go at once to the home of Peter's friend in the town but waited on the quay until the *Pretty Doe* sailed and stood there to watch the vessel put out to sea. It hurt. It astounded her how deep and awful the hurt was. It was almost physical, a dragging misery in her very guts. It was also a shadow of the long loneliness to come. He would not return to her.

He probably did love her, she thought, as much as he could love any woman. But for all his talk of jealousy, she knew he did not feel anything like the love and need she felt for him. The very way he had spoken of his marriage, the way he had parted from her, kindly but without anything like the grief she felt, had told her the truth. He was the kind of man who kept love in a separate compartment, while practical living, war and adventure and advantageous marriage were on the other side of a dividing wall.

And she must endure in silence. She could confide in no one. If she cried, she must do so secretly. Unless, of course, there was a baby and she had to go to his family, and they were not likely to show her much sympathy.

That, as it turned out, was not required of her. She knew two days later that there would be no child. It was a great relief. As well as a sorrow.

CHAPTER TWENTY-EIGHT
Blanche in Bloom
1554

"When the cows are in milk again," Jane said to Blanche as she showed her around the dairy, "I'll teach you to make clotted cream. You were never shown at home?"

"No." Blanche shook her head. "The chaplain taught me reading and writing and Latin, too, because Mother said that these days, ladies are supposed to know some Latin. Embroidery, music and dancing, things like that, she taught me herself. But I'd like to learn dairy work."

"And so you shall. And you'll go on with the other things. Your father would want that. Dr. Spenlove will study with you and I can teach you the rest—that is, if you stay here."

"I'd like to stay. I don't miss my mother much," said Blanche sadly, looking down at her feet. "Is that very wrong?"

"Well…" Remembering what Dorothy had been like, Jane found this difficult to answer. "Many people would be upset to hear you say so, so perhaps you shouldn't. She was very ill, you know. You can say that her sickness made you unhappy, and you are glad she isn't suffering anymore."

"Thank you. I'll do that," said Blanche, brightening.

She was a very pretty child with no trace of Dorothy's sullenness, and she was slender where Dorothy at her age had already been plump. She had had smallpox at one time, but it had left only a few tiny marks near her hairline and her skin was otherwise clear.

Her hair was a pleasing fawn colour, richer than Dorothy's mouse, and her eyes were beautiful. Dorothy's had been an indeterminate grey and Ralph's were dark, but Blanche's eyes were the subtle green-brown shade known as hazel. The effect was changeable—sometimes dark, sometimes a shifting green like the light under the trees in Allerbrook combe in summer. When she laughed, they sparkled like sunshine through leaves. But she didn't laugh as often as a child should. Jane thought it a pity.

Dr. Spenlove had noticed Blanche's eyes. He had now completed his second set of handwritten and illuminated Gospels, for another Taunton gentleman who loved the beauty of such manuscripts. Having done so, he asked if he might make a miniature portrait of Blanche. "I make tiny drawings for my illuminated capital letters and borders. I'd like to try my hand at a portrait and Blanche would be a charming subject." He had just finished the miniature, producing an excellent likeness, delicately drawn and painted. He had even caught the rare sparkle of laughter in those eyes.

In time, Jane hoped, it would appear more often. Blanche had probably not had an easy, certainly not a frivolous, childhood. She danced well, but seemed to regard it as just another accomplishment she was expected to acquire, like embroidery stitches and Latin grammar. She was shy and very well behaved. Spenlove had remarked that the child often seemed older than her years.

Jane sometimes felt older than her own years. For there was still no news of either Ralph Palmer or Stephen. Whatever had happened about the intended rebellion, no word had found its way to Allerbrook.

The dairy was cold. "We shall have snow by tomorrow," she said. "Come back to the hall—it's warmer there."

Peggy was sitting by the hearth with Lisa. Since Christmas, Peggy had slowed down a great deal and Jane had told her to take her ease; Letty and Beth were there to do most of the work. Letty, though pockmarks were common enough and she was not as unattractive as she thought, had resisted all approaches, while Beth had married one of the Searle family two years ago, but had lost her husband to a winter fever and had not remarried. Lisa was staying on as well, to help out with sewing. There was always plenty of that. "The house isn't short of hands," Jane had said, reassuring Peggy. "You'll always have a place here."

Lisa was leaning forward to put more wood on the fire as Jane and Blanche came in, and Jane, glancing at the wood basket by the hearth, saw that it needed replenishing. Peggy, whose eyesight was still healthy enough, saw the glance and laughed.

"There's more wood bein' chopped. See out of the window."

Jane went to look and saw Tobias and Tim Snowe's eldest son, twelve-year-old Paul, pulling branches out of the woodshed and hacking them into convenient sizes. Every autumn, branches were cut in the woods of the combe and stacked in the shed to dry. "Excellent," said Jane. "We can be generous with the fuel. Blanche, if you take a candle and sit by a window, you can still be warm but you'll have light enough to practise your embroidery."

"My workbasket is in the parlour," Blanche said. "I'll fetch it."

"She's a sweet-natured child. Nothing like her mother," Lisa said, watching her go.

"Was Dorothy very difficult?" Jane asked. "I've never discussed her with you, but I imagine caring for her wasn't easy."

"No, it wasn't," said Lisa truthfully. "But she was a sick woman the last couple of years. She suffered. It was bad for the child to see it. She'll blossom here, given time."

"Yes, indeed. I've been thinking of her future. If—"

"Mistress Allerbrook!" Blanche, without her workbasket, came tearing down the steps from the parlour. "There's someone coming! I saw him from the parlour window! He's wearing a helmet and he's on foot and Tobias and Paul are running to meet him!"

"What?" Jane made for the yard. Tobias and Paul were coming across it, helping another man, who could only walk slowly and whose cloak seemed to hang awkwardly over his left arm. "Stephen!" Jane gasped.

"Hullo," said Stephen. "Sorry to come back like this. Wounded, I'm afraid."

"Bring him into the hall!" said Jane.

When they got him inside and onto a settle, Jane lifted the cloak away and saw that his left arm was awkwardly bound across his chest on top of a stained breastplate with some alarming scratches on it.

"What happened?" she said.

"I've been chased," he said. "The queen's men are everywhere. It's all over. Thomas Wyatt's in the Tower. Lady Jane Grey's been beheaded—the queen won't let anyone live who might be a focus for another rebellion. Her husband, Guilford Dudley, he's been beheaded, too. Lady Jane's father, he's to go the same way, for supporting Wyatt. I was with Wyatt— he was taken near London. I got away. So did others, but…"

His voice faded and his eyes closed. His head sagged forward as though the helmet were too heavy. Jane removed it and then gently unwound the wrappings around his left forearm, uncovering an ugly slash from the elbow almost to the wrist. It was on the outer side and had not touched an artery, but it was inflamed and suppurating. What could be seen of his face, under several days' growth of beard, was grey-tinged with a flushed patch on each cheekbone.

"I'll get some medicines for him," said Peggy. "Come, Blanche. You can learn something about remedies. And he'll need hot water, too."

"Thought I'd got away," Stephen said, opening his eyes. "Tried to avoid towns. But I ran into a squad of local soldiers near Taunton, and they were after me at once. A man with armour on, scurrying along with his back to London—he's a suspicious object."

"Did they know what had happened in London?" Tobias asked, puzzled. "Did they know fugitives would come this way? But how?"

"Royal messengers ride like demons and every fair-sized town has an innkeeper paid to keep a fresh horse or two in his stable. County towns have their own teams of messengers. News can spread fast."

Stephen closed his eyes again, but went on talking. "Long before I got to Somerset, it was known there'd been west-countrymen with Wyatt, and that some of them had got away. I fought my way free of the soldiers near Taunton— that's where I got wounded. But they wounded Ginger, too.

He got me to safety, clever little pony, but he fell down under me half an hour later. He's dead. That was yesterday, in the evening. I walked on through the night. I haven't eaten since midday yesterday…."

Lisa and Peggy arrived with steaming water, herbal ointment and a feverfew tincture. "Where's Blanche?" Jane asked.

"Tearing up an old sheet for bandages," said Peggy. "Let me see that wound."

"It's a wonder I got here," Stephen said. "Is there any news of Peter Carew?"

"He escaped to France," said Jane briefly.

"Good." He didn't ask how she knew. "The men I fought… they might track me here. Can you hide me? I shouldn't have come home—put you in danger—but I felt so ill."

"Do these soldiers know your name?" Tobias sounded remarkably firm and more grown-up than his real age of twelve. "Would they recognize your face?"

"Doubt it. They were strangers. Anyhow, helmets change faces and I can shave this beard off. But they do know they wounded me."

"You mustn't be caught," said Tobias. "Yes, you've put us in danger, but here you are. We'll hide you somehow. We'll find a way."

"There's one more thing," said Stephen. He moved sharply as Jane bathed his arm, and sweat broke out on his forehead.

"The sooner you're in bed, the better," she said.

"There's *one more thing*. It's Ralph Palmer. Must tell you before Blanche comes back. He's dead. He was with me when I fled from London. We had money. We bought food in small villages and slept mostly in barns. But we met trouble just as we came down off Salisbury Plain. We were ambushed in some woodland. We fought our way out, but a musket shot got Palmer and he fell out of his saddle…."

"You left him?" said Tobias sharply.

"*No.* I know what you're thinking, but I never held Palmer responsible for my mother's death. We'd been comrades, fighting side by side. Ginger was a steady pony but he bolted then…frightened…all too much for him…I swear I didn't abandon Ralph Palmer."

He swallowed and then said, "I turned back when I'd got Ginger under control. I thought they'd simply arrest him and perhaps I could follow and rescue him…but I found him. Dead. Hanging from a tree. Awful musket wound in his side. I suppose they reckoned he wouldn't last, so there was no point in keeping him captive and he'd thrown a lot of insults at them, too, during the skirmish. They'd strung him up and left him. He's dead, and when I met that other lot of soldiers at Taunton, I had to fight my way out on my own. I could have done with Ralph's swordarm there."

There was a silence, while Jane, horrified and anguished, tried to imagine Ralph's last moments. Seized, roped, his life suddenly at an end. Poor Ralph, terrified, probably in great pain from his wound, hardly able to believe what was happening to him, and then left swinging, choking…

Ralph. He had used Sybil so badly that if Stephen really had deserted him, it would have been understandable. He had made unforgivable approaches to Jane herself. He had stirred her against her will, he had…

Been known to her all her life. He was Ralph. Aloud, as though he were there and she were speaking to him, she said, "I will look after Blanche. I promise."

"Don't tell Blanche what happened to him," said Stephen. "Say he fell in London, with Wyatt. It's kinder."

"I agree," said Jane.

Blanche, when they told her that her father was dead, wept bitterly. Dr. Spenlove was fetched from his room, where he had been reading, and offered her the consolation of prayer. "We are allowed to pray for the dead, now that the laws have been changed," he said.

Blanche grew calmer, but the next day, when the household met in the chapel for the early Mass that Dr. Spenlove now held each morning, Lisa said worriedly that the child was still abed because she hadn't slept. "I think she cried all night. I told her to rest. How is Master Stephen?"

"Improving, I think," Jane said. "And I've posted Paul Snowe on top of the tower to watch for soldiers. If any come this way, I want to know in good time. If they're looking for a wounded man and they find one here…! We'll have to think of something, but God alone knows what!"

After Mass, while breakfast was being prepared, Jane and Lisa dressed Stephen's arm again. His fever seemed to be down, but he was clearly still very unwell. Blanche had come downstairs by then. She looked pale and tired, but she apologized for missing Mass and asked after Stephen's health.

Jane began to tell her, but before she was half finished, Paul Snowe came down from the tower at a run. "There's men on horses comin' over the moor from Withypool way. Air's clear, though there's snow on the wind. It's that dark to the north."

"He'd best take to the moor," said Tim. Paul had fetched his father, who had come inside to join them.

"A sick man can't hide on the moor in a snowstorm!" said Jane, horrified. "And I think there's going to be one."

"I've an idea. He could have got a slash like that by
chopping wood," said Tobias. "We've got to say he's been
here all the time and the wound's an accident, the sort that
happens on farms. What else can we do?" he added in a dis-
gusted voice.

Blanche timidly said, "The room he's in has those green
curtains around the bed, but your bedcurtains, Mistress Allerbrook, are crimson."

They all looked at her in astonishment. "What I mean
is…well…" said Blanche, and then turned scarlet and lost
herself in stammering.

"Have you lost your wits, child?" demanded Lisa indignantly. "Jabbering about bedcurtains—what's wrong with
you?"

Dr. Spenlove said, "One moment. Blanche, just put your
thoughts in order. You've had an idea, haven't you? Well, tell
us. Even if it's not a good idea, no one will be cross with
you. Come, now."

"When I had smallpox three years ago," said Blanche, "I
was put in a bed with crimson hangings. The physician said
that would bring out the spots and the poison would come
out with them, and with care, I still might not be badly
scarred—and I wasn't. I just thought…"

A few moments later, when Blanche had finished her
timid explanation, Jane said, "In North Molton Master
Grede had a similar idea as a way of keeping the crowd from
finding me. Blanche, my child, we've hoped you would
blossom in our care. You're in bloom now, my dear!"

"Blanche," said Jane, "cry for your father if you like, but
pretend the tears are for Stephen." Jane was finding in herself
a surprising degree of generalship. "We'll have the story of

the accident with the chopper as a second line of defence," she said. "It could easily happen if a man were beginning to feel ill."

"We need a bloodstained axe blade," Tobias said. "I'll see to that." And he added, surprisingly, "Chicken for dinner?"

"Well done, Toby," said Jane. "That shows spirit."

"We'd better explain to Stephen," Spenlove said.

Stephen greeted Blanche's idea with relief. "It's better than lying out in the heather! Or being dragged out of a clothespress or a hayloft! Thank God Tim managed to clean my beard off last night."

"Give me ten minutes," said Spenlove, "and I'll make Master Stephen look like nothing on earth. I'll get my paints."

CHAPTER TWENTY-NINE
To Live in Peace
1554

aptain Herbert Clifton of the Taunton Militia was in a disgruntled mood. If the messengers from London were right, southwest England was swarming with stray fugitives from the queen's justice, but the only miscreant he'd even glimpsed had cut his way out through Clifton and six troopers and vanished into the dusk. A little later, trying to give chase through a wood in the hope of catching the fellow before it was too dark to see a hand before a man's face, they'd found a dead pony which was surely his, lying in a pool of blood from a sword slash in its belly.

Wanting to look closely at the animal, though, in case it needed to be released from pain and also to ascertain that it really had belonged to their quarry, he dismounted and called for a light. Someone produced a tinderbox and lit a flare for him. Kneeling beside the pony, he saw that it was dead and no longer suffering, for which he was glad. Then he saw that it was a moor pony with a brand mark on one haunch—two parallel lines and a slanting line through them. Clifton was Somerset born. He had never visited Allerbrook or met anyone who lived there, but he knew every brand mark on the moor.

It proved nothing, of course. The pony could have changed hands half a dozen times since it was taken from its herd, but it was a starting point. "We make for Exmoor and a place called Allerbrook," he said as he got to his feet. "Our man must be making for somewhere, and that just could be the place. We'll start first thing in the morning."

He searched the hamlets along the way, which held the pursuit up to some extent, but by the second morning he and his men had reached Clicket. Here he became more thorough and began by investigating Clicket Hall, where the butler cooperated with the utmost grace and nothing of interest was discovered. He then took his men up to Rixons, where the Haywards were sullen but seemed unfeignedly astonished by the intrusion. He told his men not to do too much damage.

When Rixons yielded nothing, they made for the big house above it.

Snow began to fall as they rode in. The place seemed orderly, with poultry and animals all shut inside as they should be in such weather. The yard was untidy, though— God's teeth, they'd left a pile of chopped firewood out in the snow and a perfectly good chopper on top of it, getting rusty. Could that be a sign of disturbance—a task interrupted by the arrival of a fugitive, perhaps? He'd soon find out.

Dismounting, he handed his reins to the nearest man and advanced to hammer on the iron-studded front door. There was a delay before it was finally opened by a middle-aged priest who stood nervously fingering his pectoral cross and looking at Clifton in a distracted fashion.

"I am Captain Herbert Clifton, Taunton Militia. We are searching for a fugitive believed to have come this way. This is Allerbrook House?"

"Yes. That's right."

"I have a warrant entitling me to search any premises where such fugitives may be hidden. The man we are looking for had a pony bearing the Allerbrook brand. We must search your house and outhouses forthwith."

"I'll have to ask."

"You will not have to ask. I said I have a warrant." He glanced over his shoulder and called to his men to find a barn for the horses and search the outhouses. "And then follow me inside. You!" He turned back to the priest. "What's your name?"

"Spenlove. Dr. Amyas Spenlove. I'm the chaplain here. But we're all in confusion just now and…"

"Are you, indeed? Well, you'll be in even worse confusion if you don't stand aside and admit me into the house at once. You may announce me to your master."

"It's Mistress Allerbrook, Captain. She is a widowed lady."

"Then take me to her."

Spenlove shrugged and led the way into a panelled hall, with a good fire in the hearth and plenty of rushes on the floor. And a distracted air.

For one thing, though the morning was well advanced, there were still people around what was presumably the breakfast table. There were three women servants, one of them apparently a nurse or tirewoman, since she was sitting protectively beside a girl child who seemed to have been crying. There were two youths, one dressed like a son of the house and one like a groom, and an older man, very like the young groom, and probably his father.

And just crossing the room with a steaming bowl of something on a tray was a lady wearing a plain dark dress and no cap at all on her brown hair, which was knotted up so roughly that some of it had slipped loose and was trailing over her shoulder.

"This is Captain Clifton, from Taunton, m'am" said the chaplain in a flurried way. "He has soldiers with him. They're searching for fugitives. It will be something to do with this Wyatt rebellion, I suppose."

"We're behind the times with the news here," said the lady. "We leave the farm so rarely in winter. I am Jane Allerbrook. Why have you come here?"

"Wyatt has been taken, but some of his followers got away. We're chasing a fugitive who was wounded in the left arm when we tried to seize him. He escaped us, but his pony was killed and bore the Allerbrook brand."

"Indeed? And you come here on that account? We often let our colts run on the moor till they're old enough to be broken to saddle and sold as riding ponies. My late brother Francis said we made more money from them that way. You'll find ponies bearing our brand all over Somerset. Excuse me, please. I must take this to my nephew. He is sick."

"Ill?" said Clifton sharply.

"Yes, very," Jane told him with equal sharpness. "You may see him if you wish, but I trust you have had the smallpox. If you have not, then you had best be careful."

"I haven't. Nor have any of my men, to my knowledge." Clifton had paled. An uncle of his had died from the pox, and had caught it simply by entering a house where someone was abed with it. "You are sure it is smallpox?" he said.

"I fear so, and we are all very concerned. I want him to eat this broth if he can. I am going up to him now."

"I can't send my men to do what I dare not," said Clifton, "and pox or no pox, this house must be searched. I must see this nephew of yours."

"Then you had better come with me now," said Jane. "Beth, go to the kitchen and soak a cloth in herbal water—use the mixture in the jar at the end of the top shelf. Captain Clifton can hold it to his nose and mouth for protection."

Clifton, with a wet and astringently scented cloth clutched to his nose, accompanied his hostess upstairs and was led to a large bedchamber. Inside was a bed with crimson curtains, drawn close. A good fire blazed in the hearth and because the day was now becoming murky, there were candles. Jane, telling him to stay in the doorway, went into the room, drew the bed-curtains back and held a candle where the light could fall on the patient's face. Clifton took one appalled look and then retreated.

He went straight down to the yard, told his men to stay out there but to look down the well in case they found anything suspicious dangling in it, such as a helmet and breastplate in a bucket, and then searched the rest of the house himself.

In the kitchen an old woman he hadn't seen before was plucking a chicken, and cursed him because he threw the door open too roughly and the draught sent feathers flying. After that he found a dairy, a cider press, a small family chapel very properly appointed with crucifix, candles and a statue of the Virgin; a ladies' parlour containing nothing more suspicious than a lute and two workbaskets; a study where there was a desk with an abacus; some bedchambers used and unused; a privy and a spartan-looking chamber which evidently belonged to the chaplain.

He did not find any wounded fugitives and was very aware of the fact that to the inhabitants of the house, he was a thoroughgoing nuisance.

He apologized for the inconvenience caused, and left.

"It's over," said Lisa, watching Clifton and his men ride off.

"Don't be too sure," said Spenlove shrewdly. "We wait awhile."

With his companions, Clifton went on through the steadily falling snow, over the ridge to Hannacombes, where, once more, he found nothing. He gnawed his lip, overcome by misgiving. He had heard of people being fooled by the pretence of disease. He hated the thought of going back, hated the very idea of looking at that sick man again, but just in case…

"The people at Rixons said that as well as this place, there's one more farm on this estate," he said to his men. "Over the other side of the combe. Go and search it. I'm going back to Allerbrook House."

Spenlove admitted him with a look of sheer exasperation. "You've been gone only two hours. What can you want with us now? Haven't we trouble enough without all this?"

"I regret it," said Clifton stiffly, pushing his way inside and stamping the snow off his riding boots, "but I wish to see your sick man—the nephew of your mistress, I believe—once again. Please show me to his room."

"Only with the mistress's consent. She is in the hall. I'll call her."

Once again Jane—in stony silence and this time without offering him any perfumed cloths—led the unwelcome visitor up the stairs to the room with the crimson-hung bed.

The patient moaned in protest when she opened the bed-curtains and in a hoarse voice begged for water. She gave him some from a flask at the bedside. His right hand emerged from the covers to take it and the back of the hand, too, was dotted with pustules. Clifton once more retreated in haste.

"I am sorry," he said over his shoulder as Jane followed him down the stairs. "I will not trouble you again."

At the threshold he paused to make a bow to her and Jane, looking at him tiredly, said, "Do you not know, Captain, that all most people really want is to live in peace? We wish the laws would stop changing, so that we knew for sure how we should worship. We want to raise our crops and our children, conduct business, enjoy festivals, celebrate marriages, baptize our babies and mourn our dead. Rebellions happen because we grow weary of never being let alone."

"Madam, the queen, and no doubt her prospective husband, too, wish all people not only to have happy lives but the promise of heaven for their souls."

"I'm sure they do. I rather wish they would leave our souls to us. Now, Captain, please go away and don't come back. I hope you don't take the pox. I wouldn't wish that on anyone. But I would rather not set eyes on you again. Ever."

"Will he stay away this time, do you think?" she asked Spenlove when, once more, the invader had gone.

"I hope so, but we'd better wait till tomorrow. Master Stephen must stay abed, anyway."

They went together up to what had been Jane's room until they'd moved Stephen into it because it was easier than exchanging the bedhangings.

"For the love of heaven," said Stephen, "can I have the curtains drawn back? I'm so *hot*. I'm not feverish now—it's that huge fire."

"You're luckier than Clifton is," Spenlove said. "He's ridden off into a snowstorm. He's going to Greys now, I gather. They'll probably be saddled with him until the snow goes away. Let me have a look at your smallpox rash, though—just in case he makes a third visit."

"You look horrible, Stephen," Jane remarked. "I congratulate you, Dr. Spenlove. How did you do it?"

"My pigments are good," said Spenlove. "And I'm used to getting the results I want, after all."

He had made a most artistic job of Stephen's face, strewing it with a realistic set of smallpox spots, and he had also adorned the backs of Stephen's hands and added, for good measure, a few more spots on his chest, even though his bedgown hid them. Most were simply red, but some had yellowish centres, as though they were filled with pus, and a few looked as though pus was dribbling from them. Even at close quarters, the impression was both convincing and revolting.

"I've hidden my paints," Spenlove told him. "Just in case they gave our good captain ideas. I made sure they were all locked in their cupboard, and I put a cloth over my paint-stained old table and set a statuette on top. It's the one Father Drew gave me at Christmas."

Stephen moved uncomfortably. "It was a good idea to hide my breastplate inside this mattress, but it's a nasty hard thing to lie on. What did you do with my helmet?"

"It fits neatly into one of our cauldrons," said Jane. "I put it inside and tipped a lot of pottage in on top. It's bubbling away now. We shan't eat the pottage—the pigs can have it."

Stephen began to laugh. "I'd no weapons when I came home. I had a pike, but I lost it in that last fight. What would you have done with that?"

"Pushed it up a chimney, I expect," Jane said. "He didn't

look up any chimneys. But I heard him tell his men to look in the well."

"Cunning bastard," said Stephen. "I wonder if he *will* come back a third time?"

"He'll find everything just as he found it before," Spenlove said.

Jane gave him a grateful smile. Dear Spenlove. She might well owe to him the fact that Allerbrook was still hers. She'd never know, because he wouldn't tell her and she would never ask.

Spenlove smiled back at her, happy to have defended not only her nephew but Jane herself, happy that he had once broken the law to keep Allerbrook safe for her. He had a curious idea that there had been something between her and Peter Carew. On board the *Pretty Doe,* she had been alone with Carew for over an hour and she had emerged—transfigured. Well, he would never speak of his guess. He was growing old and he was celibate, but he was glad that, after all, he knew what it was like to fall in love.

Captain Clifton did in fact consider going back for a third time, but Dr. Spenlove had painted Stephen's face extremely well. The captain's nerve failed him. In fact, it was nearly a month before he stopped examining himself every morning to see if he had come out in spots.

CHAPTER THIRTY
To Love at Will
1560

"*I* like April," said Blanche. "The skylarks are singing and you can hear the lambs bleating miles away and the flies aren't a nuisance yet and even the wind isn't cold."

She and Tobias were on the ridge above Allerbrook, walking toward the barrow. She turned to him, smiling.

"You've been home from London since last December, but somehow I haven't yet told you how much we all missed you. We did, you know."

"I was glad to be back," Tobias said. He looked at her, returning her smile. It was six years now since a solemn little girl named Blanche had astonished them all by inventing the scheme that saved the life of Stephen Sweetwater. She was a little girl no longer, but had grown into a pretty young woman, who had a clever way with her hair and clothes. She had herself put the line of embroidery around the front of her cap, and she had skilfully trained a curl of light brown hair to fall a little way over her forehead, to hide the very few traces of childhood smallpox.

Much else had happened in those six years, too, to him and to Stephen. They were travelled young men now, who had seen the royal court and crossed the channel to visit France.

"It was interesting, seeing other places," he said, "and I liked the Flaxton family, but I was happy when Mother wrote saying that I'd had enough polishing and asking me to come home and take charge of Allerbrook."

"I hardly knew you when you rode in," Blanche said. "You looked so smart, and you had a goshawk! I felt shy with you. I think that's why we haven't talked together very much. Today, when you asked me to walk, I wondered what I'd find to say!"

Toby laughed. "I've noticed how elusive you are, always either in the dairy or else earnestly embroidering. But I'm just the same old Tobias at heart. I've got velvet doublets and fashionable ruffs, but they're all put away. You haven't noticed me wearing finery, have you? I've learned about falconry but I don't call it sport—just a way of bringing down game for the table. I'm still Tobias, even though Sir Giles Flaxton took me to the court of Queen Elizabeth."

"Did you see her?" Blanche asked. "What is she like?"

"She's young, but there's something frightening about her," said Tobias thoughtfully. "A kind of glitter…and a way of compelling people to do her will. She gives an order and even the most powerful courtiers jump. She is determined to swing the whole country back to the Protestant faith, you know."

"That's a good thing. Isn't it?" Blanche sounded worried. "I miss the Mass and the incense," she said. "But still, when I think of the things that happened in Queen Mary's reign…"

They were both silent, thinking of the horror that had

hung over the land in those days, which were still so recent. Mary's laws had condemned over three hundred of her own subjects to death by fire, only for the crime of disagreeing with her in matters of faith.

Blanche shivered. "There was a man, John Hooper, who was once in the abbey at Cleeve. After the abbey was closed he went out into the world and became a bishop. Anyway, he turned away from the old faith and Queen Mary had him burned. It must be such a terrible way to die. And there was Andrew Shearer, in Minehead, and Master Luke Palmer only escaped because he died in his bed before he could be arrested. There was a warrant out for his arrest on a heresy charge. And he was eighty years old!" said Blanche.

"Really? I didn't know about Palmer. He was lucky," Tobias said soberly. "But Hooper and Shearer…poor devils. I heard about Hooper through a proclamation, and Mother wrote to me about Shearer. It happened only just after she sent Stephen and me to London. He'd been making public speeches against the old faith—gathering crowds in the middle of Minehead and shouting his head off. Stupid of him! But yes, it was a vile way to die. Mother said Tim Snowe rode over the shoulder of Dunkery hill that day, and swears he saw the smoke rising in the distance. Does Stephen know?"

"Yes," said Blanche. "Mistress Allerbrook wrote to him, too, because she said he'd be sure to hear it from someone anyway when he came home. He wrote back that Master Shearer had scarcely acknowledged him and meant nothing to him, but when he came back and the Hannacombes asked us all to dine, by way of welcoming him home, Will Hannacombe mentioned Shearer. He meant no harm—he was just talking about the past and saying he'd heard that Mistress Shearer had married again. But I saw Stephen's face go hard and shut-in. I think he minds a good deal. No one wants those days back again."

"But it doesn't have to be like that, Blanche. I have visited France," Tobias said, "and seen the young king and queen there. They are Catholic, naturally, but I don't believe either of them would wish to persecute those who think differently from themselves. Young Queen Mary—she's queen of Scotland as well as France—no one could be sweeter. Did you know that many Catholics believe she is England's rightful queen, as well? They say that King Henry and Anne Boleyn were never lawfully married, so that Elizabeth is only a love child. But Mary would never harm anyone—I'm sure of it. Couldn't a nation be led back to the old faith, without being terrified into it? I miss the old rituals, you know, just like you."

"It's all so confusing," Blanche said with a sigh.

"Don't trouble yourself over it. Live your own quiet life. If that's what you want. Or do you wish that you, too, could go away to another household, or go travelling? Have you been happy with us?"

"I have been happy," said Blanche, "and fortunate. Your mother has been so kind. She has treated me like a daughter, though I'm only a penniless orphan now."

"Don't talk of yourself like that. You are *Blanche,*" said Tobias indignantly.

"My father was never tried or condemned for being part of Wyatt's rebellion," said Blanche sadly, "but all my lands were confiscated just the same. I really am penniless, whatever you may say. But at least it meant that Mistress Allerbrook could be my guardian and the authorities didn't interfere. She says she'll plan a happy marriage for me one day. I hope not too soon, though. I'll have to leave Allerbrook then."

Tobias glanced quickly at her, but her face was turned away from him, looking toward the sea.

"Stephen hasn't changed much," he said, changing the subject. "He was always one to want adventure. I've a feeling that he won't stay here long."

"I know. He came home two weeks before you did—in November—and he was hardly back before he got that look of his again, as if he were gazing toward a distant horizon and wishing he could set off for it."

"Yes, that's Stephen! How old is he now? He's older than I am. I'm not quite nineteen. He must be…oh…about twenty-five. Here's the barrow." He held out a hand to her. "Let's climb it."

Up on the barrow the wind was stronger, whisking Blanche's skirts about. The day was clear, too clear; the horizon of the sea was a hard line and usually that meant rain was coming. But for the moment it was sunny and dry. Three young stags, still carrying last season's antlers, started up from behind a gorse patch farther along the ridge and stood staring, poised for flight, at the human figures outlined against the sky.

"Look, deer," Blanche said, and then, in practical tones, "I hope they don't get into the wheat again this year. They're so greedy."

"There's a kestrel," said Tobias, looking upward and narrowing his eyes against the light. "See it? Hovering over the farmland. Kestrels can be greedy, too. Once when I was out on the moor with our sheep, I saw one try to snatch a weasel."

"It couldn't! A kestrel wouldn't be big enough. They just seize mice and things like that."

"It wasn't big enough," Tobias agreed. "It got the weasel a few feet off the ground and then the weasel broke free and fell. It was all right. They're as clever and supple as cats. It hit the ground, sprang up and vanished into a clump of bushes."

"I would never have thought it! Something new always seems to be happening, here at Allerbrook," Blanche said. "I'm not like Stephen, wanting to explore beyond the skyline. The moors are beautiful enough for me. I said that once to Tim Snowe, but he shook his head and said *Ah, I be too busy to have time to look at they hills.*"

She imitated Tim's voice but then stopped, embarrassed. "I mustn't make fun of him. He's kind, and Mistress Allerbrook might think I was rude."

"I think there's a merry young girl inside our solemn Blanche, trying to escape into the open," said Tobias, and they both laughed, until Tobias suddenly stopped laughing, reached out and turned her to face him.

"You're beautiful, too," he said abruptly. "When I came home, the moment I set eyes on you I thought how lovely you had become. Your eyes fascinate me. They change colour according to the light and your mood. If you missed me while I was away, being polished in a gentleman's house, then I missed you. But I only saw how much I'd been missing when I came home. So, you'd like to stay at Allerbrook?"

Blanche, startled at what sounded like another sudden change of subject, said, "That's so. But…"

"Well, why should you not stay? Blanche, haven't you seen me looking at you? Haven't you realized…?"

"Realized…what?" Blanche almost whispered it.

"That I love you. Well, all right, I only knew it myself when I came home, and I'm sometimes shy, too. I've hidden my feelings so well that you haven't guessed at them, it seems and nor, I think, has my mother. Well, it's time to speak. Blanche, my dear little love, you're seventeen now, quite old

enough to marry. I am already the young master of Allerbrook. Why not marry me? Then you will be penniless no
more, but part of Allerbrook, and we can live here together,
for always!"

The stags watched, confused, as the two human creatures
drew together and united into a single silhouette, with not
the smallest chink of light between their two bodies. The
creature thus formed did not seem to threaten them, but it
was too strange to be trusted. The trio fled, vanishing down
the far side of the ridge in a series of swift leaps.

The kestrel had drifted away, as well. Tobias and Blanche,
engrossed in each other, never noticed any of them go.

"We were all surprised, you know," Jane said over the wine
and cheesecakes which Idwal Lanyon's wife, Frances, had
brought out for her, "that Idwal and you finally decided to
live in Lynmouth instead of Bristol though Idwal sails from
Bristol whenever he goes overseas. Why was it?"

"We like it here," said Frances, looking contentedly
around the comfortable parlour. "We came back originally
when Idwal's father died, ten years ago. My mother-in-law
wanted to stay here, but she needed our help. Now that
Mistress Katherine has gone as well, we agreed to make this
our main home. Bristol is just for business. We have many
friends here and I like this house. It creaks like a ship at sea
when the winds blow, but I don't mind that." She smiled.
"It reminds me of the pleasant part of being in a ship, without
the uncomfortable things, like floors that won't keep still. I
am not fond of travelling."

"I am beginning to find journeys tiring myself," Jane
agreed. "I'm nearly forty-two now and I must admit I find
the ride over from Allerbrook a trifle long these days."

"Perhaps it's because we're women. Idwal never seems to tire…ah," said Frances. "Here he is."

"I see Cousin Jane has arrived." Idwal, striding in through the street door, greeted her with a bow before sitting down and reaching out a large hand with ginger hairs and freckles all over the back of it to pick up a cheesecake while Frances poured him some wine. "Forgive me for not being here when you arrived, Mistress Allerbrook. I was interviewing a couple of seamen I might take on. One of them will do, but the other won't. He's a mass of useful muscle but no brains and a nasty streak as well, I fancy. He's been a seaman for nearly twenty years and been getting on captains' nerves for the same length of time, I'd say. I believe he comes from your district, Cousin Jane. Name of Hayward."

"If it's Tom Hayward," said Jane, "I remember him well. An unpleasant man. He attacked one of our maidservants." She never liked to talk in detail of Francis's death. "But I'm sure you could control him and make use of him," she said, looking at Idwal, who was a big man and looked even bigger in his padded brown doublet with its puffed and slashed sleeves.

"I prefer seamen with some sense in their heads, and I certainly don't want to hire a man who attacks young women. Never mind about him. You timed your letter well, Cousin Jane. I shall be at sea within a month. Travelling with a fleet of other ships, since we're bound for the Mediterranean. Trouble with pirates is getting worse these days. No wise captain sails alone. Now, about this letter…"

"Yes. You wrote back," Jane said, "and invited me here, so I suppose you're not opposed to the idea, but you didn't actually say that."

"I couldn't. It's years since we've seen your Tobias. Where did you send him? He and Stephen went together, didn't they?"

"Not quite. Tobias joined Sir Giles Flaxton's household. Sir Giles is the son of Sir Edmund, who once arranged for me to go to court, though I didn't stay there. Sir Edmund died a few years ago. Tobias has had some experience of the world now. He's been to London, travelled in France and attended both the English and the French courts. He's seen Queen Elizabeth face-to-face. Stephen went to a different household, though. Sir Giles made the arrangements, but I said it was best that Stephen and Tobias should be separated, because they've never been really friendly."

"I must say I'm glad you're not suggesting Stephen," Idwal said frankly. "He was a wild little boy, always in trouble! And if you'll forgive me for saying so, Mistress Allerbrook, when I saw him last—about three years ago it was—I still sensed something wayward about him."

"He's not the owner of Allerbrook, anyway," Frances said mildly.

Jane smiled. "No. And he still uses the name of Sweet-water. In fact, he's turned out well in his own way and I intend to do something for him. He's my nephew and he has nothing of his own. But I didn't come to talk about Stephen. It's Tobias that I'm offering you. He's educated and he knows the world and yes, I now regard him as the master of Allerbrook."

"What kind of life would our Gwyneth have there?" Frances asked.

"A good one, I promise. Allerbrook is prosperous these days. My brother began to improve our fortunes when he bought sheep from Cleeve Abbey, and my husband, Harry, made some wise decisions, too. I've tried to follow their example. Toby's not a great landowner but he's a yeoman in comfortable circumstances. I realize that Gwyneth has grown up in merchant circles and our way of living is different, but it need not be too different. She need not do farm work unless she likes. There are others to do that."

"No one will ask her to feed the pigs or stand on a hilltop throwing grain into the wind to winnow out the chaff?" said Frances, quite seriously. She added, "That happened to a cousin of mine. She was married into a farming family and they did expect just that. She hadn't been brought up to an outdoor life at all and it was too hard for her. She died after two years and she never had a child."

"Gwyneth, I promise, need not lift a finger," said Jane firmly.

"Gwennie can cook and run a household," Idwal said. "And make bread and grow herbs, and she embroidered all the cushion covers on this settle where I am now. We never reared her to be idle. Our Nicholas will inherit my business, of course, but Gwyneth will have a dowry in coin, jewellery, plate and linen. She has good health, too. Would she have Blanche for a companion? Our Gwennie will be nineteen this year, but Blanche is younger, surely."

"Seventeen. She may not be at Allerbrook much longer, but I hope she'll be near at hand. Her family held the lease of Clicket Hall but we own it, so it wasn't confiscated with the rest of her property. I intend it to be her dowry. It has tenants just now, but only on short leases. I hope Blanche will always be close by. In fact, I'm thinking to marry her to Stephen. It's a way of providing for him and settling them both."

Frances considered, her head on one side. "We originally planned to marry Gwennie into another merchant family. Isn't that so, Idwal? In fact, we'd chosen the young man— the eldest son of a family in Bristol. But…"

"Mediterranean pirates," said Idwal shortly. "He was lost last year. I think Tobias sounds suitable, Cousin Jane."

"We must arrange for her and Tobias to meet," said Frances. "They haven't seen each other for years. I hope they'll like each other. We wouldn't force her into a marriage against her will."

"Gwennie's a biddable girl," Idwal said. "She has my red hair but not my explosive nature, and though we've never seen much of Tobias, what we've seen we've liked, I agree."

"I'm sorry we've met so rarely over the years," Jane said. "But after my brother sent Sybil here, he wanted to keep us apart, and then I came and removed Stephen and—well, I suppose your parents were offended."

She did not add that for her part, she had never wanted to set eyes on Katherine or Owen again because she couldn't forget Stephen's sticklike legs and the feel of his thin body in her arms. This was not a time to stir up old, bad feelings.

"It wasn't so much a matter of taking offence," said Idwal, "as feeling awkward. I think they didn't know quite how to behave toward you. Still, that's all in the past now. Families shouldn't be estranged."

Beyond the windows, gulls drifted on the gusty winds, calling in plaintive voices, their white wings flashing in the sun. Sensible people, however, did not envy seagulls. Sensible people sat in well-kept parlours and made wise arrangements for the young folk in their care. The three adults nodded to each other, satisfied with the plans they had laid.

On the barrow high above Allerbrook, Tobias and Blanche at last ended what was surely the longest and sweetest kiss in history. They made their way down from the barrow and then, without speaking, he took her hand and together, utterly at one and utterly at peace, they began to walk back to the house.

CHAPTER THIRTY-ONE
Threefold Resolution
1560

*J*ane, riding homeward over the moorland tracks with Tim Snowe as her escort, was happy. When they reached Allerbrook, she left the ponies to Tim and Paul and went into the hall, where she found a pleasant, homely scene. Her three young people were talking and laughing around the hearth, Lisa, though aged now and equipped with strong eyeglasses, was stitching in a window seat and there was an enticing aroma of supper in the air.

From the kitchen came a clatter of pans and the sound of cheerful female voices. Not Peggy's voice. Peggy had died three years before. But Beth and Letty were still here and Susie Snowe had returned to work in the house when her children were grown, bringing her daughter Phoebe with her. Phoebe was married and her husband, Mark Edwardes, was an Allerbrook ploughman. Paul Snowe was married, too, and his pretty young Nell, from Clicket, was also among the chatterers in the kitchen. Jane, looking and listening and holding her momentous news in readiness, felt the greatest affection for them all.

Momentous news should be broken at the right moment, however. She did not want to disturb this amiable domestic atmosphere by speaking of serious matters at once.

Instead, she merely answered questions about her visit by saying that yes, it had been pleasant to see the Lanyons again and that they all hoped the two households would meet more often in the future. After supper, however, she said, "Blanche—and Tobias and Stephen—I have news for the three of you. Come up to the parlour. I've asked Phoebe to light a fire and put candles there."

In the parlour she bade them all sit down, settled herself on a window seat and told them of the plans that had been made that day.

"Idwal and Frances suggest, Tobias, that you should visit them soon and talk to Gwyneth. You haven't seen her since you came back from London and you didn't know her well even before that. I spoke to her before I came away, though, and she says she remembers you and is happy with the idea. She is a charming girl. Blanche and Stephen, of course, do know each other well. It has always seemed to me that the two of you liked each other. So, what do you all say?"

She smiled brightly around at them, although throughout her little speech she had been increasingly aware that something was amiss. Eyes had not lit up, mouths had not begun to smile, as she had expected. Instead, all three faces had become oddly wary. Now, as she awaited comments, a dreadful silence had fallen.

"Well?" she said impatiently, at length. "What is it? Will somebody please say something?"

"When you came home, Aunt Jane," said Stephen, "Blanche and Tobias were telling me something. I appreciate the offer you are making me and I'd like to accept it—"

"Stephen!" gasped Blanche, while Tobias sat up straight and clenched his fists.

"No, Blanche, sweetheart, it's all right. Tobias, lower your hackles. I only meant that I'd be honoured to accept Blanche's hand if it were available. But it isn't. I'm sorry, Aunt Jane, but you really should have discussed this with us before you went to Lynmouth."

"Stephen, what do you mean?"

Tobias cleared his throat. "He means," he said, "that today, up on the barrow on the ridge, Blanche and I betrothed ourselves to each other. We love each other. Blanche only realized it today, but I—well, when I went away, I thought of her only as a sister. But when I came home again and saw her with new eyes, I knew almost at once that I loved her. I was waiting for the right moment to approach her and today that moment came, and now I find to my joy that she loves me. If you had spoken to us beforehand, I could have warned you."

"You said just now that the Lanyons don't want to compel Gwyneth into marriage," said Blanche. "Please don't compel me, either. I think of Stephen as a brother. It's Tobias that I want."

"And I want Blanche," Tobias said. He reached out for her hand and took it into his. "And," he added, "I mean to have her."

Jane stared at her son. It was as though she had never seen him clearly before. He had always been just her Tobias, whom she sometimes called Toby—quiet, inclined to piety, with soft hair that had to be kept short or it would fall into the brown eyes that were so like her own. A good, obedient son. Now something hard was emerging from him, like one of the rocky outcrops on the moor. The set of his jaw was belligerent. He reminded her suddenly of his father, Harry Hudd.

"What am I to do?" she said. "I have reached an agreement with the Lanyons!"

The silence that followed this was eloquent. No one repeated the phrase *if you had spoken to us beforehand,* but she heard it inside her head.

For a brief but awful moment she was angry. It was the duty of parents and guardians to settle young people in life. She had tried to do her duty, and heaven knows she had considered everyone's happiness. She wasn't trying to thrust Blanche into bed with a red-faced old man with bad breath and half his teeth gone, which was what Francis had done to her. She wasn't asking Tobias to marry a girl with a crooked spine or a shrewish temper. She had done her best to plan wisely and responsibly.

Oh, Peter, what would you say to this? Sir Peter Carew, she knew, had come back to England even before Queen Mary's death, because his wife had worked hard for his reinstatement. He was high, now, in the favour of the young Queen Elizabeth, and news of him reached her sometimes, for he was Deputy Lieutenant of Devon. But he had never come near her, never even contacted her by letter. He had held fast to his sound, practical marriage. He understood how marriages should be planned.

In the eyes of many, she was entitled to be firm, to say that she had made good arrangements and that they must stand. People would think her perfectly justified in locking

Blanche up with just bread and water or even beating her, in order to insist.

It would be useless, of course. It wouldn't make Stephen agree to marry Blanche or Tobias agree to marry Gwyneth. Judging by the expression on Toby's face now, he was capable not only of saying no, but saying it directly to the Lanyons and possibly launching a new family feud.

Besides…she knew what being compelled was like. In any case, Jane couldn't imagine herself taking harsh action against the girl.

But as the silence went on and on, it occurred to her that they were probably fond of her and that none of them was stupid. She had startled them. They hadn't had time to think. This unsuspected attachment between Toby and Blanche was very recent. It might not yet be deep-rooted.

Stephen was the first to break the hush. "I am not going to argue," he said. "Tobias and I have disagreed often enough, but we're not going to squabble over Blanche here. She's not something for sale in a cattle market. I'd have taken you gladly if you were agreeable, Blanche, but I wouldn't want an unwilling bride. That's no recipe for happiness."

"I think," said Jane, "that we should not go on discussing this now. You three should have time to consider, to talk to each other. Leave me now, all of you. Ask Lisa to come up to me."

Without a word more, all three of them went.

Lisa, making her way up the spiral staircase to the parlour a little later, arrived somewhat breathless, as she always did these days after tackling it, and reported that Stephen, Blanche and Tobias were once more gathered around the hall fire, deep in earnest conversation.

"Master Stephen's doing most of the talking. Dr. Spenlove was with them for a while but they sent him off, said they wanted to be private together. He's gone to bed, I think. What's going on, ma'am?"

Jane, who had been sitting with her hands in her lap, raised them despairingly and then let them drop. "I've been trying to arrange marriages for them all. But…"

And then, without warning, she burst into tears. Lisa came to her, sitting down beside her and taking her hands and rubbing them as if to warm them. "I thought I was doing right!" Jane sobbed. "I thought they'd be glad, pleased. I thought I was making wise plans for them!"

"When you were at Rixons, living there, I mean, you reared ducklings, didn't you?" Lisa let Jane's hands go, found a handkerchief in her reticule and handed it over.

"Yes, there's a duck pond," Jane agreed, wiping her eyes. "But why are you talking about ducks?"

"Ever put a clutch of duck eggs under a hen?"

"Lisa, you're not talking sense!"

"Yes, I am, ma'am. Well, did you?"

"Yes, sometimes, if we had a broody hen and duck eggs to spare. But what on earth…?"

"Hens get upset when their little ducklings go off into the water. They get agitated and cackle. But the ducklings go just the same, following their nature. Seems to me that young folk these days follow their own nature, too. Best leave them be."

Jane heaved a sigh. "I've left them to talk. Perhaps after a while they'll see things differently."

"I wouldn't count on it," said Lisa.

Lying in bed that night, Jane longed for sleep, but her legs and back ached. She was no longer young. The ride to and from Lynmouth had been a strain. Nothing could stop the advance of the years.

Sleep wasn't elusive just because of the twinges, though. It was also because of her disappointment. She had expected pleasure, interest, questions. Not those appalling, frozen silences!

She sank at last into a thin doze, but just after midnight a small sound started her out of it. She lay listening. There was a low murmur of voices, and then soft laughter. Jane sat up sharply.

Her bedchamber was between two smaller rooms. Lisa occupied one; Blanche had the other. The sound had come from Blanche's.

There had been a fire in Jane's hearth the evening before and its red embers were still glowing. She got into an overgown, lit a candle at the hearth and went out.

Originally all the bedchambers had led directly into each other, but when the wing was rebuilt by Jane's father, he had said that he saw no reason why anyone who wished to sleep early should have to put up with people walking through their rooms and disturbing them. Now the bedchambers opened into a passageway, which ran the length of the wing. Here Jane stopped to listen again, before moving to Blanche's door. Yes, the voices came from here. Without knocking, she walked in.

The curtains around Blanche's bed were fully closed, but the voices undoubtedly came from within them. Jane marched forward, jerked the hangings apart and stood there, candle in hand. Blanche and Tobias, lying side by side, sat up with a jerk, eyes wide with alarm.

"I see," said Jane. "All too clearly."

There were footsteps behind her and a brightening of the light. Lisa, also carrying a candle, had followed her into the room, and behind Lisa was Stephen, similarly equipped.

Hard on Stephen's heels was Dr. Spenlove, blinking and half-asleep. They clustered around the bed.

"What's going on?" Stephen demanded. "I heard a noise…dear God, what are you doing here, Toby?"

"It seems plain enough to me!" Lisa snapped at him.

"I agree," Stephen said. "That was a silly question. Well, well. This seems to be the end of all discussion about who is going to marry whom. I'm sorry, Aunt Jane, but though I will always be fond of Blanche, I must withdraw what I said about being willing to marry her, if she were agreeable, too. I can't possibly do that now, even to please you. She may be already with child by him, for all we know!"

"They will have to marry," said Spenlove. "I will wed them myself in the morning if you wish, ma'am."

"You…you…!" Jane could not remember ever being so angry in her life. She stepped close to the bed and would have struck Blanche except that Stephen's hand shot out and caught her wrist.

"Please don't, Aunt Jane. It isn't the end of the world. She and Toby are a perfectly suitable match. You're not concerned about her dowry, surely. Toby has enough."

"I wanted to marry her to *you,* to give you a place in the world, property!" Jane stared furiously at her nephew. "I made these arrangements because they were best for all three of you, including *you!* How can you be so blind to your own interests?"

"I'll make my way," said Stephen calmly. He released her wrist and looked at Blanche and Tobias. "Should I say something formal? *Bless you, my dear children,* or something like that?"

"How can you make jokes about this?" Jane cried, and then once more she was really crying, the tears streaming down her face. Through them she had the oddest impression that Stephen and the two culprits in the bed were exchanging glances that she didn't understand, that looked conspiratorial, but the need to get herself and her pathetic outburst of emotion out of their sight came first and stopped her from thinking about it.

She ordered Tobias back to his own room, saw him go and then turned away and let Lisa guide her back to her own bed. Spenlove, shaking his head and murmuring about the shamelessness of the younger generation, pottered away to his chamber. Lisa saw Jane into bed and then went down to the kitchen, to return with a warm wine posset.

"Don't fret too much, ma'am," she said. "It will work out well in the end."

"But I wanted to do something for Stephen! I had that in mind all the time!" Jane was still shedding tears. They splashed into the posset.

"Well, can't you? You were going to make Clicket Hall and its land over to Blanche when she married. Can't you make it over to Stephen instead? Blanche is getting Allerbrook along with Tobias. She'll be none the worse. Give Clicket Hall to Stephen outright," said Lisa. "He's your sister's son."

In the morning, dressed in her best velvet gown, with her face washed and her dignity restored, Jane summoned the recalcitrant younger generation into the hall before breakfast and there, in the presence also of Dr. Spenlove and Lisa, she formally accepted their threefold resolution and told them that she would arrange for banns to be called for the marriage of Tobias and Blanche. "I'll go to St. Anne's today and see Mr. Honeywood," she told them.

She would have liked to hear Father Drew's opinion but Drew, old and tired, had gone to sleep one evening a few months previously and failed to wake in the morning. Young Reverend William Honeywood was his replacement.

"All must look normal in the eyes of our neighbours," Jane told her hearers. "Dr. Spenlove would marry you privately and at once, but that would start gossip. Tobias and Blanche, you will behave yourselves meanwhile. No more midnight wanderings, if you please. Lisa, you will share Blanche's room, small though it is. Stephen, I can't offer you Gwyneth Lanyon in place of Blanche, because...well..."

For the first time during this solemn speech, Jane faltered. Stephen grinned. "I know. The Lanyons still think of me as the tiresome child Idwal's parents didn't really want to adopt. And I don't like red hair, anyway."

"Instead," said Jane, recovering, "I will grant Clicket Hall to you and the land that goes with it. That will give you some status and a chance of a good match, I trust. You, Blanche, have forfeited Clicket Hall. You must accept that. Oh!" Her voice was exasperated. "I did my best, but...well, yes, I know what it's like to fall in love."

Astonished, Tobias said, "Mother, I am sure you were a good wife to my father. Peggy told me that. But she also told me how you came to marry him and surely..."

"I did my best by your father, yes," Jane said. "But there was someone I'd rather have married."

"Who was it?" asked Stephen inquisitively.

"That," said Jane, "I shall keep to myself. It's all in the past now."

They went about their various tasks and in the end, it was a moderately pleasant day. It wasn't until she was once more in bed that it occurred to Jane that last night, Toby and Blanche had behaved very oddly. They were both so conventional and well behaved. That they should kiss for the first

time in the morning and fall into bed together the very same
night was out of character.

Thinking about it, she remembered that they had been lying
side by side but not embracing, and there had been that conspiratorial glance between them and Stephen. Was it possible
that Blanche and Tobias had only pretended to be lovers that
night, and at Stephen's suggestion? That they had laughed and
talked noisily on purpose, and if she hadn't woken, Stephen
would have roused her, claiming that he had caught them in
the same bed? All so that he could take a virtuous stand on *I
can't possibly marry Blanche now even to please you, Aunt Jane,* and
she may be already with child by him, for all we know!

It was entirely possible. He didn't love Blanche, but he was
probably fond enough of her, in his careless way, not to
stand in her light.

It was something else that she would never know.

Not too bad, Stephen thought as he mounted his horse—
a sixteen-hand dapple grey which he had bought in London—
and rode out for a morning's hawking. He, too, had brought
a goshawk home. Not bad at all, he repeated to himself as he
cantered across the moor. He had gained property without the
encumbrance of a wife, and it was best this way.

He unhooded his hawk so that she could rouse and look
at her surroundings. He had never seen himself as a family
man. He wanted to see the world. Had he married Blanche,
he would probably just have got her with child and then left
her to look after her baby and the property, and gone off adventuring. He wouldn't have made her very happy.

Or been happy himself, come to that. She was pretty and
sweet, but dull. So, to his mind, was Toby. Toby was tediously
interested in religion and Blanche was biddable to boredom

point. When he'd set out to persuade them into being found in bed together, Toby had talked about mortal sin, while Blanche seemed as horrified as though he had urged her to stow away on a ship bound for Cathay. He didn't care either way but he was sure that the two of them had merely staged their scene, as though it were something in a masque, and not actually done anything.

Stephen laughed. His hawk was ready now to fly, and seeing a rabbit in the distance, crouching nervously at the sight of the approaching rider and about to flee, he loosed her. It was pleasant to think that he would soon be master of Clicket Hall, but he had his own plans and they didn't include staying anywhere for long. Sometimes, at night, he dreamed of the sea and of sailing the Atlantic, crossing it, perhaps, to see the strange lands on the other side. One day, soon, he would make that dream reality.

"We are grateful, Mistress Allerbrook. We promise you will never regret letting us marry," Blanche said timidly to Jane. Stephen had gone hawking; Tobias was out on the farm. Blanche and Jane were in the parlour, sewing.

"I hope not. I don't want you to be unhappy, but I shall have a difficult letter now to write to the Lanyons," Jane said.

Blanche said, "This morning Tobias and I were talking and we thought, if you would let us, there was something we'd like to do for you."

"Yes, Blanche?"

"I still have the miniature portrait that Dr. Spenlove made of me. It's so good. We think Dr. Spenlove could vie with any court painter. Why shouldn't we ask him to paint a proper portrait of you, Mistress Allerbrook—something to hang in the gallery upstairs? It could be beautiful because you're beautiful, Mistress Allerbrook, and it would be a way for us to say thank you."

"Well," said Jane, startled. "It's a very kind thought. If Dr. Spenlove agrees…well, yes. Perhaps."

"I'm sure that Jane Allerbrook is telling the truth when she writes that she had no idea of what was going on," Frances Lanyon said, once more scanning the letter that Idwal had handed to her.

It had been delivered by a grave-faced Tim Snowe, and it said, apologetically but plainly, that it would not after all be possible for Tobias to marry Gwyneth because, without Jane's knowledge, he had betrothed himself to Blanche Palmer.

"I daresay you're right," Idwal agreed. "She is probably most embarrassed. We can be glad that Gwyneth is so well behaved and wouldn't dream of going behind our backs as Blanche and Tobias have apparently done to Jane."

"Well, it may be best after all for Gwyneth to marry into a merchant family," Frances said. "It was a pity that our first choice didn't live to marry her. But surely—isn't there a younger brother?"

"Well, yes. And he's still single. I saw the family on my last visit to Bristol." Idwal considered. "The younger one's only about five years older than Gwyneth. In fact, it crossed my mind just before Mistress Allerbrook arrived with her proposal. He's a handsome young fellow and he has a share in the business. He won't be pushed out to make his way as best he can. Yes, Frances. You may have a good idea there."

"I should be delighted to paint a portrait of Mistress Allerbrook," said Dr. Spenlove, entranced at the suggestion. "I only hope my ability is equal to it. It will be a pleasure."

CHAPTER THIRTY-TWO
Unexpected Events
1562

The Lincolnshire house that Peter Carew shared with his wife, Margaret, had once been splendid, but nowadays the dining hall had woodworm, the fine tapestries were fading and there were loose slates on the roof. And no spare cash to deal with any of it.

"I've given Her Majesty good service," he said to Margaret. "I've done a survey of the Tower of London for her and chased pirates out of the Irish Sea for her. I am loyal to her, as well she knows. Yet she's paid me the minimum possible for my work, while you nearly beggared yourself campaigning to get me forgiven by her sister—or rather, her sister's husband, Prince Philip—and allowed to come home."

"She has promised a formal reversal of the attainder on you," Margaret said soothingly. "Perhaps she sees that as making up for the lack of financial reward!"

"You are philosophical, my love, considering how much

you've lost for my sake. I'm grateful to you," Peter said. "You used your wealth and your family's influence and stopped the Crown from seizing my property when I was in exile. Elizabeth is mean and you are generous." He shook his head worriedly. "We shall have to raise money somehow," he said.

His lady set her round embroidery frame down on her knees and looked gravely at him across the parlour hearth. Margaret Carew was no longer young but, perhaps because she was childless, her waist was still slim. Her brown hair, neatly packed into a gold net (a memento of more affluent days) was not yet greying. She was still an attractive woman.

"You are Deputy Lieutenant of Devon but you work mainly through agents," she said. "I saved Mohuns Ottery for you, but you rarely go there. Would you consider selling it?"

Her voice was perfectly tranquil. She smiled at him and resumed her embroidery. And he wondered, not for the first time, what the thoughts behind that smile really were. Margaret was a good wife: dignified, well dressed, competent, amiable. She had worked indefatigably to get him home from exile and when at last he returned, she asked no awkward questions. Nor did she reveal her inmost thoughts.

Or knowledge. How much did she guess? While he was overseas, living as best he could, as a guest of friends first in this country, then in that, he had often—in fact, usually—had to share bedchambers and even beds with his companions, and they had warned him that he sometimes talked in his sleep. As far as he knew, the habit had faded out before he returned to Margaret. As far as he knew.

She was aware that Jane Allerbrook had helped him to escape. Since several of his men had been there, he had felt it best to be open. He had represented Jane as a respectable widow from a Protestant family which had long been friendly with his own.

But just occasionally, when some reference to his escape from Weymouth was made, usually by guests intrigued by his past, she would glance at him and look away and then try, gently, to turn the talk into other channels.

He also knew that now and then he dreamed of Jane Allerbrook.

He could not fault Margaret and he had no wish to hurt her. He knew there had been no awkward results from the episode with Jane. During his rare visits to Devon he had avoided Exmoor, but he had made discreet enquiries. Margaret could not have been alerted by scandal.

And yet, now that there was a question of raising money, she wanted him to sell his west country property.

"Well, what do you think?" she enquired gently.

He owed it to her.

"It's worth considering," he said. "As a matter of fact, I believe there's some land in Ireland which belongs to my family, although it has never been claimed. We might journey there and see if we can trace it. I may have a title to it." He paused, and added, "If I'm to sell Mohuns, I'd better see what order it's in. Before we go to Ireland, I must visit Devon."

He would so like to see Jane, just once more.

In a tavern in Plymouth, Stephen Sweetwater was sitting in the company of a sea captain by the name of John Hawkins and discussing slavery.

"We're on quite good terms with the Spaniards at the moment. There was even talk for a time of King Philip marrying Queen Elizabeth," Hawkins was saying. He was a small, flaxen-bearded man with humourless stone-coloured eyes. "The Spanish have sugar plantations in the New World and they need men to work them."

"Isn't there a local population of savages?" Stephen asked, sipping strong cider. "Won't the Spaniards use them?"

"There aren't many left, it seems," said Hawkins. "Where the Spaniards have settled, they've wiped most of the native population off the face of the earth."

"Careless," Stephen remarked.

"You could say so, but it was to my father's advantage and I trust will be to mine. My father has left me his trade connections and his capital. I intend to use them. I'm sailing in the late summer, collecting some Spanish seamen who know the route across the Atlantic, and going on to Africa to gather up a cargo of strong slaves, with some women, so that they can perpetuate themselves. We sail west in the autumn to land our goods. You say that when you were being educated away from your home, your mentor took you to sea and that you know something of the business?"

"I know one rope from another. I've learned navigation and I've been working as a sailor on a coastal trader for nearly two years," Stephen said. "And, as I said, I have a little money to invest. I leased my house and farmland out before I went to sea, and I've been saving my money and building up capital to invest in real adventuring when the chance arrives. This sounds like the opportunity I want. I'll leave my property in the hands of the agent who arranged the leases, let him go on gathering capital for me while I'm gone and then I'm your man."

"I'm taking a good fleet. I've leased my flagship, the *Jesus of Lubeck,* from the queen. But I haven't got all the men I need yet. If your captain gives you a good reference, I could do with a first mate for the smallest ship—the *Sweet Promise.* A little joke of mine," said Master Hawkins, to Stephen's surprise, as he had already decided that John Hawkins didn't know what a joke was. "Sugar is sweet," Hawkins explained laboriously, as though Stephen wouldn't see the point without help, "and the rewards that this expedition promises should be just as sweet, in a financial sense."

Dutifully Stephen laughed. He was relieved to think that he and Master Hawkins wouldn't be on the same ship, though. Stephen Sweetwater—his own name seemed to fit in well with Hawkins's clumsy jest—gazed out the small and grimy window beside him at the glitter of the spring sunshine on the waters of Plymouth Sound. In the distance, there were hills.

The hills of England, where the man who had fathered him had died so horribly. Soon he would be gone, sailing for strange places where there would be trees and flowers and birds and animals that were never seen here, monsters maybe, and mountains and jungle forests and mighty plains.

His spirit was reaching out for them already.

It was the spring of 1562 when Sir Peter Carew first considered selling Mohuns Ottery, but he didn't actually set about it until a rainstorm brought water pouring into the top floor of his Lincolnshire house. Only the alternatives of costly repairs or keeping buckets in rows in two useless bedchambers for the foreseeable future finally clinched his decision.

Once in Devon, he launched the business of surveying and valuing Mohuns Ottery, and then set out, alone, for Clicket.

His conscience wasn't easy. *You shouldn't be doing this,* it said to him sternly as he rode across Exmoor. But it was always exhilarating to ride across hilltops. It raised the heart, this feeling that one was up on the roof of the world. The moorland was golden with moor grass and rust-patched with autumn bracken; the sky was close overhead and the distant sea was a haziness with a trace of sparkle. It made him happy, and the happiness coloured everything around, including his intended destination.

Jane.

It was only a social call, of course. But she might ask him to stay for a few days.

She might even…

What did she look like now?

He used the tracks he knew best, and came into Clicket from the western end, becoming at once aware of a mild stir near the church of St. Anne's. Some ponies were tethered near the gate and there was a litter, which had been set on the ground while the two ponies that carried it, fore and aft, had been released from its shafts and were enjoying nosebags.

He drew to a halt just as the church door opened and a young priest came out. Behind him came a young woman, pale but smiling happily and leaning on the arm of a young man, perhaps her husband. Next came an elderly priest and an older woman, carrying a baby in her arms. A straggle of others followed.

There were people near enough to speak to. "What's afoot?" Carew enquired of a man with a leather apron and a blacksmith's build.

"Ah, it's the christening. Stranger here, be you? Master Tobias and his wife, Mistress Blanche—their first baby. Wed over two years they've been, so it's about time."

"But she had a bad childbed," said a woman on Carew's other side. "They had to bring her by litter. That's Tobias's mother, carryin' the baby and walkin' with their chaplain."

The little procession was out in the street by now. The elderly priest and the woman with the child were at this moment passing close to him, though neither looked his way. The woman was a step or two ahead and Carew saw both their profiles clearly. The priest was Dr. Spenlove, though the years had taken away his rosy chubbiness. The woman was Jane.

Like Spenlove, she had changed. Peter had last seen her when she was only in her mid-thirties, still with a bloom on her. Now she was in her forties and celebrating the birth of a grandchild. Her new status had settled on her like a rich but not a youthful mantle. He was experienced enough to know that he was seeing a woman whose world was complete.

The ponies were being put back into the shafts of the litter and the pale girl was being helped into it. Jane had gone over to her and the girl was holding out her arms for her child.

"She and Master Tobias married for love, folk say," the woman beside him remarked, "and they were so grateful to Mistress Allerbrook for allowin' it that they had her portrait painted, as a thank-you gift. The chaplain, Dr. Spenlove, he's clever at such things and he did it. I've not seen the picture, but it's said it's a fine likeness of Mistress Allerbrook. But the lass almost got her death, bearin' that first child. Still, here she be after all, and the child's healthy, so I hear."

Carew cleared his throat and said, "What name has he been given?"

"Robert. Robert Allerbrook," said the man. "Vicar told me that."

"I used to know the Allerbrook family slightly," said Carew with caution.

"You on your way to visit them, sir? Well, you've timed it right. There's to be a feast now up at Allerbrook House."

"No," said Peter Carew. "I'm just passing through on my way to...to Withypool. I don't intend to intrude. I don't know the family now, not really. It was all so long ago."

★ ★ ★

"Land ho!" croaked the exhausted man at the tiller, and
added, "Dunno where it is, but God be thanked anyhow."

God be thanked indeed. Stephen and the two men who
were the only survivors of the storm in which the *Sweet
Promise* had foundered, stared longingly ahead at the hazy
outline of land on the horizon. Stephen was so grateful that
he could have cried, and actually did pass a hand across his
face, to wipe this enfeebling impulse away. His skin was
peeling where sun and wind had left their marks, and under
his palm he felt the stiffness of his untended, salt-caked beard.
His gums were swollen and bleeding from scurvy. They had
been at sea for what felt like eternity. It was a week since the
storm had separated the *Sweet Promise* from the rest of Master
Hawkins's fleet, and two days since she had finally ploughed
her bows under the wave and never recovered herself.

It had been a time of the most appalling responsibility for
Stephen, since by then he was no longer the first mate, but
had become the captain. The original captain had suc-
cumbed to a fever when they were two weeks out from
Africa. He had probably caught it from the black slaves in
the hold, among whom sickness was already raging. They
had all died before the storm, along with many of the crew
and the ship's Spanish pilot.

Stephen had been made captain by vote, partly because
he was the first mate anyway and partly because he was
popular with the crew.

The popularity had soared just after the captain fell ill.
Stephen, going below to tend him, heard curious noises
coming from his own cabin and went in to find the most
disagreeable sailor on the vessel, a powerfully built but extremely stupid man called Tom Hayward, on Stephen's

bunk—where he hadn't the slightest right to be—with a frightened and tearful cabin boy, both of them devoid of all their nether garments.

The captain being out of action, Stephen dealt with the situation. He hauled the boy off the bunk, told him to get dressed and then shouted for assistance and had Hayward put in irons. There was an impromptu trial, held on deck in the presence of the surviving crew, and it soon transpired that he had molested all the younger men at various times. He was too big and strong to argue with, they said, and he'd sworn that if they told, he'd say that they had propositioned him, and not the other way about. Stephen had ordered Hayward to be hanged.

Hayward, sobbing and then howling, pleaded wildly that he came from Stephen's own home, at least from Rixons, which Stephen's aunt owned, didn't she? It made no difference. Hayward's body was thrown to the sharks and half the crew looked on Stephen as their saviour.

But he couldn't save them from the storm. The *Sweet Promise* had carried three small boats, including the one he was now in, but when she finally sank, it had happened so fast that only two were launched, and Stephen had seen the tempest overwhelm the other one before his eyes. He and his two companions were now the only survivors, and they wouldn't last long unless they found land. Provisions and flasks of fresh water had been kept in the escape vessels, but they were all gone now. If only that distant land proved friendly. "Out oars!" he barked.

The coast, as they neared it, seemed to consist mostly of sandbanks, and when at last they saw an opening, they had to row against wind and tide to get there. But once through, they found themselves in a lagoon. Worn out, they shipped oars and drifted, looking for a landing place. The country in front of them looked green and fertile; there might be game there, and fruits that were good to eat.

It was then that one man said, "If that ain't the smoke of cooking fires, I'm the King of Spain." The other added, "Someone's comin' out to meet us. Look there. In rowing boats. What travellers call canoes."

It was going to be all right. The natives were amiable, even kind, though strange to look at, with their coppery skins, high cheekbones and dark almond-shaped eyes. The head of their chieftain was shaved at the sides, leaving a narrow crest of hair like a horse's hogged mane across the top of his scalp, and in his ears were copper earrings.

They all shook their heads at the filthy and sickly state of the mariners, and Stephen and his companions found themselves being towed ashore by the canoes, taken to a village of wooden houses, then led into one, where golden-brown women, themselves decently wrapped in leather cloaks, fetched warm water so that they could wash, took away their dirty clothes and brought deerskin tunics for them to wear instead.

Then there was food—a feast served on the beach and cooked there over a big outdoor fire. There was venison, some kind of porridge and melons, wonderful melons, which every one of the men seized with instinctive gratitude, as though their bodies had been crying aloud for fruit.

The chief had a wife, who sat beside him, and a young girl, who was evidently their daughter and looked very much like the chief, seemed delighted to serve them.

Halfway through the meal Stephen, rather as Jane had done when she came home from court and fell in love with

Peter Carew, became suddenly aware of two surprising things at once.

One was that for the first time in his life, he was homesick. He had never thought he would yearn to be at Allerbrook again, never thought he would miss Exmoor. He had spent most of his young life wanting to get away from it, and when he'd learned of the way his father had died, he had never wanted to see southwest England again. He had returned from London, when summoned by his aunt Jane, with reluctance.

It was odd that Andrew Shearer, who in life had been so little to him—one could hardly count a few grudging words of well-wishing on one isolated occasion—should in death persistently haunt his imagination. He could not bear to think that the body which had given life to his own should have died in such agony and indignity and been turned to ash so that there was not even a grave by which a son, who liked being alive, however it had come about, could kneel to pray.

Now, in this strange, far land, images of Allerbrook House, of the racing peat stream in the combe, of Dunkery outlined against a lemon-tinted evening sky, rose unbidden before his eyes and the thought that he might never see them again filled him with sorrow.

In the same moment he realized that the chief's daughter, who at that moment was offering him some more melon and smiling at him, was breathtakingly beautiful.

Part Four

ENDING AND BEGINNING
1585–1587

CHAPTER THIRTY-THREE
The Hills of England
1585

"What I need," said the swarthy, dark-gowned man whose principal purpose in life was the protection of his sovereign lady Queen Elizabeth, and—as a corollary—the entrapment and destruction of her rival, Mary Stuart of Scotland, "what I need are eyes and ears in every house of any standing, in the whole of England. All of them—not just most. I am fortunate in the agents I have in France, but I need more in England. The country is riddled with these dangerous Jesuits."

Irritably he paced around his study. "They're like mice in the woodwork. They slip ashore in disguise and creep from house to house, charming money out of purses and promises out of gullible romantics. They are vermin!"

He stopped pacing. This office in Whitehall Palace had

linenfold panelling, exquisitely patterned leaded windows and a view of the rippling Thames. Its beauties, however, mattered little to its proprietor. It was not overlarge and he had stopped pacing because, apart from the fact that the place contained a lot of shelving, several wooden stools and a big desk piled with documents, there were a number of other people present and he kept having to walk around them.

They included two competent secretaries—highly gifted both in code breaking and forgery—and an individual who was supposed to be another member of the secretarial suite but spent much of his time interrogating suspected Jesuits. He was small and inoffensive looking, and skilled at setting verbal traps so subtle that his victims often did not know they had been caught until their questioner himself, smiling pleasantly, pointed it out.

These were all official employees. The others were less official, though equally valuable in the eyes of the queen's spymaster, Sir Francis Walsingham, albeit not in all cases for admirable reasons.

No one knew the details except Sir Francis himself, but rumour had it that Walsingham possessed knowledge that would have had several of them in prison on serious charges, except that they had talents that Walsingham valued. He employed them to seek out treachery and keep him informed.

One particularly valuable agent was Bernard Maude, who had once tried to blackmail the Archbishop of York over an amorous intrigue between the prelate and an innkeeper's wife and spent three years in Fleet prison for it. Maude had blue eyes with the unwavering stare of inborn dishonesty. He had been released early, after Walsingham, trawling legal records for likely recruits, had picked out his name and interviewed him. Walsingham was prepared to go personally into the most repulsive, damp and rat-ridden dungeons in order to provide himself with useful spies.

There was also one woman, a lady in her fifties, dressed in a dark blue gown over an apple-green kirtle. The over-gown, if one looked closely, hung just a little awkwardly. This was because Mistress Ursula Stannard had a pouch sewn just inside the front opening of all her overdresses, in which she habitually carried, among other things, picklocks and a small dagger.

Mistress Stannard, unlike Maude, was entirely respectable. She was a long-standing agent and had penetrated many con-spiracies simply by virtue of being a woman, apparently interested in embroidery and music and the fortunes of her daughter and grandchildren. Behind this harmless facade she watched and listened, examined other people's corre-spondence and identified dangerous patterns in seemingly unconnected facts.

Her loyalty to Elizabeth was absolute. She was a love child and it was said that she was related to the queen, though there were varying theories about what the relationship actually was.

"The situation," said Walsingham, sitting down behind his desk, "is becoming more and more perilous. Ever since that damnable papal bull, practically ordering every Catholic in the land to turn into a potential assassin or risk excommu-nication, I have hardly had one good night's sleep for worrying. Nor has Her Majesty, courageous though she is. We have already had two dangerous plots, both centring around Mary Stuart. She is always the focus. There are rumours of further plots. But unless she is implicated in something unquestionably treasonable, the queen will never agree to cut off her head. It needs doing, but..."

He brought a fist down on the desk. "She has been nearly

twenty years in England, ever since the Scots threw her out
because her husband had been murdered and she was
probably a party to it. She is a simpleton. She was foolish to
marry Henry Lord Darnley—a spoilt degenerate if ever there
was one—and more foolish still to marry James Bothwell.
There's little doubt that he was the one who had the gunpowder put under Darnley's bed. She fled to England. Elizabeth has taken care of her because Mary is a queen and also
a cousin, and she repays by scheming and plotting...arghhh!"

He interrupted his diatribe with an exasperated snarl. His
audience, who had heard it all before, was silent. "The plots
have always been foiled—so far," he said. "But she never
learns. She is an ingrate and a wantwit and a threat. So I have
called as many of you as were to hand, for this meeting. I
want you to go out to towns and villages and farms, and find
me further aides—as well as seeing what you can learn on
your own account, of course."

After a thoughtful pause Mistress Stannard said, "Which
districts are the worst off for eyes and ears? The north, I
suppose? The Catholic faction has always been strong there."

"Yes, the north." Walsingham nodded at one of the secretaries, who fetched a scroll from a shelf and unrolled it on the
desk, weighing down the corners with inkpots and books.

The scroll was a map of England, on which circles had
been drawn in thick black ink. One big circle embraced most
of the north, and the secretary pointed to it. "If a Catholic
rising is fomented, much of its support will come from there.
However, there are also suspicious households in the south—
here...here...and here....." He indicated three small circles
in the home counties. "We have no agents in any of them.
And we're very short of agents in the southwest peninsula.
We know too little about the major households there."

"The kind of people we want to recruit," said Walsingham, "are people who know their districts and have the entrée to the right houses. I'll send two of you north. See if you can discover any useful men there. You will receive payment, plus funds for your journeys. Another of you had better deal with the home counties. Find excuses to visit those three houses and do your best to enlist people there who will act for me. Also, enquire about vacancies for butlers, grooms, tutors and the like. I'll try to find applicants. Now, Mistress Stannard…"

"You have left the southwest for me, have you?" said the lady serenely. "My daughter and her husband are at the moment visiting his cousins in Plymouth. I could certainly decide to join them for a while. They have a wide acquaintance in Devon."

Walsingham, with a slight smile, said, "I know."

Mistress Stannard nodded. "Of course you do, Sir Francis. Plymouth will make a good starting point. Once there, I may be able to arrange other visits, to households in Somerset as well as Devon." She studied him thoughtfully. "The danger is really serious?"

"The queen," said Walsingham, "calls me her Old Moor because of my dark hair and complexion. Some people think it's a discourteous nickname. But it could be worse. She could have called me Spider. I myself think I am very like a spider, crouching in the middle of my web of spies and waiting for a careless fly to touch the web and make it quiver. It is quivering, Mistress Stannard. There is trouble on the way." He looked around and addressed them all equally. "How soon can you all set out?"

Almost in one voice they said, "Tomorrow."

Have I done the right thing? Stephen, leaning on the rail of the *Santa Maria* as she glided slowly nearer to Plymouth, turned to look at the young woman beside him. She was tall for a girl, only a little shorter than he was, straight of back, slender but strong. Her amber skin, the curve of her aquiline nose and the set of her long dark eyes told of the foreign blood she carried. She was so like her mother. But when she also turned her head and looked back at him, he saw himself in her expression. In mind, in character, she was very much his daughter. She had both an English name and an Algonquin one. She was Philippa as much as she was Golden Bird.

"Should I have let you come?" he said. "It's too late now, but I find myself wondering—will you be happy in England? Will you settle? Are you already pining for your home?"

"I chose to come. I didn't want to be parted from you," said Philippa. "And it was you or my birthplace. I couldn't have both, could I?"

"Perhaps I should have stayed." But even as he spoke, he was glancing beyond her, at the distant hills, green under the October sunshine, drawing closer every moment, and he found himself adding, "Look, there are the hills of England. We're nearly into Plymouth."

"You always wanted to come back to England," Philippa said. "Round the fire in the evening you talked endlessly to me and to my brothers about it. You taught us English, and all about Christianity."

"I baptized you all. It's allowed if no priest is to be found. Yes, it's true. I always hoped that somehow, sometime…but your mother could not have borne to be uprooted. I told her that I wanted our children to understand their father's world as well as hers, but I hoped she didn't know how desperately I wanted to come back."

"She may have guessed," Philippa said. "She spoke to me once, about the way you so often used to stand on the shore and stare out to sea, toward the east. But I think she knew you wouldn't leave her."

"I'd never have done that. Never!"

"I know. But since she died you've been waiting for your chance. My brothers knew, too. When this man Sir Richard Grenville sailed in on the *Tiger* with those people you called colonists, we all realized at once that when he left, you'd go with him."

"I wish the boys had come, too," said Stephen. "But they are men of the Algonquin, through and through, and it's in the nature of things for young men to choose their own path. Philippa, I *pray* you will be happy. You will have to make your life in England now. I will try to find you a good husband, who will understand."

"Thank you. Don't worry, Father. I shall be all right," said Philippa, and smiled.

And then looked away, because although she was with her father, the voyage on the big ship, surrounded by strangers from his homeland, had been confusing and sometimes frightening, especially when Grenville turned pirate and boarded the *Santa Maria,* on which they were travelling now. It came home to her, suddenly, just how far she was from her birthplace, and that it was to be forever.

She had known that all along, of course. *But I didn't understand what it meant!* The realization almost stopped her breath. She held on to the rail, her knuckles turning white, and swallowed hard. Then her head came up and her face was tranquil. The Algonquin rarely showed their feelings. She would not show hers.

Footsteps came toward them along the deck and they turned to see who it was. And then blinked in astonishment, scarcely recognizing the handsome, sunburnt but neatly shaved gentleman who was approaching, his beautiful buckled shoes tapping on the planks, his muscular calves outlined by fine knitted stockings and the rest of him adorned in puffed hose, tight velvet doublet, pristine ruff and wide-brimmed black hat. The last time they had seen him, he had been in seaboots, scruffy knee-length hose and a leather jerkin which gave a good view of his hairy chest, while most of his face was obscured by a mass of beard.

"Sir Richard?" said Stephen. "But…!"

"I had my best clothes in my trunk, waiting for the day of my return," said Sir Richard Grenville. "I got them out yesterday and went to the galley to steam the creases out. We've been sighted—can't you see the crowd waiting for us? It looks to me," he added with satisfaction, "that the news that I boarded a Spanish vessel on the way home and seized her cargo of treasure must have got here already. Via Spain, no doubt, since I left the crew alive and allowed them the *Tiger* to get home in. We've got gold, silver, pearls, sugar and ginger in the hold and I fancy we're going to be welcomed with trumpets and speeches. I wonder if the news has reached the queen yet? I wish you'd let me take Philippa to court."

"Certainly not," said Stephen.

"Well, you two had better go below and tidy yourselves up. Philippa, my dear, the colonists I brought over gave you some women's clothing. You had best get into it."

Philippa looked down at the breeches, shirt and jerkin she was wearing. "English women's clothes are not comfortable."

"You'll have to accustom yourself," said her father firmly.

Once ashore, they were plunged into the midst of the crowd. People pressed around her, and stared. She was conventionally dressed now, but she did not look English and she walked with a lithe step like the prowl of a cat. Few Englishwomen, encased in their boned stays, their stomachers and farthingales, could move in such a fashion.

She kept her head up but stayed close to her father's side while, as Sir Richard had prophesied, trumpets sounded and a man wearing a chain of office of some kind stepped forward, unrolled a prepared speech and proceeded to read it aloud.

After that, the situation began to resolve itself, but new surprises awaited her. Many of the people on the quay were known to Sir Richard, who rapidly set about arranging lodgings for himself and his companions by parcelling them out among the many households offering hospitality. Stephen and Philippa found themselves taken in hand by a couple called Bartholomew and Thomasina Hillman, a pleasant, neatly dressed pair who looked as if they were in their early forties. They led their guests toward a coach, at which Philippa looked in wonder.

"Horses!" she whispered to her father.

"You've seen horses before," said Stephen. "You saw the ones Sir Richard Grenville's colonists brought with them."

"But I didn't know they were used to pull things. You told me about people riding them, but not that."

"Did I not?" Stephen chuckled. "They're used for both, though not on Exmoor. The tracks there are no good for things like that coach. You'll have to learn to ride."

"I wonder if my brothers will learn to ride the colonists' horses."

"I'd take a wager," said Stephen, "that many of your tribe are already learning to ride the colonists' horses. It won't be so very long before all your people take horses for granted and wonder how they ever lived without them."

"But the colonists didn't bring that many."

"They brought three yearling colts, male, and some of the mares were in foal. In other words, breeding stock for the future. The lives of your people are going to be changed. Not as much as your own," he added with a touch of compassion, "but changed, all the same."

"You told me about the house you own on the place you call Exmoor." As they came up to the coach, Philippa changed the subject. "Will we be going there soon?"

"Yes, as soon as possible, and to that house—that is, if I still own it! Twenty years—it's more than that!—is a long time. Meanwhile, we can stay with my aunt Jane—at least, I trust so. I hope she's still alive. Let me hand you into the coach."

The house to which they were taken overawed her because of its size. Their small cedarwood home in the Algonquin village of Secotan would have fitted easily into the main hall of the Hillmans' home. The room she was given impressed her as well, with its glossy wooden panels and velvet bedhangings. She stroked them admiringly.

She was uneasy, though, because she was now separated from her father, and she felt constricted by the stiff English clothes, even though she had firmly declined to wear stays. Nevertheless, she took care over her toilette. She must fit in with this English tribe to which she had come—and come of her own free will, too. She must make herself acceptable to them, and if she felt homesick, no one was to know it. If they did, she would be letting her mother's tribe down.

It was midafternoon before dinner was served. Mistress Hillman fetched her and took her down to the dining hall. This was better. Though it had tapestries instead of the deerskin curtains which adorned the tribal houses, and its oak beams lacked the cedarwood scent, the hall nevertheless reminded Philippa of the longhouse in Secotan, where meetings and communal feasts were held when the weather wouldn't allow gatherings out on the beach.

The Hillman household seemed to be large. The people at the table included not only Bartholomew, Thomasina and numerous children, varying in age from late teens to a small girl of about six, but also a chaplain, a secretary, a tutor, a man who apparently worked for Bartholomew as a land agent and some relatives who were staying in the house.

These consisted of a couple in their thirties, who were introduced as Bartholomew's cousin George Hillman and his wife, Margaret, and Margaret's formidably dignified mother, who made Philippa feel bashful. She was a widow and her name was Mistress Ursula Stannard. She called her daughter Meg.

At table, Mistress Stannard and Meg, who was apparently pregnant although this was not yet visible, discussed suitable names for the forthcoming offspring. Mistress Stannard, having declared that the names of Katherine and Elizabeth were being used far too often and it was causing confusion, drew Philippa into the conversation by saying that hers was a musical-sounding name and a little less commonplace.

"Meg has two sons and a daughter already, and the girl is called Ursula, after me. They're at home with their tutor just now. Meg, why not call the new one Philippa, if it's a girl? What do you think, George?"

George said amiably that he liked the name. Philippa, trying not to stammer with shyness, and thankful that her father had made sure she spoke good English, said she would be honoured. Even when Mistress Stannard was being kind, it was like being addressed by royalty.

The food was ample but not quite unfamiliar. The roast lamb was very like roast venison and there were oysters, too, to which she was accustomed. She sipped some excellent wine, which warmed her and made her a little less timid, so that after a while she was able to talk quite easily to Meg Hillman, who wanted to ask questions about her early life, and the voyage to England.

Stephen watched her with approval. This was her first introduction to English society and she must be bewildered, for she had been cast into it straight from the ship. She was doing very well.

He then became aware that from across the table Mistress Stannard was addressing him. The Hillmans seemed to have told her something about him. She was asking just where in the west country his home was and what relatives he had there. Indeed, she was enquiring about his religion. He wondered why, and with vivid past recollections of religious squabbles in England, became wary.

"I am very out of touch with English affairs," he said evasively.

"Really? But you sailed across with Sir Richard Grenville. He must have told you what to expect when you arrived, surely?"

"Well, I know that Queen Elizabeth still reigns and that England is officially Protestant. I asked Sir Richard about that before we sailed. I'd have thought twice, if England had been Catholic. I am not of that persuasion. I've taught my daughter to be Protestant, as well. My father…"

He stopped. Mistress Stannard said enquiringly, "Your father?"

"I didn't know him well. He and I…were not on good terms. But all the same, he was still my father and but for him, I wouldn't be here. He was burned for heresy, by Queen Mary Tudor. I was away from home and I learned of it only later. As I said, we were far from close, but after I heard what had happened to him, I couldn't forget it or forgive it."

"I see," said Mistress Stannard, and sounded as though she did indeed see something interesting, though what it was he couldn't imagine. She said, "Is your family well-known in Somerset?"

"He's connected to the Allerbrooks, who are quite a power in the district called Exmoor," Bartholomew put in. "I believe Stephen is going first to Allerbrook House, where his aunt Jane Allerbrook lives."

"She is still there, then?" Stephen said, his eyes brightening.

"Oh yes, indeed. I've never met her personally," said Bartholomew, "but we have acquaintances in common. Her son, Tobias, attends court at times, I have heard."

"Tobias is my cousin," Stephen said. "It will be interesting to meet him again. Or is he away at court now?"

No one knew. Mistress Stannard, however, seemed interested in the social circle around the Allerbrooks and nodded thoughtfully when the chaplain observed that not long ago he had met Mistress Jane Allerbrook at Dunster Castle. "The Luttrell family reside there sometimes these days. This was a dinner to celebrate completion of some rebuilding they've had done at the castle and I was a guest of their own chaplain—he and I trained together. Master Hillman kindly gave me leave of absence to attend."

"When I was young," Stephen remarked, "the Allerbrooks were acquainted with the Carew family, as well. I knew Sir Peter Carew."

"He was part of the Wyatt rebellion against Mary Tudor," Mistress Stannard observed. "Were you in that, Master Sweetwater? It's quite safe to say so nowadays," she added.

"I was young and wild. Yes, I did ride with Carew for a time, though I ended up having to flee ignominiously for home and pretend I'd never been away. Where is Sir Peter now, by the way?"

"Dead and gone these many years," Mistress Stannard said. "There are other Carews still in the west country, however. Perhaps you will meet them. Tell me—" she was looking at him now in a very speculative way indeed "—did Grenville ever speak to you of Mary Stuart?"

"The former queen of Scotland? Yes. She is in England as a guest of the queen, isn't she?"

"Mary is half guest and half prisoner and altogether dangerous," George Hillman said. "She thinks the crown of England should be hers, and she has friends who every now and then lay plots to put it on her head. Many people think England would be a more restful place if she didn't *have* a head, but our merciful queen is reluctant to execute her cousin."

Mistress Stannard and George Hillman were gazing at him intently as though they were wondering something about him, and Stephen began to feel more at sea than he had in the middle of the Atlantic. Something was afoot here but he didn't know what it was, and no one, it seemed, was going to explain. The chaplain now observed that Mary still practised her Catholic religion despite all attempts to convert her, and the tutor joined in with some general remarks about the number of Jesuit priests who were stealing into the country to encourage treasonable plots. George Hillman declared that there would probably be a respite during the winter. "Nothing like bad weather to keep pests at bay."

The conversation shifted away then from politics and religion to talk of London and the company of players who were becoming famous for the dramas they put on to amuse the queen. But after the meal, when Thomasina and Margaret Hillman had taken Philippa off to show her around the house, George Hillman and Ursula Stannard quietly steered Stephen out into the grounds. The sunshine was still warm, and they strolled through a topiary garden, chatting idly, until, when they were thoroughly out of earshot of anyone else, Mistress Stannard finally came to the point.

"I am not merely paying a visit to relatives," she said. "I have a purpose in coming to this part of England. I have confided it to my son-in-law here, though not to anyone else. You seem, Master Sweetwater, to be both adventurous and intelligent and it seems, too, that you have good reason to dislike and fear the prospect of a new Catholic regime."

"Well, I do. When I think of what my father must have suffered, I feel a horror and an anger beyond words. But may I know…?"

"I have a proposition," said Mistress Stannard.

CHAPTER THIRTY-FOUR
A Sense of Familiarity
1585

"You need a map," said Mistress Stannard. The sun had set and mists were drifting in from the sea. They had come indoors, to a small study, where George Hillman had left them. "I'm not really concerned in this," he said. "Mistress Stannard's secret world is not to my taste. I prefer to keep out of such things."

"A map of what—or where?" Stephen asked. The little panelled room was warm, firelit and candlelit, and there were padded seats and a table laden with miscellaneous items, but no maps that he could see.

"I don't mean a map of places," said Mistress Stannard, seating herself at the table. "I mean a map—in a way—of names and connections. There are things you can't know, having been away so long. If you are really ready to help us— and I have rather pounced on you when you can hardly have got your land legs yet—then you need information. The names of people in key positions, for instance, and the names of those under suspicion. Are you serious about accepting this commission?"

"I was unsure at first. But then I thought of my father. Yes, I am serious. That is, if I can be of real use."

"You'll be paid a retainer. That might be an added induce-ment," said Mistress Stannard with a smile. "In one way," she said, "it's a drawback that you've been out of England for so long, but there are advantages, too. No one will suppose that you're in the queen's employ. You are a hunter whose scent your quarry will not recognize. Be seated and I'll instruct you."

He sat down. Afterward he said to George Hillman, "Your mother-in-law is the most frightening woman I have ever met. She talked of being in the queen's employ, but she has such an air of command that I could almost believe she *was* the queen!"

"Half-sister," said Hillman.

"What?"

"Elizabeth and Mistress Stannard are half-sisters. Mistress Stannard's father was King Henry and her mother was one of Queen Anne Boleyn's ladies. She was a love child. Her early life, when she was brought up on sufferance by her mother's family, was very hard, I believe."

"Good God. So was I—a love child—as a matter of fact," said Stephen. "And my early life wasn't easy either. We have something in common, she and I, it seems. I still think she's terrifying!"

She had taught him much during the evening in the little candlelit study. He knew now who Walsingham was, and the names of his senior staff. He also had a written list of Mary

Stuart's principal agents in France and England, and another of people in England whom Walsingham considered dubious. He had heard for the first time of Jesuit priests.

"There are openly Catholic households," Mistress Stannard said, "and no one interferes with them if they at least attend Anglican services sometimes or else pay their fines. And keep the laws of England, of course. But these priests move from one household to another, holding illegal Masses and preaching sedition. If holding religious services was all they ever did, the authorities would probably wink at it, but it isn't. They talk of Mary Stuart's rights and the duty of all good Catholics to uphold her. They imperil the peace and security of England."

"I can see," said Stephen doubtfully, "that in some circumstances I might have to pretend to be a Catholic sympathizer. It makes my gorge rise when I think of my father at the stake, but I suppose, if it were necessary..." He stopped. "But what if I were arrested in error?"

"I think not," said Mistress Stannard, and from the box on the table took a couple of rings. "See if one of these fits any of your fingers."

The rings varied in size but were otherwise identical. Each consisted of a piece of faceted amber set in elaborately patterned claws, on a wide band of gold. One of them went smoothly onto the middle finger of his left hand. "That fits. But..."

"Take it off again and look inside the gold band," said Mistress Stannard.

He did so. Engraved on the inside of the hoop was an ornamental capital *E,* followed by a curious elongated pattern of entwined loops. He looked up at Mistress Stannard, puzzled.

"It's part of the queen's signature," she said. "The initial *E* of Elizabeth, and the pattern with which she always finishes her name. When she signs documents, the pattern goes underneath. Here, because there isn't room under the *E,* it goes alongside. It really is her signature. I mean, she created the design for the die, with her own hand. I held the magnifying lens for her. It would be very hard to imitate. Such a ring will gain you entry to Walsingham's presence at any time, or even the queen's, in an emergency, and it will assure anyone who tries to arrest you that you are accredited by Walsingham's office. The existence and description of these rings are known to senior military ranks from captain upward. And there is one more thing."

"Yes?"

"You must take care, if you have suspicions of anyone, *not* to warn them, even by accident. This is important, Master Sweetwater."

There was a pause, during which Mistress Stannard's hazel eyes looked very steadily into his. "Much may depend on not alarming the enemy before time," she said. "It is Sir Francis Walsingham's wish that if there is indeed a plot, it must be allowed to ripen, because that is the only way he will ever get the queen to put an end to Mary Stuart. Mary is an anointed queen. To execute her would set a terrible precedent. Sir Francis understands that—we all do. But Sir Francis also feels that until Mary's head is off, there will be no safety in this realm. This is crucial, Master Sweetwater! Fail in this and you yourself would become a traitor."

So here he was, Stephen Sweetwater, agent in the pay of Walsingham, riding home on the bay gelding he had bought in Plymouth. It was an expensive animal, but he had his share of the Spanish treasure, plus a first payment from Walsingham, via Mistress Stannard. Philippa was on the pillion and a hired man on a cob rode behind, leading a packhorse. They were crossing the moorland toward Clicket, and Stephen had an amber ring on his left hand and a head full of names and the task of getting himself invited to dinner by as many influential families as he could, in order to sift their conversation and find out who their friends were.

Here on the moor it all seemed unreal, as remote as the moon. Heather and gorse and bracken, ouzel and kestrel and coney, stag and otter had nothing to do with wrangles about queens and popes. He turned his head to speak to Philippa.

"Well, this is Exmoor. The dark low-growing plant is the heather. It blooms in August and its flowers are purple. The spiky bushes with the yellow flowers are gorse. Some of them are always in flower, but in August they all are. The whole moor turns to purple and gold. Next year you'll see."

"It's wild and open," said Philippa simply. "I didn't like Plymouth, but I like this. You've described it to me many times, but seeing for myself is different! I feel better," she added.

Yesterday evening, in the inn where they had spent the night, her father had come to bid her good-night and found her crying. Homesickness, the knowledge that an ocean lay between her and her birthplace, had suddenly descended on her. Stephen had comforted her as best he could, but he had gone away looking worried. She had made a great effort that morning to appear cheerful. Now, out on this open moor, her spirits had genuinely risen. Something in her answered to this place. Something in her was saying, *Don't be afraid. This is home. You have made the right choice.*

Her father had done his best to prepare her. He had told her and her brothers as much as he could about Europe, its peoples and its history. He had even taught them to read and write, using charcoal and pieces of pale deerskin leather in lieu of paper. But her brothers had never taken to it, and although

Philippa had wanted to learn, she had not had sufficient practice. In the Hillmans' house, when offered the chance to read a book of verse, she had realized just how slow she was.

Thomasina had told her that Clicket was remote and that countrywomen often couldn't read or write, but Bartholomew had said—jovially, yet not as a joke—that hers was a good family and she would be expected to have some learning. She would have to study hard, and she wasn't used to that.

She would have to master horse riding, too. The near future looked alarmingly full of new skills to be learned. But the sense of homecoming remained. Something deep within her recognized this place.

CHAPTER THIRTY-FIVE
Hellspawn
1585

*J*ane Allerbrook was in the parlour, adding up accounts. She rarely used the study, though Tobias did. She liked the parlour because it was in the tower, above the high-ceilinged chapel, and had such glorious views. She often sat there, even though it sometimes brought back memories, not all of them happy.

She was not entirely happy now, either. She knew she was lucky to have reached her mid-sixties and remained in good health, but there were things that troubled her.

For one thing, although many years had passed, she had not forgotten Stephen. She had learned through the agent who had charge of Clicket Hall that her restless nephew had sailed for the New World on a ship called the *Sweet Promise.* Eventually, word had reached England that the *Sweet Promise* had been separated from her companion ships and was presumed lost. That had been two decades ago and she had long since accepted that he was dead, but privately she still mourned him. His life and death both seemed so pointless, such a waste.

Nor was that all. Jane broke off her work in order to spend a few moments in worrying and also in being annoyed because she was worried. Jane longed above all for a peaceful life, but she had repeatedly been compelled to abandon domestic calm in order to look after those around her, as she had long ago promised herself she would. She was afraid now that such a time might come again. The world, as ever, was troubled and there were those in her household who might very easily run into danger. Sometimes Jane felt that her family—and in some cases her friends—lacked a sense of self-preservation. Why could they not just live and be happy instead of allying themselves with this faction or that?

They probably imagined that she didn't know how their minds were working, but long experience had taught her that to have any hope at all of safeguarding the wayward spirits around her, she must be aware of what they were thinking. She knew more than they supposed.

Well, this was no day for fretting, with the moorland lying so serenely under a mild blue autumn sky and quietness all around. She bent her head once more to the ledger, pushing her eyeglasses more firmly onto her nose. Eyeglasses were one of the blessings of modern knowledge, allowing her to go on reading and studying accounts, which she needed to do to help Tobias. As a boy, he had tried to master arithmetic but had no aptitude. He was thankful to leave the ledgers to her.

This year the figures were good. The wool clip had sold well. An old arrangement under which they sold fleeces cheap to a weaving family in Dunster and took a cut from the profits on the finished cloth had been terminated by Jane's father, and Jane had always been thankful for it. Now they could haggle and get the best prices. This year the harvest and the cider apple crop had also been good. Most of the women—Blanche, Nell, Letty, Phoebe and Phoebe's twenty-year-old daughter Eliza—were at this moment down in the orchard, gathering the fallen apples for the cider press. There were some fine young bullocks and fat pigs, too, to provide salted meat, hams and bacon for the house, with a few animals over to be sent to market. They were well set up for the winter.

Tobias and his son, Robert, were out on the farm. Blanche had been unlucky with children and there had been no more since Robert, but he had grown into a good-looking young man, dark haired and brown eyed as his grandfather Ralph had been and with something of the same swashbuckling nature, yet with a kindness in him, a touch of genuine romance that Ralph had certainly not possessed. Jane was proud of her grandson.

She was concentrating on some addition when the noisy lowing of cows broke out somewhere, followed a few moments later by excited shouting. Startled, she peered from the window but could not see what was happening. However, the sounds were depressingly familiar.

"Hellspawn again!" said Jane, and casting her work aside, she made for the spiral stairs down to the hall, and out across the yard to the track beyond. Where she stopped short, annoyed but not surprised. She had seen it all before.

Riders were approaching: a man on a big bay horse, with a girl on his pillion, and a second man on a cob and leading a packhorse. Between riders and house, however, there was an obstacle, in the form of a herd of black cows. They were blocking the track completely and one of them, as though she were some kind of ringleader, had planted herself right in front of the horses with the air of a besieged medieval castellan watching the advance of enemy forces.

The man on the bay was shouting at her to move over. But, as she possessed a discouragingly large pair of horns, she stayed put. The man tried to ride round her, but she shifted her position and got in the way again. The girl began to laugh.

The last time this had happened, Jane herself had been caught on the wrong side of the cows with their belligerent warrior queen, and had had to take to the fields and approach her own home by another path. Now, although she knew it would be of little use, she marched forward and shouted at the cows, as well. None of them took the slightest notice.

She was looking round for assistance and wondering where her grooms had got to when a small, weather-beaten man appeared on foot, panting up the slope from the direction of Rixons and waving a stout stick. Behind him, also waving sticks, came two hefty, flaxen youths, and loping after them, barking noisily, a hairy black-and-white dog.

"Sorry...sorry, zurs, madam." He was addressing the newcomers, not Jane, who needed no explanations. "Bloody animal. Had the devil in her zince she wur calved. Get out of 'un's vield, her would, even if I'd got a castle wall round 'un, 'stead of a vence. Others all vollow 'un, like she vor their queen. But I don't call she Elizabeth. Hellspawn, I calls she, *and* a bloody nuisance, that's what!"

"Master Blake!" said Jane indignantly. "Get those animals off the track, will you? *Now!*"

He and the youths, with shouts and curses and the not very

efficient aid of the dog, which was clearly ill trained, set about rounding up the cows. They were phlegmatically reluctant to move, except for the overintelligent ringleader, who turned around and lowered her horns at the dog, which yelped and retreated. The weather-beaten man stopped short to mop his brow and then, with relief, to greet reinforcements.

"Ah, Master Toby, canst thee help? They'm out again and blockin' the way for thy guests yur. I'd turn she into collops and joints, so I would, 'cept she'm a good milker and her calves, they do be beauties!"

Tobias, bestriding a pony, had come from the Allerbrook fields to help. He joined in vigorously with the farmer, thwacking the bovine ringleader off the track, and helping the youths to herd the other animals out of the way, as well. In the middle of it all he glanced toward the riders and called out that he was sorry for all this, and would welcome them properly in a moment. Then his gaze sharpened and he pulled his pony up. "I do believe—I'm not mistaken, surely? God's teeth! You're *Stephen.*"

"Good day to you, Tobias," said Stephen, manoeuvring the bay in order to prevent the ringleader from trying to break away in the wrong direction. "And to you, Aunt Jane!" he added in a shout, across the backs of half a dozen cows. "I've come home!"

"Stephen!" said Jane, at once astonished and slightly disbelieving, as she stood beside the tall bay horse, looking up at its riders. "It really is you? After all these years? And who is this young lady?"

Amid the usual cacophony of dogs and geese, the travellers had come into the yard. Paul Snowe and Robert had appeared on foot and Tobias was just getting off his pony. The man who had been leading the packhorse was dismounting, too, and moving his charges out of the way. Blanche had arrived as well, and so had most of the other women, now including Jane's maid Alice. They stood in a cluster, as wide-eyed as Jane herself, wondering at the sight of Stephen Sweetwater, who hadn't been heard of for twenty years, and agog to know who the girl on his pillion might be.

The girl was wearing a green velvet cloak and her head was adorned with an elegant green hat with a long brown feather in it. Robert was looking at her with immense interest and had already swept off his cap in order to bow to her. Stephen was grinning.

"Yes, it's me. Really me." He was brown from weather, and his face had unfamiliar lines, but his voice was the same. "Let me present my daughter, Philippa."

"Your daughter!" said Jane wonderingly. Robert, mean-while, had stepped forward to help the girl off the horse, and once down, she curtsied very correctly to Jane and then stood up, throwing back her cloak.

She was as straight backed and slender as a young pine tree, with a look of lithe strength which was somehow foreign. Jane was sure she was not wearing stays, and furthermore, that she had no need of them. Un-English, too, was the amber skin and the curve of her nose, the high cheekbones and the set of her dark eyes. Her shy smile, though, was enough to bridge any gap of strangeness. Jane found herself smiling back.

Stephen dismounted in turn. Paul Snowe went to help the hired man with the horses and the luggage. Tobias said, "I see that Simon Blake's cows are still being a nuisance. I suppose that infernal animal Hellspawn led them out again. I don't know how she does it. It isn't that he doesn't look after his fences, but if she finds a fence post that rocks just a little, she'll lean on it till it gives way. Blake swears she goes around the field testing the posts! He ought to train that useless dog of his better, though."

"Blake is the tenant at Rixons now," Jane said to Stephen. "The Haywards are both dead. Blake is a widower with two sons, and is making a good job of Rixons, except for this trouble with the cows and the dog."

"Many things will have changed," Stephen said. "I'll have a thousand questions to ask, I can see that."

"We'll all have questions!" said Blanche. "You must have had some adventures since we last saw you."

"Adventures and dangers, too," said Philippa, speaking for the first time. Her voice was clear, faintly accented, but not hesitant. She had turned her shy smile to Robert. "But we have come through safely."

"I shall light candles in our chapel in gratitude," Robert said.

"That is an excellent plan. We are all glad of your safe homecoming," Tobias said a little stiffly. "Well, the two of you had better come inside. Your man will see to your animals, and our groom, Jack Edwardes—he's Phoebe's boy, Tim Snowe's grandson—will help him and see that he is given refreshment. Here's Jack. Welcome home to Allerbrook, anyway, Stephen, and Mistress Philippa, too."

As a greeting it was polite and correct, but the tone was hardly effusive, all the same. Stephen glanced at Jane and winked. Clearly he had noticed. Was this, Jane wondered anxiously, going to be a really happy homecoming or not?

As they went toward the hall, Robert walked at Philippa's side. He was smiling and talking to her and the dark, graceful girl was responding, turning her head to look up at him. Walking beside Jane, Stephen once more caught her eye. He nodded toward them and raised his eyebrows, grinning more widely than ever.

"Nonsense," Jane whispered. "It's true that Robert has a romantic streak, but they've only just met."

"I fell in love with Philippa's mother and she with me at our first glimpse of each other. She was the daughter of a tribal chief and I was a stranger from the other side of the world, but it made no difference. We knew at once."

"Oh, really, Stephen!"

"I promise you," said Stephen. "I know the symptoms. It might even be a good thing. I've brought Philippa to England and I have to see her settled. She's been homesick, but falling in love is a good cure for that, given the other party is suitable. Is this one suitable? Who is he?"

"He's Tobias's son. He and your daughter must be second cousins!"

"What of it?" said Stephen. "They won't need a papal dispensation these days, will they?"

"Oh, dear God," said Jane as the anxiety which had troubled her mind as she sat doing accounts in the parlour suddenly sprang into new life.

CHAPTER THIRTY-SIX
An Interest in Gossip
1585

tephen stepped out of his bedchamber into the long gallery and took in what he had not noticed the previous night: the presence of a picture on the wall almost opposite his door. Placed between two windows and framed in gilt, it measured about nine inches wide by a foot high, and it was a portrait of Jane Allerbrook.

She wore golden-brown damask, with a divided front to reveal a cream kirtle embroidered with small flowers, and short, puffed damask sleeves over long undersleeves of the same embroidered cream material. She had a neat white ruff and a moderate farthingale, and her hair was netted in silver. The painted brown eyes smiled at him as though they could actually see him. He was studying the picture when Philippa came out of her own room and joined him.

"Do you recognize her?" he asked, remembering that Philippa had never seen a portrait before she came to England. There were a couple in the Hillmans' house, but he did not know if she had noticed them.

"It's Great-Aunt Jane, isn't it?" Jane, welcoming Philippa to Allerbrook, had asked to be called that, and explained how relationships were named in England. "But it must have been painted a long time ago," Philippa said. "It's like her, but...she is older now, surely."

"Yes, I think you're right. It wasn't done recently. She must be well into her sixties by now. I must ask her when it was painted."

"Her dress is beautiful," Philippa said sincerely. "Though it can't be comfortable!" She looked down at the quite simple gown she had put on, which had a very small ruff and no farthingale. "I have had such a struggle to get into these things this morning and they are so stiff and scratchy. Will I really have to wear such clothes forever?"

"I'm afraid you must, my dear. You will get used to it. If you had grown up in England you would never have known anything else."

"I will *not* wear those things called stays. I don't need them and I hate them," said Philippa, for once abandoning her usual impassivity. "I don't come down into a point where my stomach is!" She looked again at the portrait. "But it is a lovely picture of her, although she looks worried. Look at the lines around the eyes."

"You eagle-eyed Algonquin! But yes." Now that he looked closely, he saw that Philippa was right. Well, it was natural enough.

"She has had her troubles in the past," he said. "Plenty of them. I suppose they left their mark."

★ ★ ★

Jane, sitting by the fire and sewing, paused, needle in hand, as Stephen came into the hall. He stopped, wrinkling his nose. "I can smell apples. I remember that aroma so well. You've begun making cider."

"Letty and Robert are showing Philippa how the cider press works. She must feel very strange among us all. You have brought her a long way from her home, Stephen. Her childhood must have been so different from life here that however hard I try, I don't suppose I'll ever imagine it right. I thought that if she had something practical to do, something new, it would help her. Tim Snowe's lending a hand, too, loading apples into the hopper. He's become our indoor man now—our butler, so to speak. Stephen, why did you come back? And why did you bring your daughter?"

"I was shipwrecked, as I told you yesterday evening. I was taken in by a friendly tribe and had to make the best of it, but I missed England badly and I taught my children all about it. When the chance came to return…well, I took it. Philippa wanted to come mostly because she wanted to be with me. She'll adapt—you'll see. Are you not glad to see me, Aunt Jane?"

"Of course I am!" said Jane, and then wondered how true it was. She had sometimes dreamed how she would rejoice if Stephen suddenly walked in the door. But a curiously unpredictable atmosphere had always surrounded Stephen, and it hadn't changed. Here it was again. She was overjoyed to see him, oh, of course, but if only she could shake off this absurd feeling that in these troubled times, to have him in the house was somehow to open the door to disturbance.

"Your daughter is very beautiful," she said, and then hesitated before adding, "Stephen, my grandson, Robert, has promised to give her a first riding lesson this morning. I could hardly object, because she must of course learn to ride. I said that she can use my pony Beechnut—he's descended from Hazelnut and is just as quiet. It was kind of Robert, but…"

"Why are you worried?" Stephen asked, sitting down. "Because you obviously are."

"Because of Tobias, mainly. If…if they are attracted to each other as you thought yesterday they might be, I don't think Tobias will like it. Where is he, by the way? I thought you two were riding around the fields together."

"He's looking at the fence around the sheep pen. He hasn't changed much, has he? I don't think he's over-delighted to see me back again. Still, I won't be under his feet for long. I'll move out into Clicket Hall as soon as I can if I still own it. Do I? Look, Aunt Jane, Philippa is young and marriage is the natural thing for her. She understands that she will live in England for good and will be wed here. Back with the tribe, she would be expected to marry soon. It seems quite natural to her. But England must seem strange to her and I'd like her to be with someone who won't make her feel even more strange. Now, Robert is part of the family."

"Oh, you are going too fast!" said Jane irritably. "You've scarcely arrived! Let the poor girl get used to us all! I have kept an eye on Clicket Hall, by the way. We all thought you were dead but I have never put it up for sale and the agent— it's still the same man—has gone on following your orders and letting it only on short leases. The rent has been mostly used for upkeep but some has been separately banked—just in case. Somehow, I never wanted to…"

"Shut the door on the hope that I would turn up after all? Thank you for that, Aunt Jane."

"But the existing lease has only just been renewed. It won't run out till this time next year."

"Indeed? That's a pity. Aunt Jane, what would Toby's objection really be, if I'm right about Robert and Philippa? Why should he mind? He's never liked me, I know, but surely he can't hate Philippa herself?"

"Stephen, please slow down! Philippa has much to learn before we worry about Robert or anyone else. I have been talking to her this morning and she seems intelligent and has a great natural dignity, and those are assets. But she can hardly read!"

"Yes. She needs a tutor. Have you any ideas?"

"Our chaplain, Gilbert Mallow, can instruct her. He educated Robert for a time."

"You say your chaplain is called Mallow? What happened to Dr. Spenlove?"

"He died in 1574—he was about seventy-four himself. I miss him. He was a good friend." Jane paused, looking back at memories. "When he was near the end—we both knew— I thanked him for all he had done through the years, and he was able to understand me, for which I'm glad."

We understood each other. Our eyes said all that we would never put into words. I had so much to thank him for and he…I never knew it before, but I really think he loved me.

He had committed a crime for her. Many times over the years she had studied Francis's will, and lately she had noticed as the ink aged, the writing in the final paragraph had faded a little more than the rest. It was evidence enough for her.

"Have you noticed my portrait in the gallery upstairs?" she asked. "He painted it—Blanche and Tobias asked him to do it at the time of their marriage. It's a pleasant reminder of him."

"Where is this man Mallow now? He obviously isn't here."

"He's visiting a friend in Plymouth. The friend has a guest he wants Gilbert to meet, I understand. He'll soon be back. Mallow's been with us for ten years, but he's still quite young and full of energy. He's a good teacher. Philippa needs advice about dress, too, but she can share my maid. Alice is a good helpful girl. I miss Lisa as much as I miss Spenlove. She died just after he did, during a bad winter. They both caught cold and it turned to lung congestion. Stephen, I think I must be frank. If Philippa and Robert really are attracted, Tobias will dislike the idea principally because he disapproves of cousin marriages. He says that the old faith was right about that."

"The old faith? Are you telling me," said Stephen, "that Tobias has Catholic leanings?"

"I'm afraid so, and they're not wise opinions these days. I worry about it. It came about when he was visiting the royal court in London, about two years ago. He made friends with a young Catholic gentleman there. There are Catholics at court, Stephen. They're not all the queen's enemies, I do assure you...."

"Didn't the Pope issue orders at one time that they all ought to be, and would be excommunicated if they weren't?" enquired Stephen.

"Yes, but many of them still manage to walk a fine line. Toby's friend is like that. I haven't met him, but I know it was he who finally converted Toby to his faith. Toby says he is charming and cultivated."

"I see. Well, we must take things one step at a time, I suppose."

"We certainly must." Jane pushed her needle into the case that was lying on a table close to her, and laid her work beside it. "Now, Stephen. Let us talk of other things. What has been happening to you all these years? You told us yesterday that you had been wrecked on a New World coast and had lived with the native people, but then you began to ask questions about Allerbrook. I want to know more. What kind of ancestors does Philippa have on her mother's side, for instance? You said yesterday that her mother was the daughter of a tribal chief and that you fell in love on sight. But that means your wife's relatives were people of some importance. How did you come to marry into a family like that?"

"We both knew at once what we wanted," said Stephen. "But I dared not approach her, of course, not then. Anyway, I knew nothing of the language! But I hadn't been with the tribe long before I was taken on a hunting trip, after deer. The tribe uses bows, quite powerful ones. Most of the arrows have stone tips...."

"Stone?" said Jane, astonished.

"Yes. The Algonquin haven't much metal, except for a little copper. Some axes and arrowheads are copper, but believe me, the first time I tested a stone arrowhead with my finger, I cut myself. They build cedarwood houses and they can cut down trees and split logs with stone-headed axes as easily as with copper ones! On this trip, one of the men was attacked by...oh, it was like a tawny panther. I've seen lions and panthers in the menagerie at the Tower of London. This was lion-coloured and panther-sized. It just sprang out of the undergrowth, onto the fellow's back. I chanced to be well placed for shooting at it, so I did, and saved the man's life."

"Was the man the chief?" Jane asked.

"No, just one of the tribesmen, but a good hunter. The others valued him. I didn't kill the beast outright. It leaped off its victim and charged *me*—came at me snarling, with my shaft sticking out of its side. I was terrified! But I just had time to nock another arrow into place and loose again, and this time I got it in the chest and it rolled over. The man it attacked didn't die. He'd been clawed—that creature had claws like iron hooks! But we carried him home and he recovered. Everyone was pleased, and there was a ceremony. They managed to convey to me that they were making me a member of the tribe. They gave me a name, though I didn't find out till later that it meant Swift Arrow. And then..."

Stephen sat by the fire with his hands, brown and calloused from the hard outdoor life he had led for so long, dangling between his knees. His brown eyes looked into the flames, as though he saw pictures there. "That was when Running Doe—that was what her name meant in their tongue..."

"The chief's daughter?"

"Yes. She was there. All the villagers of Secotan had been called to this gathering—it was held on the beach. She went to her father and spoke to him, pointing at me, and then came over to me and took my hand. There was some talk and some argument, a few cheers and a good many head-shakings, but she went back and knelt before her father and two days later there was another ceremony, of which I hardly understood one word, but her father put her hand in mine and there was a feast and from then on, she was my wife. I learned enough of her tongue to talk to her eventually. She never learned much of mine."

"If Robert has a romantic thread in his character, I think it must be a family characteristic! You've got it, as well."

"We had two sons as well as Philippa," said Stephen reminiscently. "They're grown up now—but they are Algonquin to the bone. I was never really close to them. Running Doe died two years ago and I still mourn for her, but if she'd lived, I couldn't have come home and I'm glad I have." He lapsed into silence, still gazing into the fire. Jane sat quietly, studying him.

He had changed. He was…she groped for a word…mature. Well, he had travelled to far-off places and lived a life she could scarcely imagine. He must have learned much. He had come back knowing that he wished to live at Clicket Hall and see his daughter married and absorbed into England. The child Sybil had borne out of wedlock and then abandoned had gone away to find himself, and done precisely that.

But that atmosphere of disturbance was still there. It was already making itself felt, in the matter of Robert and Philippa. She had watched Stephen and Tobias yesterday, listened to their voices as they made conventional conversation, and she knew perfectly well that they were as they always had been: as incompatible as oil and water, as dissimilar as day and night. Their minds could not meet. Tobias would not welcome Stephen's daughter as his son's wife.

Abruptly Stephen withdrew his gaze from whatever imaginary worlds he had seen in the glowing logs and looked at her. "Aunt Jane, I believe you are acquainted with the Luttrell family now?"

"With Lady Margaret Luttrell, yes. It's a slight acquaintance—it began when I bought a farm from the Luttrells. I've done my best to build up the Allerbrook fortunes over the years and with some success, though I say it myself. Toby and I are invited sometimes to Dunster Castle. Lady Margaret and George Luttrell—that's her son—are there quite often these days. Lady Margaret's husband died a good many years ago, when George was still a boy."

"Are you likely to be asked there again soon?"

"I have been invited to a gathering in November, yes. With Toby and Blanche."

"Can I come with you? They might be interested to meet the adventurer who spent over twenty years with the Algonquin tribe and has come back with a half-Algonquin daughter. Would you ask them?"

"Are you trying to tell me that if Robert doesn't ask for her hand after all, you might try to find Philippa a husband in the Luttrells' social circle? That's aiming rather high! It's true that George's wife, Joan, is only the daughter of a lawyer, but I understand that the lawyer concerned was George's guardian. Everyone says he foisted the girl on to him. She's poorly educated, and last time I was there, her gown was all splashed with whatever meal she'd eaten last. Hmm." Jane put her head on one side. "Maybe Philippa has a chance in that company after all. With a little teaching, she'll leave Joan Luttrell far behind."

"My dear aunt, what glorious gossip!" Stephen began to laugh. "This is nothing to do with Philippa," he said. He paused, looking with great affection at his aunt Jane, remembering how she had protected him from Captain Clifton, knowing that he could probably trust her and knowing, too, that he would be wiser not to trust anyone, least of all someone whose son was a Catholic.

He was not going to include Tobias's religious beliefs in any kind of report to Walsingham. He didn't intend to point the finger at his own relatives, but he must still be alert to learn whatever he could about other people's families, and that would be easier if Tobias had no suspicions of his newly returned cousin.

"I just want to get to know my new neighbours," Stephen said. "I'm interested in local affairs—local gossip, if you want to put it that way."

"I see," said Jane.

She wished she knew why she felt that something was being kept from her. She wished she knew why that feeling of disturbance had suddenly increased and why, deep within herself, she felt afraid.

CHAPTER THIRTY-SEVEN
The Worm at the Heart of the Apple
1585

The news that Stephen Sweetwater was home, accompanied by a daughter whose mother had come from a New World tribe, spread rapidly around the county. Allerbrook tenants, Clicket villagers, acquaintances from Withypool, Dulverton and Winsford all found excuses to visit the house. "I knew this would happen," Jane said resignedly, despatching Paul Snowe to Dulverton for extra stores.

The news penetrated as far as the coast, causing Nicholas Lanyon, his wife, Agnes, his two young sons, his sister Gwyneth Mercer and her husband, John, along with their daughter Nicola and her newlywed husband, Will Steadman, to arrive at Allerbrook unheralded and in force.

"It was sheer curiosity that brought us," they said candidly, beaming and shaking Stephen's hand with enthusiasm.

Stephen the difficult child who had caused a rift between the two sides of the family was forgotten. He was now a returned traveller from exotic lands and they were delighted to see him. Jane graciously accommodated them overnight and Philippa bore up well under their interested scrutiny, dressing carefully, answering questions politely, speaking only when addressed and smiling at everyone. If she felt she was being put on display, she didn't say so.

The November gathering at Dunster Castle duly took place and as Stephen had hoped, the Luttrells, too, had heard of him and his unusual daughter and were only too pleased to extend the invitation to them. The event was a success from a social point of view, but from the point of view of espionage it was a complete blank.

Stephen thought it over as they jogged home afterward, through the woodland tracks that wound their way up the Avill valley toward the moorland, reviewing it in his head, putting the dinner table conversation through the sieve of memory, and finding nothing.

Nothing! He had promised to send reports direct to Sir Francis Walsingham in London, using the royal courier service from Taunton. Any report he sent now would be as bland as plain blancmange.

None of the numerous visitors to Allerbrook had said a single word out of place, and at Dunster Castle young George Luttrell had talked mainly of plans for reconstructing Minehead harbour, while his mother, like most older ladies of standing, was interested only in the household and estate. As for George's wife, Joan, she was as Jane had implied—uninformed, untidy and lacking in any opinions whatsoever.

Walsingham's retainer was of course useful, but Stephen,

owner of Clicket House and some useful profits from the *Santa Maria,* could do without it. He was beginning to think that he should write to Mistress Stannard and ask to be released from his task.

Jane, riding beside him, was thinking how pleased she was with Philippa, who was already promising to become a dignified and cultured young woman. She had begun to learn how to brew cider and cure hams and she had been studying dutifully. Even a few weeks of lessons with the chaplain, Gilbert Mallow, had developed her mind considerably. He had started her on Latin and French, and her reading and penmanship had already improved a good deal.

And if she had also spent a good deal of time in Robert's company, he seemed to keep her cheerful. Tobias didn't like it, and showed it, but the couple took little heed and Jane, gently, had told him to let them alone. "He's good for her. Stephen told me she was homesick at first. Now she's beginning to put down roots at Allerbrook and Robert is helping her."

"Gilbert Mallow is doing more," said Tobias. "And he's brought a musician back from Plymouth with him. I've been talking to the man and he's willing to start Philippa on the virginals and the lute."

The musician was the man Gilbert Mallow had gone to Plymouth to meet. He had come back to Allerbrook with Mallow, and Tobias had granted permission for him to stay for a while. His name was Charles Dupont and he was half-French but preferred, he said, to live in England. He was young and quiet but gifted, since he was a composer who had written a number of pieces for various instruments.

"I believe," Jane remarked now to Stephen, "that Philippa is showing some aptitude for the lute. I must give her some lessons in dancing, too. Mallow and Dupont are doing well by her."

"I'm sure she'll become a graceful dancer," said Stephen somewhat distractedly.

He had nothing against Dupont, but he was less enthusiastic about Mallow. Philippa, when talking to him of things she had learned from Mallow, had remarked that he admired Mary Stuart of Scotland. "Father, he says that in England she is wrongfully imprisoned, and ought to be restored to the Scottish throne."

"Those are unwise remarks," Stephen told her. "Naturally you mustn't contradict your tutor, but don't repeat them." He had wondered if here, at last, was something he should mention in a report to Walsingham, but had decided against it. He certainly did *not* want the authorities to begin eyeing his own home with suspicion. Yes, it would be better if he withdrew from the business of being an agent. Then he wouldn't have to take these inconvenient decisions.

"You are very quiet," Jane remarked. "By the way, I must tell you—I overheard George Luttrell asking Tobias when he next intended to visit the royal court, and Toby said perhaps at the end of the winter. It could be a good thing for Philippa to have relatives who attend court. Toby goes most years, for a while. He likes to visit his friends there, too."

"Including the one who turned him into a Catholic?" Stephen asked.

"Oh yes, indeed. He finds Sir Anthony such good company, he said. Anthony Babington—that's the name of his friend."

Stephen lay in his bed in the dark, and could not sleep. He had been so glad to come home. During the long years of homesickness he had begun to understand what he and Hawkins had done to their cargo of enslaved and kidnapped Africans and to know it for an evil. He would never take part in such a trade again—even if he ever had the chance.

He had not been a slave, but the pain of separation from his homeland and all familiar things had been intense. He had not even had the other survivors from the *Sweet Promise* for company, for both had died, quite soon, of some local fever.

He had made a life among the Algonquin and, blessedly, there had been Running Doe to help him, but because of her, he had had to keep out of the way the first time a ship from England put in, and let his first chance of getting home slip by.

He knew very well that her death had spared him from an agonizing choice when, later, the *Tiger* sailed in with Sir Richard Grenville. He had brought a group of men and women who wished to found a New World colony, and had chosen Secotan because of a report from the earlier ship. Grenville himself would be sailing back to England, and now Stephen was free to approach his countrymen, free to leave. And Philippa, his dear Philippa, had chosen to come with him.

Home. *Home.* He had been near tears when he'd seen Plymouth come up on the horizon. And now...

It was like eating an apple and coming across a wriggling white worm inside it. Tobias, whom he had never liked, had been paying visits to court and making undesirable friends there. Tobias had been consorting with Sir Anthony Babington.

Hidden in his room was the list Mistress Stannard had given him, of people in England who were under suspicion because, although they had as yet done nothing questionable, they had strong Catholic sympathies and contacts among doubtful characters, including Mary Stuart's French agents, and certain priestly agitators in Catholic Europe.

Sir Anthony Babington was on that list.

A few doors away from Stephen, Jane Allerbrook was also awake. She was worried and puzzled. On the ride home, when she'd mentioned the name of Anthony Babington, Stephen's face had changed, as though a shadow had crossed it. She did not know why, and before she could ask him what was wrong, he had begun to talk of Philippa's music lessons and the dances Jane might teach her, and the fact that Philippa had a good sense of rhythm and back in Secotan had played the drums among the other women. The moment they were home, Stephen had gone to his room and she had seen him only at supper, when the whole household was gathered around the table to enjoy an excellent welcome-home meal. She had had no chance to question him.

But something was wrong. She knew it, though she didn't understand it. She tossed restlessly, wondering what the time was. Probably not yet midnight. A long night lay ahead. She closed her eyes resolutely, courting sleep, but opened them again almost at once. Nearby, a door had softly opened and closed, and she rather thought it was Philippa's.

Philippa! She and Robert had ridden together on the journey home today. Had Robert just gone into her chamber?

If those two wanted to wed, whatever Tobias might say, Jane would support them. But she didn't intend to support any unlawful lovemaking before the ceremony. Sybil had suffered from that. She got out of bed, pulled on a robe and slippers and stepped out into the gallery, to come face-to-face at once with Stephen, who was holding a lit candle and staring in the direction of the stairs down to the hall.

"Stephen?"

"Softly. Don't disturb Philippa."

"Her door opened!"

"I know. That was me. I heard footsteps passing my door and glimpsed candlelight beneath it and I wondered if, well…"

"You wondered if Robert had gone to her room? So did I!"

"Well, he hasn't. I looked in, and she's fast asleep and all alone as a young maid should be. But *someone* went along this gallery and presumably went down to the hall. I'm wondering why."

"Gone to the kitchen for something to eat?"

"After that enormous supper?" Stephen whispered. "Anyone who's still hungry would have to be a gannet. No, someone's prowling about and I want to know why. You go back to bed. I'm going downstairs."

"I'm coming with you."

"There's no need, Aunt Jane. I'll go down and…"

"This is my house," said Jane with determination. "You may regard yourself as my escort."

Aunt Jane in this mood was not to be gainsaid. Together they made their way downstairs. The hall was empty and dark except for the red glow from the banked fire. They made for the kitchen wing, just in case someone really had failed to eat enough at that laden supper table, but the kitchen was deserted. They were returning to the hall, puzzled, when Stephen put his hand on Jane's arm and whispered, "Light. Coming through the door to the tower. Where the parlour and the chapel are. Over there."

They stood still. Faintly, they heard the murmur of voices.

"It's all right," said Jane in a low voice. "Tobias has gone to the chapel to pray. He does that sometimes. Even at night, just occasionally. There's nothing to worry about."

"But I think someone else is with him." Stephen blew out his candle. "I mean to know what's afoot."

"But Stephen…"

"Sssh!" said Stephen, softly and yet so commandingly that Jane fell silent. Like a shadow, he moved toward the tower door and Jane, bewildered, followed him.

Beyond the door was the foot of the spiral stair to the parlour, but beside it, recessed into an archway, was the chapel door. It was not perfectly closed, and the glimmer of light came from within. Stephen drew it open another inch and peered in.

There were candles and an embroidered cloth on the altar and the Catholic Mass was being said. Gilbert Mallow, Charles Dupont, Tobias, Blanche and Robert were all present, but Mallow was not officiating. Dupont, in priestly garb, was elevating the host.

So Dupont was a priest as well as a musician.

If holding religious services was all they ever did, the authorities would probably wink at it, but it isn't. They talk of Mary Stuart's rights and the duty of all good Catholics to uphold her. They imperil the peace and security of England.

"It's just a Mass." Jane, who had followed close behind him, whispered into his ear. "I…I guessed that Dupont was a priest. But there's no harm in it, surely. Toby likes to hear Mass when he can."

Stephen did not answer. There had been an uncertainty in Jane's voice, and now Mistress Stannard's words were repeating themselves relentlessly in his mind. Whatever was happening here, and even though this was his own home, his own family, he had to know whether it stopped at holding a Mass, or not. He gripped his aunt's wrist to keep her still.

The service ended. Dupont removed his vestments and

put the ornate candlesticks, the cloth and the chalice into an oak chest which lay against the chapel wall. The chapel was still lit, for those attending had brought their own candles, which stood in a row on a small table close to the chest. They were now picking them up.

"It has been a great pleasure to say this Mass for you," Dupont said. He turned as he spoke, to address the others, so that he was facing toward the door, and though his voice was low, it came clearly out to the eavesdroppers. "I am more grateful than I can say for your promise of help. I shall leave here a week from today and go on to Salisbury. But you will not be forgotten. You will hear when the moment ripens. It will not be before next spring, which is some way off. But you will not change your minds? I have your word?"

"You have our word," said Tobias. "My son and I will set out as soon as you summon us. Will we not, Robert?"

"Yes, of course." Robert's low voice was eager. "We can bring no force of men, but we can bring ourselves, and offer our services in any way that may be useful."

"It will be dangerous," said Blanche, "but I pray that all will go well. I shall be waiting in fear but also in hope. I am glad that Mallow is staying. It will make the household feel more normal."

"God be with you all," said Dupont, and Mallow said, "Amen."

All five of them began to move toward the door and there was no time to get back across the hall and out of sight. Instead, swiftly and silently, Stephen, propelling Jane ahead of him, ascended the spiral stair, halting just around the first curve and sitting down on the steps, setting his unlit candle down beside him. Below, they all came out of the chapel, closed the door and went off across the hall toward the other stairway, and their beds.

"Did you know?" Stephen whispered. "Did you know, Aunt Jane, that Tobias—and Robert, too, it seems—are not just men of harmless piety who like to pray with candles and popish symbols around them?"

Jane was shaking—with the night chill which came through her robe from the stone stair beneath her, but also with shock. For so long she had feared that something like this would happen, that Tobias's convictions would lead him into danger, and now her fears seemed to be coming true and this nephew of hers, Stephen, sitting beside her on the steps, knew about it, too. He had been away for twenty years. She could not guess what he would do.

"I didn't know," she said. "I only…worried. But Stephen, they didn't say much, did they? Perhaps it doesn't mean anything very serious."

Stephen put his face in his hands. It was true that they had not mentioned Mary Stuart, or Babington, or any other name of ill omen. He could not put his hand on his heart and swear that what he had overheard was part of a plot to enthrone Mary and thereby to destroy Elizabeth.

But to a Jesuit—and Dupont was surely that—what other ripening would matter? Would need the force of men which Robert was clearly sorry they couldn't produce? Would be, as Blanche had said, dangerous?

And if this really were a plot, then the worm at the apple's heart was big and greedy and might consume his own kin. Traitors died terrible deaths. He did not care what happened to Mallow or Dupont, but every instinct cried out to him to protect the others. As an agent he was, quite clearly, useless. Almost a traitor himself.

"Whatever you know, or fear," he said, "understand this, Aunt Jane. You must never, never admit to knowledge of any kind, never admit that you suspected Tobias's beliefs. You must be innocent, Aunt Jane. If…if the worst happens…"

"Stephen, don't!"

"I will never betray my own kin," Stephen said. "Don't worry. But Philippa can't marry Robert now. You realize that?"

"Yes. And tomorrow," said Jane decisively, "I shall talk to Tobias."

CHAPTER THIRTY-EIGHT
Just a Simple Tournament
1585

"Yes," said Jane, sitting wearily on her favourite parlour window seat. "Yes, Stephen, I have spoken to Toby. It was like talking to a stone wall."

A carefully limewashed stone wall. Clean, superficially innocent and concealing God alone knows what.

"I didn't mention you," she said. "I said that I had been alone when I followed him downstairs and overheard what was going on in the chapel. He said I had misinterpreted everything. He said that his friend Sir Anthony Babington was organizing a tournament in London next spring and that he and Robert were going to take part. Sir Anthony has said he will lend them suitable horses, since none of our own horses are chargers. Blanche is worried because tournaments are dangerous and she doesn't think that either her husband or her son will have time to get into practice. She means to pray for their safety. Gilbert Mallow much regrets that such sports are unsuitable for a chaplain and so he isn't going."

"And it's natural, in a chapel, just after Mass, to start discussing arrangements for a tournament?" said Stephen grimly.

"I know. What are we to do? I know what I'd like to do," said Jane. "And that's to order Mallow and Dupont out of this house. At once."

"Please don't!" If she did that, it would alarm the quarry, the very thing that Mistress Stannard had insisted must not happen. "It could make Toby and Robert angry. In anger, they might plunge in deeper than they already are. Better wait," Stephen said. "If we do nothing, it may all come to nothing." He, too, was weary. He had not slept at all the previous night. "At least," he said, "Tobias must now realise that you are—making guesses. Perhaps he and Robert will think twice. They mentioned next spring and that's a long way off, as yet."

A week later, the night before Dupont was expected to take his leave, Stephen, who was still sleeping badly, once more heard, some time short of midnight, the sound of feet going past his door. This time he let them go. No doubt Dupont was holding another illegal Mass before departing. Later he heard the feet returning. Eventually, he slept.

In the morning Tim Snowe, who now had a ring of thin white hair around an otherwise completely bald pate, but who was still remarkably active, rang the usual bell for breakfast and then stood ready to help serve it. Philippa and Robert came to the meal last, hand in hand, their eyes at once bright and bashful, and on the table before the rest of the household they laid the certificate of their marriage, carried out the previous night by Gilbert Mallow.

"I feared that you wouldn't agree, Father," Robert said as Tobias stared at the scroll and then at the couple, opening and closing his mouth as though unable to find words. "I know, Father, that you don't like cousin marriages. But they are lawful."

"Is that…?" Jane began.

"It's a document declaring that they were married last night," said Tobias, and then shot to his feet. "But it's not lawful in my eyes! I can hardly believe this!" He picked up the certificate and brandished it. "How dare you, Robert? I will have this annulled! And you, Mallow—what were you thinking about? I am your employer!"

"Tobias!" Jane protested. "Please don't. They look so happy!"

"It's outrageous! What will folk say in Clicket? No banns were called, no feast held! They'll say there's scandal behind it!"

"Well, there isn't, and it's our business, not Clicket's," said Robert. "And it's legal, banns or no banns. Even if you are angry, Father, it can't be undone."

"I am angry, very!" Tobias shouted. "And it *shall* be undone." He had not even looked at Philippa, who was listening, motionless, impassive of face as ever. "I said," shouted Tobias, "I'll have it annulled!"

He turned to Blanche for support and Blanche promptly gave it. "How could you, Robert? How *could* you, Philippa? As for Gilbert, I'm ashamed of you, sir!"

"There are no grounds for an annulment," said Robert calmly. "We are fully man and wife, and there is evidence."

"You mean you…last night, after…?"

"Yes," said Robert, and grinned and Philippa smiled, too, looking at him with affection.

Dupont, visibly embarrassed, rose to his feet, murmured

something about leaving the family to its private affairs and left the hall. Jane's maid Alice, who was at the table as well, stayed where she was, bright eyed and young enough to be rather thrilled by all the drama. Tobias turned to Mallow, who had been warily holding his peace.

"What have you to say for yourself? How dare you perform such a ceremony without my permission?"

"If I hadn't," said the chaplain, "I feared from what they told me that they might fall into sin. The marriages of second cousins are perfectly in order these days."

Philippa turned to Stephen. "Father? Will you not give us your blessing? I am so happy."

He should have known she might do something of this kind. She was his daughter and in her was a little of his own adventurous streak. Philippa, not her brothers, had been prepared to leave her birthplace behind and travel across the ocean to a new life. This was another adventure, another brave throwing of the dice.

"Philippa," he said, rising from his place, "come with me. Don't be afraid. I want to speak with you alone for a few minutes, that's all."

He took her into the chapel, as it was the nearest quiet place, and having closed the door, said, "My dear daughter, I was not against your marrying Robert until a week ago, but then I found out something."

He hesitated. He couldn't say to her, *Your bridegroom is probably part of a treacherous plot against Her Majesty Queen Elizabeth,* though he knew at heart that he had not misunderstood those few words he had overheard. For one thing, he couldn't calculate what she might do. Would she abandon Robert? Turn on him? Inform on him?

Or warn him.

*It is Sir Francis Walsingham's wish that if there is indeed a plot,
it must be allowed to ripen, because that is the only way he will ever
get the queen to put an end to Mary Stuart…until Mary's head is
off, there will be no safety in this realm. This is crucial, Master Sweetwater! Fail in this and you yourself would become a traitor.*

The Algonquin, he thought bitterly, had more sensible
gods. Their principal deity was Wakonda, who had made and
watched over the forests and rivers, the plains and creatures
and the Algonquin tribes. Stephen had long ago concluded
that Wakonda had much to be said for him. He got on with
maintaining the world he had created without having hys-
terics over whether people believed in him or not, or in the
fine detail of how they worshipped him.

The only hope now was that the plot was only the feverish
dream of a few foolish priests and their pious followers and
that it would prove impossible and never be put into action.
Or that the ringleaders would be caught before anything
could happen, anyway.

But he couldn't see the future. He was like a traveller
picking his way, step by step, through lethal marshes, in a mist.

"Did you know," he said carefully, "that Robert is a
secret Catholic?"

"Oh yes," said Philippa. "I know. So are his parents.
Blanche has become Catholic to please Tobias. Robert told
me. He says he doesn't know if his mother is Catholic at
heart, but she stands by his father, whatever he does. Robert
said that his father would not consent to our marriage—
because I'm not Catholic and because we are cousins—so
we chose to wed secretly. I thought you would understand.
Father, I can't explain what happened, but from the moment
I first saw Robert…well, it was the same with him. It was

how things were, from what you've told me, between my mother and you."

"Did the pair of you really threaten to become lovers if Mallow refused to marry you?"

"Yes," said Philippa, looking him in the eyes. "We did. Side by side and hand in hand, we swore it. Robert has a sword with a cross-hilt. You told me, long ago, what the cross means to Christians. He had the sword with him and we swore on the hilt."

"I hope to God," said Stephen, "that no harm comes of this. Go back to your Robert. I daresay Tobias will soften, given time. I expect his mother will persuade him. Aunt Jane was always a peacemaker. But..."

"What is it?" Philippa was looking at him keenly. "Father, you're afraid of something! I know you are. But what?"

"These are dangerous times for Catholics, that's all. Go back to Robert. You're his wife now. Look after him and try to keep him safe."

"Safe from what?" She was genuinely puzzled, and that at least was a comfort. If there was a plot, she clearly knew nothing about it.

"From the perils of the age," said Stephen steadily. "Go, my daughter. Go back to Robert."

When she had gone, however, he stayed in the chapel for a long time, not praying but simply trying to quieten himself. He did not want to see Philippa's heart broken. He was so afraid for her.

CHAPTER THIRTY-NINE
The Summons
1585–1586

After grumbling and sulking—there was really no other word for it—for two days, Tobias capitulated, called the entire household into the hall and there declared that although it was not his choice, he accepted his son's marriage and would welcome Philippa as his daughter-in-law.

He performed his climbdown with a degree of grace, and Blanche seconded him, giving Philippa a kiss. As Jane and Stephen watched, Robert's wide smile and Philippa's transfigured face fell upon them both like a burden.

Stephen knew now what he must do. Through wakeful nights and miserable days he had faced it. It looked impossible, but he would have to try. First, he must *know*. He must know exactly what scheme was being planned, and if it was dangerous he must...

Try to detach his relatives from it, but without warning them that official suspicion existed already. Even if he had to drug them, knock them on the head, kidnap them by force. And after that (but not before) he must report what he knew. And faced with what might be a genuine danger to the realm, he could not resign from Walsingham's employment.

He could see only one way to acquire certain knowledge. He went to Gilbert Mallow.

His stomach was churning and his palms were wet in a way which astonished him. Nevertheless, he spoke the necessary words steadily.

"Gilbert, I have come to know that Tobias and Robert both follow the old faith. Do you follow it, too? You are clearly on good terms with both of them."

He had found the chaplain in his chamber, reading by his fire. Mallow put a marker in his place, laid the book aside and considered Stephen thoughtfully. "May I know why you ask?"

"There was a sailor in Sir Richard Grenville's crew who believed in the old faith. During the fight with the crew of the *Santa Maria*," said Stephen, surprising himself with his own fluent mendacity, "I heard him praying to the Virgin Mary to protect us, and saying to her that he knew he shouldn't be doing this, the Spaniards being Catholics like himself, but he had to, to survive. He fought well, I have to say that. He wasn't the sort to let down his shipmates. But afterward, I saw that he was unhappy."

I ought to join a company of players and write their dramas for them!

"I liked the man," Stephen said. "I'd been so long away from England—but I remembered how it was in Queen Mary's day, and how I missed the rituals of the old faith afterward. I don't remember the details well, though. I wondered if...if you could explain to me."

"You are truly interested?"

"My daughter has married Robert. She may well adopt his way of worship in due time. I would like to understand."

He was careful not to overdo the haste. It was a fortnight before he told Gilbert that he was so impressed by what he had learned that he wished to become a Catholic himself. It was another week until, after listening to an account of how King Henry VIII had put aside his Catholic wife, the Spanish Catherine of Aragon, in order to go through a form of marriage with Anne Boleyn, he said, wrinkling his brow, "But in that case—our present queen can't be legitimate!"

"That is indeed the Catholic view," Mallow agreed. He stopped there, however, as if wary.

Careful. The stalking hunter must not move too fast. "But there are stories about Mary Stuart," said Stephen hesitantly. He had heard them from Mistress Stannard. "About…the death of her husband Lord Darnley. Didn't she marry the man who was said to have arranged it?"

"Slanders!" said Mallow, suddenly angry. "Yes, James Bothwell had Darnley killed. Then he kidnapped the young queen and raped her and she married him to save her honour. She is all honour and delicacy as young women ought to be."

"I can hardly imagine a young woman conniving at a murder," Stephen agreed solemnly. "Poor lady."

After that, it was simple. Astoundingly and alarmingly so.

Robert and Tobias were essentially simple souls. In his own way, Mallow was simple, too. In the New World, Stephen, finding his way through an unfamiliar culture, had learned how to tell liars from honest men by signs that did not vary between nations. This trio, even though Tobias had spent time at court, remained uncomplicated. It was easy, so easy, to deceive them.

Two more days, and Gilbert had admitted that Charles Dupont was a Jesuit priest. Stephen, looking earnest, said, "Aren't they supposed to be trying to encourage support for Mary Stuart?"

When told that they were, he said, "It's so puzzling. If she is the rightful queen, then shouldn't something be done to put her into her rightful place?"

"Many think as you do," Gilbert said. "But we shall have to see."

Stephen asked no more questions. The stalking must be very cautious now. He must wait to let himself be drawn in further. He changed the subject to a discussion of the forthcoming Christmas celebrations.

Snow set in early in the new year of 1586. The fields vanished under a white blanket. Getting to church in Clicket was impossible for three Sundays running. The thaw was no better, for it came accompanied by pouring rain. The hills were lost in cloud; fields turned to quagmires, and in the combe, the river spated, roaring like a lion.

But when the rain had gone and the flood had subsided, there was a further invitation to Dunster Castle, to join a small house party. This time, by hobnobbing with the servants of the other guests, Stephen picked up the information that Mass had been illicitly said at a house in Wiltshire and that a Jesuit priest had visited a home in Hereford, disguised as a pedlar.

Here was something to report, and thereby earn his retainer.

But his anxiety for Philippa was eating into him. Philippa and Robert were not only deeply and obviously in love, but also prospective parents. Philippa had conceived very quickly, and the child would probably come in September. He must not, *would not,* do or say anything to harm her or Robert, even if…

Even if kept him awake at night. When he did sleep, his dreams were often unpleasant. He dreamed one night of his father's execution, which he had not seen or even had described to him, but which imagination ruthlessly re-created for him.

The year began to climb toward the spring.

Sergeant Gervase Wells of the Taunton Militia was young and single. He had dark auburn hair, kept short and clean, chestnut eyes and clear tanned skin. He was not tall and his build was wiry, but just because of this he was active on his feet, handy with a sword and an excellent dancer.

He had indeed been accused, by a well-educated colleague, of resembling the squire in Geoffrey Chaucer's *Canterbury Tales.* "You'd sing or whistle, anyway, all the day if you were let, and yes, *as fresh as is the month of May* just about describes you. Do you have to be so damned cheerful," demanded the colleague, "when we're got up before daybreak to go on exercises in the pouring rain?"

"But I rarely get the chance to love hotly till dawn," said Gervase regretfully. "Much as I'd like to. And my hair isn't curly."

"Oh, trust you to know the *Tales* better than I do!" growled his friend, but without rancour.

Most people liked Gervase, and knew that he was not as frivolous as he seemed. Despite his habit of bursting into song at odd moments and being merry over the bread and small ale before training exercises in the dark of wet winter mornings, he had grieved and been silent and quite unlike himself for weeks after the death of his mother.

He had respect and affection in his voice, too, when he spoke of his father, who was a prosperous tenant of the Luttrell family and rented a sizable farm a couple of miles from Dunster. Since he knew the Exmoor district well, having been brought up on the edge of it, he was often chosen when a messenger was needed to go in that direction.

The messages were supposed to be official ones, such as proclamations emanating from the royal court. Local militiamen were sometimes co-opted to help disseminate them to various towns. It was not part of their duties to carry private letters about. However, if a chance acquaintance made in a tavern, someone who didn't know Exmoor well, heard a man was going that way and asked him to drop a letter at such and such a house, no one would question it, as long as it caused no delays.

Gervase had such a letter with him when he set off through a spring morning to deliver to the town criers of Minehead, Dunster, Dulverton and Clicket a proclamation concerning the duty of all citizens to be alert for Jesuits and to report anyone who might be suspect.

Gervase put Clicket last on his list, rode back to it from Dulverton, delivered the proclamation and sought directions to Allerbrook House. Armed with instructions, he set off whistling and turned his horse onto the track up the combe. Before long he was within sight of a crenellated tower and from that surmised the existence of a tiled gatehouse in the latest style of black beams and white plaster, and a handsome courtyard.

He was surprised to arrive in due course at an unremarkable gate into what looked like an ordinary farmyard, where geese and hens pecked at grain. Two large dogs came galloping out of nowhere to bounce around his horse and bark, and the geese, led by an aggressive gander, abandoned the food and came cackling to join in. Two black-and-white cats asleep on the roof of a stone-built stable raised disapproving heads at the racket.

Gervase, however, was farm-bred and unimpressed by either dogs or geese. Swinging out of his saddle, he feinted a kick in the direction of the gander and shouted, "Quiet, you noisy curs!" at the dogs. On the other side of the farmyard rose the house, as splendid as it had seemed from a distance, but clearly occupied by unpretentious people.

The livestock having retreated out of his reach, although they were still making a noise, he took the letter from his saddlebag and led his horse toward the front door. It was opened before he got there, by an elderly man with a bald head and a butler's chain of office dangling over a business-like black doublet.

"Is Master Tobias Allerbrook at home? I have a message for him," Gervase said, holding it up. "I am Sergeant Wells of Taunton Militia, not that that's important. I'm just the messenger."

"You'd best come in. Dogs! Silence!" The dogs stopped barking at once. "Jack! *Jack!*" The butler raised his voice to a startling shout and a groom appeared. "This here's my grandson, Jack. You can trust your horse to him. See to the gentleman's animal, my lad—now, rub 'un down well. Come inside, sir. We'm due to dine any minute but there's always enough for a visitor."

He hadn't eaten since early that morning and was hungry. He let the butler lead him into a well-appointed hall where

THE HOUSE OF ALLERBROOK   445

a table had been laid for a meal and there was an agreeable smell of cooking.

The butler showed him to a seat, fetched him a glass of cider and went off to call Tobias, who presently arrived, accompanied by a lady whom he introduced as his wife. By the look of them, both were in their mid-forties. Tobias had a slightly chubby, earnest face and soft, greying hair that needed trimming. A lock of it kept falling into his eyes. His wife, who was a trifle plump but held herself with too much dignity to be called cuddly, was one of those calm women who kept their thoughts to themselves. Pleasant, ordinary-looking people, Gervase thought

Tobias took the letter with a word of thanks, read it immediately and then passed it to his wife. Having read it and handed it back, she moved to stand at her husband's side in a way that suggested she would always be his supporter. Gervase wondered what had been in the letter.

Tobias, meanwhile, was repeating the invitation to dine, and presently the rest of the family appeared. A smiling older lady with a neat white ruff over her tawny gown was introduced to him as Mistress Jane Allerbrook, Tobias's mother. A tough-looking man in middle life was apparently her nephew, Master Stephen Sweetwater.

The younger generation was represented by Robert Allerbrook—"My son," Tobias said—and Master Robert's wife, Mistress Philippa, who appeared to be Stephen's daughter. Tobias handed the mysterious letter to Robert, who read it without comment and then passed it to Philippa. Gervase noticed this in distracted fashion.

The sight of Philippa had nearly stopped his breath.

He saw at once that she was expecting a child and as they took their places at table, he noticed that she and her dark, good-looking husband constantly exchanged glances and were assuredly as deeply in love as a young couple well could be. On the instant, he found himself envying Robert Allerbrook. He had never seen a girl like Philippa in all his life.

Despite the curve of the coming child beneath her green gown, she still looked as lithe and lean as a young cat. She had an amber complexion, not through sun and wind but because her skin was naturally thus, and her eyes were darker and longer than purely English eyes could ever be. Her long hair was contained in a caul of silvery net which only accentuated its thickness and its remarkable blue-black colour. He bowed low over her slender brown hand, glad to look downward in case his eyes revealed his admiration.

Gervase's admiration, indeed, was so intense that he found himself unwontedly tongue-tied as dinner began, although he observed that the two couples were a little quiet. He wondered if that were normal, or had something to do with the letter.

It was private, anyway. He mustn't wonder about it and he mustn't stare at Mistress Philippa, either. Pulling himself together, he exerted himself to answer properly when Mistress Jane asked him questions about his life, and his errand to their district. He also gathered from the family's oddly stilted conversation among themselves that Mistress Philippa's foreign beauty was because her father had been to the New World and her mother came from a native tribe there, the Algonquin.

But he feared that he had still been too quiet and had turned his eyes too often toward Philippa. After the meal, he pretended to be in more haste than he really was, and took his leave quickly.

He rode away with his mind full of Philippa. He had never

seen such a girl, never. Her face in repose was like a beautiful sculpture, but when she smiled, her eyes shone as though sunlight were playing on pools incalculably deep. When she moved, even now, when her movements could hardly be as graceful as they normally would, it was like music translated into motion.

Had anyone guessed his feelings? He thought not, because he also thought that if there had been constraint at the table, it wasn't due to him.

Just what, he asked himself, dragging his mind resolutely away from Mistress Philippa, had been in that letter?

CHAPTER FORTY
Strange Gods
1586

"Well, Master Sweetwater, are you with us?" Gilbert Mallow asked Stephen. "Or rather, with Tobias and Robert here? Sir Anthony Babington has bidden them to London, but I have been told to stay here and continue my duties as chaplain. Matters are moving. Will you join with us—and go with your kinsmen to London to offer your services, perhaps your sword?"

"I am with you," said Stephen gravely.

Tobias said, "We have talked among ourselves and decided to trust you with the knowledge of what we are doing, but *are* you with us, truly? Or have we put our necks in the noose in speaking to you of our plans?"

"I am with you. Truly," said Stephen, meeting his cousin's eyes with, he hoped, what looked like honesty.

He had waited, and his quarry had come to him freely. Indeed, Tobias had begun to change toward him, to become more friendly, from the very day Stephen first told Mallow that he wished to become a Catholic. When Stephen expressed interest in the cause of Mary Stuart, it was rapidly clear that Tobias was so enamoured of it that he was prepared to trust and to embrace anyone who shared his feelings. Even, Stephen thought cynically, if the person concerned reeked of sulphur.

As for Robert, the romantic streak that Jane had once mentioned seemed to have been aroused by Mary Stuart, though he had never met her and knew only that she was beautiful, imprisoned and, from a Catholic point of view, wronged. He had once spoken of the fact that her husband Henry Darnley had been murdered, but apparently believed that it had been done without her knowledge by her nobles, one of whom had then captured her and married her by force. "She is a tormented heroine," he had said. "She is like a lady in a legend. I long to serve her."

Now, in solemn tones, Stephen said, "I repeat, I'm with you, if you'll have me."

"Our sovereign lady Mary," said Tobias, "needs as many men as possible, to support her in the conflict to come."

Stephen looked up at the windows of the chapel, where they had forgathered. Sunlight poured through the stained glass, making coloured patches on the tiled floor. One very fine window had always intrigued him. It showed an angel standing before a building with arms outspread, denying entrance to a man who held a flaring torch aloft. It was said to commemorate something, now forgotten, that Aunt Jane's grandmother Quentin had done for the family. Looking at it, he thought of Aunt Jane, who loved them all so well and had taken risks in their defence more than once. Now she was threatened with more trouble. Poor Aunt Jane. At her age, she was entitled to some peace.

"It will be a perilous enterprise," he said. "Robert, you especially should take care of yourself. You're a husband and will soon be a father. Let me go in your stead."

It would have relieved his mind immensely if Robert had agreed, but his son-in-law only shook an emphatic head. "I have to go. I'd be ashamed to be left out," said Robert. "Philippa understands. I've talked to her. She realizes how much it means to me and she has given me her blessing."

It occurred to Stephen that however much in love Robert might be with Philippa, there were things he didn't know about her. He had never lived with the Algonquin. Of course Philippa, the granddaughter of a chief, had not wept or shouted or even protested. Algonquin women didn't. They hid their feelings when their men went into danger, but some of them burned inside, and their eyes betrayed them.

Philippa was and always would be partly Algonquin. So Philippa knew what this venture meant to Robert and was happy to see him go, was she? Robert was a fool. What Philippa felt and what Philippa said were two completely different things.

Robert was still talking. "It is such a privilege! To be one of the instruments, however humble, in bringing Queen Mary Stuart to her rightful power and the old faith back to England! How could any man worthy of the name give up the chance, even for the greatest domestic bliss? It would be like a knight refusing his lord's summons to go to war. Wives and homes and children had to be left behind then. Their honour was at stake as well as the man's."

Dear God, said Stephen to himself. He had been frightened for his daughter when she married Robert, but this was worse. He had never known such dread.

"So," said Jane furiously, marching into Stephen's chamber with only the briefest of knocks. "So you and Tobias and Robert are all off to London tomorrow and Tobias is still talking nonsense to me about going to a tournament. You, apparently, are going along to give general help with the organizing, meet some of Toby's well-bred friends and renew your acquaintance with London. Am I expected to believe a single word of this?"

Stephen, who was packing clothes into a hamper, straightened up and said, "I don't expect it, Aunt Jane. It's spring, and that was the season we heard mentioned when we stood outside the chapel door that night. And now the summons has come. What you and I fear may well be true. I have managed to make Toby believe that I think as he does. I am going with him and Robert in the hope, mainly, of protecting them. If they need protection, that is. I need to know how real, how serious, this is—this thing they seem to be involved in. It's my duty, anyway, Aunt Jane. It's every citizen's duty."

"You mean that if it's serious, you'll run to the authorities. You'll admit what you've learned! You'll throw Tobias and Robert to them!"

"Hush!" said Stephen. Jane's voice had risen alarmingly. For a moment they stared at each other in silence and Jane, watching her nephew's face, thought that he was about to speak but had checked himself.

"Stephen..." she said pleadingly.

"If the thing is truly serious," he said, "and not just foolish dreams and unworkable schemes, then yes, I must report what I know. But first I'll get Tobias and Robert out of it if I possibly can. If they'll let me!"

"What if you can't? What if they *don't* let you?" Again Jane's voice had risen, and there was a note of hysteria in it. "And what if you run into danger yourself? Aren't you putting yourself at risk of arrest?"

"I hope not. Aunt Jane, please. Try to trust me. As a young man," said Stephen, trying to smile, "I was an adventurer. I still am, but a more responsible one than I was then. You *can* trust me, Aunt Jane. At least to try as hard as I can to do what is right."

"What is it you're not telling me? There's something. I know it!"

"Dear Aunt, I beg you. Ask no more questions. If Tobias and Robert are running into peril, then I'll do my utmost to get them out of it but…no, Aunt Jane!" She had begun to protest again and he caught hold of her, grasping her upper arms strongly. "Listen to me, please, please listen. If this plot is serious, then it is a terrible thing. The future of the *whole realm* may be at stake. Do you want the Inquisition here in England? Do you?"

"The Inquisition!" Jane's eyes widened in horror.

"Yes," said Stephen relentlessly. "The Inquisition. Like the days of Queen Mary Tudor, but worse. You remember those days, don't you? So do I! My father…!"

Jane began to sob. He held her firmly. "Hear me out. If I learn of a real, dangerous plot and hold my tongue, even to save Tobias, even to save my own son-in-law, and the plot succeeds and the Inquisition comes here, then every hideous death they bring about will lie at my door, and if I hold my tongue for your sake, then it will lie at yours, as well."

"What?"

"I mean it. You *must* listen." He released his grip and put his arms around her instead. "It is because of those terrible memories, because of what happened to my father that I must tread so carefully now. Only believe that I will do my best for us all. Don't betray me to Toby or Robert. Let me deal with this in my own way. Don't meddle! I *will* try to save them—if only they'll listen. If they don't, then the choice will be theirs and only theirs."

"I have tried already to talk them into backing out!" said Jane wretchedly. "I said I didn't believe the tournament story, that I suspected they were in a conspiracy, and pleaded with them to abandon it. They treated me as though I were a stupid woman who knew nothing! They just shook their heads and Toby said he hoped to win a trophy in the lists. *Tournament!*" She almost spat the word. "Very well, I won't *meddle* further." She drew herself away from him and wiped her eyes. She was trembling. "I understand what is at stake. At stake! Horrible word! I know why Mary Stuart must never rule here. But I charge you with this duty, Stephen. Get them out. *Get them out.*"

"I have called you here for a very important reason, Gilbert," said Jane, standing behind the desk in the study. "You are dismissed."

"Dis...?" Gilbert Mallow, who when Tim Snowe came to fetch him had been on his knees in the chapel praying for the success and safety of the three men who had just left for London, looked at her in bewilderment.

"Yes, Gilbert. *Dismissed* is the word I used. I want you out of this house. Here are the wages you're owed." She picked up a small bag from the desk and held it out to him. "You need not fear betrayal. I can't denounce you as a conspirator against the queen without also implicating my own family. I know perfectly well why my son and grandson and my nephew have gone to London. Don't try to deny your part in it. I can never forgive what you and that man Dupont have done between you. I won't have you here any longer. Not another day."

"But…!" Gilbert seemed genuinely amazed.

"How many people do you imagine want the kind of rule you wish to inflict on England? I pray, night and day, that the conspiracy fails without bringing about the deaths of Tobias, Robert and Stephen."

Though so angry that she was shaking, Jane had remembered to include Stephen in the list. Gilbert must not suspect that there was a cuckoo in his little nest of traitors. "Dear God, how could you and Dupont behave like this, confusing their minds with wild dreams? Yes, dreams! Like the visions of someone in a high fever!"

"Mistress Allerbrook, that isn't so!" Mallow did not seem to understand how outraged she was. His voice was as eager as ever and he even smiled, trying to win a smile from her in response. "Dear Mistress Allerbrook, they have gone on a quest, like King Arthur's knights, like the crusaders, to restore the true faith—"

"Whose true faith? You mean your faith. Do you also hope to see the Inquisition installed here, to see heretics hunted as they were in the days of Queen Mary Tudor?"

"It wouldn't be like that, Mistress Allerbrook! Our gracious lady Mary is gentle and merciful…."

"So was Mary Tudor, to start with. I don't care about your faith, Gilbert. What about mine? How dare you be so arrogant? And how dare you call me *dear* Mistress Allerbrook? Neither I nor my family are very dear to you if you are prepared to hazard our lives—to hazard the whole country— like this. If my family were not virtually hostages, I *would* denounce you. You have misused my hospitality and led my kinsmen into terrible danger. I wanted to throw you out long ago but—" *careful, don't say it was Stephen's advice* "—I feared it would anger Toby and the others and maybe drive them further into danger. However, they couldn't be deeper in than they are now! Pack your belongings and go."

He had still not taken the money. She shook it at him. "*Take* this. Take it!" Reluctantly he did so. "Be out of this house within one hour," she said grimly, "or be ejected by force, by the Snowes and Jack Edwardes. Now, leave me. I wish never to set eyes on you again!"

"I have ordered Gilbert Mallow out of the house," Jane said some time later, walking into the hall where Blanche was putting a bunch of gold and purple heartsease flowers into a little bowl of water. "I trust he has gone?"

"Yes. Whatever did you say to him?" Blanche turned a worried face toward her mother-in-law. "I saw him going off on his pony, with all his belongings. He looked terrified."

"I daresay. He's probably afraid that I'll denounce him, although I said I wouldn't. I hold him responsible for the way your husband and son and Philippa's father have been drawn into this dreadful situation."

"What do you mean? What dreadful situation?"

"If you suppose, Blanche, that I don't know that this talk of tournaments is all a taradiddle, then think again. I know very well why they've all gone to London. I tried to talk sense into them before they left, but they wouldn't heed me. I think they want to be martyrs! I'm furious with all of them and afraid for them, too. Aren't you?"

"Yes," said Blanche in a low voice. "And if you think I haven't tried to talk Tobias and Robert out of going, you would be wrong. I did."

Blanche put the last flowers in place and looked at them miserably. "Flowers! What's the use of women making a home pretty when the men would rather ride off on demented quests? I agreed to become a Catholic to please Tobias, but when all this business began—well, I pleaded with them both but I failed, and then I promised all three of them my prayers. They don't know I've been praying they'd change their minds! I don't understand it all," said Blanche, "but I think that the plan is to free the queen of Scotland from her prison. After that, I'm not sure what is intended. Are you?"

"No, but isn't it obvious? Dupont was a Jesuit, and Jesuits believe that Queen Elizabeth is baseborn and therefore has no right to the crown. In which case, the rightful queen is Mary."

"She can't be put back on the Scottish throne," Blanche said. "Her son has that one. If she doesn't choose to go into exile, then…"

"Quite. The Jesuits want her on the *English* throne."

"But that can't be," said Blanche, "unless the present queen is deposed and shut away or worse. I can't sleep at night for worrying. I don't know about Philippa. I didn't want this marriage because Tobias didn't, but there it is and I've tried to make friends with her, as a mother-in-law should with her son's wife, but she keeps her own counsel so much. She doesn't confide."

"I know," said Jane. "But to my eyes, she's been mopish since Robert rode away. Where is she now?"

"I think she went out for a walk. She's been gone some time."

"Has she? She shouldn't walk too far. I know she's strong, but all the same, she's big, for five months. I think," said Jane, "that I ought to go after her."

Philippa, as Jane had once done, liked to walk up to the ridge. She might have done so now. Jane made her way out to the track up the combe. She had guessed right. Before she was at the top, Philippa was in sight.

She was on the skyline, facing the east, holding up her hands, palms outward, as if in supplication. Jane, disconcerted, quickened her pace, wishing she were as active as in her youth. She had put on weight in the past few years, and going uphill made her breathless.

She was too short of breath to call out as she came up behind Philippa, but a moment later she was glad, because it would have seemed somehow a mistake to break in. Philippa was talking, apparently to the sky.

Another moment and she realized that whatever her great-niece was saying was not in English. She was speaking a language that Jane had never heard before. And it was an invocation; Jane knew that at once, by the intonation and the rhythm of the words. She stopped and waited.

The prayer ended. Philippa's hands dropped. "Philippa!" Jane half whispered. "My dear, what are you doing?"

Philippa turned quickly. "Great-Aunt Jane! I thought I was alone!"

"Obviously. But what *were* you doing? It looked— sounded—like…praying."

"It was."

"But…people don't pray like that. Not standing out in the open and…and looking up at the sky. Philippa, people pray on their knees. In church, or at least indoors."

"I was praying to the greatest god of my tribe, if he can

hear me. England is far away from his territory. But he is very powerful. His name is Wakonda. I was praying to him."

"But…" said Jane, and then stopped, words failing her.

Philippa was standing straight-backed as she always did and her face was so calm that it might have been carved from wood. "I was asking Wakonda," she said, "to look after Robert, now that Robert is going into danger."

"Philippa!" Sheer horror gave Jane back her powers of speech. "My dear, dear girl. You must forget your heathen gods! Something terrible could happen to you if it were known that you said such prayers! You must kneel in the chapel and ask the true God to look after Robert. There isn't any other, my dear, and no one must ever, ever know about this."

"The gods of my people," said Philippa, "are more merciful than your god. I have learned how the queen who loved the old faith persecuted those who preferred the new—and sometimes it was the other way about, was it not? Not so often, perhaps, but it happened. And when we were on the *Tiger* with Sir Richard Grenville, I heard how the Spaniards had treated other tribes like mine, farther south, because they were not Christians. They did such terrible things. Even worse than the Inquisition in Spain. I heard about that, too, on the ship."

"I know, my love. We all know how the Spaniards have conducted themselves in the New World. Our vicar, William Honeywood, has spoken of it from his pulpit."

Philippa shuddered. "I was frightened when Sir Richard attacked the *Santa Maria,* but I was glad, too. I had already learned to hate the Spaniards. He was generous, letting her crew go once he'd got hold of the treasure."

"If the plot in which Tobias and Robert are entangled should succeed," said Jane slowly, "we may find ourselves

with the Inquisition here in England. We must pray, Philippa—
in the chapel, not up here—but we must pray for more than
the safety of our menfolk. We must also pray that their plot
fails, so as to keep the Inquisition out. Do you realize that?"

Philippa's dark eyes widened.

"Gilbert Mallow—whom I have just ordered off the
premises, by the way—says that won't happen. But I fear it."

"I didn't understand. I mean, I didn't know that if…if this
Queen Mary Stuart that Robert has talked to me about
were to take the throne, then it might mean the Inquisition
coming here. But Robert wouldn't…his father wouldn't…"

"I think they are deluded," said Jane unhappily. "They
don't see, or won't see, that Mary could not take power here
without bringing civil war on us all, and that if the Catholics won, then the Inquisition would most likely appear in
England. It's even possible, if she succeeds, that it would be
with the help of Spain."

"I can't think in that way," said Philippa. "I can't think
about inquisitions and rival faiths and a queen called Mary
Stuart. I am simply afraid for Robert and lonely without
him. If you're right, then what he is doing is…is dreadful—
madness…but it makes no difference to the way I love him.
Great-Aunt Jane, did you ever love anyone like this? Your
husband?"

"No, dear. Not my husband. Mine was a forced marriage
and I never managed to be more than mildly fond of him,
though he was good to me in his way, I suppose. I loved
someone else. I do know what it means."

"Was he your lover?" Philippa asked it outright.

"Once," said Jane, meeting candour with candour. "Once
and once only. He made the marriage his family expected,
for money and position, and I went on living here at Aller-

brook. He died far away in Ireland. The news didn't reach me for months and then only by accident, when I was dining with the Luttrells and someone casually mentioned him. I cried so bitterly that night. I could bear being without him as long as he was still alive, still under the same sky as I was, sharing the sun and the moon with me. To know that he wasn't here anymore…that was dreadful."

"I'm sorry," Philippa said.

"Well, it was years ago now. It's a strange thing, but it's possible to love a man steadily lifelong, even when the time the two of you had together amounts only to a few days. It kept me from ever wanting to remarry. That and loving Allerbrook so much and having three young people to look after, as well! Now, we must get back to the house. We will go to the chapel." Jane studied the younger woman with concern. "Are you still homesick, Philippa?"

"Not now. I was at first but this is my home now, the home I want to share with Robert, forever. If only he comes back! I suppose I was—calling for help from every possible direction. Old habits…"

"Come back to the house. You shouldn't walk far just now anyway. Philippa, never, never invoke these strange gods of yours again. Promise me!"

"I promise," said Philippa.

CHAPTER FORTY-ONE
Nightmare
1586

*T*his, said Stephen Sweetwater to himself, *is a nightmare. I never knew before what that really meant.*

It had been nightmarish enough when the *Sweet Promise* was blown off course in the storm and finally swallowed by seas like hungry mountains, to leave her last survivors huddled in an open boat with no means of knowing where they were, let alone where they were going.

It had been nightmarish to find himself cast away and dependent on the hospitality of a savage New World tribe, nightmarish when Sir Richard Grenville made up his mind to attack the *Santa Maria,* not because Stephen himself was averse to the venture, but because Philippa was there and he feared for her if the Spaniards won.

But this...

The parlour at Sir Anthony Babington's London lodgings in Holborn looked civilised enough. It was panelled and painted, with a Turkish carpet patterned in red and black and slate-blue hanging on one wall by way of decoration. There were cushioned settles and a spinet and a shelf of books, and in the centre of the room stood a polished table whose surface reflected the flames of numerous candles, burning in an array of chased silver candlesticks. A set of upholstered chairs stood around it. This was a place for friendly gatherings, for conversation and games of cards and backgammon, accompanied by tasty snacks and flagons of good wine.

This evening, despite the cultured atmosphere and the sparkle of candlelight on the company's jewellery, the parlour was the scene of the deadliest conspiracy.

One of the most dreadful things was the naïveté of the participants. Since Stephen and the Allerbrooks had only just reached London, this was the first meeting they had so far attended and it was Stephen's first glimpse of Sir Anthony Babington. Babington was twenty-five years old, with a wife and small daughter, who were at his country home. He looked younger than twenty-five, however, and his mind, too, was youthful. He was delicately made and refined, fair-haired, with manicured hands and innocent grey eyes. His expensive sky-blue doublet and starched ruff were in the latest fashion, his faith in his cause as ardent and simple as the faith of a child.

"If God is with us, how can we fail?" he had said, twice, in the first ten minutes of the meeting. Stephen, who had in his time heard men and women pray to quite an assortment of deities and not be heard, wondered on which remote mountain or lonely island Anthony had spent most of his life.

At Anthony's side was a priest, John Ballard. He had the eyes of a fanatic. Stephen had seen such fanaticism before. His own father, Andrew Shearer, had had eyes like that, and so had Danny Clay and their companions when they burst into Allerbrook on the day Harry Hudd died. Looking at Ballard now, he even found himself wondering if his father had not rushed headlong to his own death. Not that that excused his executioners. No doubt their eyes had looked the same.

Ballard had spoken with joy of the day when the old faith would be restored, and of the sixty thousand Spanish troops who were being gathered and made ready to land in England in September to support the gallant heroes, Sir Anthony and the six noble young Catholic gentlemen, who were to undertake the task of destroying the heretic queen, to make way for Catholic Mary Stuart. The gigantic difficulties were to him no more than molehills. He was innocent as well as fanatical, and doubly alarming because of it.

Restoration of the old faith would assuredly need the help of the Spanish Inquisition, if it were to take place at all. Stephen smiled with false approval and longed to thrust a dagger through Ballard's pitiless heart and empty a musket into his simpleton's brain.

The six noble young Catholic gentlemen were not present, because Anthony was still recruiting them from among Catholic friends at court. Her Majesty, Stephen thought, had displayed a remarkable degree of tolerance. According to Mistress Stannard, this was not the first Catholic conspiracy.

Tobias and Robert were seated opposite Stephen, their faces both serious and eager. Beside Tobias was another young Catholic gentleman, Bernard Maude. He was not a prospective assassin but was assisting John Ballard, who had been living abroad, as companion and guide through England. He had come to take notes and had writing materials in front of him. He had a round, unlined face and innocent blue eyes. There wasn't a morsel of common sense, thought Stephen despairingly, among the lot of them.

"The outlines of the plan are clear," Anthony was saying, "and I should have my six volunteers sworn in within a week. Then I will gather them to discuss details. Meanwhile, you, Father Ballard, intend to alert the Catholics in the north, is that not so? We should find ample support there."

"I shall tell them to be ready to rise when the beacons are lit on the death of Elizabeth," Ballard said.

"The actual date for her death must wait on news from France about the readiness of the troops and, of course, on acceptance of the scheme from Queen Mary. A means of communicating with her has been found," Sir Anthony said, beaming. "A man called Gil Gifford, who has wormed his way into Walsingham's favour, is acting as a courier between Walsingham and Chartley mansion in south Derbyshire, where Queen Mary now is. He says that Chartley gets its ale from an outside brewer. If we pay him, the brewer will arrange for letters to go in and out in ale barrels. Gifford will see that the letters get to their proper destinations."

"When the time draws near," said Ballard, "bid your young men to attend court regularly, with weapons concealed about them, so that when the day is declared, one or more may seize whatever chance presents itself to shoot or stab the usurper. I can provide an extra helper for them, a man called John Savage. He will also attend court and can count as a seventh assistant. But when the task is done, Babington, you and your men will have the further task of riding to Chartley—or wherever our sovereign lady then is—gathering as you go those supporters who live along your route, to rescue the queen from her imprisonment. And now we come to a very important matter. Whoever kills the usurper queen must be able to escape afterward."

"It will be a moment of great danger." Stephen felt that it was time he made a contribution. "She will have people with her. They will fall on anyone who attacks her."

"You are right," Ballard said. "Our men must pick a time when she is out walking in some open place and they must have horses nearby. More than one may be involved in the actual killing. We need men who are apparently not connected with any of them, to cover their flight. This is where you three, our good friends from Allerbrook, come in."

"We will do our part," said Tobias. "Rest assured of that."

"You will be introduced to our men so that you can recognize them, but you must not appear to know them. Stay close to them, however, because your part will be to appear to give chase but in reality to hinder their capture, by whatever means you can."

Tobias smiled. "Clutch at a flying cloak and miss and fall over in the path of those coming behind. Start a hue and cry after the wrong man—that would be a good trick to play. We will confer and think of many plans."

"We are so very privileged!" Robert was excited. "To be chosen from so many for a task so vital!"

"You have the entrée at court," Anthony pointed out. "That is valuable. I must write to Charles Dupont and congratulate him on the work he did in drawing you Allerbrooks into our scheme. It *cannot* fail. Before Christmas, the English crown will be on our sweet Mary's head. She was in the care of the Earl of Shrewsbury for a time," he added. "As a boy, I was one of his pages. That was when I first met her and

gave her my heart and my allegiance. She has such enchantment. Her faith in her God was an inspiration to me. And
her smile! I would die for that smile, gladly! What an adventure this will be, and what a triumph!"

He looked around at the gathering, bestowing on them a
delightful smile of his own. His charm and his devotion to
Mary Stuart, his passionate belief in his religion and his joy in
sheer adventure came at them all as if a wave had broken over
them. For a moment Stephen felt the undertow, almost understood. Indeed, he understood the urge to adventure, all too
well.

But he had also become a realist, with loyalties of his
own—to the memory of the father who had kindled his life,
however casually, to Aunt Jane, to Philippa. He saw Tobias
and Robert nodding eagerly back at Sir Anthony and hope-
lessness overwhelmed him. Just what, he asked himself, had
he achieved by joining them? He had wanted to know if the
conspiracy were serious, and if so, to learn the details. Well,
learned them he had, and it could hardly be more serious,
but what chance did he have of dragging his kinsmen out of
this mess in time to save them? Look at them—all aglow with
fervour! Must he choose between their lives and betraying
England by keeping silence? He could *not* keep silence in the
face of this. The danger was too great. He had hoped, and
Aunt Jane had begged him, to find a way of keeping faith
with both sides, but...

Stephen sat there, his face expressionless, and wished the
Sweet Promise had taken him with her to the bottom of the
sea.

"The timing is important," said Maude. "We must have a
date on which the Spanish troops—they'll be coming from the
Netherlands—will move, given fair winds. We shall have to

say that from a certain date onward, the first day when the wind is right, will be the day to strike. Do you agree, Sir Anthony?"

"Yes. Word must be got to the Spanish ambassador in France, Bernardino Mendoza, since he is preparing the force. He must name the date for us. Note that, if you will."

Maude dipped his quill pen and began to write. A moment later he paused as if to consider a word, looked up and let his eyes meet Stephen's fleetingly before dropping his gaze to Stephen's hands. Then he shifted the paper in front of him nearer to a candle and once more resumed his notations. As his right hand moved, guiding the pen, the light from the candle flashed on a ring. Stephen glanced at it and a shock went through him. It was a wide gold band with a stone of faceted amber set in elaborate claws. It was the exact twin of the one he wore on the middle finger of his own left hand. The ring that Mistress Stannard had given him.

He had been wrong to think that Maude's sky-blue eyes were innocent. They were not. They were merely plausible. There was a spy already in the heart of the conspiracy.

As they were leaving at the end of the meeting and going down the steps from the main door a little way behind Ballard, he found Bernard Maude at his side.

"Two of the clock. Tomorrow afternoon. I'll have horses. This end of the Strand. Don't fail." The words were breathed rather than spoken and Maude looked straight ahead all the time. Then he brushed past Stephen and rejoined Ballard, leaving Stephen to wonder if he had really heard Maude speak at all.

The time had come to do some speaking of his own. He knew now as much as he needed to know and it was worse than his worst imaginings, and if his kinsmen would not abandon this madness now, they were doomed. He could not think of a way to lead into the subject smoothly. He must simply say what must be said, and hope for a response.

On the way back to the Green Dragon inn in Bishops-gate, where the three of them were staying, he suddenly said, "This is a very elaborate scheme. We have to put together our own strike with promises of support from abroad, yet what proof have we that the support will come? I don't like it. Do you? We could back out now and go home. I don't mean betray anyone—just withdraw ourselves."

It was the best he could do. Bernard Maude's presence was evidence that Walsingham almost certainly already knew all about the plan and who was in it, but he dared not tell them that.

If there is indeed a plot, it must be allowed to ripen…until Mary's head is off, there will be no safety in this realm…. Fail in this and you yourself would become a traitor. He must not warn his cousins, or they would warn their fellow conspirators and the chance of removing Mary, the head of the serpent, would be lost.

But if Toby and Robert simply backed out now, at once, it was just possible that Walsingham might not pursue them. It was worth trying.

They were looking at him, however, with scorn. "We never thought you would turn craven," Tobias said.

"And of course the scheme will work!" Robert was alight with the excitement of it all. "Why should it not? God will see to that."

"I think," said Stephen, "that we should not trust too much to God. God," he added grimly, "seems to have a liking for martyrs. Do you want to be martyrs? Because I do not."

"We might have known you'd fail us," said Tobias contemptuously. "Why did we ever let you in on our plans? Are you going to go running to Sir Francis Walsingham now?" His hand was on his dagger hilt.

"No, I am not," said Stephen, privately blessing the existence of Bernard Maude, who had freed him from the hideous choice between kinsfolk and country. Maude would do all the betraying that was necessary. "You can leave your dagger alone. What do you take me for?" he demanded, hoping his indignation sounded real. "I shan't run to anyone. I am simply saying that this is a highly perilous plan. I am reconsidering and I urge you to do the same. Have you thought what you'll do if it goes wrong?"

"It won't!" said Robert.

"I have," said Stephen, ignoring this. "I shall make for home. The authorities will think first of Dover, or a ship down the Thames. I shall ride for Somerset. Nicholas Lanyon might help. He has a ship."

"Why do you expect things to go wrong?" Tobias said. "When Babington's men strike the usurper queen down, will you be with us to help them escape? Or not?"

"Oh, yes," said Stephen, vigorously and mendaciously. The Queen's Players, he thought, that band of actors now dedicated to entertaining Her Majesty, had not only missed a good playwright in him; they'd missed a good performer, as well. "If you mean to go through with this, then I stay with you. If the day comes and nothing has gone amiss, I will do my part."

"Good," said Tobias pugnaciously. "God will be with us. You'll see."

"I pray it may be so," said Stephen piously.

Well, he had planted the seed. He could do no more.

Force was hardly practicable. The final decision must be theirs. There was a chance that the seed would grow. He would wait a few days, to nurture any promising shoots, before he betook himself to safety.

At two of the clock the next day, having slipped out of the lodging unnoticed, he was at the Strand, the long row of fine riverside houses between the City and Whitehall. Maude was awaiting him, with the promised horses.

"Where are we going?" Stephen asked as he mounted the nag whose reins Maude had handed him. "If it weren't for that amber ring on your hand, I wouldn't have come."

"I daresay. We're going to Richmond, to see Walsingham."

"What for?" demanded Stephen.

"You'll find out. Don't even think of arguing, if you value your life. Come on. It's a long way and horses are the quickest method. It's miles and *miles* by river even when the tide is right. The old Thames winds so much," said Maude. "It'll still take us about two hours."

"As a matter of interest," said Stephen as they rode, "where does John Ballard think you are now?"

"Wenching," said Maude succinctly. "He believes I have a girl—a maidservant in one of the houses along the Strand. It's a useful pretence when I want to get to Richmond."

Stephen had not seen Richmond Palace since his educational sojourn in London, but he remembered it as beautiful, with graceful turrets, ample windows, ornamental fountains and weather vanes that chimed in the wind. Today he hardly noticed its charm. He felt like a poor swimmer out of his depth and caught in a current. He wished he were back among the Algonquin.

Once in the palace, their horses were taken by royal grooms, and at the sight of their amber rings they were shown without delay, first into a room where secretaries were working, and then into an inner office.

It was graciously proportioned but its beauty had mostly disappeared behind furnishings which declared that it was used by someone who had no time for frivolities. Shelves laden with ledgers and books obscured the panelling; tables were strewn with documents and writing sets; a blackboard on the wall had curious symbols chalked on it.

The man in charge matched the scenery. His hair was black, except for some silvering at the temples, his skin nearly as brown as Philippa's, and his gown was of black velvet. He was as dark eyed as any Algonquin. So this was Walsingham, the famed and in some minds infamous Sir Francis. He was seated at the largest table, writing, but raised his head as the secretary showed the new arrivals in. When those eyes looked at him, Stephen felt as if they had impaled him.

"Master Bernard Maude and Master Stephen Sweetwater, Sir Francis," said the secretary, and withdrew, bowing.

"Ah," said Walsingham. "Thank you, Maude, for bringing Master Sweetwater. You have the amber ring, sir? May I inspect it?"

Mutely Stephen took off the ring and held it out. Walsingham examined the engraving inside and returned it with a nod. "Good. So much for your bona fides. Be seated. Master Sweetwater, through Maude here I knew in advance who would attend yesterday's meeting in Holborn. I had been disquieted to learn from him that you would be there, without official sanction. And that you were in the company of relatives who are sunk to their eyebrows in the conspiracy. I ordered him to make contact with you and bring you to me. Explain yourself!"

One did not lie to those eyes. They belonged to a man whose mind was acute and who had the Tower of London and the royal rackmaster at his command.

"I came with my cousin and his son, who is my own son-in-law," Stephen said. "I did so to find out exactly what they were about. I hoped to persuade them—without warning them—to back out before I brought my report to you."

"You intended to bring it, then?"

"I first wanted to find out exactly what I was dealing with. Having done so, then, yes, I saw that I must report what I knew."

"I see." Walsingham looked as though he really did see. "Yes, that makes sense. No doubt it was distressing to find yourself investigating your own family."

"Yes, sir."

"A case of divided loyalties." Walsingham steepled his long fingers and rested his chin on the tips of them. "You have been in a dilemma. Trouble yourself no longer, Master Sweetwater. Through Master Maude, I know already what is being planned, and by whom. Also, a Jesuit priest named Charles Dupont was arrested in Salisbury and has spilled some names, including those of Tobias and Robert Allerbrook. You need not put yourself on the rack, wondering if you should betray your relations or warn them. There is no need for the one and no point in the other. They are doomed."

"If they were to change their minds and withdraw now..." Stephen began.

"They would be too late," said Walsingham. "I hope for your sake that you *haven't* already told them that I am privy to their detestable ambitions! Did Mistress Stannard not make it clear that nothing—*nothing*—must suggest to these plotters that they are under suspicion?"

"Yes, Sir Francis. And I have not done so."

"I'm glad to hear it." He paused, transfixing Stephen with that sharp dark gaze. "How much do you know?" he asked. "Mistress Stannard's report said you had been in the New World for many years, so perhaps you are not aware that Mary Stuart's husband Henry Lord Darnley was strangled in a garden in Edinburgh while trying to flee after being warned that his bedchamber was about to be blown up with gunpowder. He escaped the explosion but not the assassins. *Did* you know?"

"Yes, sir. It was part of Mistress Stannard's briefing."

"He was an unpleasant young man, but there were other ways of dealing with him," said Walsingham. "Instead he was murdered. Mary then married the man who almost certainly organized the murder, the Scottish lord James Bothwell. He abandoned her, the Scottish people understandably threw her out and she came to England to be a nuisance to us for two decades, representing herself as pathetic and hard done by. In some gullible quarters she is considered a martyr and almost a saint. *Saint!*"

There was another pause. Then Walsingham said, "Just what *did* you say to your relatives?"

"That I thought the scheme too unwieldy and we should withdraw—just us three, the Allerbrooks. I didn't suggest trying to dissuade anyone else. My kinsmen are thinking about it, I hope," said Stephen unhappily.

"In vain," said Walsingham. "Nothing whatsoever is going to interfere with my plans. I intend to pile up such evidence against that woman that even Queen Elizabeth cannot argue with it. You are lodging, are you not, at the Green Dragon in Bishopsgate?"

"Yes, Sir Francis."

"Not any longer. You will remain here tonight, under guard. Bernard Maude will go to the Green Dragon to pay your bill for you and collect your belongings. He will bring them here tomorrow and you will then return to the west country, under escort. Bernard, whom your relations believe to be a fellow conspirator, will tell them that you have decided to back out and go home. It might be safer for you," Walsingham added. "You took a risk, my friend. Men who are willing to overturn the realm might not stop at putting a dagger into an unreliable associate and dropping him into the Thames, even if he's a family member."

Sir Francis had remained seated throughout the interview. He now reached for a quill and began to trim it. "You can keep the amber ring," he said. "You did send some useful information regarding a house in Wiltshire and a so-called pedlar in Hereford. You are a competent enough agent, I think. Continue your work, if you will. It could be worth your while. The property of traitors is often confiscated, but out of respect for your services, perhaps Allerbrook may be exempted."

"I will continue," said Stephen.

"Good. But don't even think of attempting to contact Tobias and Robert Allerbrook. That is all. You may go."

They were dismissed. It was over. Robert and Tobias, unless they had after all listened to what he had said to them, and ran for their lives now, at once, were already as good as dead.

The devil take you, both of you, for what you will do to Aunt Jane and poor Philippa and that unborn child.

But he quelled the thought quickly. Philippa loved Robert, and in any case, the devil had his talons in them already and the devil bore the name of Sir Francis Walsingham.

CHAPTER FORTY-TWO
Contingency Plans
1586

"*I* did my best," said Stephen. "Aunt Jane, Cousin Blanche, Philippa, my dear, dear daughter, I did my best. Toby and Robert were determined to go through with it. I could do no more. I left without them." He had managed to persuade his escort to part from him when once they were in Clicket. Explaining Walsingham's two dour soldiers to his family could have been difficult. "One thing I can swear," he said. "I did not betray them. It didn't come to that. I had...heard things. This man Walsingham—he is said to have spies everywhere. It is very likely that the plot is known already. I just backed out. Toby and Robert despise me for my cravenness."

"Craven? *You?*" said Jane. But her attempt to laugh was a failure. Her face was white.

They were in the Allerbrook parlour, all four of them.

He was telling as much of the truth as he could. He wasn't sure what impression he was making. On Philippa, it seemed, not enough.

"You should have *made* them come home!" Philippa shouted. She had abandoned impassiveness. For once she was behaving like an Englishwoman, not to say an English fishwife. "Didn't you *tell* them you thought they were discovered?"

"They would have asked me how I was so certain, and I would have had no answer."

"But if you thought they were betrayed already, just *why* did you think that?" Philippa almost screamed. "*How* did you know?"

"Philippa, be calm!" Jane put an arm around her great-niece. "You will harm your child. I told you—do you not remember?—what such a conspiracy could mean, if it succeeded. Your father knows that, too. It must *not* succeed. You were not here in the days of Mary Tudor, but he and I were. I think he may know more than he has told us, but he has done his best. I know he has."

Philippa, breaking down at last, began to sob. Stephen said somberly, "Don't hate me, Philippa, please. *Please.* If they are rushing to destruction, it's their choice, my dear. I wonder myself why they can't see it. Dear God, even if someone did assassinate Elizabeth, Mary would simply be carried off to a dungeon and the whole country would spring to arms to hold off any foreign invasion. I fancy the council would send to Scotland for Mary's son, young King James. Her *Protestant* son. He'd have to decide what was done with her, but I doubt if he'd hand her the crown! The conspirators are living in a dreamland. They'll awake to…a nightmare. But I did do one thing that might, just might, be a help."

The three pairs of eyes, brown and hazel and night-dark,

fastened on him in wild hope. "What did you do? What?" demanded Philippa. She wiped her eyes.

Stephen looked at his daughter with tenderness. "I suggested that if things went wrong, they should make for Somerset and ask Nicholas Lanyon to help them. He's family, after all. In fact, I suggest that we approach him ourselves, in advance. At worst, I think he would say no. Exmoor people don't hand their kinfolk to the hangman willingly."

"We could do that, yes," Jane said.

"If it comes to it, I will do all I can to save Tobias and Robert," said Stephen. "I promise you, all three of you. I swear it."

Jane said, "Well, I can still ride a pony. Stephen, you and I will go in search of Nicholas tomorrow. We'll try Lynmouth first."

Nicholas Lanyon was also of the opinion that his supplicants knew more than they were telling him. "A great deal more, I suspect," he said candidly.

The fiery Lanyon hair had faded to a brownish-chestnut, but he was still fit and muscular, with good biceps under the sleeves of his brocade doublet. Jane and Stephen, who had duly made for Lynmouth first, had had the luck to find him there. He sat in his parlour with an ankle crossed over a knee and looked intently at them. Jane sat opposite, hands clasped nervously in her lap while Stephen stood protectively beside her.

"You say that Robert and Tobias may have run foul of the law," Nicholas said. "In what way? Have they turned footpad? Has one of them murdered a rival in love or an importunate creditor? Or have they been plotting a Catholic coup? I am aware that they are Catholic. Tobias told me, as a matter of fact, a year ago."

The stillness and the silence which greeted this were his answer.

"I see," said Nicholas. "And you expect me to give them aid if they ask for it."

"They are on the edge of a plot, but not among the ring-leaders," said Stephen. "I found that out in London. I told them they were running headlong into danger but they didn't listen. All the same, I must, *must* do what I can for them if they need help. Nicholas, they're family. Yours and mine. My daughter is Robert's wife, and she expects a child in September."

"You are asking a great deal. I have a reputation to maintain and a family of my own to care for."

Stephen said persuasively, "Aunt Jane says you have a boat."

"My *White Wing?* Yes."

"Is she a seagoing vessel? Can she cross to France? Is she easy to put to sea at short notice?"

"She has been to France often and she can indeed put to sea quickly. I have studied the art of sailing and how to make use of crosswinds."

"Nicholas," said Jane, "*please.* We will do all we can to protect you. If…if they do reach you, asking for aid, couldn't you get them away to France?"

"I could. My crew are loyal. If I carry passengers, it's my own business. *If* I carry them."

"How would you feel," said Jane, "if the people you were being asked to help were your own sons or grandsons?"

"I trust that none of my family would be stupid enough to indulge in conspiracies. I am sorry if this hurts your feelings, Mistress Allerbrook, but I have never thought highly of Toby's intelligence."

"Nor do we," said Stephen. "I regard him as a nitwit, if

you want to know. But he's still Toby. My cousin. And his son is my son-in-law."

Nicholas sighed. "If they come to me, I will make my final decision then. I'm not promising that I won't fling them into my cellar and send for the local constable, but that's a chance they'd take, whoever they asked to help them. Probably I won't betray them. I'll also keep you informed of where I am, whether here or in Bristol, or anywhere else. That is as far as I'll go."

On the way home Jane said, "I have a feeling that when it comes to the point, Nicholas won't let us down."

"I hope not," said Stephen.

They rode on in silence, through the world of late May, brushing past the young green ferns and the white cow parsley that edged the steep lanes out of Lynmouth and then taking a track over the high ground where the moor grass was mistily purple as it always was so early in the summer.

It was the seventeenth day of August, just before midday, when Tobias and Robert came home.

"Sir Anthony Babington was arrested on the fourteenth," Tobias said. Unshaven, red-eyed from fear and sleeplessness, long hours in the saddle and scanty food, he and Robert sat in the hall, consuming the hot chicken soup that Blanche had brought to them, and pushing dunked pieces of bread hungrily into their mouths. As he ate, Robert leaned against Philippa, who sat beside him with an arm across his shoulders, looking at him as though she couldn't believe he was there. Once in a while he turned to look up at her, and once he spared a hand to reach out and gently, wonderingly, pat the bulge beneath which his child was growing.

"One of his servants warned us," Tobias said. "And told

us that we had been betrayed—he didn't name the man but it was someone in Sir Anthony's confidence. The wretch was in Walsingham's pay all the time. Another of Sir Anthony's servants told the authorities where to find his master. Is there a house in the land where Walsingham doesn't have a spy?"

"Very few, I fear," said Stephen dryly. Jane glanced at him sharply and then looked away.

Tobias, spoon in hand, also looked at him thoughtfully. "You were so very sure that things would go wrong. What made you so certain?"

"I was simply afraid. The plan relied too much on too many people with too little communication acting together on a given date. You called me craven. You were right," said the man who had fought Spaniards hand-to-hand on the *Santa Maria* and stood fast to loose two accurate arrows when a tawny panther charged him.

"Tobias. Are you pursued?" Jane asked suddenly.

"I should think so," said Tobias, turning to her. Letty, who was still active and no more patient with the male sex than she had ever been, brought a fresh platter of bread and dumped it roughly on the table. "If anyone is taken by Walsingham," Tobias said with his mouth full, "they talk. I daresay someone has talked about us. There is a rackmaster in the Tower, they say, someone called Sir Richard Topcliffe, who could make stones speak."

"I've heard that, too," said Stephen, who knew what they did not, that Dupont had been taken and had most certainly talked.

"I can't bear to think of it," said Blanche. She had seated herself opposite Tobias, and was filling her eyes with him.

"No one interfered with us on the way here, but we travelled fast," Robert said. "We've barely eaten or slept. We rode all night once. It was cooler than in the daytime, though not much. The weather's so hot. There's been a fire over toward Dulverton. We had to ride across a whole blackened hillside. Thank God it didn't affect Allerbrook. What put it out?"

"We had a storm two days ago," said Jane. "We hoped it would cool the air, but all it did was make things sticky as well as hot. The rain put the flames out, though. We saw the smoke and had fire brooms ready, just in case, but we didn't need them."

"But we had to keep hiring horses, and that leaves a trail," Tobias said. "I think we will be hunted. We don't mean to stay here. We only came to let you know we were still alive, and to ask for fresh mounts. Then we're going across the moor to Lynmouth to ask Nicholas Lanyon for help. Your idea originally, Stephen. You seem to have instincts about saving your skin." The sneer was unmistakable. "Aren't you under suspicion yourself?"

"As far as I know," said Stephen, "by leaving London so soon, I avoided becoming a suspect." Privately, he recalled how he and they and Bernard Maude had all met round Sir Anthony's table, and sent up a silent prayer of gratitude that they evidently didn't know that Bernard Maude was their principal betrayer. If they had, they might have found Stephen's escape from suspicion very hard to believe. "But while I've been here," he said smoothly, "Aunt Jane and I have called on Nicholas. He is in Lynmouth now and I think he'll get you to France."

"We'll work to get you pardoned," Jane said. "One day you'll be able to come home."

"We need some rest, at least for a few hours," Tobias said exhaustedly. His hunger was assuaged, but his eyes were hot and sunken with weariness.

"What about the hirelings we rode here?" Robert asked suddenly. "They must go back to their stable in Taunton! It's the Sign of the Falcon."

"Jack put them in the paddock," Stephen said. "They're commonplace nags. No one can prove they're any particular horses."

"Commonplace is the word," muttered Robert, gulping more soup. "Mine was the worst slug I ever got astride."

"Leave all that to us," said Blanche. "Eat and rest. We'll set a watch, won't we, Mistress Allerbrook? We'll rouse you if there's need."

"Yes," Jane said. "Where's Tim Snowe?"

"Here, ma'am." Tim had been hovering close at hand.

"Send Paul up to the tower to watch and tell him to report to us at once if he sees anyone riding toward the house. Tim…"

"Ma'am?"

"I know you don't know exactly what has happened, though it must be obvious to you—to everyone here—that something serious has. I can only say that your master, Tobias, and Robert my grandson have been involved in dangerous matters in London and are fleeing for their lives. Can we trust you?"

"Of course. We know 'ee've tried to keep it from us," said Tim, "but we all know what's been afoot. None of us would betray you."

"I've just noticed," interposed Tobias, "that there is someone missing. Where's Gilbert Mallow? He hasn't been arrested, has he?"

"No. I dismissed him," said Jane shortly. "But for him, you would never have run into this danger. I ordered him out of the house the day you left for London."

"Mother! You shouldn't have done that."

"Oh yes, I should. As far as I'm concerned," said Jane grimly, "he has thrown us all to the wolves. Why did you listen to him? Why couldn't you leave crowns and religions to others and just live your own lives? And how dare you entangle yourselves in plans that could have brought a Spanish army onto English soil! Are you both insane? God's teeth, I've tried to keep these everlasting squabbles over power and faith from intruding into my home, and again and again one or other of my family has let them in! Sometimes I think of Allerbrook as a castle under siege, with people inside it who are willing to unbar the gates to the enemy! I will do all I can to protect you, both of you, but make no mistake about it—you have been a pair of fools."

"Mother!"

"I'll say it again." Jane had never been so formidable. "Fools and simpletons! The only one with any sense is Stephen. Do you hear me, Toby? And you, Robert! Don't you dare sneer at Stephen now, either of you. Blanche, do you intend to go with Tobias and Robert? Philippa obviously can't, as yet, though perhaps she can follow later."

"Yes. I'll go," Blanche said. Tobias reached out a hand to her and she took it, though hers was trembling. "*Where* will we go?" she asked him.

"France and then Paris. We have money enough to last a few months. We'll find a home to rent and I'll try to place myself and Robert in some great seigneur's household. Don't be afraid."

"I'll try not to be." Blanche's voice was shaking as much as her hands. Bravely, however, she said, "I'll put some things together, as much as can go into the saddlebags."

"Meanwhile," said Jane to Tobias and Robert, "go upstairs, both of you, and rest. Philippa, go with Robert."

"I'll send hot water up, and soap and clean towels with it," Jane said to Stephen. "They mustn't arrive in France looking like scarecrows. Let us hope that Nicholas stands by us and…Robert?"

Robert had come running back down the stairs, his face aghast. "Grandmother…Mother…it's Philippa! I think…"

CHAPTER FORTY-THREE
The Decree of Exmoor
1586

*I*n after years, Jane said that on that August day in 1586, it was no human agency that decreed which of the Allerbrooks should live and which should die, but Exmoor itself: wild, beautiful Exmoor, ruthless as a hunting falcon, and seemingly possessed of a diabolical sense of humour.

The afternoon was hot and the room where Philippa lay, struggling with agonizing birth pangs, was sweltering. She had been labouring only for five hours, which in itself was normal, but she was having a very bad time.

"The child's coming early. I'd say by about three weeks," Jane said as Blanche, upset to the point of wringing her hands, came into the kitchen to join an anxious conference. Jane was heating water while Phoebe and her daughter Eliza cut up a linen sheet to make extra cloths and Alice stirred broth. "It need not be a disaster," Jane said, "and she's strong. This isn't Sybil all over again. You say there's been no change, Blanche?"

"No, she's just…battling. Letty and Nell are holding her hands. I think it's worse than when I had such trouble with Robert! Tobias doesn't know whether to go or wait," said Blanche distractedly. "Whatever he does, I need to be with him, but to leave you now…"

"You must go and so must Tobias. He can't be put at risk, as well. What about Robert?"

"Robert!" Blanche wailed. "He has no shame. He's in Philippa's room, too, as if a man had any business in a birth chamber, except for a physician or a priest! Nell is shocked and Letty is furious—well, you know Letty! He says he won't leave Allerbrook until his wife is safe and the child is born. I can't make him listen and nor can Philippa. She's tried. She's a good girl. I didn't know how good. She's longing for him to stay, I can see it, but still she urges him to go with Toby, for his own sake. Oh, what a toil we're all in!"

"You *must* go! You *must*. Oh…damn these sodding pains… hell and damnation…!"

Stephen did not wish to eavesdrop, but as propriety forbade him to intrude on this female mystery and he was desperate to know what was happening, he was standing miserably outside Philippa's door and listening. He thought wryly that although he had taken good care, when instructing his daughter in English, never to teach her any oaths, she had clearly learned some since she came to England. He had wasted his caution.

"I'm staying till this is over," said Robert staunchly. "My parents can go, and should, but if anyone comes searching for me, I'll just have to hide. It's been done before."

So it has, thought Stephen. *As well I know. Can we get away with it again?*

Inside the birth chamber, Philippa might never have heard of Algonquin stoicism. "Why did you do it?" she shouted at Robert. "All this wrangling over what rituals you pray with, all this quarrelling over which queen should wear a gold crown and a purple cloak! What does it matter?"

"Hush, hush. You're wasting your strength." Letty squeezed a damp cloth over Philippa's wet brow, but Philippa pushed her away and with an effort raised herself against her pillows. She pointed to the leaded window, beyond which the August moors could be seen, drenched in sunshine and glowing with heather and gorse in full summer bloom. "There's purple and gold out there, enough to satisfy anyone, and it belongs to us all. People don't have to murder each other for it!"

"Now, now. This is no time to be thinking of such things, anyway." Paul Snowe's wife, Nell, who was a conventional young woman and rarely did any thinking at all on abstract matters, tried to soothe her.

"How can I not think of them?" Philippa shouted at her. "Oh, dear God! Here it is again...! These bloody pains! Oh no...*damn...damn...!*" Words dissolved into a wail.

Robert stepped swiftly outside the room and, finding Stephen there, grasped his arm. "Father-in-law! Please go and tell my parents to set off at once. I'll follow when I can, but they mustn't wait for me. The evenings are still long. They can reach Lynmouth before dark, just. My mother has told me that's where Nicholas Lanyon is now. Get them on their way!"

There were times when one didn't argue. Robert might not understand Philippa as well as her father would have liked, but it was certain that he loved her, and that was good enough. Stephen made for the stairs down to the hall. He was halfway across it, looking for Tobias and Blanche, when Paul Snowe came racing down from the tower.

"Soldiers, Master Stephen! Comin' across the moor from the north. God's teeth, it do be hot up there on the tower. They'm about fifteen minutes away, but they'm comin' this way."

"What is it? I heard Paul's voice." Tobias came hurrying from the chapel. Blanche and Jane, carrying cloths and a steaming ewer of water, appeared from the kitchen and Tim Snowe ran in from the yard, where he had been collecting fresh wood for the kitchen fire "Soldiers?" said Tim on a note of fear.

"Tobias!" Stephen took command. "Go to the stable. Jack's there. Get ponies saddled for yourself and Blanche. Robert refuses to go and there's no time to argue! Go on! At once!"

"Blanche has packed the saddlebags and they're with the saddles," Jane said. "There are cloaks as well—it'll be cooler at night and on the ship. If Robert isn't going, tell Jack to bring his saddlebags back inside. I'll empty them. Blanche, you and Tobias just go. *Go!*"

"Out by the back way," said Stephen. "Straight up the combe and over the ridge. Then no one coming in by the main track will see you."

"But Robert!" Blanche cried.

"We'll protect him if we can," Stephen barked. "Just *go!* Now!"

"There isn't time!" gasped Blanche.

"There is if you move fast enough. Paul, go back up and keep watch. Come down again when they get close."

"But..." Blanche looked terrified. She stared at the cloths in her hands. "Just to go...like this...without Robert..."

Jane took the cloths, put them and her ewer down on the table and then took Blanche in her arms. "Don't stop to wrangle. Do as Stephen says. You'll be with Tobias. You'll come home one day and if we can save Robert, we will. Godspeed, both of you!"

There was just barely time for Jane to give parting hugs and kisses to Blanche and to Tobias and then they were gone. "I'll get Robert hidden," Jane said. Snatching up jug and cloths, she made for the stairs.

In the bedchamber, Philippa was once more convulsed with pain and Robert had given her his hand to clutch. Nell was clucking in disapproval and Letty looked murderous, but he was taking no notice.

"Soldiers are coming. They're nearly here," said Jane briefly, putting down the jug. "Paul saw them. Robert, your parents are leaving now. I hope they're in time. I suggest that you get under Philippa's bed. The flounce of the mattress covering hangs well down and you'll be completely hidden."

"If they do find me," said Robert, "you had no idea I had done anything in London that anyone would call wrong. You're my innocent grandmother. You're astonished to find that I'd hidden under the bed. You thought my father had gone straight from London to visit friends in France."

"They won't find you," said Jane. "Surely they won't! The one place that no gentleman is likely to intrude himself is the room where a young woman is in childbed."

She had, however, not reckoned with Captain Adam Clayman.

Or with Exmoor.

When Adam Clayman was a small boy, trailing along the shore at Minehead behind his parents, Danny and Eva, and digging clay with his own little trowel, he had decided that one day he would have a different life. Becoming a soldier had given him that life. It had also got him away from the west country altogether.

He hadn't been pleased, three months previously, just as

he was approaching forty, to find himself transferred back
to it, when a captaincy fell vacant and someone suggested
him as a suitable replacement because he had come from
there in the first place. He had no interest in going back.
He hardly remembered the area and he certainly didn't know
his way around it. He had kept nothing from his old life
except that he called himself Clayman—and even then he
had added the last syllable because it seemed to him that it
sounded more dignified than just Clay.

Now he'd got to find a house called Allerbrook. The Babington plot had burst into his world like a clap of thunder
when a Queen's Messenger arrived on an exhausted, sweat-
soaked horse with rolling eyes and foam around its bit. The
messenger, having once delivered his news, had all but collapsed, so hard had he ridden from London.

But he had picked up information on the way. It was
certain, he said, that two of the conspirators had fled
westward. He had found an innkeeper who had hired horses
to gentlemen who met the description of a father and son
called Tobias and Robert Allerbrook. They came from Allerbrook House and could well be making for home. It
would be Captain Adam Clayman's task to bring them in.
Here was a warrant.

His father had known the district, but Danny was dead
long since. However, among the soldiers at Taunton Castle
he found a Gervase Wells, who said he had once taken a
letter to Allerbrook. Gervase could guide them. With six
men, therefore, including Gervase, he set out.

As he rode along through the August heat, Adam found
himself intensely disliking his county of origin. He hated the
bleakness of the hills and the darkness of the wooded valleys,
and the barrow mounds made him feel creepy. He had been

told as a child that they were haunted, and the sight of them produced atavistic twinges in his guts. He would if necessary have bivouacked on top of a barrow mound, he said to himself, and was irritated to find that he was lying.

There were also other causes of annoyance, and Captain Adam Clayman had a short temper.

On a day like this, the open hillsides were like a griddle. Distances wavered silkily in the heat. At one point they found themselves on a pebbly path across a hillside which had lately been on fire. To either side stretched blackened expanses of what had been heather, with here and there the charred skeletons of gorse bushes. It was like a country of the damned.

He felt—they all felt—as though they were being cooked in a monstrous pan to provide dinner for some ferocious sun god, and as if that were not bad enough, there were the flies. There were clouds of them, especially when the path led through bracken. He and his companions were driven to pulling bracken fronds and waving them about as fly switches to ease both their own misery and that of the horses. They even went to the lengths of pushing fronds under the edges of their helmets, to keep the humming pests out of their eyes, although it meant peering through a green fringe to see their way.

The wooded combes were less fly-ridden until the track took them deep into one, and across a river ford, when a new horror appeared in the shape of huge black horseflies that bit. One landed on Adam's wrist. He knocked it off, but not before it had drawn blood. Another actually managed to bite his thigh through his breeches. The man just ahead of him was bitten on the neck and snarled with disgust as he smashed the insect away.

None of them crossed the ford without being attacked by

the bloodsucking terrors, and their curses made birds fly out of the trees.

When he reached this place Allerbrook, Adam said to himself, he would enjoy arresting those two fugitives. He hoped they would be there! It would pay him for this ride through such a scorching, fly-infested hell.

The afternoon was passing but it was still stiflingly hot when Gervase brought them to a track across the moorland above Clicket, and pointed out the church tower in the village below. "We'll see Allerbrook House in a moment," he said.

Gervase was not happy. One part of him had welcomed the idea of going to Allerbrook, because perhaps he might see that amazing young woman, Mistress Philippa, again. But she would not be glad to see him; he would be an enemy, one of the men sent to arrest her husband and her father-in-law. There would be an unpleasant scene if they did find the wanted men at the house, and it would be worse if Clayman gave way to his temper.

They jogged on. Few birds sang in this heat, but a corn-crake gave its harsh call from a barley field as they rode past, and a buzzard drifted overhead, hunting for prey. The cren-ellated tower of Allerbrook House came into sight. For a moment Gervase thought he glimpsed someone on top of the tower, but if so, the figure vanished almost at once and he couldn't be sure he had really seen anyone.

The house also went out of view as the path changed course and a spur of hillside came between. As they rounded the spur it reappeared, but now there was a new obstacle. They pulled up sharply. The track was bounded on one side by a ditch dividing it from a field of rye, and on the other by a steep heather-covered drop, and the way ahead was blocked by a herd of black cows. The foremost cow, which had impressive horns, was right in their path, staring at them with more intelligence in her eyes than any mere bovine had the right to possess.

"Get out of the way!" bellowed Clayman, brandishing his riding whip. There were clouds of flies around the cattle and a detachment came to reinforce those already buzzing around the horses. Clayman swept them away with his bracken fly-swat. The lead cow regarded him with contempt and turned broadside on, lowering her head to pull at some clover by the wayside. He whacked her flank, whereupon she turned and once more presented her horns to him.

"Brutes!" Clayman spluttered. "Where's their herdsman? God damn these bloody flies! Move aside, you stupid animal! *Move!*"

The cow lowed at him and stood firm. Behind her, her sisters browsed placidly on the verges of the track. They formed as solid a barrier as a bramble hedge. "For the love of God!" bawled Clayman.

Gervase pushed his horse up past his captain, came along-side the obdurate ringleader and by shoving and prodding, at last induced her to turn around. Her tail flicked him across the face—purposely, he suspected—and made his eyes water, but turn she eventually did, and slowly the entire herd was induced to shuffle around and start back along the way it had come. Presently shouts were heard in the distance, and a small, walnut-complexioned man accompanied by a pair of flaxen-haired youths and a black-and-white dog came puffing up the hill on foot, gasping apologies.

"Are these animals yours?" Clayman shouted at them.

"Aye. Simon Blake I be," said the small man. "They'm my cows, right enough. Allus gettin' out, they are."

"Can't you keep your fences in repair?"

"That there lead cow, Hellspawn I call she, she'll wreck a fence soon as look at it. Her 'ud get out of the Tower of London, her would."

"I doubt it," said Clayman coldly. "For the time being, though, I'd be glad if she'd just get out of our way! We're on the queen's business!"

"Ah, well. We be just country folk, zur, Exmoor folk. Don't know nothing about queen's business round here."

"Just get that bloody herd off this path!" Clayman made a swipe with his whip and Simon Blake only just succeeded in evading it. "Now! Hellspawn, you call her! Very apt!"

"Where are the soldiers? Shouldn't they be here now?" Jane said, hurrying down into the hall. Tim Snowe and Stephen met her. They were grinning.

"I've just been up on the tower," Stephen said. "Paul came halfway down and called me and he was laughing. They've fallen foul of Blake's cow Hellspawn and the rest of the herd. She's got out again and taken the other cows with her. Thank God for it. Tobias and Blanche have only just got away. They wouldn't have been in time, but for Hellspawn! The cows blocked the soldiers' way and held them up just long enough. Hellspawn's done us all a favour. But Blake and his sons are there now and they're shifting the herd. We'll see the soldiers at any moment."

Paul came rapidly down from the tower. "They're well nigh here!"

"Go to the stable and find something to do," said Stephen. "Something ordinary. We must all look innocent. Aunt Jane, here are Robert's saddlebags. Quick, go upstairs and empty them in my room and then go back to Philippa. Look after her! I'll let our visitors in and be polite to them."

"Call me when they arrive," said Jane shortly, and with that seized the saddlebags and hurried away.

Emptying the bags took only a few moments. She threw the contents into suitable chests and presses in Stephen's room, dumped the bags themselves in a cupboard and sped back to Philippa.

She found the drama there quite bad enough, without soldiers to complicate matters. Robert was under the bed; on it, Philippa was suffering so intensely that Jane found herself fearing for the girl's life. Nell and Letty, now reinforced by Phoebe, all much distressed, were alternately murmuring prayers and applying warm wrung-out cloths to Philippa's distended stomach. Downstairs, Jane had left Eliza and Alice still occupied with heating more water and stirring more broth. Eliza was in tears.

Philippa's room did not look toward the yard, but Jane's ears, straining to hear, picked up the whinny of a strange horse and the barking of the dogs. She went down at once, trying to arrange her features into an expression of surprise and preoccupation. The preoccupation was real enough. Philippa's condition was alarming.

Out in the yard she found Stephen talking to half a dozen soldiers, who were still on their horses. Jack had ordered the dogs to lie down, but the geese, led by the gander who was always a feature of Allerbrook, had gathered around, cackling in their usual fashion. The soldiers looked strange, not to say absurd, for they were very dusty, except where sweat had made rivulets down their grimy faces, and most of them were peering at the world through fern fronds stuck in their headgear.

"Er…good afternoon," Jane said, placing herself in front of them, aware that she must look harassed and dishevelled and not much like a lady of standing. "Did…did you want shelter for the night? Is the White Hart in Clicket full? Rixons might be a better place for you—we're in confusion here. My grandson's wife has been brought to bed and…and we are worried…we can't very well…"

Clayman brushed all this aside. "We have a warrant for the arrest of two men wanted for complicity in a serious plot against Her Majesty's person and realm. Their names are Tobias and Robert Allerbrook, father and son. Are they here? Is this man one of them?" He pointed at Stephen.

"I am Stephen Sweetwater, Mistress Allerbrook's nephew," said Stephen. "I am staying in the house. Tobias and his son Robert are my cousins."

"They're not here," said Jane. She raised her chin. Clayman's bullying tone had warned her not to seem vulnerable. He was not the kind to pity weakness or even age, if it looked pathetic. She must somehow impersonate a lady of position and authority even though her knees felt as though they were melting. "They were in London but my…my son Tobias wrote that they were going on to visit friends in France. They can't be involved in a plot, anyway! That's absurd!"

"I agree. It sounds most unlikely," said Stephen coolly.

"Indeed! We think otherwise." Clayman slid his feet out of his stirrups, preparatory to dismounting. "We must search these premises—house, outhouse and fields. I warn you not to hinder us—"

He stopped short as a shadow swept over him. Then something plummeted out of the sky and landed struggling at the feet of his horse.

The falling object consisted of a buzzard with an adder in its grasp. The adder in turn had fastened its fangs in the buzzard's throat and the bird was dying. It lay twitching, wings spread in the dust and a little blood oozing from the poisoned wound. The snake, very much alive, still twisted in the raptor's talons. Clayman's horse, horrified to see a snake only three feet from its front fetlocks, reared up with a squeal and plunged sideways, and Clayman fell off.

He landed well clear of the snake, but lay gasping and winded, for a moment unable to move. Gervase's own horse had shied back, but as Gervase still had his feet in his stirrups, he kept his seat. Having steadied his mount, however, he dismounted, drew his sword and swept the snake's head off. At the same moment Clayman recovered himself and got to his feet, whereupon the gander shot out his neck and tried to peck the intruder. The attempt failed because Clayman, scarlet with fury and embarrassment, moved faster. He seized the bird by the neck and wrung it.

One of the men started to laugh, but the laughter stopped short. Clayman identified the source of the snigger and threw the dead gander to him. "Take charge of that. We'll take it back to Taunton to eat later."

"Excuse me, Captain," said Jane. "That bird belongs to me."

"You can call it a fine for attempting to assault a member of Her Majesty's militia. Is that snake dead?"

"Yes, sir." Gervase was brisk and expressionless. "Buzzards and hawks sometimes overreach themselves, grabbing prey that's too much for them."

Clayman, still scarlet, visibly quivering with fury, dusted himself down. His men watched him uneasily, knowing the signs. "This place is an anteroom to hell! Heat, burnt hillsides, flies that bite, cows and geese that scheme against men, snakes falling out of the sky! Madam!" He glared at Jane. "Bid your grooms see to our horses. We will search the house. Every room and every alcove, no matter who is there already, or why. Now!"

CHAPTER FORTY-FOUR
A Savage Business
1586

"Don't provoke them," Stephen whispered to Jane, standing at her side while they both watched the soldiers with mounting terror. "It would be dangerous."

"This is hateful!" said Jane, trembling.

This search was a far more savage business than the one carried out by Herbert Clifton long ago. The chapel was invaded. The locked chest was broken into without anyone even asking for the padlock key, and the discovery of embroidered vestments with a crucifix and a statuette of the Virgin beneath them was greeted with shouts of "Hah, popish symbols!" from three of the men and "Confiscate them!" from Clayman.

After that, parlour, hall, study, kitchen and servants' quarters were torn apart. Presses were flung open. Dairy and kitchen were ransacked, food and drink seized and messily consumed on the move by men who were hot, hungry, thirsty and angry.

Jane and Stephen followed them about, both wondering how far this search really would be carried, whether decency would halt it at the door of Philippa's chamber or whether these men had gone beyond decency. The man who had killed the snake glanced at Jane apologetically as he went past, but he did not try to restrain his comrades. She recognized him as the young soldier who had once brought a letter to Allerbrook, but he wasn't trying to behave like a friend of the household now. Wise of him, no doubt, she told herself.

However, when they had finished with the ground floor and were striding toward the bedchamber stairs, she broke away from Stephen's restraining hand and ran to block the way.

"Captain Clayman! Please! My grandson's wife, Philippa, is having her child up there. If you must search, then do so, but I beg you, show a little respect. Try not to disturb Philippa."

"Out of the way!" said Clayman.

The soldiers thrust her aside and poured up the stairs. Jane followed. Stephen, catching up with her, said grimly, "I said it was useless. But if they harm Philippa…somehow I'll see they'll regret it if I have to complain to Walsingham himself!"

Upstairs, the sounds of anguish from Philippa's room made Stephen stop short, stricken. Jane once more threw herself into Clayman's path. "This is the lying-in chamber. Can't you hear? Have you no shame? I will open the door so that you can look through it and see for yourself what is happening, but no honourable man can enter that room. What would your wife say, or your mother? What…?"

"I will search this room as I would search any other!" Clayman snapped. "Step aside!"

Gervase protested for the first time. "Sir, surely we shouldn't intrude on this? A woman in childbirth…"

"Don't argue with me!" shouted Clayman. "And remove that woman from the doorway!"

Gervase obeyed, but as he did so, he looked into Jane's face and in his warm chestnut eyes she once more saw apology. He drew her aside, firmly but not roughly, and held her while the others marched in through the door. "There's nothing you can do," he said. "Please don't try."

He was right, of course, just as Stephen was. "I know. But I must still go to her," said Jane. "Unhand me."

He nodded and released her and she followed the soldiers into Philippa's room.

The women round the bed were staring at the invaders in outrage. "What is this?" Letty demanded wrathfully. "How dare you? Men! Can't you see…?"

Philippa's amber skin was grey-tinged and her face was sunken. Stephen had followed Jane through the door, but stopped just inside. Jane, glancing back at him, saw tears in his eyes. Clayman, still aflame with anger, paid no heed to any of them. Gesturing to his men to open the clothespress and the chest beneath the window, he marched straight up to the bed and tossed the curtains about, to make sure that no one was standing on a corner of the bed with folds of the bedhangings drawn around him.

There was nothing. Then Adam Clayman knelt on the floor and lifted the flounce that hid the aperture under the bed.

"Let me stay to see my wife through this. Under guard if you like, but let me be with her till this is over! Can't you see the state she's in? Please!"

"Please!" came the soft, tormented echo from the bed.

"Please let Robert stay. It may not be for long. I think I'm going to die. The child won't come out. Let him stay. I need him. Please, please!"

"No," said Clayman savagely, and with a jerk of his head told the men who were holding Robert to take him away. He turned to Jane. "It seems, Mistress, that you were lying! And so was your nephew!" He glared at Stephen. "You said your son and grandson were not here. I am placing all three of you under arrest. You hid Robert Allerbrook. Where is Tobias?"

As Robert was dragged out, Jane had seen the despair in his face. She felt the same. Her world was collapsing. Long ago she had made herself a private promise to love and care for her home and those she loved. She had taken chances to keep that oath. She had taken risks for love itself, with Carew. In her way, she was as much of an adventurer as Stephen had ever been, as Tobias and Robert apparently were. So far, she had usually won. At least she had survived. But here, finally, was defeat.

She could hear them forcing Robert down the stairs. Clayman, standing in front of Stephen, was once more demanding to know where Tobias was. Ahead of all of them— Robert, Stephen and herself—lay prison cells, trials and death, the manner of which she did not dare to contemplate. If she could find a way to die before then, she thought frantically, she had better take it. She hoped the others would do the same.

"My cousin Tobias really is in France," Stephen was saying calmly. "As for Robert, you clearly meant him no good, so my aunt Jane said he wasn't here. He's her grandson! He was in this room with his wife, in the circumstances you see. I held my tongue because I considered it rude to call my elderly aunt a liar. What would you have done?"

Clayman looked him up and down, and Stephen, staring him out, held out his left hand with the amber ring still in place upon it. "You know the meaning of this?"

"What? What is it?"

"Please look at it, sir." Stephen drew the ring from his finger. "Kindly examine the engraving inside the band."

Clayman, glowering and puzzled, took it from him. There was a pause while he held the ring in the light and studied it. Then he handed it back. "So Walsingham is your master. You are in his pay."

"That is so," said Stephen. He did not look at Jane, or acknowledge her sharply indrawn breath. Privately he thanked God that Robert was out of earshot. "I can assure you," he said smoothly, "that I have no reason to suppose that my cousins are involved in any wrongdoing. Since my return from London earlier this year, I have in fact sent information to Sir Francis concerning two Devonshire households where there are Catholic sympathizers. Frankly, I find it very hard to believe that there are conspirators in my own family. I fancy Aunt Jane does, too."

There was a pause. Philippa moaned and the women gathered around her were suddenly intent, glancing over their shoulders at the other drama in the room, but too concerned about the girl on the bed to do anything but tend her. Clayman, meanwhile, was at last hesitating.

"My nephew's telling the truth! I've never heard of any conspiracy! It's all a lot of nonsense! Conspiracies indeed!" Jane followed Stephen's lead and tried to sound scandalized. "I said Robert wasn't here so as to stop you taking him away from Philippa at such a time. I would have lied to God himself to prevent that! And I wanted to keep you soldiers out of this room. You shouldn't have entered it. You should *not!* This is a respectable household and your intrusion here is improper!"

"There I must agree. None of us men should be here," said Stephen. "I can assure you that my aunt knows nothing of any conspiracies."

Wells, looking with distress toward Philippa in her travail, said in anxious tones, "Sir, I hardly think this elderly lady can be a conspirator. I'd say she's just a misguided grandmother, and her nephew, of course, is obedient to her. The warrant doesn't name Mistress Allerbrook, does it?"

"She's been sheltering dangerous fugitives!" Clayman pointed out.

Philippa screamed. Nell cried, "The babe's coming. Yes, it's coming. Oh, God be praised, I see 'un's head...." Jane, galvanized, actually thrust Adam Clayman out of her way as she rushed to Philippa's aid. Clayman would have pulled her back, but one of the other men barred his way and in broad west country tones, protested.

"Sir, let be! Wells is right. She'm a proper lady—oh, and maybe a doting grandma but I'd wager she don't know aught about any plots. And if this here fellow is really Walsingham's own man—well, is it likely that if he knew anything, he'd keep it to hisself, relatives or not? Walsingham's men don't, from all I've heard. Too scared of him, folk say."

Clayman had the look, by now, of a bull surrounded by a pack of baying dogs. But Jane, ignoring him, was stooping over Philippa and all the women were exclaiming. Stephen, too, had stepped in front of Clayman, and the captain's own men were edging away from this scene of female mystery. A bloodstained cloth slipped off the bed and fell at Clayman's feet, causing him to step back in loathing. He snarled.

"God's death, let's get out of here! We've got one of them,

anyway. He'll be for London and the Tower! You two!" He pointed at a couple of his soldiers, one of them Gervase Wells. "Search the rest of the rooms up here. You just might find the other one! I don't believe he's in France!"

He strode out. Jane, turning to pick up the fallen cloth, found herself briefly face-to-face with Wells. Softly he said, "If everything—heat, flies, the snake, all those things—hadn't made him so angry, he might not have searched this room at all. He's a respectable man really, only he's hasty."

"That's a great comfort," said Jane sarcastically.

"I'm sorry," said Wells. He added, "I pray all will go well with the young woman and the child." Then he went.

Manhandling Robert down to the hall had taken some time. Stephen, racing after him, caught up as his son-in-law was being forced out the main door. "The family will do their best for you, Robert! Be of good heart!"

"You be careful," said one of Robert's captors over his shoulder. "Offering succour to a traitor's no way for an honest man to behave."

Stephen, strategically, withdrew and found Alice crying in a corner of the hall while Tim and Paul Snowe tried to quieten her. "They'll do some more searching, I think," he said to them, "but they won't find anyone this time. Just don't get in their way. I'm going back upstairs to see how Philippa is."

Upstairs, jubilation was taking over and Nell was exclaiming with sheer delight. "Go on, Mistress Philippa…again… yes, go on…! That's it…a girl! Oh look, what a lovely little girl. There, there. It's all over, my love, it's over…."

"It's not!" Philippa gasped. "It's…not…I'm still…"

"God's teeth, she'm right. It b'ain't over!" Letty squealed. "There's another coming!"

"Twins?" gasped Jane. "No wonder she was so big."

"Twins it is!" said Eliza excitedly. "The other one's comin' already! And this un's coming easy."

A short time later Jane was holding a boy-child in her arms and Philippa, shaking and exhausted, was at last released from her agony. "You're going to live," Jane said to her. "And you have twins, a boy and a girl. What will you call them? Did you and Robert talk of names?"

"Sybil for a girl," Philippa whispered. "After my grand-mother. Robert for a boy—Robin for short, so as not to make a muddle with two Roberts. But he never saw them! Robert never saw them! They've taken him away, haven't they? Haven't they?"

"Hush, dear Philippa, quiet now. You mustn't give way. You could shrivel up your milk, and the babes will need it."

"Great-Aunt Jane...!" Philippa clutched at her. "Will you go after them? If they take Robert to London will you go, too, and plead for him? Try to bring him back to me. He ought to see his children. I want him to see his children. Will you try?"

CHAPTER FORTY-FIVE
Looking into a Pit
1586

"Did you betray them to Walsingham?" Jane asked. "Tell me."

"No," said Stephen. "Someone else had already stolen into the midst of the conspirators and Walsingham knew their names and the details before ever I reached London."

"I want to see Walsingham myself," said Jane. "Can you arrange it?"

They were not in the parlour, but sitting in Jane's bedchamber, to which she had summoned her nephew the morning after Robert's arrest. He hesitated and she gave him a grim look.

"If not, why not? Since you're one of his men. I may tell you that I have half guessed at it, ever since that night when we listened at the door of the chapel downstairs. You were so determined to find out what was afoot, like a hound on a scent. You had no fear of arrest when you went to London with Toby and Robert and I remember you agreeing, the day that Tobias and Robert arrived here, fleeing, that there were few houses where Walsingham does not have a spy. I realized all along you knew more than you would say."

He looked at the amber ring on his left hand. "I really did try to save Toby and Robert, but I was too late and in any case, they would have none of it."

"Why did you agree to work for Walsingham? Who recruited you?"

"Someone I met in Plymouth, when I first came back to England. I agreed because of the way my father died…. Aunt Jane, please don't cry."

"I hate this—hate it! I don't want my family mixed up in these religious and political confusions anymore, but you all keep doing it. You won't stop! You…!"

"Please," said Stephen, and knelt to put his arms around her. Her body felt stiff. "I promise you that I did not betray my own kin. Now, I think I'll be able to get you an interview with Walsingham, but can you do the journey? You're not far off seventy. You can ride short distances, but this would be two hundred miles!"

"Make me a litter!" said Jane. "The Snowes built one for Blanche to go to Robert's christening in. Even with a litter, we can do at least twenty-five miles in a day. There's plenty of daylight at this time of year."

Within ten days they were in London. It was the twenty-seventh of August when at last the sturdy Exmoor ponies bore Jane's litter into the city. Paul Snowe rode alongside with Alice on his pillion and Stephen led the way. He and Paul had changed mounts several times on the way, but the ponies seemed to be made of iron.

"I must find an inn with good stabling," Stephen said. "And I need to enquire where the court is. Walsingham will be with it. In such a time of crisis, the queen will probably be in London. I hope she is. Well, the landlord of any good inn will know. They always do."

The landlord of the Green Dragon in Bishopsgate did know. "In Whitehall," he told them.

"Can you hire me a sidesaddle?" Jane asked. "I am going to court. I'll ride one of our horses and I wish to arrive with dignity."

The landlord, who had at first considered that this elderly woman with the country accent didn't resemble a lady of consequence, met her eyes and changed his mind. "Reckon I can oblige you," he said.

The next morning, on horseback, Jane and Stephen presented themselves at Whitehall and the amber ring did its work. With very little delay they were ushered into the presence of Sir Francis Walsingham.

Jane had expected that such a high court official would have more sumptuous surroundings, and Walsingham's businesslike office surprised her. Walsingham himself, however, dark of complexion and gown and radiating power which was almost visible, stood out from his background. He rose as they were brought into the room, and politely handed Jane to a seat.

"You are Mistress Allerbrook, I understand," he said to Jane, "and Master Sweetwater here, with whom I am already acquainted, is I believe your nephew. How can I serve you?" The courteous air with which he had greeted them hardened. "Though from what I have heard, I am not sure if you have served me well, either of you. I wonder if any member of the Allerbrook family can be considered a trustworthy citizen."

"I provided you with what I hope was useful information, gleaned during the summer, sir," Stephen said.

"Yes, you did. It's where your own family are concerned that you suffer from conflicting loyalties. I sent you out of the way, Master Sweetwater, to make sure you didn't warn your foolish cousins—useless though such a warning would have been—but it seems that both you and this lady here, your aunt, lied to Captain Clayman and told him that Robert Allerbrook was not at home. I am well-informed, you see. He was found there and dragged from under a bed. Tobias Allerbrook has disappeared and so, I hear, has his wife. Perhaps I had better not enquire too deeply into how they got away."

There was a brief and awkward silence, until Jane, looking gravely and very directly at Walsingham, said, "Tobias is my son and Robert my grandson. If I had refused aid to them, Sir Francis, what kind of mother or grand-mother would that make me?"

"The safety of the queen is involved. This is a matter of treason. It is my business to bring traitors to justice."

"Of course," Jane agreed. "That's your duty. But mine is to love and to protect my own kinfolk, whatever they may do. It's my business to try to prevent things like realms and queens and conspiracies from destroying the peace of my home and my family. We don't all have the same duties in this world, Sir Francis."

There was a pause. Then Jane added, "I believe, in ancient Rome, there were stern matrons who would have put Rome before their own families and handed their own children over to justice if they broke the law. Perhaps that is admirable, in a way. But I can't do it. I have come today to plead for my grandson's life and to ask if I may see him. I doubt if he's seen a kindly face since he was taken from his home."

"You think I am a heartless monster," Walsingham said. "I am not, not quite. As an upholder of the law, I deplore what you have done. As a man with a family of his own, I understand your feelings, Mistress Allerbrook, and to some extent I understand yours, Master Sweetwater. If I didn't, I would have you both arrested now, for hiding Robert Allerbrook and—probably—for spiriting his father away. Very well. I won't pursue that subject. I will tell you something. Anthony Babington, a principal leader in this shocking conspiracy, is in the Tower, but at the last moment I weakened and tried to keep him out of it. By then we already had Mary Stuart in our trap and we could have snapped it shut without Babington. We could have kept up the correspondence in his name. He destroyed his own chances."

"Kept up the correspondence?" Stephen said as Walsingham paused. "Oh! Courtesy of one Gil Gifford?" He remembered that nightmare conference, and Babington, eyes shining, explaining that letters to and from Mary Stuart could be transported in an ale barrel, with the help of someone called Gifford.

"Yes, Gifford is one of mine," Walsingham said. "He led Babington on very well. Babington is a young man I could have liked in other circumstances. He has a wife and child whose hearts I am now obliged to break, and if you think I don't regret that, you are wrong. Well before his arrest, I called him to my presence and reminded him of his duty to be faithful to our queen. I told him he could do so without fear, even if it meant confessing knowledge of a plot, that he could speak to me freely. I hoped to save him, and perhaps to learn the names of conspirators I hadn't yet identified. But he denied all knowledge of any treachery—and then went away to continue with it. I am sorry, and I am sorry, too, for your grandson."

"You will do what you can for him?" Stephen asked.

Walsingham shook his head. "It is out of my hands. Robert Allerbrook will be tried along with the rest of the traitors and cannot be given special treatment. You can see him, Mistress Allerbrook, but not until after the trial, which can only take place when we have finished interrogating the prisoners. They are allowed no contact with visitors while this is being done."

"Is Robert…has he been…racked?" Jane asked in a whisper.

"No, Mistress Allerbrook. He has made a confession, in writing."

"When…?" Jane began.

"I will have you informed. Where are you staying?"

"At the Green Dragon. Bishopsgate," said Stephen.

"You should return there," said Walsingham. "When the trial is over and the verdict and sentence pronounced on all the plotters, you will be sent for." His dark eyes held something near to compassion. "You may well find you are visiting your grandson only to say goodbye. I have no power over the outcome of the trial and would not use it if I had. I will say this. Because Master Stephen Sweetwater here is in my employ and because he did not, in fact, betray my trust although he could have done, I am overlooking the way you both tried to deceive Captain Adam Clayman. As I once hinted that I might, I have recommended that the Allerbrook estate should not be confiscated. This recommendation has been accepted. I can offer you that much balm for your sorrow. But Robert Allerbrook cannot be saved."

"Thank you," said Stephen. Jane said, "Could we not appeal to the queen for Robert's sake?"

"The amber ring would ensure you an audience," said Walsingham. "But I don't advise it. She is bitterly angry. She is a courageous lady but the last few months have been terrible for her. Until Mary Stuart's guilt was fully certain, we had to leave the conspirators at large. Her Majesty was in danger for a long time and knew it and has suffered. She won't forgive those months of fear. She's in no mood for clemency. I counsel you to keep away from her. My secretary will see you out."

Three weeks later, in bed at the Green Dragon, listening to the even breathing of Alice in the truckle bed by the door, Jane lay wakeful, trying not to imagine where she would sleep tomorrow night. By then, she might well be in chains.

Was it treachery against the realm to save a condemned man from death by disembowellment? And could she do it? Stephen probably could, but she must not put him in danger. Philippa needed her father now that her husband was to be taken from her. No, this was Jane's lonely duty to her family, out of the love she felt for them.

It's like looking into a pit. Oh, God, help me.

But God, of course, wasn't going to do any such thing. God hadn't kept that man Clayman from looking under Philippa's bed. God didn't answer prayers. Experience had cured her of any real belief.

The moon was moving on. The night was going by. The passes had come at last and tomorrow they had permission to visit the Tower and see Robert. The day after that, the twentieth of September, Anthony Babington and six of his foremost coconspirators were to die. The rest, including Robert, would follow the day after. There would be only one chance.

In the morning, as they set out for the Tower, nothing seemed real. She was a sixty-eight-year-old widowed lady, of good reputation. Such people simply did not go about with daggers hidden in their clothing and the intention of driving them into any human heart.

At the Tower they were handed over from one guard to another and then to a turnkey, who led them to a low door in one of the towers that studded the massive outer walls. Taking a flambeau from a wall bracket just inside, he lit the way down some steep, dark steps. There was a dank smell, as of dirty river water.

The turnkey was a scrawny individual of doubtful age. His teeth were brown but his smile seemed friendly and he had a pink, positively wholesome face. At the foot of the stairs he showed them through two more doors, which he unlocked and then locked behind them with a great clanking of keys, and then, at last, they were in Robert's cell.

It was a horrible place, of bare stone, the only light a gleam from a small grating high in the wall. The reek of the nearby river was very strong. So was the smell of human ordure, from the pail that stood beside the cot on which Robert was lying.

He lay on his back, on a coarse blanket. He was staring into space as though at some nightmare vision. His wrists were manacled together and an ankle chain, long and heavy, was fastened to the wall. He had grown a beard, thick and black, obscuring half his pallid face, and his hair straggled greasily close to his shoulders. He wore only a filthy shirt and breeches.

"We don't treat 'em badly," said the turnkey. "See, he can move about a bit, to the length of that there chain, and there's blankets on 'is bed. They get food and water, too. That's orders, that is. So as they don't get sick and die afore the law deals with them. If you've brought any extra comforts, there's no rule against it, long as you slip me a little something." He beamed, and the grinning face was suddenly wholesome no longer, but sly and acquisitive.

"Robert!" Jane made toward him, with Stephen following.

Robert sat up, withdrawing his fixed gaze from whatever evil visions had filled it. "Better not touch me," he said as he brought his feet to the floor with a clatter of chain links. "You'll get lice. You've come to say goodbye?"

"We've been waiting here over three weeks, for passes," Stephen told him, evading the question. "Philippa is safe," he added. "You have twins, a son and a daughter, Sybil and Robin."

"Have I? And Philippa came through! Thank God! I wish I could see them. I wish…"

His voice cracked. He raised his chained hands and pressed them to his face, and began to lurch from side to side. Jane, ignoring the lice, put a hand on his shoulder.

His voice came to her, muffled by his hands and his tears. "Do you know what the worst thing is? It's not even the fear, though God knows the fear's well nigh beyond bearing. I've not slept more than an hour at a time since I heard the sentence, nearly a week ago. But worse than that—yes, I mean it—is…I want to go home. I want to be at Allerbrook again. I want to hear the river in the combe. I want to see the gorse and the heather. I want Philippa."

He dropped his hands and looked up at her. His eyes were wet. The turnkey was standing back, by the door. Jane moved so that her wide skirts shielded Robert from him and pulled the dagger out of her sleeve. Stephen whispered, "What…Aunt Jane!"

"Be quiet!" muttered Jane fiercely. *Quick, quick, I must be quick. Don't think about it. Just do it. It's easy. One hand firm on his shoulder and thrust with the other. Pretend you're driving the* *blade into a…a…pillow. Just do it!* "Shut your eyes, dear Robert. Shut your eyes and go to sleep. Goodbye."

"Aunt Jane, you can't—!" Stephen was gaping, unable to take in what he was seeing. Robert said, "Thank you," and closed his eyes.

And I can't do it. Oh, my God, I CAN'T DO IT. I can't kill *anyone, least of all my own grandson, even to save him from…I* *can't…I can't…*

"Here now, none of that!" Suddenly there were footsteps behind her and a pair of strong hands had reached past her and clamped themselves on her wrists. The turnkey, who was much more powerful than his scraggy build suggested, removed the dagger from her grasp. "I've seen folk try that before," he said reprovingly, "but we don't allow it. You'd get into trouble, you would, if I let you get away with that."

Robert opened his eyes. "Thank you, Grandmother. Thank you for trying, at least." He was shaking.

"Aunt Jane!" Stephen was staring at her. "I never thought…I couldn't believe what I was seeing. And I wish you'd moved faster or else asked me to do it!" He glowered at the turnkey.

"It had to be me," said Jane, weeping. "But I…couldn't… do…it."

"So I'd hope, a lady like you," said the turnkey, shaking a scandalized head. "Think you'd best say goodbye now. Give him your blessing, promise your prayers and then let this fellow take you away. This is no place for a lady, anyhow."

Gently, tearfully, Jane kissed Robert's brow. Stephen patted his shoulder. They said words of blessing. They promised to pray.

Once they were outside again, however, Jane's tears ceased and she squared her shoulders.

"I said nothing to Robert because I didn't want to raise false hopes, but if you can get me into her presence with the help of that ring, I'm going to the queen. It's the only thing that's left. I'm a woman. She's a woman. We must have some common ground somewhere!"

So this, Jane thought as she sank into a very deep curtsy, was Elizabeth Regina of England. She didn't know what she had expected, but the reality was overpowering. Elizabeth had not ruled England for nearly thirty years without acquiring an aura of power that reduced Walsingham's aura almost to nothingness.

She had received them in a small audience chamber at Whitehall. She was splendid in black-and-white brocade, with a huge farthingale and ruff, and ropes of pearls. She was seated on a throne, with arms and a pointed back and a canopy, and the throne itself was on a dais.

Courtiers stood about, though not too close. Most of them had stared in surprise when Jane and Stephen were led into the room, but the red-jacketed gentleman pensioner who escorted them in had spoken to her quietly, and with a movement of her head she had signalled that she wished for some privacy with her visitors.

Only when she had curtsied deeply and been bidden to rise did Jane dare to look closely at Elizabeth's face. Then she saw what had not been apparent at first—that the enthroned person inside the magnificent black-and-white gown was a tired woman past fifty. Time, that destructive force, had erased all resemblance to the solemn, red-haired little girl Jane had glimpsed at the court of Queen Anna, long ago, or to the magical young princess whom Carew had once described as having hair like red-gold satin. This aging woman's crimped red hair did not look real. "Madam," Jane said, and then found her tongue refusing to form another word.

"Mistress Allerbrook, we understand. And Master Sweetwater. You have one of Walsingham's rings, we believe, Master Sweetwater, which gives you the right to enter our presence in emergency. May we take it that this is an emergency?"

"To ourselves, ma'am." Stephen had kept hold of his self-possession. "It is an emergency for us, but only you can help."

"Well, let us hear what you wish to ask." The queen's face, which was pale, was shaped like a shield, Jane thought. In fact, it *was* a shield. The lines of tiredness were plain to see, but there was no knowing what mood the owner of that face might be in. Her golden-brown eyes were unfathomable. "The name Allerbrook," Elizabeth said, "is familiar to us. Is there not a man of that name in the Tower now, under sentence of death, to be carried out tomorrow? Are you related to him?"

"Mistress Jane is his grandmother, ma'am," said Stephen. "I am her nephew—he is therefore cousin to me. Aunt Jane…"

"I have come," said Jane, finding her voice at last but with difficulty and having even so to clear her throat before she could get any words out, "to ask…not for his life—I know I must not ask that—but for some mercy. For a quick death and not…not…"

She couldn't go on. Tears blinded her. If the answer was no, then there was nowhere else to go and Walsingham had said that Elizabeth was angry, too angry for clemency.

"Don't be so afraid of me," said Elizabeth, abandoning the royal plural and sounding now as weary as she looked. "Babington and his principal plotters died today, and at my orders, the extreme of agony was their lot. It did not meet with the approval of the Londoners, I hear, and having been told of the details, I find that after all, it does not meet with mine, either. You need not have come to plead with us for this. Those who die tomorrow, and they include the man Aller-brook, will die quickly." The formal plural had reappeared, but this time by way of an assurance that what she was saying was official. "We promise."

CHAPTER FORTY-SIX
The Apologetic Visitor
1586

"I failed him. I'm sorry," Jane said to Philippa. "Allerbrook itself is safe for your son, at least. But I hadn't the courage to do what I meant to do. It was the queen who saved him from the knife. She kept her word and he did die quickly. That I can vouch for."

"We were both there," said Stephen. "Robert had friendly faces in the crowd whether or not he knew it. He wasn't alone at the end."

"I know you did your best." Philippa's voice was flat.

"Rest against it if you can," Jane said, and knew, from the fierce agony in Philippa's eyes, that it would be long before peace of any kind would come to her.

Jane knew something of the grief and rage seething inside her great-niece. Philippa had known of Robert's death before her father and great-aunt returned home. The news had been proclaimed in Clicket. Letty had said that when

Philippa heard of it, she had shut herself in her room for hours, and Eliza, going worriedly upstairs with hot milk, had found her not only weeping but storming about the room, beating her fists on the wall. Eliza had had great difficulty in soothing her.

"I had a word in the village with a woman there as has a new baby," Letty had told Jane. "Just in case Mistress Philippa's milk failed, but it didn't. A mercy that—it might well have, the state she were in at first."

Philippa had, however, become quiet after a time, had emerged from her room, and busied herself with the twins instead. But passions so violent would take a long, long time to dissipate, if they ever did.

They were once more in the parlour, where, over fifty years ago, Francis had been told that his sister Sybil could not go to court after all, because she was expecting an illicit child. Who had eventually turned into Stephen, this man in late middle life, whose face was hollowed by the memory of his cousin Robert's execution.

Philippa turned her head and looked across the room to where the twins lay in basket cradles, side by side.

"Robert has an heir, at least," she said. She glanced at her father. "Are we going to move into Clicket Hall soon?" she said. There was a silence, and then she added, "Well, it will be something to do—arranging the house to your liking."

Stephen said slowly, "I shall certainly go to Clicket Hall shortly—the tenant has agreed to move out early. He is to have a refund. But, Philippa, if you and Aunt Jane are agreeable, I would like you to stay here. For the time being, I think you'll be better in a familiar place. You both loved Robert. Perhaps you can comfort each other. Also, there's another reason I would rather you stayed here. I'm thinking of getting married—or remarried—myself."

Jane and Philippa stared at him. Philippa looked as if she had actually been jolted into genuine surprise. "Who to?" she asked.

"When we were in London," Stephen said, "I sometimes went out for walks, leaving Aunt Jane in the inn. Did I not, Aunt Jane?"

"Yes. It worried me, in case a messenger came saying that we could go to the Tower to see Robert forthwith."

"On one of my walks," Stephen said, "I met Mistress Ursula Stannard again, the lady who recruited me for Walsingham. She was at court to be with the queen until the Babington business was all over."

"You mean…Mistress Stannard is a widow, I take it?" said Jane.

"Oh, I wouldn't dream of proposing marriage to Mistress Stannard!" Stephen suddenly laughed. It was the first laughter there had been in the house since the news of Robert's death had reached it. "That woman petrifies me," he said. "But one must be polite, and when she invited me to take refreshment at a tavern with her and her son-in-law, Master Hillman, who was escorting her, I agreed. Over our wine I mentioned to them that I had ideas of marriage. Why not? I am not young but I'm still—well, capable. I fancy I can still have children."

"But Stephen," Jane said, "a young girl, and a man your age…do you think it's wise?"

"Oh, a young girl wouldn't be suitable, but I thought, perhaps, a widow in her thirties—something like that. Master Hillman suggested one at once. She's aged about thirty-five and living near Barnstaple. She's a distant connection of the Carew family. She has two sons, aged fifteen and thirteen, well provided for under her former husband's will. Master Hillman said he knew her, and that she is good-natured and agreeable to look at, and wishes to wed again."

"Her name?" Jane asked, bemused.

"Silvestra Hapgood. I sent her a letter, through Master Hillman, and I hope to meet her soon after I move into Clicket Hall. If we take to each other, the hall will have a mistress—and...well..."

"Two women trying to run one house?" said Philippa. "No, it might not work. It's different with Great-Aunt Jane. We...belong. I'll stay if you'll have me, Great-Aunt. Tell us more about this Silvestra Hapgood, Father, please."

As a distraction from the misery of Robert's death, Silvestra was a success. Mercifully, Philippa showed no jealousy, but seemed interested in her father's plans. Jane, watching her, acutely aware of her, knew that this was not just due to generosity on Philippa's part, but owed more to the fact that since Stephen's failure to bring Robert back from London, the deep love and trust she had had for her father had cooled. She loved him still, yes, but he was no longer the lodestar he had been. Well, perhaps there were advantages in that.

It was a mercy, Jane thought, that Philippa had been spared the sight of Robert's last seconds, when he kicked on the end of a rope. His neck had broken in less than a minute, but that minute must, to Robert, have felt as long as eternity. It would have done Philippa no good to witness that.

A little feverishly, but glad to lead Philippa's thoughts away from Robert, Jane, too, began to ask questions about the unknown Mistress Hapgood. They were still discussing her when Nell came up to announce that a visitor was asking for Mistress Allerbrook. "A Master Wells, he says he is."

"Wells?" Jane broke off in the midst of trying to ascertain exactly what relation Silvestra was to Sir Peter Carew. "Not Gervase Wells?"

"That'll be him, ma'am."

"But…he's a soldier! Sergeant Wells, that's his rank. Nell, are the soldiers back?"

Philippa put out a hand and clutched at Jane. They had both gone pale and Stephen's expression was grim. Nell, however, was shaking her head. "No, ma'am. He'm alone and in ordinary clothes, ma'am, and he's calling hisself just Master Wells."

"Shall I see him?" suggested Stephen.

"No, bring him up here, Nell," Jane said. To Stephen, she added, "As it happens, he brought the letter that called Tobias and Robert to London, but he didn't know what was in it. The next time he came it was with Clayman, but he tried to keep them all out of Philippa's room. He spoke up for me when that man Clayman wanted to arrest me. I shouldn't think he means us any harm. Though I don't know which Mistress Allerbrook he wants to see."

He came into the parlour apologetically, carrying a brown velvet cap. He was very much a russet-coloured gentleman today: hair, eyes and velvet doublet. His small ruff was the only touch of white.

"Master Wells?" said Jane uncertainly.

He bowed to them all and greeted them. His eyes rested on Philippa for several seconds, Jane noticed. Then he said, "I only came because I wished to know—how you all were."

"Why should you want to know that?" Stephen asked coldly. "And how is it that you are not in the gear of the militia?"

"I've bought myself out. My father needs help on his farm. He's not a young man now. I was born when he was already nearly forty. He's a Luttrell tenant at Foxwood Farm, near Dunster, on the side of Grabbist Hill. I'll inherit the tenancy one day. I wanted to apologize."

"For inheriting the tenancy of Foxwood Farm?" said Philippa, genuinely bewildered.

"No." Master Wells smiled. "I put it badly. The last time I came here—you will recall the circumstances—well, I want to apologize for them. I was sorry then and am sorry now for that intrusion into a lady's room at such a time. Whatever the law may say, I think it was wrong. I am sure, truly, that Captain Clayman wouldn't have done it, except that he was so angry because of the heat and the flies and…"

"The snake and our gander and Hellspawn?" said Jane. "We haven't replaced the gander yet."

"As I observed," said Wells, smiling. He became serious again. "I know what happened to Robert Allerbrook," he said. His eyes were once more on Philippa. "The proclamation was given out in Taunton as well as here. I can't regret that a plot was foiled, but I do regret what happened in this house, in the presence of both of you ladies—above all, Mistress Philippa, at such a time for you. I also offer my condolences to Robert's family, if you will accept them. I wouldn't blame you if you ordered me to leave, but when I say I did not like what was done here, I mean it."

Jane said, "Master Tobias Allerbrook really is in France. We hope, in time, to win a pardon for him."

"I wish you well, madam. And I am happy to see that Mistress Philippa is recovered." He looked toward the cradle. "Is that your…but there are two of them!"

"Twins. Sybil and Robin. One of each," Philippa said.

"I hope," said Wells soberly, "that they may be a comfort to you in years to come."

"I think," said Stephen, "that we had better have some cider—and a tisane or some milk for you, Philippa."

Nell said, "I'll get it," and vanished down the stairs.

In the kitchen she said to the others, "It's hard to believe, so soon, but there it do be. One man's wiped out of the world and afore his widow's had time to turn round, another turns up. September it were when Master Robert died and now, before October's out…well."

"He's never said he's here after Mistress Philippa!" said Letty, aghast. "Is there a scent blown on the wind, or what? The way men'll come sniffing round…"

"All he said," Nell told them, "was how sorry he was about the way Master Robert were dragged off. That's all he's *sayin'*. But he's lookin' at Mistress Philippa in *that* way, and he's admirin' the babes, and he's got smart velvets on, that show him off, and he's shaved as smooth as cream. I know the signs!" said Nell.

"That man," said Philippa to Jane later that day as they walked in Jane's garden, examining the herbs. "The one who came today. Gervase Wells. What did he really want?"

"To say he was sorry—about Robert," said Jane carefully.

"He kept looking at me. It was noticeable. But I can't think of anyone but Robert and I don't believe I ever will."

For a moment Jane said nothing. When she did speak, it was with some difficulty, for it had been suddenly borne in on her that Stephen was right; Philippa, who shared Jane's grief for Robert, would indeed be a comfort. She didn't want even to think about Philippa one day leaving her. In the same moment she knew that she must not say so. The right words were quite different and only the right words must be spoken.

"My dear, you are young and your life stretches far ahead. Even the worst memories grow less as time goes on. I've lived long enough to know it. I thought when I heard of the death of my lover that I couldn't go on living. Yet I did go on. One does."

"He wasn't executed! He wasn't dragged from your bedchamber and...and...!"

"No, I know. But the years lie before you. You won't want to look over your shoulder forever."

"If Wells comes here again, I don't want to see him."

"Then you need not," said Jane.

CHAPTER FORTY-SEVEN
The Time Has Come
1586–1587

Master Wells reappeared a fortnight later. During that time, Stephen had ridden to Barnstaple, stayed for three days at an inn there and called on Mistress Hapgood every day, returned home announcing that he was betrothed and moved into Clicket Hall forthwith, to prepare it for his bride. He was therefore not at Allerbrook when Wells once more rode into the yard and asked to see Mistress Jane Allerbrook.

"I just came to see how you were all faring," he said when he had again been shown into the parlour.

Jane had been sitting there with Philippa and Alice, while all three of them worked on the stitchery which was always part of their lives. From the window they had seen Wells approaching, and Philippa had at once retreated to her chamber. Jane, clicking a thoughtful tongue, sent Alice away, too, and welcomed the visitor alone.

"The weather has turned cold," Wells remarked. "I noticed a rich crop of berries on wayside trees and bushes. It means a hard winter to come, so it is said. Nature feeds the birds and squirrels well, in readiness."

"It's kind of you to come so far, just to ask after our health," Jane said dryly.

"Is Mistress Philippa in the house? May I pay my respects to her?"

"She is in the house, but…Master Wells," said Jane, picking up her embroidery frame and looking at it as though not certain what it was, "why have you come? It was courteous to visit once, to express your regret for that unhappy scene when my grandson was arrested. But what, really, brings you here again?"

"You have an acute mind, mistress," said Wells, sounding uncomfortable. He didn't seem anxious to go on.

Jane laid the frame down on her lap. "Is it Philippa?"

"I know it's much too soon. I wouldn't say anything to her—not yet. I just have a hope that if I visit occasionally, and see her now and then, she may grow used to me, and perhaps begin to think of me when I'm not here, and that one day, when time has passed… I was enchanted by her the first time I saw her. She was another man's wife then. But that's not so any longer and surely, one day, she must marry again. Might it not be me—eventually? I would like to say," he added, "that Foxwood Farm, where I shall inherit the tenancy, is a worthwhile place. My family has money and we own the stock. I would see that the boy, Robin, was trained to inherit Allerbrook in due course. I would be an honest guardian."

Jane was silent.

"Mistress Allerbrook?"

"Master Wells, it would rest with Philippa. Are you sure about this, though? Philippa is only half-English. She grew up with a New World tribe. Her father was with her and told her as much as he could about England—instructed her in Christianity, taught her to read and write—but she will never be wholly English. There will always be something different in the way she looks. And thinks. She has memories we can't share, pictures in her mind that we can't imagine. Is that truly what you want?"

"I think it is," said Wells soberly. "I want to marry. I want a wife who is affectionate—well, she seems to have loved her first husband wholeheartedly. She has some education, too. All those are things I value, and as for the differences you speak of, I value them, too. They are something to marvel at and be forever just a little surprised by. I like a little salt on my table."

He paused and then added, "I would wish to be her friend as well as her husband. Believe me, you can entrust her to me."

"I see. Well, if you feel the same when you come to know her better, you are free to pay court to Philippa. The rest will depend on her. Yes, you may visit us now and then. She has sensed your interest and has hidden from you this time, but that's because she's still raw. Later, I daresay she'll be willing to greet you in a normal way. But mark one thing. Say nothing to her of your feelings until you are quite certain they will not change, and indeed, until Philippa has had time to heal. In fact, please say nothing until I give you leave."

"Very well," said Gervase.

★ ★ ★

"Aunt Jane, I was coming to see you!" said Stephen, pulling his horse to a stop on the track from the combe to Allerbrook House. "Should you be wandering about in the cold?"

It was a grey December day with an edge on the wind. Jane, wrapped in a cloak, was walking restlessly along the path. She had no basket or sign of any other errand, and Stephen was surprised to find her out of doors in such discouraging weather.

"I can't walk as far as I used to do, but it helps me to think," said Jane. "I wanted to think."

"About what? I was coming to ask for some advice about my wedding feast next week. You look worried."

"It's Wells. He's been here three times now. Stephen, he wants to court Philippa. At first she hid from him. I told her that she couldn't go on doing that, and since then, she's sat with us and talked to him, but she's wary. She makes conversation cheerfully and she never mentions Robert—it's heartbreaking sometimes—but she's careful not to be left alone with Wells. Not that it would matter if she were. I've warned him to say nothing to her until I give permission, but it ought to be your permission! You're her father. I was thinking I must come to see *you*."

"Wells has called on me already," said Stephen. "He wanted to give me details of his finances and expectations and to convince me that he would be a trustworthy stepfather! He suggested that you and I should be trustees of Allerbrook on Robin's behalf."

"I see," said Jane thoughtfully.

"The man's in love with Philippa—that's true enough, Aunt Jane. I told him that it would rest with Philippa herself. Since Tobias is in France—I bless Nicholas Lanyon for that, for he stood by us nobly in the end—we shall have to settle a way of looking after Allerbrook anyhow. You and I could do it well enough together, that's quite true. But at a guess, I'd say that Philippa needs a year at least before she will be ready even to think of a new marriage. Then let him try his luck."

"Stephen…"

"Yes, Aunt Jane?"

"It's terrible," said Jane. "I ought to want Philippa to find a new husband. But sometimes the idea makes me angry. It feels as though she would be forgetting Robert, being unfaithful to him! I know I'm being unreasonable, that Robert is gone and Philippa has her life ahead of her. I've even told her she can't always be looking over her shoulder at what she's left behind! And then I think of Robert, and how he died and…I should miss Philippa so. She's like a daughter, and I've already lost my son and Blanche, though I know they're safe enough in Paris. You were right—Philippa does comfort me and I hope I comfort her. I dread the thought of losing her. It's wrong to feel like this, but I do."

Calmly Stephen said, "Tell Wells to wait until the first anniversary of Robert's death has passed. I fancy you need that year as well as Philippa! Wait and see how all three of you feel then."

The winter deepened. Just before Christmas, Stephen's marriage took place and he and his bride were snowed up in Clicket Hall during Yuletide. Jane and Philippa, equally snowed up in Allerbrook, laughed about it.

"No one will interrupt their honeymoon in this weather," Philippa said. "Well, I wish them happiness. I like her."

Silvestra had turned out to be a good-tempered, firmly

built, bouncy lady with a gurgle of a laugh and a gift for managing a household. Her two sons were both away, acquiring polish in an uncle's home in London. Between the absence of the boys and the presence of the snow, Silvestra and Stephen would have every opportunity to build their own private world, uninterrupted.

On the eighth day of February, 1587, Sir Francis Walsingham finally achieved what he had set out to do and Mary Stuart, formerly Queen of Scotland and pretender to the throne of England, laid her head upon a block in the great hall of Fotheringay Castle in Northamptonshire.

She dressed for the occasion in red, the colour of blood but also the colour of martyrdom, declaring that she died a martyr for the Catholic faith. If at any point she thought of the men she had enchanted and dazzled and led to their deaths, it was only to regard them as fellow martyrs, and hope that they would all meet, crowned with gold, in heaven. Mary Stuart never had possessed more than a nodding acquaintance with reality.

The news was proclaimed through England and, since the snow had gone by then, reached Allerbrook within two days. Philippa, for once breaking her silence on the subject of Robert, said savagely, "If he had been royalty, perhaps he could have died that way. The axe is swift. The rope was surely horrible, even without…the other."

"Try not to think too much about it," said Jane awkwardly, and did not say how often, in her dreams, she saw Robert die all over again, and how often, in secret, she wept for him.

The days lengthened. Spring came, and then summer. It was July when Jane noticed that Philippa had once more begun to go up to the ridge alone. When she had done so for four mornings in succession, Jane, ignoring the breath-lessness which was now a serious affliction, plodded up the combe after her. She found her great-niece standing on top of the barrow, staring out toward the sea. "Philippa!"

"Great-Aunt Jane! Did you follow me up here? I'm sorry. Does it worry you when I wander off?"

"A little. What is it, Philippa? You were looking toward the sea! You…you don't want to go back to the New World, do you? To your tribe?" Jane spoke hesitantly. She was more in tune with her great-niece than Blanche had been, probably because the link of blood between them was so much closer, but she had never been able to picture the world from which Philippa came.

"No, not that," Philippa said. "I belong here, Great-Aunt Jane, as I have said before. I'm sure of that."

"Then what is it? What makes you walk away from the house day after day, and come up here, whatever the weather?"

"I don't know, Great-Aunt. I want something but I don't know what. I try to think of Robert but he's slipping away from me, like a ship going out of sight over the horizon. I was watching a ship just now, doing just that. Great-Aunt Jane…"

"Yes, my dear?"

"I broke my promise."

"Which promise?"

"The one I made to you when I said I would never invoke Wakonda, the great god of my people, again. I did invoke him, only a few minutes ago. I need help. How am I to make a life without Robert—a life for myself and a life for our children? I feel so lost. I tried to pray in the chapel, but there was nothing there. It's different up here in the sun and the wind."

She made a sweeping gesture, taking in the rolling moors and the distant channel. "I can imagine Wakonda here! This barrow, where we're standing—someone is buried here, so Robert told me once, perhaps the chief of a long-ago people who lived here, and they weren't Christians, so he said. But I suppose they had gods of a sort and perhaps they were gods like those of the Algonquin. Gods of that kind would feel at home here."

"Philippa, you mustn't…you *mustn't!*"

"Do you really, *really* believe in the God you worship?" Philippa asked suddenly.

"No one has ever asked me that question before," Jane said. "The answer is…I don't know. Perhaps not. But we live in dangerous times. It's wisest to do what everyone else does, worship as everyone else worships, and keep your own counsel. Philippa, when I look back, I see that a great deal, perhaps most, of my real life has been lived inside my head and my heart, in secret. For instance, you are the only person in the world who knows that once—and once only—I had a lover."

And no one at all knows, or ever will know, that if Robin one day inherits Allerbrook, it will be because Dr. Amyas Spenlove almost certainly forged the last paragraph of my brother's will, so that Allerbrook became mine to hand on. The secret foundations of Allerbrook must remain secret, forever.

Most unexpectedly, Philippa said, "Was his name Spenlove? Was he the man who painted that portrait up in the east gallery?"

Jane laughed. "No. No, Dr. Spenlove was our chaplain and a fine artist, and I think, yes, that he understood me as well as anyone ever has, but he was not my lover. Just a very good friend."

"People can be both," said Philippa, once more gazing out to sea. "Robert was." She sighed. "Dear Robert. His only fault was that he was too honest. He wouldn't pretend about what he believed. Must one pretend, in order to belong?"

"Or to survive. Yes. Captain Clayman went away thinking I was just a grandmother who was too respectable and too doting, both at once, to believe that her grandson was trying to overthrow the queen! I did a good deal of pretending that day," Jane said.

"I want to survive—anyone would. But above all, I want to belong!" Philippa said it passionately. "And I want to belong here on the moor, to…to put down roots…. I must anyway, because Robin will have Allerbrook one day. Only, there's more to it than just…just conforming. Something deeper. I know there is, but with Robert gone, I'm like a boat with no rudder. I can't see where I'm going. I don't know *how* to belong. I don't know *how!*"

"For the moment," said Jane gently, "my advice is to conform in matters of religion, to recover from your grief and live from day to day. Your future will become clear. You'll see. Now come back to the house. But once more, please promise me never to pray to your old gods again and this time, for your own safety, my poor Philippa, keep your word!"

"I will try," said Philippa forlornly.

Alone in the study, later, Jane sat down to write a letter. Paul Snowe could carry it. She paused, struggling against a final surge of unwillingness. She *didn't* want Philippa to go away, even though it would be a matter of only a few miles. It would be as though Robert had been buried twice.

But she had never been able to shake off the feeling that she had failed Robert at the end. She had saved others in the past, but what use had she been to him? Or, looking back, to poor Harry Hudd, either. At least she now had a chance to make up for them both, to give Philippa the help she needed.

Jane, listening to her as they stood on the barrow, had understood Philippa's trouble better than the girl herself did.

She understood because she, too, had loved but, since the day she'd watched the *Pretty Doe* sail out of Weymouth, had had to do without her lover. She had learned then that people deprived of their dearest wish, their dearest love, must still find a way to live.

She had found one. She had given herself to Allerbrook and to the care of those around her, to whom she had dedicated herself already, in any case. Marriage would not have fitted with those duties and she had renounced all thought of it. But she had been older than Philippa. And she had a place where she really did belong.

Philippa had no such place, no clear path before her feet. Peter Carew, the secret love whom Jane had never named, even to her great-niece, had unintentionally made it possible for her to see the true nature of Philippa's sadness. Because of him, she knew now what she must do.

Curious, how much her two carefully guarded secrets, Spenlove's forgery and her affair with Carew, had given to her.

I want to belong…but I don't know how. Jane knew how. Philippa needed a place in the world that was hers, and for her, that must mean husband and family and a home of her own.

Gervase Wells, whose father was a prosperous farmer and a principal tenant of the Luttrells (which was nearly as good as being a landowner himself); Gervase Wells, whose home was only a few miles away, so that Robin would still be reared close to Allerbrook, his future inheritance; Gervase Wells, who had said he wished to be Philippa's friend as well as her husband, was the obvious answer.

Denied this opportunity, what would Philippa do but pine for the past and, very likely, despite her promises, turn again to her old gods? In that case, what lay ahead for her was nothing but unhappiness and, quite possibly, terrible danger. In a world where Jane Allerbrook wouldn't always be there to defend her. The tiredness and breathlessness from which Jane so often suffered now were warning signs. How long before the last sand trickled out of her hourglass?

She sat there for a long time, so still that she might have been the painted image of an Elizabethan lady, like her younger self in the portrait upstairs. She was even wearing similar colours, since her gown was a deep tawny, over a cream kirtle. They were her favourite shades.

She had, too, a modest farthingale and a neat lawn ruff with a little gold thread in its edging. The latest generation of the La Plage family had grieved over her insistence that she did not care what the new fashions dictated. She had told them roundly that she didn't want to push her head through the middle of a cart wheel, and her hips were large enough already without being expanded to elephantine proportions by a monster hoop. She knew very well that her old-fashioned moderation suited her.

One could not sit immobile forever. Presently, her right hand began to move, dipping the quill, smoothing out the paper, tracing the words that needed to be written. The future stretched ahead and must be filled.

To Gervase Wells, Foxwood Farm, at Dunster, from Mistress Jane Allerbrook of Allerbrook House.

The time has come…